BOOK ONE OF THE KAZUMI CHRONICLES

D1825648

SHADOW OF DECEPTION

Dear Dani,
Thank you so much!
Enjoy!

SOPHIA L. JOHNSON

outskirtspress

DENVER, COLORADO

Outskirts Press, Inc.
http://www.outskirtspress.com

ISBN: 978-1-4787-4284-5

Outskirts Press and the "OP" logo are trademarks belonging to Outskirts Press, Inc.

PRINTED IN THE UNITED STATES OF AMERICA

PROLOGUE

"Mommy!" little Kazumi sobs while trying to wipe off her mommy's blood. "Daddy . . . where are you?"

Squatting among the trees on the side of a narrow country road, Kazumi smudges her tiny hands on the damp grass hoping to clean off the yucky red stain.

"Run my angel . . . be strong, don't look back . . . just run!" Remembering her mommy's words, Kazumi wipes away her tears, leaving streaks of red on her rosy cheeks.

She *was* running; until she was out of breath, until she rolled off the hill and scratched up her knees pretty bad. The fall was the most painful thing she has ever experienced. If she were at home, she'd be crying a river. Mommy and Daddy would lovingly tend to her injury while singing her favourite song. But she is all alone now and needs to find help.

She slowly stands up, wincing at the sharp sting, and begins to march forward again. She knows that Mommy would be proud of her.

She looks back in the direction of her burning house and sees nothing but tall trees and thick branches. Suddenly the image of trees turning into brown, wrinkly monsters reaching out for lost children fills her head. With a loud squeak, Kazumi covers her ears to block out the howling of the tree monsters and runs toward the open road.

Just as Kazumi stumbles onto the unpaved road, she sees a big black car with black windows driving toward her in the distance. Frantically, she waves her hands in the air, trying to get the driver's attention. Then she remembers how short and tiny she seemed when standing beside Daddy's car. She wonders if the big black car would even see her. So she desperately jumps up and down in the middle of the road with the hope that the driver would help her mommy. The pain in her knees all forgotten.

"Help! Please help!" she yells as loud as she can.

The black car screeches to a stop right in front of her. She looks up slowly and realizes this car is much bigger than her daddy's. Suddenly afraid, Kazumi backs up several steps and the earlier enthusiasm has vanished.

A man steps out of the car, wearing big sunglasses even though it's an overcast day. The man is quite short compared to Kazumi's daddy. And there's something in his expression that makes her want to hide behind something, anything that can protect her.

The man kneels down so he's at Kazumi's eye level and says, "What's your name my dear?"

"Um . . ." Kazumi was never shy, but this man scares her. All she can do is stare at her dirty shoes.

"Where are your parents?" asks the stranger.

The mentioning of her parents reminds her of her mission and a rush of courage overcomes her fear. "Please . . . help my mommy."

"Tell me what happened." The man says calmly.

Kazumi takes a deep breath and begins recapping the incident, "I was picking flowers in the garden, then our house exploded with fire. It was very very loud and hurt my ears. Then I found Mommy lying on the ground with, with lots and lots of blood." She extends her palms for the man to inspect, worry that he won't believe her.

"Oh, that's most unfortunate." The tone in the man's voice changes. Kazumi cannot figure out if he's happy or scared like her. He takes off his sunglasses, revealing a pair of eyes that Kazumi finds funny-looking. They are small and far apart from each other.

"Can you help my mommy? Pretty please?" she whispers.

"Of course," the man stands and holds out his hand. "But you'll have to come with me."

Kazumi stares at the stranger's big hand with her grayish green eyes. She knows she's not supposed to talk to strangers, never mind going with them. But she's desperate.

"I can show you where Mommy is," she says as she reaches for his big, warm hand.

"Sure my dear. I would love to see your mommy and daddy . . . or what's left of them . . ." the man trails off.

Kazumi doesn't quite get what the man is saying. It doesn't matter. She found help.

After securing Kazumi in the back seat, the man drives off in the direction of the burning house.

CHAPTER 1

Eleven years later . . .

My eyes spring open and see a blurry swirl of blue, white, and gray, like an abstract painting behind a piece of fuzzy glass. Before I can remember what happened, it begins to spin. Then a wave of intense headache hits, like someone just punched me in the temple. *Aaagg!*

I shut my eyes but the dizziness doesn't stop. I have no idea where I am. All I know is that I'm lying on my back, bent in an awkward position. Jagged edges digging into my spine. I'm too disoriented to open my eyes again, so I decide to use my sense of touch, which proves to be just as useless. When I move, a surge of painful tingling rushes through my extremities like I'm being pricked by a thousand fine needles.

I curse at the bothersome sensation and wait for the tingling to disappear before trying again. But my body is not done with the complaining. A horrid aroma fills my nostrils, causing a gag reflex that churns my stomach. The smell is nauseating and sweet, putrid and meaty—like leather being tanned over fire. There's something else in the stench that I recognize—the strong metallic smell of blood.

Panic kicks in. I begin to envision horrible scenarios in my head—from kidnapping to cannibalism. If someone can see my thoughts right now, they'd be scared too.

It's all in your head. Don't be paranoid. I tell myself.

With my eyes still closed, I slowly breathe out and extend my arms to get a feel of my immediate surroundings. The extreme soreness in my muscles makes me want to stop, but I must know how dire my situation is.

My fingers feel cold and stiff like they haven't moved in days. The wet dirt underneath feels oddly warm and squishy. Patches of grass tickle my hand as I brush over them. They too, seem wet and sticky. After a brief moment of palpating the dirt around me, my right hand finally lands on what feels like someone's hand. I let out the breath I've been holding, at least I'm not alone. But my relief is short-lived. The hand I am now holding is icy-cold and too rigid.

Terrified, I immediately retract my hand. Cannibalism doesn't sound so crazy now.

Goosebumps form on my skin and I can't stop shivering even though the temperature is scorching. I want to scream for help but worry that the killer might come for me next. So I stay as quiet as possible and slowly, I open my eyes. My survival instinct trumps my vertigo.

I don't know what's worse, killers who eat human flesh or that I'm lying beside a multitude of human fragments sprawled across the field. Some are charred beyond recognition while others are pinned under sheets of metal.

"H-help!" I force the word out of my parched throat. I have never been this terrified. I thrash and push on the blood-soaked dirt, trying to get up and kicking a few body parts in the process. I call out again but I doubt anyone can hear my drowned-out plea between the crackling of the fire and whistling of the wind.

With my knees supporting my weight, I straighten my

back. Pillars of smoke rise from the ground around me, making my vision more hazy than it already is. Through the fogginess, I see more metal and more bodies. Something huge is stabbed into the ground in the far distance. At first I thought it was a fallen building but now I'm not so sure. Too far to distinguish.

I try to push myself to stand but the dizziness is pulling me down like I'm drowning in a pit of quicksand. My weak extremities give out and I collapse back onto the crimson grass. My consciousness fast fading.

Stay awake! I mentally pinch myself.

But the harder I try, the further my mind slips. I no longer see the blue sky and white clouds above, but a fast-expanding darkness that threatens to envelop me. I finally surrender and let it throw me into nothingness.

"... she doing?"

"Vital signs are normal... won't know the damage until..."

"It's a miracle that she's even alive. Page me when she wakes."

"Yes Dr. Mard."

The voices stop. I listen, but there's nothing except for the throbbing in my ear. I touch my achy head and find numerous small discs taped to my skin.

"How are you feeling?" a woman's voice makes me jump. I open my eyes and see a middle-aged nurse standing over me. Her light brown hair is short but slightly permed. Her brown eyes show concern and fatigue. They would have been beautiful if not for the dark circles underneath and the extra skin gathered on the eyelids. But I think she still looks good for her age.

She shifts a little, allowing me to see the patterned ceiling . . . wait no, it's not the ceiling. It's a flat and oval machine, about the size of my bed, suspended just below the ceiling. Blue and white dots flash randomly inside its smooth and glassy casing.

The nurse presses a few buttons on a monitor that is connected to the side of my bed by a white metal arm and says, "Your vitals are normal. How are you feeling?"

"Uh, sore. Why am I here?" I croak. My throat is so dry that my words are barely audible.

She presses another button and the head of my bed begins to move, slowly folding me into a semi-reclined position. Now I can see her and the rest of the room without straining my neck. Behind her is a big circular window, tinted so dark that the view is blocked. I wonder what's on the other side. Across from me is the washroom, with its door slightly ajar to reveal part of a toilet. On my right I'm shocked to see a hectic hallway, separated by a glass wall. Despite the busy traffic, none of the noises make it through the glass.

"You're in Intensive Care. You were in an accident," the nurse says.

Accident?

My sluggish brain is having trouble processing. I try harder and the scene of the wreckage surfaces.

"Dead bodies . . . were everywhere." I test the words in my mouth like I've never pronounced them before.

She wraps my hand in hers. Her warm touch feels soothing against my icy fingers.

"You're very lucky my dear," she looks down, like she doesn't know how to continue. She takes another breath and says, "Everyone else on that plane didn't make it. You're the only survivor."

The words "only survivor" echo in my head. So that wasn't a dream. Those *were* dead bodies.

My hands begin to shake as I recall the hundreds of dismembered corpses and how I could have been one of them. She must feel my trepidation too because she tightens her grip on my hand. The immense confusion aggravates the throbbing in my head. I press my hands to my temples, hoping the pressure will help.

"I don't remember the accident . . . just . . . just the dead bodies." I mumble in pain. The headache is becoming unbearable.

"Deep breaths my dear. Try to relax." She gently puts a hand on my shoulder, preventing me from moving too much. "It's normal for trauma victims to lose memory of the accident."

I bury my face in my hands and let the warmth of my breath calm my mind. My heart rate begins to slow down and so does the beeping above my head. I now know what the round discs on my skin are for.

The nurse adjusts the pillow behind my head and says, "What's your name? We didn't find any ID on you. Is there anyone you'd like us to contact?"

"My name is. . ." I pause, drawing a blank.

I stare at her with wide eyes, not able to offer her an answer.

"Page Dr. Mard, stat!" she calls into a device strapped to her wrist. "Don't worry . . Dr. Mard . . . Neurologist . . help . . ."

I know the nurse is speaking to me but my mind has already shut her out, making her words sound like discordant notes in the distance. All I hear are the same questions looping over and over in my head. *Who am I? Who are my parents? What is my name? Who am I? Who are my parents?* . . .

But it doesn't matter how many times I ask myself, I still can't remember. What if this is permanent?

Out of nowhere a dark, bald man in a white coat appears in front of me. DR. JONANTHAN MARD is visibly printed on a transparent tag attached to the pocket of his coat.

The sight of a doctor completely erupts my nerves. I grab onto his sleeves so forcefully that he steps back. There's a thousand questions I want to ask. But he stops me before I can open my mouth.

"I'm Dr. Jonathan Mard," he says. "I know it must be very confusing for you right now. We've already done some tests on you and there's no major tissue or bone damage, which is *very* fortunate considering what you have just been through. But it did show some swelling in your brain, which may explain your memory loss. Don't worry, you're already under constant monitoring." He points to something behind me. I turn my head slowly so as not to aggravate my headache and see a tall plastic screen extending from the head of my bed all the way to the ceiling. Projected on it is me—the hollow, skeletal version of me. Everything is on display—bones, organs, arteries. I can even see the blood flowing through like mini crimson rivers, some going upstream and some going downward.

Instinctively, I pull my blanket up, like it would cover the nakedness on the screen. But of course it does nothing to hide it. My inner workings are completely exposed and I can't help but feel violated.

"Now that you're awake, I want to do more memory tests to further determine the severity of this, so we can devise a treatment plan to help you." Dr. Mard zooms in and the screen now shows a gigantic version of my brain.

It takes me a few seconds to digest his words as I study the projection. One side of my brain is yellow but it quickly turns orange while the other side changes to green and vice versa. How can they tell what's going on in there by just looking at the colours? Which part is the damaged portion?

I feel a tug and realize I'm clutching on Dr. Mard's sleeve with one hand and wrinkling the blanket in another. He gives the nurse a look. She leans in to peel my hand off but I'm reluctant to move. He's the only person who can decipher my brain. He's the only person who can help me.

"Sweetie, it's okay, it's okay," the nurse whispers. "Let Dr. Mard go so he can get you the brain scanner okay? He can't help you without the scanner. Alright sweetie?"

I slowly shift my gaze from the doctor to the nurse, and back to the doctor. After a long while, I release my breath and reluctantly let go.

While waiting for the brain scanner, nurse Linda gives me a shot of mild sedative to settle my anxiety. Now I no longer feel the need to grab onto someone for dear life.

Linda says that I was on a plane, departing from Nice in the Republic of Europe to Toronto in the United Nation of North America. But the plane crashed just outside of the city during its descent.

They're investigating the cause as we speak. All five hundred and forty-two passengers died in the crash and they managed to find me, relatively unharmed near the crash site. Then they air-lifted me here, the largest hospital in Toronto. Reporters have already gathered in the lobby, anxious to get the full story on the lucky girl who survived. Dr. Mard has deemed me unstable hence stalling their harassment for the time being.

While Linda checks on her other patients, I make my way to the washroom and see myself for the first time since I woke up. The stranger staring back at me certainly doesn't look like someone who just survived a plane crash. Only a few faint bruises are apparent under that dull and pale complexion. She looks young, eighteen maybe? But there's something behind those eyes that show otherwise—something dark and heavy, like she's been carrying a hefty weight all her life. Her features look somewhat oriental but those green and grayish eyes suggest she's not of pure Asian blood. Her hair is wavy and hangs below her shoulders. I grab several strands and twist them between my fingers. They feel dry and full of split-ends.

"Who are you?" I whisper at the mirror. "Why are you here?"

My fingers begin to trace each feature, hoping the touch will spark something in my memories. I start with my tired eyelids and round down to the dark circles underneath. My eyes are big and round but my lashes are short. Then my fingers trail along the bridge of my nose and drop down to my thin, pale lips. Finally, I stop at my pointy chin. I press my lips in a hard line and the apex of my chin becomes pointier. How cute.

I'm actually quite attractive if not for the layers of exhaustion and melancholy carved in every inch of my face. Did I have a hard life leading up to now? Why do I look so miserable?

"Dr. Mard is ready for you." Linda says softly. I wonder how long she has been standing by the door, watching my meet-and-greet with myself.

I follow her out of the washroom and see that Dr. Mard is already waiting by my bed. Beside him is a white cart on four silver wheels. Three glass drawers occupy the top half and the bottom half is an empty shelf. Sitting on top of the cart is a silver box bigger than Dr. Mard's head.

Linda pats the bed signalling me to get in. As I'm about

to settle in, I spot a scalpel sitting inside the first transparent drawer. A chill creeps through my spine like someone's sliding an ice cube down my back.

Seeing my nervousness, Linda asks, "What is it dear?"

"I . . ." I can't even explain. I don't know where my fear is coming from.

"Don't worry," Dr. Mard says, "it won't hurt. I'm just gonna put this on your head." He pulls out a white helmet from inside the silver case. The glossy finish makes it look brand new. "While the screen behind you gives us important information about your health status, this will give us in-depth analysis of your brain."

Linda fluffs a couple of pillows behind my back and leans me against them. Knowing that he won't be using a scalpel on me, my anxiety disappears. But I still feel uneasy around so many medical tools.

Dr. Mard punches a series of commands on the attached keypad and that's when I notice his unusually long fingers. Too long for a guy who's only a bit taller than me, and I don't think I'm all that tall. When he's finished, dots of green and blue lights begin chasing each other around the helmet, making it look more like a toy than medical equipment.

"See, it's not that scary." Dr. Mard smiles, showing his perfect white teeth.

I tense up as he fits the helmet on my head, fully expecting its weight to strain my neck. But it's surprisingly light. The soft foam lining of its interior molds to my head comfortably.

This is not so bad, I can do this. I tell myself.

But I change my mind soon after. The helmet itself is comfortable enough to wear for the hour long assessment, but the tedious questioning that comes with it is what bothers me the most.

Dr. Mard begins flipping flash cards to test my knowledge from basic math to history to general knowledge of the world. I can do most of the maths but only some of the history and general knowledge. I'm also able to complete the memorization tests without too much difficulty. Just when my confidence begins to build, Dr. Mard moves onto the questions about my past. That small hint of hope quickly evaporates like a drop of water on a sizzling hot plate. Why do I remember all the irrelevance of the world but not my own life? How would knowing the square root of 81 or that the Earth is round help me in any way?

Maybe it'd been better to die in that crash. A voice in head says.

A sense of impending doom boils over, taking control of my body. I can feel my rapid heartbeat in my throat and my hands are clamped together, nails digging into skin. *I'm doomed. Why couldn't I just die like everyone else on that plane? Why . . .*

A prick in my arm, then everything slows down. My heart rate normalizes on the screen.

I stand before the circular window, twenty storeys high. Linda turned off the tint before she left so I can soak in the view. It would be a better view if not for the rain that's casting a layer of haze on what seems to be a dense, hectic, and overpopulated city. According to Linda, we're in downtown—the most crowded part of Toronto—which explains the intimidating number of skyscrapers that blocked off the sky.

I don't know what to make of this. Everything seems new to me yet familiar. Maybe I've been here before. Or maybe I was coming home from a vacation. This city could be my home.

A few storeys down I spot a light rail track, supported by massive concrete and steel pillars. Below it lies another track closer to the ground. Underneath the tracks are cars and pedestrians that fill the streets. I watch as the tiny people down below go about their business. It's six o'clock in the evening, they must be anxious to get home from a hard day's work. How lucky. I bet every single person down there has a place to call home. Even the homeless would have a spot reserved at a street corner or in an alley. Yet here I am, with absolutely no idea where I belong.

A train zooms by on the top track. My eyes follow as it snakes around a bend and quickly disappears behind a huge screen fastened to the side of a building that shows a picture of a hand holding a flat, plastic card. A second later, the picture transforms into words that says: MUD VERSION 10.5 IN STORES NOW! I immediately recognize the gadget they're advertising. Multi-Usage Device. A transparent plastic card that allows you to make calls, to make payments from a bank or credit account, to gain access to multi-media and to serve as personal identification. It's almost mandatory to have one these days.

I shake my head in disbelief. I can recite the definition of a MUD but not my own name.

"We have your results," Dr. Mard walks in with Linda in tow.

I didn't expect them to be back so soon. It's only been an hour since the tests. But now that they're here, I feel nervous. I've been mentally preparing for the worst—for him to tell me that I'm unfixable.

"Looks like you are suffering from retrograde amnesia." Dr. Mard begins as I sit down on the side of the bed. "Our tests show that you are able to retain new information and memory, but you can't recall any past episodic memories before the crash. This is due to trauma inflicted on the limbic system of your brain during the accident. Seems like most of your semantic memories are still intact, which relates to your abstract knowledge of the world. That's why you can still talk and have a general understanding of your surroundings."

He then goes on to explain how memories are formed and organized in the limbic system, but I tune all that out as my emotions override my need to learn. I don't care about the limbic system, I just need to know how he plans to fix me.

"Will I recover?" I cut him off in mid-sentence.

"It depends." He doesn't look bothered by my interruption. "Some patients have recovered some or all of their memories over time, but there are also patients who lost their memories forever. On the bright side, you survived. That's a miracle in itself."

"Great! When's the party?" I roll my eyes at him. "How are you going to fix me?"

He shakes his head. "Sorry. I'm afraid there's nothing I can do at this point. We'll just have to wait and see."

"What do you mean you can't do anything?" I raise my voice. "With all your high-tech gadgets, can't you go into my brain and do *something*? Put in a device . . . take something out. Anything!"

Dr. Mard and Linda exchange a look. Then he says, "Sorry, there's really nothing more we can do."

And you call yourself a doctor? Is what I want to say to his face but I hold my tongue. I'm still in his domain. But he pretty much just pulled every ounce of hope out of me, wrapped it in a ball and threw it out the window. I don't want to look at him anymore. I don't want to look at anyone. I feel like wrapping myself in a blanket and tune out the world. So I do just that.

They get my hostility and excuse themselves, giving me the

space and privacy I need. The room suddenly becomes so quiet that I can hear whispers in the hallway. They must have left a gap in the glass sliding door.

"Do you think she's one of them?" a woman whispers.

"Shh. . .don't let them hear you." Another woman replies.

"All I'm saying is, if she is, then we should get rid of her as soon as possible. I mean, we don't want to attract more of them here. Those things freak me out. They're not normal."

I have a strong suspicion that they're talking about me. Part of me wants to storm out there and slap those two bitches for calling me a thing, but I'm too tired to do anything about it. I stay curled up in my blanket and eventually I drift off.

CHAPTER 2

It has been four weeks since the crash. No one has answered to the ads the hospital put up for me. Plus my story must have appeared on the news a couple times more than I would like. No one wants to claim me. I don't blame them. Who wants to take home a broken amnesiac, especially one who's prone to anxiety attacks and occasional temper tantrums?

They moved me from Intensive Care to Recovery the day after Dr. Mard gave me that brain scan. It was like being thrown into a pit of chaos filled with inquisitive patients and loud nurses—a complete opposite to the serene and private room I woke up in. Recovery is pretty much a massive room with medical pods in cubicles, clustered in groups of four or six. It is enclosed by floor-to-ceiling windows which provide ample light during the day. Then they'd darken the windows at night for sleeping. I'm tucked in the far corner with other neuro patients. To my right is the cardiac section and the oncology wing is to the left. No distinct partition, no walls, no privacy screens between each division. Just a big hologram lit above its corresponding section. The nurses in my department reassured me that no one on this floor is contagious. They have a separate quarantine zone for that. But still, I don't like to be surrounded by so many people, sick or healthy.

They put me in a pod right next to the window which offers me a view that is more or less the same—tall skyscrapers, light rail tracks, colourful advertising signs—except not as high up as Intensive Care.

From my exploration, I found out there are over two hundred medical pods on this floor and each single one is occupied. They let you roam free within the huge room but there's no getting out without a doctor's permission. I also discovered that the crash made me famous, within the hospital at least. People were staring everywhere I went. Some stopped me to ask questions and some gave condolences. It got irritating very fast.

I sit in my pod with its lid open. They don't recommend closing it unless you are sleeping or being scanned. It's two o'clock in the afternoon, the busiest time for visitors. This is when I'm extra grateful for the sound-cancelling headphones and the MUD provided at each cubicle. They are my companions and life-savers for the past month. Though Linda has been my support, she doesn't work in Recovery. But she makes sure to visit at least twice a day. My panic attacks have been significantly reduced because of her. My last episode was a week ago when I read the news.

JUNE 3RD, 2153 was marked on the corner of the screen. The headline of that day was about how the United Nations of North America had sent troops to the Republic of Europe to aid in the rescue and clean up of a fallen city destroyed by a major earthquake. That same day, the cause of my plane crash was announced. They claimed it was due to multiple-engine failure.

Reading about the accident brought on a wave of anxiety and despair. But I didn't need the needle. Linda's presence and her comforting words were enough to calm me down. It was a huge improvement for me and Linda was proud.

As far as temper tantrums go, I'm getting better at managing them but there are still times when I feel like punching someone. The psychologist they had me seeing taught me how to meditate whenever anger rises. I didn't trust her at first, she looked a little flaky to me. But if I were to survive on my own, I'll have to learn to control my emotions. I'm sure the hospital won't keep me here forever.

Today, Dr. Mard is paying me a visit. I don't remember the last time he was here—maybe a couple weeks ago. Time is of little meaning to me now.

"Hello Gabi, how are you feeling today?" he says as he walks into my cubicle.

"Same old." I put down the MUD and swing my legs off the pod so I'm sitting on its edge. They decided to call me Gabi, short for Gabrielle. Linda said it means Strong Woman of God. But I don't think God has anything to do with what I'm going through. If he does, then he's a sick man. The name is too feminine for my taste, but I don't care what they call me. I will never know my real name anyway.

"Sorry Gabi," Dr. Mard says, "but the hospital can no longer keep you here. Our resources can barely manage our current demand."

See, I knew it. The inevitable is finally here. I'm about to ask where exactly do they expect me to go when Linda appears, "We have arranged for you to stay at a nearby foster facility for the time being. The place only accepts children under sixteen but the hospital persuaded them to make an exception for you. Afterall, you don't look that much older than sixteen."

How wonderful. I get to live in a building full of annoying, noisy brats who probably ran from home because they didn't know how to appreciate what they had.

"Alright." I lean back, pick up the MUD and resume the game I was playing.

Linda and Dr. Mard both stand there, caught off guard by my reaction—or lack of. They probably had a speech prepared thinking I would put up a fight. I probably would have a week ago. But since then I have learned to accept reality. If I were to become homeless, then so be it.

The next day, Linda shows up with a backpack full of clothes, snacks and a MUD preloaded with money. She has gone above and beyond for me. At first I thought this is how she treats every patient but I soon realized I'm more than just a patient to her. She's been taking care of me like a mother would of her child. I know she also feels sorry for me. I appreciate her gesture but hate the sympathy. I feel sorry for myself every waking minute already, I don't need others to join in.

"I'll walk you out dear." Linda says after I changed into a pair of dark green shorts, a beige sleeveless top and a pair of sandals with thin colourful ropes overlapping on the top of my feet.

"Thank you for all you've done. I appreciate it. But I don't want to take up any more of your time." My expression appears cold and unattached compared to her loving smile.

"I *will* walk you out," she insists.

I care about her, I really do. She's the only person I grew to trust. But for some reason, I don't want her to know, like she would care for me less if she knows how much I will miss her. It's twisted, I know, but that's how I feel.

I see moisture building up in her eyes and I have to look

away. The last thing I want is for her to see me cry. So far I've only shed tears in private, in the dark, under my blanket. I would like to keep it that way.

Linda and I exit the hospital together. This is my first time outside since the accident and it feels good. I fill my lungs with fresh air and don't care that it smells like exhaust fumes. I just stand there, letting the warm summer breeze caress my skin. I know the sun is out because of the clear blue sky but its beams can't quite make it to the ground with so many tall buildings surrounding us.

Linda suddenly grabs my arm and pulls me the opposite direction of the foster home. There's a sense of urgency in her that I've never seen before. I just follow her lead without objection, curious as to where she will take me. I am in no hurry to go "home" anyway.

We turn a corner into an alleyway where a black car is parked about thirty feet ahead. This area smells even worse, like inside a dumpster of leftover dinners.

A man, slim and tall, gets out of the car as soon as he sees us. His gray-to-almost-white hair stands out from the black of the car as well as his dark suit.

Linda's hand still on my arm as we walk toward him. I have a bad feeling about this, but I find myself trusting Linda at the same time. We stop just steps from the man, who looks older now that I can see his face. Linda turns to me, her usual calm demeanour is replaced by caution and seriousness.

"Listen carefully Gabi," she grabs my shoulders. "You're not going to the foster home." I arch my brows but let her finish. "I found you another place where you can be safe and maybe even recover your memories."

My eyes widen at the sudden change of events. "Where? And why won't I be safe at the foster home?"

"The people at the new place will tell you everything you need to know. Hopefully I'm not wrong." She looks down, mumbling to herself. "It can't be wrong. All the results show up positive."

"Positive for what?" I ask impatiently. I hate ambiguity. My life is puzzling enough as it is.

"I . . . I ran some other tests on you. Trust me, this is for your own good." She glances back to where we just came from. "We're running out of time. They'll wonder where I am. Bill here will take care of you. Just remember, no matter what happens, you belong with us." She gives me a hug and a kiss on the cheek, then she runs off. So quick that I didn't get a chance to say my goodbyes.

What did she mean that I belong with them?

"Let me get that." Bill says as he takes my backpack and opens the car door for me. Based on his wrinkles, my guess is that he's in his sixties. Despite his age, he looks immaculate in his fitted black suit. His face shows indifference but his stance is firm, like he won't take no for an answer.

I don't trust him, why should I? I just met him. But Linda was pretty insistent that I go with him for my own sake. To be honest I will go with anyone who claims they can help recover my memories. So what the heck.

"So where are we going?" I ask casually. Don't want to come off being scared.

"The Rockies," he replies curtly.

There's that sense of familiarity again. I want to ask Bill where this place is but decide not to. He doesn't look like the talkative type. I will find out soon enough. I get into the car and we drive off.

CHAPTER 3

I thought our destination was somewhere in the city. But it turns out Bill is taking me to a private jet. This is the first time since I woke up that I don't mind not remembering the accident. I don't know if I have the courage to get on a plane if I remember what happened.

We've been driving for more than an hour now. I no longer see high-rises or crowded city streets. Instead we're surrounded by nature. Green and beautiful.

We turn left onto a narrow path that can barely fit our four-door luxury sedan. Tall trees line both sides, blocking the sunlight. We stay on the path for another ten minutes then it suddenly opens up into a wide field. A silver jet sits in waiting. It looks like a cross between a helicopter and a fighter jet. It has four huge propeller engines extending from its short and slender body—two on either side. Four circular windows run along each side of the body. The cockpit is entirely made of glass, revealing a pilot wearing blue, talking into his headset.

Bill parks the car next to the jet then leads me to a metal staircase extended out from its belly. I stand on the first step, hesitating. If I want to run, this is the time. But the truth is I'm more curious than scared. What do I have to lose? My life? One that I don't even know if it's worth living?

With a deep breath, I walk up the stairs. Once inside, the rumbling of the engines becomes barely noticeable. A spacious and modern interior is the last thing I expect to see inside such a powerful machine. It reminds me of a comfortable living room with cream, plushy carpet and white textured walls. Eight white leather armchairs fill the cabin in two groups of four. A bar sits in the back, with bottles of alcohol secured inside a glass cabinet.

I pick a chair that faces forward and Bill sits directly across from me, with a white table in between. I almost roll my eyes at him. Out of all the seats, he has to sit so close. It's not like I can escape, unless I want to fall out of the sky again.

As soon as I fasten my seat belt, the jet begins to ascend like an elevator. Then I'm pushed back into my seat as it accelerates forward in high speed.

Just when I sink into my chair comfortably, the pilot's voice rings loud in the speakers. "Bill, there's a storm ahead. We'll be hitting some heavy turbulence."

Bill pushes a button on his armrest and replies, "OK Zach."

"How can we be hitting a storm already? It was sunny when we boarded." I say.

"Well weather is hard to predict nowadays," he relaxes into his chair like he's not a bit concerned about the impending turbulence.

I turn the tint off on my window and see nothing but dark gray. For a second there I thought the button malfunctioned and I'm still staring at the tinted window. The storm clouds thicken by the second and the jet begins to shake. I don't need to remember the crash to feel anxious at this point. My stomach twists as the plane drops, and when it quickly regains altitude, I feel like my gut is being pushed into my throat. I have to keep reminding myself to breathe. I don't want a panic attack when Linda is not here to calm me.

I want to ask Bill exactly what's going on, but if I open my mouth, my breakfast will likely make a reappearance. I'm sure whoever owns this jet will not appreciate me ruining the plush white carpet and the expensive-looking leather chairs.

Bill frowns when he sees my pale face. My deadly grip on the leather armrests doesn't help my case either. He leans over and says, "Have you been to the Rockies?"

I shake my head. The truth is I don't remember what the Rockies are and I'm too nervous to talk right now. I try not to show my fear but I'm quite sure the layer of cold sweat gleaming on my forehead just gave me away.

Bill pulls out a drawer from under the table and produces a pink pill and a bottle of water.

"Take this. It will help." He hands me the pill.

I eye him suspiciously. He opens the drawer again and picks up another pink pill and pops it into his mouth.

"It's to help with motion sickness," he says after he swallows.

I take a deep breath, grab the pill and wash it down with a gulp of water.

He's right. After about five minutes, the knot in my stomach is gone. I'm still nervous about the turbulence but at least I don't feel the need to vomit.

"Thank you." I say.

"Help yourself to drinks and snacks back there," he points to the bar behind me, "and the washroom is just up ahead." He reclines his chair.

"Wait, so you're not going to tell me where we're going?" I ask with annoyance in my voice.

"You'll find out in a few hours. Just relax and enjoy the ride." He closes his eyes, telling me the conversation is over.

After four hours of twirling my fingers, doing the brain exercises on my MUD Dr. Mard suggested, and more twirling of my fingers, Bill finally wakes up. He rubs his eyes with his hairy knuckles and says, "You can see it out the window now," he points to what looks like a mountain just below the blanket of clouds. "Well, what's left of it. Mother nature has not been kind. Earthquakes and landslides did a good number to what used to be a splendid World Heritage Site," he sighs. "The beautiful mountain ranges, the serene valleys, the picturesque lakes and national parks . . . all gone. We're lucky if we can still find a clean pond or two." The despair and longing in his voice are obvious.

It's about ten in the morning when we finally begin our descent. We emerge through the clouds into a vast view of an endless mountain range. Rays of sunbeam cascade through the canopy of clouds, casting bright spots along the peaks like shiny scales on a sleeping dragon. As we get closer, the mighty dragon appears more rugged and damaged. Patches of burnt land are visible throughout, as if chunks of flesh are missing on the mighty creature.

As we slowly make our descent, he explains that the Rocky Mountains are a major mountain range that runs north-south in the western United Nation of North America. Our destination is somewhere in the range. I look out the window as we fly past different peaks, seeing patches of muddy banks but no lake or river. If what Bill said is true, then Mother Nature was indeed cruel for turning this pure and beautiful landscape into a lifeless piece of wasteland.

The plane hovers over a clearing high up on the mountain that's too narrow to actually land on. Just when I fear that we might have to jump, a short ladder appears from below our opened door. Gusts of wind rush in, blowing my hair sideways.

I brush strands of hair from my eyes and look down. The drop is not that far but I'm still feeling queasy. I hesitate when Bill tries to guide me out onto the extended step.

"Just hold on tight. The ladder will lower us down," Bill yells over the wind and engine noise.

I release a stifled breath and put my feet on the extended step, which can easily fit the both of us. The metal ladder slowly lowers us to the ground.

As soon as my feet touch down, the plane takes off, leaving just me and Bill on the mountain top.

"Well, this is not awkward at all." I mumble.

A young girl with a crusty old man in the middle of nowhere. But I keep this comment to myself.

Though I have to admit, Bill doesn't come off being like that. He has a kind face, like a loving grandfather, and there's also a sense of dignity to him.

He pretends he didn't hear my comment and walks to the edge, "Shall we go?"

"Where?" I don't see anything nearby except for a steep drop of who knows how far.

"Our headquarters." Then he steps off the edge.

"No!" I scream, wanting to catch him before he falls.

But he doesn't. He just stands there in mid air, extending his hand to me.

I gape in disbelief.

"Come on, don't be afraid." He beckons.

I shuffle closer to him and look down. There's still nothing under his feet other than the intimidating cliff that drops into a dark chasm.

Looking at my reaction, he grins for the first time since we met. "Care to join me?" he says. "Come closer and you'll see."

I may have lost my memories, but I know this is exactly

what someone who's about to kidnap you would say. Except I already got into the car willingly, and boarded the plane. I'm already half way into whatever mess is waiting for me. I don't have any other options. I grab his hand and tentatively, I extend my right foot out into the thin air.

I squeeze my eyes shut as I step next to him. Something hard and steady, like a slab of concrete holds my footing.

I open my eyes and almost lose balance as I stare down into the haunting chasm. Under my feet is a flat panel that seems to have appeared out of nowhere. It's a combination of concrete and steel I think. It's big enough for the two of us with railings to my left and right. I grab on tight as it begins to move.

"It's pretty clever isn't it?" Bill asks. "Our engineers created this ten years ago to protect the headquarters from outsiders, mainly from our enemies. It uses active camouflage technology to create an illusion to the naked eye so you can't see its existence until you are on it." He waves a small device strapped to his wrist. I saw it earlier and thought it was a watch. It must be the remote control used to activate the platform.

The metal track that secures our platform becomes visible when we're about half way down. Sunlight begins to fade as the elevator takes us deeper into the chasm. Broken branches protrude from crevices all around us, like skeletal arms reaching out from their prison cell.

The darker our surroundings become, the more anxious I get. The metal railing turns slippery under my sweaty palms but I don't dare to let go.

The platform suddenly shifts horizontally, almost throwing me off balance. I hold my breath as we move *into* the mountain, passing through stones and gravel like they're not even there. It must be another ingenious illusion, a camouflage tunnel into the heart of the mountain.

As impressive as it seems, I can't help but wonder who they are trying to keep out? What is this secretive organization that Linda so wanted me to join? I feel myself getting increasingly agitated by the second. I need answers.

When I'm about to ask, Bill beats me to it. "Celine will be the one to answer all your questions."

"Why can't you just tell me what's going on?" I don't bother to hide my frustration. I'm surprised this hasn't turn into an anxiety attack yet.

"I'm not authorized to. I'm sorry. My job is to bring you here safely." He says impassively.

The fact that he needs authorization to speak is ridiculous. What kind of a control freak is running this place?

"Is this some kind of a cult?" The words rush out of my mouth. But he cleverly ignores my comment.

After a brief moment in darkness, I begin to see rows of moving platforms similar to the one we are on. We have arrived.

The room we're passing through is easily six or seven storeys high, but only about thirty feet wide. Numerous platforms are parked on the top portion of the room with tracks climbing up the side of the walls. Our track sits along a wall on the left, which will lead into a bright tunnel. Another two tracks branch off from the same hidden entrance and weave into two different tunnels to the right.

"The platforms will only go in and not out." Bill says.

Great, a one-way entrance. That means I'm not getting out that easily.

The track that carries our platform ends about ten feet into one of the three tunnels. I follow Bill as he makes his way down the corridor. A big medical lab appears on my right, encased by glass. Inside, people in white uniforms are working away. A few of them see Bill and wave. Then they dip their heads at me with a smile. I do the same with half of the enthusiasm. The area on my left is much less exciting. Though the white wall does have little circular patterns on it, like ripples in water.

We walk past a silver door that says: MEDICAL ROOM 10. It's closed so I can't see the inside. But its name is pretty self-explanatory. I look past Bill and see more silver doors coming up. Where is he taking me?

Just then Bill stops in front of a silver door that says MEDICAL ROOM 8.

"Here we are." He says while holding a MUD in front of a device above the door handle. It beeps and the door clicks open.

The strong smell of bleach and rubbing alcohol permeates the room. I have to shield my nose as I walk in. The room is about the same size as the one in Intensive Care but more welcoming. Directly in front of the door is a medical pod, similar to the one I used at the hospital but slimmer. Tucked in the opposite corner is a white reclinable armchair that looks soft and inviting. Beside it is a long, oval console table, white and glossy. An abstract painting that covers half of the wall is hung above the table. I think it's a beach at sunset—colourful yet serene.

Just when I think this is a room I don't mind staying in, my eyes fall on a series of glass drawers fastened on the wall next to the comfy chair. In them are sharp, gleaming medical instruments ranging from syringe to scissors, to scalpels. Then there it is again, that unexplainable fear. I close my eyes and tell myself that they're inside a drawer. They can't hurt me. But that's not exactly true, because I still don't know what these people want from me.

"You alright?" Bill asks.

"No." I say.

"Have a seat. You'll find out soon."

"Not soon enough." I mumble.

I sit and purposely turn my head so I'm facing the opposite wall where I don't see the surgical blades. I just can't shake the nagging feeling that I'm being tricked. Scenarios of them dissecting my brain or injecting me with various test drugs flash in my mind like a slide show. My instinct tells me to run. Kick Bill hard in the groin and run. But where to? The moving platform is no longer there and the way we came from is a one-way route. I'm trapped.

A young man walks in, wearing a black asymmetrical zip-up jacket with slim-fit black pants. My eyes go straight to the long sword slung across his back and the two guns hanging from his hip holster. I won't be surprised if he has a grenade tucked in his crotch too. Why on Earth is he so heavily armed? Who, or worse, *what* are they fighting? The more I think about it, the more I want to get out of here.

"Hi, I'm Finn," he extends a hand to greet me.

Still sitting, I slowly shift my gaze from his guns to his face. He looks a few years older than me. Somehow his sweet, handsome face doesn't quite match the deadliness the rest of his body portrays. He's also quite tall. I probably only go up to his shoulder if I stand. His facial features are delicate and well-proportioned, with captivating dark blue eyes, tall straight nose and nicely sculptured lips. He has a certain presence to him that captures my attention.

After staring at him for a little too long, I finally say, "They call me Gabi." Then I shake his hand firmly, letting him know that I'm strong and will not go down without a fight.

"Thanks Bill, I'll take it from here. They want you at Recruitment," he says.

Bill nods and shuts the door behind him, leaving only me and the assassin in the room. A sense of dread washes over me as I study him. I might be able to fight Bill because of his age. But now I might as well surrender and beg for mercy.

"So you're the one who's supposed to tell me what's going on? Speak then." I demand, trying to mask the fear in my voice.

"A little respect goes a long way." He says with a smile while sorting through a few syringes in the drawer.

"You're the one to talk?" I jump up from the chair. My fear is replaced by anger. "I've been pretty much hijacked from the hospital with no recollection of my entire life, almost fell to my death on that stupid illusion platform, and now in a medical room, about to be cut open by a psycho with deadly weapons. So ya, you sure have my respect." I stand tall and stern, but almost have to tiptoe in order to stare straight into his eyes. Every muscle in my body has tensed up, ready for fight or flight.

"Take it easy there you little firecracker," he chuckles. "I promise you won't feel a thing." He takes a scalpel from the drawer and twirls it between his fingers.

Blood drains from my face and he sees it too.

"Alright alright, sorry. I was just joking." He puts the blade back in the drawer. "No one is cutting anyone open today. We're not going to hurt you."

Now my face goes from white to bright red. I would have pounced on him if not for his weapons.

"Okay. I see someone can't take a joke," he says. "Actually, we're here to help you. Celine is usually the one in charge of this, but she's preoccupied at the moment. So here I am."

"Fine, then what is this place? Who are you guys? Why am I here?" I ask.

He looks at me, then tilts his head toward the chair.

With a sigh, I sit down again.

"Have you heard of the Sarcomeres?" he crosses his arms and leans back on the medical pod.

I shake my head. "I might have before the crash, but now I don't remember anything."

"Right, I almost forgot about that. Alright then, I guess I'll have to give you a quick lesson about our kind." He presses a button on the side of the pod and out comes a cushioned seat. He sits down and rests his elbows on his knees. "Everyone here is different than your average human, whom we call Ordinaries by the way. Go figure. Anyway, we are born different. Our genes are superior. The Ordinaries don't know too much about us and those who know are somewhat afraid of us. We call ourselves Sarcomeres."

"What makes you guys so superior?" I ask.

"Well, we move faster, we have higher dexterity and strength. Also, we recover faster from most soft tissue injuries." Finn says.

I wait for a moment, thinking he is going to add more, like they can fly, or time travel or something. But he just stares at me.

"That's it?" I say. "You made it sound like you guys are super-humans or something."

"We *are* super-humans, if you want to call it that. Stuff we can do, the Ordinaries can't. Not even if they train their entire lives." He gets up from his seat. "I can tell you need some convincing. Follow me, I'll show you something."

"Okay. I thought you were going to use the medical pod on me."

"Nah. I trust Linda, she's never wrong. If she said you're positive, then you are," he says.

"Wait, Linda is a Salmonere?"

"Sar-co-mere." Finn enunciates.

"Are you saying I might be a Sarcomere?"

"Well, don't jump the gun just yet. Even if you have the gene, it doesn't mean your body can utilize its full potential. Not all Sarcomeres have the same level of strength and ability."

He leads me out the room and we walk down the long hallway together.

"So what does Sarcomere mean?" I'm struggling to keep up with his long strides.

"The basic unit of a muscle," says Finn.

"So . . . you called yourselves Muscle?" *What a stupid name.* I think in my head.

"Hey, I didn't make up the name okay," he frowns. "And no, not Muscles, Sarcomeres. And that's because our special ability has to do with the way our muscle cells are structured. We have one particular gene that regular humans don't. We call it the Prime Gene, short for neuronal nitric oxide synthase prime, or nNos-Prime, which provides our muscle with extraordinary properties. Ordinaries only have nNos-alpha and beta, but not the prime."

I blink a few times. All that science talk just went over my head like a gust of wind, come and gone. All I care is whether I have that prime gene or not. I know something about me is different, maybe this is it.

"So Linda, she said I'm positive? Meaning yes to the prime gene?" I ask.

"Seems that way."

"Are there other types of super humans?"

"Just one other, but you don't need to worry about them at this point. You'll have enough on your plate to begin with."

He's right, I don't need any irrelevant information to overload my brain. I'm already overwhelmed.

We are now at the end of the hallway. He pushes open a set of heavy doors and we are in yet another corridor with the same white textured walls. Except this one has no rooms on either side and it bends right, then left, then right again.

He opens another set of doors after we turned the last corner and a big white dome appears before my eyes. The massive circular hall has rows of windows stacking up to six storeys high before the cone-shaped roof begins curving in. The ground level is surrounded by offices and meeting rooms, all enclosed by glass. Those with their windows and glass doors darkened, I assume, are occupied. This place is not nearly as crowded as the hospital I came from but there's still a good number of people milling about—some in white lab coats and some heavily armed just like Finn.

"We're in the Dome Hall by the way. Important announcements and town hall meetings are held here." Finn says as he leads me into the dome. The floor under my feet turns from dark hardwood that lined the corridor to glossy white tiles and I feel the temperature difference the moment I enter. Less than ten steps in and my extremities are already covered in goosebumps. I wonder if they purposely crank up the air conditioning to compensate for the lack of fresh air.

Finn banks to the left and a stage becomes visible. A large glass balcony draped with a red and white valance perched above it. On either side of the stage is a set of glass doors with block letters written above its frame. I'm still a bit too far to make out what they say.

"You said you guys are superior in strength, then why the need for so many weapons?" I ask. The thought of being underground still creeps me out, but my new found hope is keeping my nerves at bay.

"Well, there lies another specialty of ours. Weapon development." He pats his guns. "The government works closely with us on this matter. But we are highly secretive. We have an agreement that we supply them with weapons necessary for national defence, in return, they keep their noses out of our internal affairs, and keep our identity a secret. There will only be chaos if the general public knows too much about us."

This reminds me of the whispering I overheard at the hospital. The two nurses were accusing me of being something abnormal. They were afraid. Should I be afraid too? But on the contrary, I feel quite comfortable here. Maybe I *do* belong here.

A surge of hope brings light to my eyes. "So what you're saying is there's a chance I'm from here. My parents might be here?"

"Not exactly," he says. "When Linda first contacted us about you, we searched our database and found nothing. Which means you are not recorded. Chances are, you are a lost Sarcomere."

My earlier excitement quickly dissipates. I'm back to square one. This is becoming like a pattern—hope builds up, then it crashes.

At least it's a step closer to your roots. I remind myself.

If I am a Sarcomere, which they seem quite confident that I am, then I need to learn their ways and their skills. Linda even mentioned that they may be able to recover my memories.

"So all of you live here?" I ask as we approach the stage, which is almost as tall as me. The valance that dangles from under the balcony serves as the perfect backdrop to the otherwise plain stage.

"People who work here also live here, which is the majority of us," Finn says, "others live just like the Ordinaries in cities across the globe. Most of them are strategically placed in jobs that directly assist in our cause. Like hospitals, government sectors, and so on."

"What *is* your cause?" I'm curious.

"You'll learn that soon enough."

"So I've heard." I huff. "Seems like there's a lot of us around though." I say.

"Look at you, talking like you're one of us already." He

nudges my shoulder and gives me a teasing smile. I look away and can't help but feel a little embarrassed. Maybe I embraced this whole situation a little too soon.

"Actually there's not as many of us as you think," he continues. "There's only about five thousand in the system worldwide but I know there are more lost Sarcomeres out there. That's why we treat recruitment very seriously."

We stop in front of the set of glass doors to the left of the stage. Beyond them is an empty hallway that resembles the one we came out from. I look up to read the sign: TRAINING HALL.

"Well, are you ready to be blown away?" Finn arches his eyebrows.

"We shall see." I'm still not convinced that they have super strength. I certainly don't seem to possess any heightened abilities myself. I'm easily out of breath, and still quite weak from the crash. Not to mention my head still throbs from time to time.

Finn pushes open the glass doors and the muffled sounds of clanking blades resonate in the short hallway. We follow the curved corridor and end up in a big arena filled with people. Most are enclosed in the eight training chambers around the arena, sparring or throwing daggers at targets. They remind me of fish bowls, except there's no water and they are filled with super-humans. I wonder if any of them can actually breathe under water. That'd be a cool ability.

Above the glass chambers are balconies and platforms fastened to the wall, piling up to six storeys high. Some stop midway around the rectangular arena and some run the full length. Attached to each balcony or platform is a ladder. Some are fixed, some are extendable. But none leads to a door. By the look of the old copper railings and the gray brick wall, my guess is that they are for climbing.

I look around and realize there must be a dress code in effect because everyone is wearing the same outfit: dark green khakis and black fitted T-shirt. What separates them is the stripe that runs along their sleeves. Most are in blue except one that is red.

In the centre of the room are racks upon racks of weapons. The one closest to us is hung with twenty handguns of various types. I brush my fingers over a few pistols as I walk by. I don't remember if I have ever touched a gun before but I do seem to be fascinated by them. I slowly walk from rack to rack, marvelling at the assortment of firearms.

"You don't seem to be fazed by the weapons." Finn says. "That's a good sign." He nods as if he approves.

"Well, I'm not scared of them if that's what you mean." I reply.

Then something catches my eye among the sword racks ten feet away. I walk up to the rack that houses a sword and a dagger with bright red markings weaving along their blades. The symbols look similar yet different. The ones on the sword resembles ocean waves that rush toward the tip. The symbols on the dagger are more abstract, like random swirls.

"Why do these two have symbols on them?" I pick up the dagger and run my finger along the swirling pattern. It's actually infused within the blade. The surface feels smooth and cold but the red swirls seem to come alive as a faint glow pulses from within. How fascinating.

"They're not your concern at this point, or ever." Finn says with a hint of condescension.

"Wow, you guys *really* like to share, don't you?" I shake my head slightly. Then it strikes me that I'm not afraid of these swords and daggers the way I am of scalpels. This is so strange.

"Do you see that boy over there?" Ignoring my sarcasm, Finn points to a boy who looks about twelve in the far corner, standing on a small balcony about three storeys off the ground. The red on his sleeves looks prominent even from this distance. Marked on the ground directly below him is a big red X.

Without warning, the boy leaps off in a forward somersault. I let out a faint gasp as he touches down, thinking he will surely break a bone or two. Instead, he lands swiftly in a low crouch right on the mark. He then springs into action as three arrows fly toward him from behind the weapons racks. He dodges the first two with minimal effort and catches the third with his right hand just inches from his eyes. He then does a 360 spin and throws the arrow in my direction.

Jeez!

I try to jump out of the way but slam right into Finn's chest instead. I didn't know he was standing right beside me. I look up and he's laughing at me. Out of the corner of my eye I see the deadly arrow is now lodged in a target dummy's heart right behind us, between two racks. Where did that thing come from?

I look at the boy, who's making his way to the arrow with a smirk on his face. I look up at Finn again. He still has the same smile on his face, like he's looking at something funny. Maybe because I'm still leaning against his chest. I should move away. But my eyes linger and my body is as stiff as a board.

Finn shifts a little and that pulls me back to Earth. I quickly move away and pretend to look nonchalant, yet my face is burning with embarrassment.

"Liam is in the Elite Force and he's only twelve," says Finn. I'm glad he's not focusing on how long I have just been leaning on him.

"Is that what the red stripe means?" I ask.

"Yes, you've got quite a sharp eye," he sounds impressed. "Sarcomeres are divided into three ranks. Black is Touch, because they only posses a touch of the gene. They still demonstrate extraordinary strength and agility compared to Ordinaries though. Just their ability is more subtle by our standard. They are allocated to jobs like research and development or recruitment.

"Blue is Core, which most Sarcs fall under and they are responsible for security and defence. Some may go on missions depending on their experience. And red you already guessed. There aren't many Elites, they're hard to come by. Their gene is especially dominant, making them very powerful."

So Liam, at only the age of twelve, is already among the highest rank of Sarcomeres. How impressive.

My eyes search Finn's shirt to see which rank he belongs to but find nothing. He's wearing a dark blue T-shirt under his jacket and the same style of green khakis.

Blue T-shirt. Maybe he's Core.

"There you are." A woman's voice interrupts my chain of thought.

I turn toward the voice and see a short lady in her fifties walking toward us. Her blond-to-almost-white hair is pulled up elegantly in an up-do. The most striking features are her piercing blue eyes that are hard to miss. Her fitted black business suit looks flawless when matched with that pair of bright red stilettos. She carries no weapon but she can easily kill someone with those heels.

"So this is the new girl Linda brought us?" She asks Finn but fixes her gaze on me, eyeing me from head to toe.

My first impression of this woman is in the negatives. Is it her guileful eyes? Her arrogant demeanour? I don't know, but I don't like her.

"Gabi, short for Gabrielle." I answer in measured confidence.

"Nice to finally meet you Gabi. We are glad that you have

joined us. This will be your new home from now on." She extends her hand and I shake it firmly.

I don't like her assumption either. I'm about to tell her that I have yet to decide if I'm staying or not when Finn says, "This is Chief Annette Trousing."

My eyes widen for a brief moment but I compose myself quickly, not wanting to indulge her. I guess I'm not altogether surprised that she's the leader, based on how egotistic she seems. I just thought the leader of the genetically advanced humans would look more . . . deadly.

"It's an honour to meet you. Never thought the chief would meet me here in person." I say.

I figure I should stay on her good side since she'll be governing my life should I choose to stay.

"I make an effort to meet every new recruit. After all, we're like a family." She gives me a warm smile. Then she turns to Finn. "Have you done the full scan on her yet?"

"No, we got distracted," he says. "We can do it now."

"Don't worry about it. Celine's back. She'll scan her. I want you to do something for me." She signals to a girl who's standing near the entrance. I wonder how long she has been standing there, awaiting the chief's command.

"Celine, this is Gabi. She needs a full scan." The girl nods and beckons me to follow her.

Celine has a cute face with bright blue eyes, small red lips and silky blond hair. She's roughly my height and looks about my age.

As we walk out the arena, I take a last glance at Finn, who now looks focused and serious. I wonder what his role is. Will I see him again?

CHAPTER 4

"Alright, you're done." Celine hands me my shirt and shorts. I quickly change out of the thin medical robe and join her on the other side of the frosted glass.

The procedure was quick and relatively painless. Celine made the experience all the more pleasant by always making sure I was comfortable.

She first injected me with a yellow serum that tingled as it made its way through my bloodstream. Then she scanned me from head to toe with a thin hand-held screen.

I'm anxious to know the results. They will determine my fate one way or the other. But I'll have to wait until my initial evaluation tomorrow. Somehow I feel like I'm being coerced into this new life without informed consent. All I know is that everyone here is genetically advanced, quite possibly including me, and they are ranked by the potency of their prime gene. Am I cut out for such an hierarchical lifestyle? I'm not even sure who or what I am, and now I'm going to be placed into evaluation followed by training. For what?

"Shall we go for a walk?" asks Celine, breaking my reverie. "I can show you around and answer any questions you may have. I work in Recruitment."

Perfect!

Celine leads me out of the medical facility and into what looks like a small, underground village. It's a couple of blocks long with a cobblestone pathway cutting through the different shops and restaurants. Trees and various greenery are planted in pots and placed throughout the area. The sight of living plants somehow opens up my airway, calming my nerves. Above the shops are columns of windows and small French balconies. Celine tells me this is where they live. What a lovely little village. For the first time since I arrived, I can see myself living here.

I look up and see something I didn't expect to see inside a mountain.

A clear blue sky.

No wonder it's so bright in here. But where does the beaming sunlight come from? It even casts shadows on the ground.

Seeing my perplexed expression, Celine explains that it's the work of a hologram, programed to represent the weather outside.

"What if it's raining or snowing out?" I ask.

"Then we'll be wet in here too." She gives a playful smile. "We have sensors to record precipitation, wind direction and so on. And that information gets transferred to the many sprinklers and wind jets built in around this area. This is the only 'outdoor' environment in the complex."

"Then why not just live above ground? Why bother with all of this." I wave my hand around.

Celine goes silent for a moment.

Did I say something wrong? I wonder.

"Well it's complicated," she finally says. "Let's just say we are a dying breed and the chief will do whatever it takes to protect us, to give us a deserving lifestyle under the circumstance."

Celine was so cheerful for the past hour that I didn't think she was capable of frowning until now. I almost feel guilty for dragging her mood down.

"So . . . how many people live here?" Trying for a lighter conversation.

"About three thousand. We're now the only headquarters left," she says.

"What happened to the other ones?"

"Destroyed. Many of the Sarcs were killed in the process too."

So much for a lighter conversation. But it sounds too important for me to brush pass.

"Killed by Ordinaries?" I ask.

"No, by the Neuronics," she says.

I'm about to ask who are the Neuronics when she says, "Hey are you hungry? Let's grab a bite to eat. Italo has great pizzas." She grabs my arm and pulls me into a restaurant across the cobblestone path.

We sit down at a table overlooking the street. Directly across is small cafe. A woman with a newborn baby sits on the patio, drinking tea. Next to the cafe is an ice-cream shop. A middle-aged man walks out with a popsicle in his hand and sits down on a bench. They look normal compared to the heavily armed Sarcs in the arena.

Celine catches me eyeing the gentleman on the bench and says, "He used to run the Recruitment facility, but he's retired now."

"So early?"

Celine chuckles. "He retired as of last year . . . at the age of eighty."

I give a gaping "WHAT?" He barely has any wrinkles.

"That's one good thing . . . no, the *best* thing of being a Sarc," she grins, showing her cute dimples. "We age *very* well."

"You don't say." I look around. "So everyone here is actually older than they look?" It's inconceivable.

"Well not quite," she says. "The effect of the gene is more obvious in those thirty and over, because that's when the result of aging begins to show."

I nod in agreement. "Then is life expectancy generally longer?"

Celine purses her lips then says, "Yes and no. We're still prone to diseases like the Ordinaries and if the illness spreads faster than our cells can repair themselves, we die. But if all things go well, we do live longer by maybe twenty to thirty years? Something like that."

I look at the popsicle man again with new found respect. I wish tomorrow's result is positive.

Celine orders a large pizza for the both of us. Since I still have her here, I decide to seize the opportunity.

"So tell me about the Neuronics. Are they also genetically advanced?"

"Ya, but I don't know too much about them." Celine shifts the fork in front of her so it's exactly parallel to the knife. "I've never met a Neuronic before. The war happened before I was born. I only heard about it from my parents, who actually fought in the war against them. I guess a lot of people died on both sides and that was when our other two headquarters were destroyed. One was in the Republic of Europe and the other was in Greater China, I think."

This amnesia business is really getting the better of me. I have a vague memory of where these places are and that's about it. It's like I have to re-take all my history and geography lessons.

Celine quickly tells me that Europe used to be a continent consisting of many countries. But natural disasters and the Great War destroyed many of them. The surviving countries united to form the Republic of Europe about twenty years ago. The United Nation of North America was formed under similar circumstances. Greater China was the exception in that it was the country of China that absorbed everyone else in the former continent of Asia.

"I still remember the old map they showed us when I was in school." Celine says. "There was *a lot* more land on that map compared to the ones we have now."

"Then where did all the land go?"

"Apparently underwater," she shrugs.

I am intrigued yet disturbed that I forgot such important information. A fifth grader can easily out-smart me right now.

My agitation is quickly replaced by hunger when the waiter arrives with our pizza. It looks scrumptious and my mouth begins to salivate. Chunks of meat and mushrooms cover the round dough along with some yellow and green stuff that I don't recognize. I didn't notice how starved I was until now. This is the first decent meal I have had since I woke up from the crash. Hospital food was horrendous.

"I always wondered why they call it pizza." Celine takes a huge bite. "I heard it originated from a place called Italy. It got swallowed by a horrible earthquake some fifty years ago."

"What a shame." I say as I swallow a delicious mouthful. "Their food is good." I quickly grab another piece, as if I haven't eaten in days.

"So where are the Neuronics now? Are you guys still fighting them?" I speak with a mouthful. I'll just pretend I've forgotten my table manners as well.

"I think they're mainly situated in Europe now. I don't know much in this matter. They don't usually tell us much other than what we need to know to do our job. They say it's for our protection. The less we know, the less chance we'll get into trouble. All I know is the Elites and Cores deal with anything Neuronic related." She explains.

If only the strongest Sarcomeres are allowed to deal with these so-called Neuronics, then they must be quite formidable.

"Do they have similar abilities to ours?" I ask.

She swallows her piece so quick, she almost got choked. "No, they're very different from us." She looks around as if afraid someone will overhear. Then she leans closer and whispers. "They are mind benders."

I should have guessed that much by their name. Did I know any of this before? I doubt it. They're so secretive. I was probably just a bored teenager struggling with school and boys. One that was so rebellious that her parents didn't want anything to do with her. They probably are not even looking for me right now.

"Let's talk about something else." Celine suggests and I agree. "Like where you're going to sleep tonight."

Right. I've been so overwhelmed that I forgot about my basic necessities. I could use a nice hot shower right about now.

"I guess I do need a place to sleep don't I?"

"We have guest rooms in the Dome Hall. New recruits usually stay there until they get assigned a rank and a job. Come with me." She produces a MUD from her pocket and scans it through a small device fastened to our table. The machine beeps and a green light appears.

"Thanks for the meal." I say.

"My pleasure." Celine smiles, then leads me out of the restaurant.

The guest rooms are located on the east side of Dome Hall right next to the Training Hall. Celine says there are eight rooms but they have never been occupied simultaneously. I guess lost Sarcomeres are not common. The notion of being one of them still baffles me, and the lack of confirmation makes things worse. I have yet to be validated. Celine won't mention anything about my scan results. Am I one of them or am I not? I don't want to build my hopes up and end up falling flat on my face again. I did that once several weeks ago and it gave me amnesia.

"Here you are." Celine puts her thumb on a pad by the door and instructs me to do the same. The door swings open with a beep. The room smells musty but looks new and unused. Maybe because it looks so clean and white. White floor tiles, white walls, white desk and a white bed. I guess they don't need to beautify the place when it's only a temporary stay for the guest. An oval window sits directly across and it overlooks the Dome Hall.

Despite its simplicity, it does have everything I need. Clean linens, personal hygiene products, and even a new set of clothes and undergarments. But how do they even know my size? *I don't even remember my own size.*

"They're designed by our R&D team. One size fits all. They mold to your body." She winks, as if reading my mind. "You'll love them."

This is getting more interesting by the hour. First the invisible moving platform, then the weather-changing hologram, now the shape-changing bra and panties. I'm liking this place more and more.

"It's getting late. I should head back," says Celine. "Oh, you should sign in at the arena at 9am tomorrow. They'll give you further information regarding the scan. It's nice meeting you and best of luck. I can see you'll fit right in with us." She gives me a genuine smile and closes the door behind her.

Ahhhh! I let out a long sigh and stretch my arms. Finally some alone time. It has been a *long* day.

I jump into the hot shower and stay there until my fingers begin to get wrinkly. After drying off, I decide to try on the high-tech panties that seem big in my hands. Miraculously, they start to shrink as I slip them on. The material feels silky and smooth against my achy hips. I'll try the rest on tomorrow because I begin to see stars in my drowsy eyes. I slump onto the plush bed and fall asleep immediately.

CHAPTER 5

A light breeze carrying a fresh scent of lavender brushes past me as I lift my head to bask in the warm summer sun. A beautiful scene captivates me as I look over a ledge perched on the hillside. The high vantage point offers me a stunning panoramic view of the azure coast that stretches to the horizon. Small waves of turquoise water are rolling to the shore of the half-moon shaped pebble beach, which separates the tranquil blue sea from the bustling old town.

But not even the serene atmosphere can calm my unsettled emotions. Something inside me is gripped in fear. A bright flame ignites and I look down to find that my trembling hands have caught on fire. I frantically wave my arms around in an attempt to extinguish the painless flame but to no avail. The dancing fire rapidly snakes up my arms and ignites my torso until my whole body is engulfed in a heat-less flame. I open my mouth to scream but only a soundless exhale is heard. I pick up my legs to run but find myself immobilized. A wave of horror sweeps through me as I stand in the haunted flame, helpless.

I wake with a loud scream. I sit up so fast that the room

spins before my eyes. I examine my hands. No flame, only sweaty palms. I look down and notice that I'm drenched in a layer of cold sweat. The white bed sheet is stamped with the darker mark of perspiration. That was the first dream I had since the accident. I'm half glad that I can dream again, but the nightmare was too vivid.

I wait a moment until I regain my equilibrium before standing up. The clock on the wall says 8:05am.

Good, I still have time to get ready. I think to myself.

Showering calms me down immediately. I pretend the warm water can wash away all my apprehension and fear, at least for the time being.

After the long shower, I put on the high-tech bra developed by the Research and Development Department. It does mold to my cup size as Celine promised, and with extra give for when I need to be active. The clothes they laid out for me consist of a black fitted T-shirt and a pair of olive green khakis. To my slight disappointment, there is no coloured stripe on the sleeves.

What did you expect? You're not confirmed yet. I remind myself.

They even had a pair of black running shoes with socks waiting for me by the door. They fit perfectly. As much as I hate the uncertainty, I do appreciate their attentiveness.

I check myself in the mirror to make sure I look decent for my evaluation. But as usual, I'm a wreck. I look gaunt and pale, though better than four weeks ago. The dark circles under my eyes are still prominent, making me look lethargic. My over-grown eyebrows are like two patches of random bushes attached to my face. My hair feels dry and brittle and my lips are cracked. What would have been my nice features are now covered by the lack of maintenance.

This is what Finn saw yesterday. *Great!*

For a long moment, I'm reluctant to leave the room looking like this. After much considering, I resolve that my appearance should be the last of my priorities. I take a deep breath, tie my hair in a tight ponytail, and head for the arena.

I arrive at the training hall with fifteen minutes to spare. It's empty and quiet, unlike yesterday. I scan the hall, feeling recuperated but also anxious to get the day started. I wonder who will be my evaluator.

Please don't let it be Annette. I silently plea. For some reason that woman makes me very uncomfortable.

Or maybe it'll be Finn. As I secretly hope so, a voice startles me from behind.

"You must be Gabi," a man says. "I'm Alex. I'll be overseeing your initial evaluation and training." He says with a stoic face.

"Nice to meet you." I reply, trying to hide my disappointment. He looks older than Finn, and he's shorter and wider.

"Here, drink this." He hands me a mug of thick liquid. "It's a nutrition supplement to prep your body."

The mug is icy cold with a fruity aroma that makes my empty stomach growl. The initial sip creates a blast of flavours in my mouth that consist of assorted berries and a slight lingering bitterness. I immediately recognize the main ingredient being ginseng, and I certainly can benefit from its energy boosting property.

You remember random facts about ginseng but not your own age! I shake my head but I don't think Alex notices.

"I bet you must be very anxious to find out your results." He says while I'm chugging down the delicious drink. "I gotta say, I am shocked at how prominent your gene is. . ." he measures me up and down and appears completely unimpressed. "You know, with your physique and all."

I tighten my jaw at the unexpected insult but give no reply. *Just let it slide.* I tell myself.

"Which means you could utilize your potential to quite an extent with the right training and mindset." Says Alex. "The start may be slow because your body hasn't discovered how to use what's hidden inside those muscle cells. The hardest and longest part of the training is on how to bring out that potential. It can take anywhere from a few weeks to a few years. Today, we'll start by putting your body through some tests to see how it reacts."

"Great, more tests." I mumble.

"If you're going to speak, make sure I can hear you."

"It's not for you." I mumble again and he glowers at me. "Fine, sorry. Please continue." I want to roll my eyes, but manage to suppress the urge at the last second. There's no point aggravating my instructor, no matter how much of a jerk he is.

As I follow him into a small room on the other side of the arena, I notice the faint black stripe on his sleeves. He's a Touch, which means he possesses only a trace of the prime gene, not even comparable to twelve-year-old Liam. I wonder how he feels knowing he's at the bottom of the barrel in this super-human domain.

Wait a second, why would they send a Touch to train me? He already established that my gene is prominent, which would make me at least a Core. Do they think I'm weak?

The thought of being underestimated appals me, but there's nothing I can do about it.

We enter a small changing room with a bench on one wall and some lockers on the other.

"This is to sense your muscle movements." He holds up a stack of circular stickers, each about two inches in diameter. "Now take off your clothes."

"WHAT?" My voice is so loud that it bounces off the walls a few time in the small room.

"I need to put these all over your body at specific muscle junctions. Come on, we don't have all day," he says impatiently.

"But shouldn't they get a female to do this?" I don't appreciate his lack of sensitivity.

"Did you get to choose the surgeon who operated on your naked body? Do you specifically ask for a female doctor when you're dying? NO! Because you get what you get and you just hope to get the best in the field." His voice is loud and harsh, like he's about to explode.

Heat rushes to my face. I want to tell him that this is different, that I'm not dying on a surgical table. But instead I let out a slow breath of exasperation and swallow the impulse to punch him in the gut. If this was four weeks ago my temper tantrum would have left scratch marks on his average looking face.

"Fine." I retort. "But I better not catch you looking or doing anything inappropriate."

"Trust me darling, there's not much to look at." He eyes me up and down again.

I have to applaud myself for exerting such tremendous self-control to not kick him in the shin. If only my psychologist were here to witness my progress.

"That's interesting coming from a Touch." I promised no physical aggression but said nothing about verbal retaliation. "I wonder, how do you feel being inferior to all your fellow Sarcomeres?"

Alex doesn't answer me but I take just as much satisfaction

from his furious gaze. I can tell I have hit a nerve because his face is flushed. I don't regret my words, he should know how to treat a lady properly.

It becomes obvious that our quarrel will get us nowhere. So I finally turn around and start removing my clothes. Thank God they gave me these undergarments.

I stand with my back to him in just my bra and underwear. He begins at the back of my neck and carefully places the first disc at the bottom of my scalp where the hairline ends. He sticks a few more discs around that area then continues down my neck. I get goosebumps every time his fingers brush my skin. How many of these stickers do I have to wear?

Meanwhile, Alex is being extremely precise, taking his sweet time to ensure they are at the exact position. After a long ten minutes, he is finally finished with the back of me.

"Turn around." He orders.

I turn around slowly, making sure the stickers don't fall off. I do not want him touching me any longer than necessary.

He begins placing the remaining ones on my front. Heat begins to flush my face. I can't tell whether it's from anger or embarrassment. I take this opportunity to study his face. It's interesting how perception changes based on your emotions. He looked average when I first saw him fifteen minutes ago, but now he looks repulsive with his oversized nose and eyes that are set too far apart. I think he knows how disgusted I am with him because he's making an effort to skirt my eyes even when working on my face.

Good, make him feel guilty.

After another gruelling ten minutes, we are finally done.

"Put your clothes back on. The stickers will hold." He says. "Make sure you don't take *any* of them off until you're told to. You get that Princess?"

Breathe . . . just rise above, rise above.

After climbing multiple flights of stairs we reach a platform that protrudes from the brick wall like a diving board with railings on both sides. In big white letters painted on the edge are the words SIXTY FEET. It doubles the height from where Liam jumped off yesterday. I look over the edge and see an empty space directly below. No red X. My legs begin to go numb and I tighten my grip on the railings. I want to turn back but Alex is standing between me and the stairs.

"Jump." Alex says unexpectedly.

"What? No! It's one thing to insult me, but this? This is plain murder. If you—"

I feel Alex's hand briefly on my shoulder, then I'm no longer standing on the platform. My heart leaps to my throat as I fall backward. The end of my ponytail hitting my face. I can see Alex's face getting further and further from me, which means the hard concrete floor is fast approaching. All I can think of is how I survived a thirty-thousand foot drop from the sky just to end up being killed from a six-storey fall. I shut my eyes as I prepare for the painful impact, and an image of me staring at my reflection flashes in my head. My face was expressionless. I looked more filled in and healthy, pretty even, unlike the bony wreck that is me right now.

Before I can discern the flashback, my body hits something so hard that it knocks the wind out of me. Thankfully it gives way at the last second, absorbing most of the impact but leaving me dazed.

I open my eyes, expecting to be dead. But the concrete floor has literally turned into a hard sponge. I'm woozy but otherwise unharmed. As I try to stand, a loud thump startles me and I fall back down onto my bottom. Then Alex appears next to me. He has just jumped off the same platform and landed perfectly on his feet. The floor under him remains concrete.

"So our proud princess didn't have much to show for after all huh?" Alex says.

"You're a real piece of work, you know that?" I say through the trembling. Too shaken up to move.

"You should thank me for putting those stickers on you. They saved your precious life by activating the protection mechanism in the floor. You know how?" he crouches beside me. "Because they didn't detect *any* Prime-gene activities in your muscle cells. In other words, you're not as capable as you think. A word of advice, shut up and listen to your trainer." He stands and heads for the exit.

My mind is blank as my gaze follows Alex out the door. I feel cold and empty. I hug myself as tight as possible, not wanting to move. I don't know how long I've been sitting here but eventually the floor begins to harden beneath me, reversing back to its original form.

The cold concrete adds another layer of chill to my already trembling body. The same desolation I felt when I discovered my amnesia is sweeping over me with renewed potency. The glimpse of hope Finn and Celine gave me was crushed when I hit the ground. Alex has just proven that I am indeed powerless and feeble. But he also showed me the cruel side of the Sarcomeres. Do I really want to endure such belligerence from strangers?

I slowly lift my hands to feel my cold face and find that I've been crying. I didn't notice others have already started their training. So much for not crying in front of people. Now the whole arena knows what a wimp I am. Yet no one offered to help a sobbing girl sitting in the middle of the floor. Everyone just goes about their business as if I'm invisible.

I take a shuddering breath, wipe the remaining moisture off my face and head for the exit. This is not the place for me. I may not remember who I am or what I've done in the past but I am most certainly not heartless. I have more pressing business than standing around getting humiliated by these so-called "advanced" humans. I have no interest in going through any more death-defying stunts to *maybe* bring out my potential one day. I don't care about the gene. I just need my memories back so I can continue where I left off.

When I'm about to exit the arena, something whips by, followed by a sharp pain on my cheek. I squeak as blood trickles down my face. Lodged in the wall five feet in front of me is a dagger. A thin trail of blood coats the tip of the blade.

I spin around to seek out the attempted murderer and see a girl in her late teens walking toward me, carrying a smug smile.

"Sarcomeres don't just give up you know," she says. "We're given a special gift. We're destined to serve as guardians to this world. I'm just saying." She pulls out the dagger from the wall and resumes her training as if nothing happened.

I have only one conclusion in my mind: These people are mad, and arrogant, and have no regard for others' lives. I need to get out of here quick, before I get sliced up by more Sarcomeres.

I run as fast as I can back to the guest suite and quickly change into the clothes I arrived in. I make sure to peel off every single sticker Alex put on me. I looked like a freak with white dots all over my body. No wonder the others could mark me as a rookie.

I check my cheek in the mirror, expecting a deep bloody cut. But in its place is a thin, long scab.

Where's the cut? I ask myself.

Based on the size of the scab, the wound should be quite deep. It shouldn't have scabbed over in just—

"The prime gene!" I mutter aloud, as if a light bulb just turned on in my head.

Finn mentioned something about accelerated healing. This must be it. Could this be the reason I survived the crash? I have to test this further after I get out of here.

I stand in front of the guest building, don't know which way to go. Celine didn't mention anything about exits during our little tour. I begin to question if people are even allowed to leave.

The more I think about it, the more nervous I get. What if they mean to keep me here forever? The thought of being trapped inside a mountain is unbearable.

I look around the Dome Hall for an exit sign. There's none. I wander around the complex until I finally found the recruitment section, but Celine is not here. I try my luck in the village, checking store after store, but still no sign of her. As I exit the last store, ready to give up, I see a familiar face. I run toward him without hesitation.

"Finn!" I tap him on the shoulder urgently. Startled, he swings his arm around and elbows me right on the bridge of my nose. I fall backward. A blinding pain ignites in my head. The last thing I remember is the rugged cobblestone on my back.

"Oh crap. Gabi . . ."

CHAPTER 6

"Good, you're awake," a man says.

"Where am I?" I ask.

"Recovery," he answers. "We'll try again tomorrow."

"No, I'm ready." I try to sit up but my body complains violently.

"You're ready when I say so," he stares at me with piercing eyes. "We'll try again tomorrow."

I lie back down and close my eyes, too weak to argue.

"Gabi. . .Gabi."

I open my eyes. The bright light stings.

"Thank God you're awake." I can feel the heat radiating from someone's face just inches from me.

"What . . . what's going on?" I try to shield my eyes from the bright light but accidentally hit my nose. I wince at the sharp pain.

"Oh crap, please don't tell me I just gave you another amnesia." Finn looks flustered.

Then it comes back to me. I just got knocked out by a guy twice my size . . . in public.

"What is wrong with you people?" I push myself up with some difficulty. "The day's not even over, yet I've been pushed off a sixty foot ledge, sliced on the face by a dagger and now lying here with a concussion and a broken nose!" A lump forms in my throat. "I just want to go home." Tears collect in my eyes.

But I don't even know where home is.

The emotions I've been holding back unleash all at once, like a cracked dam finally overcome by a forceful river. I cover my face and wail without reservation. I hate all of this. I hate my life.

I feel the mattress sinking in as Finn sits down beside me and gently strokes my hair. "Shh.... It's okay. It's okay. I'm sorry."

His calming touch is nice but not quite enough to repair the collapsed dam. It won't bring back my memories. It won't take me home.

After I don't know how long, I finally pull myself together enough to speak. "Can you get me out of here? Please?"

"I know it's been hard, but you've been very strong. I'm sorry if we weren't able to make you feel more welcome." His empathy reminds me of Linda, whom I now miss dearly.

"I don't belong here," I take a shuddering breath. "I can't go through another death-defying test again. I can't . . . I just can't. Please, I just want to go." I would kneel and beg if I need to.

"We don't force people to stay if they don't wish to. But there's not many of us left and it's important to sustain our kind and to protect each other. I just want you to be sure." He squeezes my shoulder to reinforce his point. "I know your initial training was a disappointment but the gene in you *is* very strong. We don't often come across high-potential Sarcs like you. This may be premature to say, but you might have what it takes to become an Elite, you know that?"

Me, an Elite? I suddenly want to laugh at the absurdity of Finn's words, despite my profuse crying. So far the only miracle my gene gave me was scabbing over a cut in record time.

"I'm flattered. But you didn't see me at the evaluation, I was a complete disaster." I lower my head in shame. "And this." I point to my nose. "If my gene is so powerful, why isn't my nose healed by now? It still hurts like hell."

"The gene specifically targets muscles and soft tissues. It does nothing for bones. So unfortunately, you'll have to endure the regular recovery of a broken nose." Now it's his turn to lower his head in shame. "I'm sorry. I really didn't mean to hurt you. It's just . . . well, I'm known for my quick reflexes." He scratches his head in embarrassment.

If this was Alex, or that arrogant girl who cut me, I'd have bitten their heads off. But for some reason, I can't stay mad at Finn.

"Thanks for trying to take me in, but I really do wish to leave. My priority is elsewhere." I say.

He gets up, looking defeated. "If that's what you wish. I'll take you to the train station then."

I survey the area one last time as Finn leads me through the village toward a narrow path at the south end. The hologram is showing a gloomy, overcast sky, which coincidentally reflects my mood.

The short path opens up to a small station that connects to an extensive underground network of tramways. According to Finn, the network consists of various routes connecting the main hub to other parts of the Rockies. I don't know if it's the time of the day or that people here simply don't leave, the station is completely empty, which makes it eerily quiet. Despite the effort of the white glow illuminating the area, I still feel a bit claustrophobic thanks to its low ceiling.

Sitting ten feet in front of us are eight carts linked to each other by metal rods. Together they make one long tram, hovering just a foot above the track with no wheels. The carts remind me of eggs, oval and white. The mid section is made out of glass that reveals four white seats inside. It'd be funny if the seats were yellow.

Instead of going to the tram, Finn leads me to a piece of glass secured on a wall to our left. It looks about four feet long and three feet tall, give and take a few inches. He puts his palm on the lower right corner and the screen comes to life, showing what looks like a map of the underground tramways.

"I will take you into the city's train station just south of here." Finn says as he slides his finger across the screen. A few seconds later a loud click resonates in the empty station. I turn my head toward the sound just in time to see the first cart detaches itself from the group. It glides silently forward and stops.

"Shall we?" Finn gestures toward the cart in waiting.

As soon as the glass door closes, the pod begins to move. My heart sinks as it navigates through the dim tunnel at a phenomenal speed. Who would have thought that under the visage of the mighty Rocky Mountains lies a secret society of genetically advanced humans who possess the world's greatest physical abilities. And . . . I'm about to abandon the opportunity to become one of them. The conflicted emotions inside me are threatening to rip me apart. One side tells me to stay because I *am* a Sarcomere, potential or no potential. But the other side convinces me that I won't survive training. Since neither option can guarantee my safety, I'll choose the path that offers me greater freedom.

The tunnel is fifteen feet high by about twenty feet wide and travels south from the village all the way to the end of the Rockies' southern-most range. The north tramway begins from the Dome Hall and travels up toward Alaska. Our destination is a short distance to the south.

Neither of us has spoken since we boarded the tram. Then my sudden squeal breaks the silence when the tram takes a sharp right, knocking me into Finn. The dim tunnel makes it hard to see ahead, which adds to the thrill of the ride.

While I'm holding on for dear life, Finn doesn't seem to be bothered by our speed nor the unexpected dips and turns that jolt me every time. Shadows dance on his face as we zip through the flickering lights that illuminate the tunnel, creating illusions of funny faces that he could be making. But in actuality, his expression is as stoic and blank as a statue.

"You won't need any travel documents as long as you stay within the UNNA," he says while handing me a MUD. "Here. It's been loaded with enough money for you to survive a while on your own."

"No. . . I can't." I don't want to owe anyone anything. But I also just realized that I left the MUD Linda gave me back in the guest suite.

"To make up for your broken nose," he shoves the card into my hand. "Use it to contact me directly if you ever run into trouble, or . . . if you change your mind." A smile touches his lips.

I look away, not wanting to be captured by his charisma, or else I would really consider staying.

After another ten minutes of travelling through the

underground labyrinth, we finally arrive at a dead end. I follow Finn out of the egg-shaped tram and the smell of wet dirt invades my nose. Next comes the chilled air that will never hit sunlight.

Finn leads me toward a small alcove to the right where no visible paths can be seen. The only source of lighting are a few yellow orbs tucked among the spiky rocks in the rugged and weary walls. Though the tunnel is not small, the uncultivated appearance is enough to trigger fear—the fear of being swallowed by the monster that is the gigantic mountain above me. But technically I'm already in its belly.

Finn doesn't seem to be bothered by it. He's probably been here a hundred times before. He looks into a small red dot on the jagged wall and a loud click echoes through the area. It must be a retina scanner.

"Are you ready?" he asks.

I just nod, not knowing what to expect. He grabs my elbow and leads me forward. The height of the ceiling diminishes as we get deeper into the alcove. My muscles tense up and I hold my breath as we walk right through the mountain.

CHAPTER 7

I have both of my hands on Finn's forearm, squeezing it so tight that I suspect our limbs will go numb very soon. Darkness envelops everything the instant we enter the mountain. The unease I felt earlier seems trivial when compared to the terror that's mounting on every inch of my skin right now, weighing me down like lead in my blood. My imagination turns into something sinister the moment all lights go out. The fear of something unseen lurking in the dark is crippling, making my already trembling legs that much heavier. The only thing keeping me sane is Finn's calmness. I don't know how he can act like we're just taking a leisurely walk in the park. If he were to let go, I would definitely lose myself in this dark, never-ending void.

Just as I imagine the worst, Finn wiggles his way out of my death grip.

"WAIT! Where are you going?" I desperately swing my arms in the emptiness trying to claw my way back to him but he is gone. He left me by myself in this unbearable darkness. I want to scream but my voice is stifled in the back of my throat, like a plug is jammed in a bottle, preventing anything from escaping.

Just when my sanity begins to slip, Finn's strong arm is suddenly back, wrapping around my shoulder like an iron rod.

"I'm still here," he says.

"Where the hell did you go?" I shout. If he thinks this is funny, I will punch him, even if I can't see.

"Sorry. I forgot you are new to this. My GPS had an interference, we're good now. We're almost there." He pulls me in tighter as if he knows his disappearance almost gave me a heart attack. I want to say that he should have given me a heads-up, but I decide to let it go. I'm just glad he didn't abandon me.

I take a deep breath and his ocean-scent body wash fills my lungs, soothing my nerves. As long as he doesn't let go again, I should be able to maintain my sanity long enough to get out of here.

Finn squeezes my shoulder and that's when I see a faint light in the distance.

Finally. I breathe a sigh of relief.

We walk out of the mountain and end up inside a small room stacked with old, rusty items. It looks and smells like someone's storage room. I don't know how the transition happened but I don't care. I'm just elated that we're no longer inside that dreadful mountain.

Finn opens a door to our right and the musty smell somehow becomes stronger. I step through the doorway and find myself standing at the back of a small antique store.

"Wasn't that fun?" Finn looks at me with a mischievous smile. His arm still on my shoulders.

I back off from him reluctantly, "Why did we have to go through the mountain? You guys can't build a regular exit?"

"It's for our protection. All of our exits are made that way so if we've been infiltrated, our enemy will not be able to escape. It's better safe than sorry." He shrugs.

A bit of over kill is what I think but my opinion doesn't matter. The path to the front of the store is almost non-existent. The place is packed with antiques big and small, and randomly placed so we have to walk around or sometimes walk over certain objects. Finn seems to know exactly how to navigate this place so I try to follow close behind. As messy and tight as this place is, its contents are quite intriguing. Along the two walls are columns of wooden shelves and on them are books. Or at least that's what I think they are. I didn't know they still exist. I want a closer look. So I step over a silver device the size of my head sitting on the wooden floor. It has numerous buttons on the side and a circular plate on the top. Above the plate are the words CD PLAYER, so smudged that I wonder if I'm even reading it correctly. I look up to see Finn is already at the front of the store, talking to some guy. I can ask him later.

I resume my exploration and slowly brush my fingers along the spines of the dusty books on the crowded shelves, purposely avoiding the section that's covered in cobwebs. It's fascinating to see stories printed on paper and bound by pictured covers. I think I would appreciate flipping through each page as I read, feeling its texture and its weight. Something more substantial than just staring at a plastic screen.

"Are you having fun?" Finn is suddenly by my side again.

"This is quite the place." I say as I pull a book away from its neighbours. "A Song of Ice and Fire . . ." I mumble the words on the hard cover.

"Yeah, this is my favourite exit by far." Finn pulls another book from the shelf and flips through the pages rapidly so it creates a light breeze. "Every time I come here it's like stepping back in time you know, experiencing pieces of history. Like these books, as obsolete as they are now, they were once so popular that every household had at least one shelf full of them. Can you imagine?"

"They must have had big houses." I carefully put the book back to its original slot.

"Anyway, we should get going." Finn does the same then leads me to the front of the store. A lonely desk covered in gadgets sits in the corner, big enough for just one person to use. Other than the space needed for the door to swing open, every inch of the squeaky floor is smothered in stuff. I'm not so sure if some of them count as antique. They look more like garbage to me.

"John here is the expert." Finn pats the guy on the shoulder. "He tends to this little disguise of ours."

I smile a little and John reciprocates.

Finn swings the front door open and the late afternoon sun blinds me for a moment. Between the honking of cars and shouting of people, I don't need to see to know that we are now in the middle of a bustling city. The sidewalks are packed with pedestrians and shoppers. Some even venture onto the four-lane road just to get ahead. Cars and taxis form four perfect lines between the sidewalks, inching forward slowly.

"Is it always this busy?" I ask.

"More or less." Finn replies. "But also today's Sunday. So it gets crazier. You see that?" he points to the huge structure at the end of the road. "That's the station."

"Thanks for escorting me out. I guess this is goodbye." I look down.

"I'll walk you to the station." he says.

I nod, welcoming the chance to spend ten more minutes with him. I know I have only known him for two days, but my heart aches at the thought that this will be my last time seeing him. I wasn't mad at him when I yelled in the medical room. And I'm not mad that he punched me either. I hope he knows that. In fact, I don't mind the broken nose. Yes, the pain is annoying but it gives me something to remember him by. The boy who broke my nose.

We walk in silence all the way to the station. The smell of food permeates the street, reminding me that I haven't eaten much all day. We reach the train station after a short walk during which I was bumped on the shoulder twice by eager pedestrians. The impressive entrance is a stainless steel arch reaching at least five storeys high. Two massive stone pillars frame the sides, giving the station its grandeur. The inside is just as stunning. An enormous light fixture that reminds me of spinning atoms and molecules hangs from the high ceiling. Big tinted windows line the opposite wall. Through them I see the rows of bullet-trains sit in waiting. This might be one of the main stations in the nation based on the sheer number of people funnelling in and out. Most mind their own business with the exception of a few who steal a look or two our way. If Finn had brought his katana, I'm sure there'd be more than just a few stares. I don't know if it's even legal to carry weapons so openly in public. I'm just glad he's not dressed like the time when I first met him in that medical room, with weapons hanging out and about. The last thing I want right now is more trouble.

"This is as far as I can accompany you," Finn says. "You sure about this?"

No I'm not. But I have to stick to my decision.

I nod. "Thank you for everything. We might meet again one day?" I glance at him for the last time.

"I'll look forward to that day." He smiles, then walks out of the station, quickly disappearing into the crowd.

My heart wants me to run after him, but my brain reminds me of my priority, which is to set my next destination. I wish there's something in my memories that could guide me, but there's nothing. One option is to go find Linda.

What about the man in the recovery room. I suddenly remember the flashback. But I'm not sure whether that was from my lost memories or merely a dream. All I recall from that episode was a familiar man in a recovery room, not enough information to help me at this point.

Just when I look up to read the destination board, a loud explosion erupts from the entrance. I fall backward into a wall from the violent jolt, bruising my shoulders in the process. I cover my head as pieces of flying debris shoot toward me. A girl beside me gets knocked down by a slab of flying steel and lies lifelessly on the dark marble floor. I quickly drop to my stomach and shrivel into a ball, praying that I won't end up like her.

Before I have time to recover from the initial shock, another explosion blasts through the station, followed by a cacophony of agonizing screams. One more blast, this one is so close to me that the concussive force pushes me further into the wall. The brief pressure compresses my lungs until they're about to burst.

As soon as the pressure clears, I inhale a deep breath of air to ensure my lungs still work. Other than a mild ache, they seem to be fine.

Finn! I suddenly remember.

He was heading to the entrance when the first explosion happened. What if he is . . .

It's all my fault. He shouldn't have escorted me here.

Guilt and fear propel me to go search for him even though common sense tells me to stay put and wait for help. I ignore my common sense and slowly push myself up. The guilt of him dying over my selfishness will eat me alive. I need to make sure he's okay.

Please be okay, please be okay . . . I repeat the same phrase over and over in my head like a mantra for Finn's safety.

I climb over a layer of rubble that was the big chandelier. Shards of glass and snapped steel rods litter the area. One slip could cause a whole lot of bleeding. I crawl past a big slab of stone that's pinning a man down on the ground. I have no time to check if he's dead or alive.

After a few wobbly steps, my right foot slips on something wet and I tumble forward into a pool of blood. I gag as I lay eyes on a dead girl's head.

Look away. Keep pushing forward. I tell myself.

I manage to ignore the need to vomit and plow through the dust and fallen obstacles. Pieces of human remains are visible throughout the station; a few arms hanging on broken light fixtures, a leg or two wedged between piles of rocks, and I think I even see a head on the broken ticket counter. This looks a lot like the crash site I woke up in. Why do I always get sucked into gruesome situations like this? I must be evil in my past life to inherit such bad karma.

As I'm sure more people are buried under the rubble, I tell myself not to look and just keep going. But their agonizing moans are wiggling into my wavering concentration. I bite down on my lower lip and begin climbing the mountain of debris that will lead me to where the grand entrance used to be.

As I approach the half collapsed archway, the sounds of people shouting and metal clanking become audible. But my sight is blocked by a thick layer of dust and smoke, not able to see further than two feet ahead. I search the ground for signs of Finn. There's nothing except blood-soaked rocks and molten metal.

I push on, climbing and digging.

The dust finally begins to settle, allowing me to see further ahead. Vaguely, I see shadows—many shadows dancing frantically in the dispersing dust.

"Capture him! He's a Sarc!" someone yells.

I turn toward the voice and see a dozen men in dark blue uniforms ganging up on one guy. The blue soldiers carry crossbows, long swords and guns. Their opponent on the other hand looks less formidable and is covered in blood. But he doesn't seem to be backing down even though the odds are twelve to one.

The opponent begins his attacks. His movements are so quick that the blue soldiers can barely defend themselves never mind charge offensively. Realizing their lack of skills compared to their enemy, the soldiers back off to regroup and that's when I see him.

A massive stone is lifted from my chest the moment I recognize Finn. But my excitement is short-lived when another dozen soldiers charge toward him.

"Finn!" I regret speaking as soon as his name leaves my lips. Having heard my warning, a handful of men turn their attention toward me, flanking me, weapons ready.

"Get her, she's a Sarc too!" someone in the group yells.

I look around for an escape route but find none. I back up further into a fallen wall, wishing a weapon could magically appear in front of me.

This is it. This is how I will die.

In a flash of movement, Finn suddenly appears in front of me, panting, a bloody sword in his hand. It's not his katana but at a moment like this, any weapon would do.

"Stay back!" he orders through gritted teeth.

I nod, too terrified to speak.

In mere seconds, four soldiers collide with him just steps from me. I half shield my face as the brutal combat unfolds, too afraid to see what might happen. But I'm also curious. I peep through the gap between my fingers and see twelve bodies lying on the ground where I first saw Finn. I glance back at the battle in front of me and what I see blows my mind. I knew Finn could fight but I never imagined such ability coming from a human being. His movements are lightning fast yet graceful. Every strike is deadly, precise and fluid, like a gale-force wind— invisible but for the damage it evokes.

Two soldiers simultaneously thrust their swords toward Finn's torso. But they are too slow and clumsy compared to their Sarcomere enemy. Finn jumps up, kicks his legs into a high split and connects right into the soldiers' faces. The impact knocks them back ten feet, leaving them bloody and disoriented.

The next two men are upon Finn with daggers aimed at his chest. They never had a chance. Finn's sword makes two deadly swipes in the air, then two bodies collapse by his feet.

The short battle ends with Finn grabbing my arm and yanking me off the wall. We break into a sprint, leaving behind another pile of bodies. I can hear multiple footsteps chasing us but I can't afford to look back. Especially not when there are arrows whizzing past us followed by gunshots. There's so much adrenaline coursing through my veins that I doubt I would feel the pain even if I get hit. Instead of running through the panicked crowd in front of the collapsed building, Finn takes the back route that will soon lead us into the woods. Although I'm running as fast as I can, so fast that my legs feel foreign to me, I can tell I'm still holding Finn back. He can easily outrun the soldiers but he's taking smaller steps to accommodate me. He has no idea how grateful I am that he's not leaving me behind.

Despite my slower pace, we manage to put a good distance between us and the pursuing soldiers. The ruin that was once the train station is far behind us now.

Just when I think we are out of harm's way, four dark

figures emerge from the trees fifty feet ahead, blocking our path. Their faces are hooded by their purple robes.

Finn stops abruptly and I stumble forward. He tightens his grip on me so I don't trip and fall.

"What is it?" I gasp, feeling like a very large person is sitting on my chest.

"Neuronics," Finn says under his breath. "Stay close to me, don't look them in the eye, and don't believe anything you see. Use this when you have the chance." He hands me a gun.

I don't remember if I ever held a gun before, but it's heavier than I thought. The cool and smooth metal is somewhat soothing against my hot and sweaty palm. There are red markings infused into its gleaming surface, just like the blades I saw back in the training hall. The lines and curves of the characters remind me of ancient runes. And the red ink inside seems to be moving, like a mini river flowing through a maze. This is *his* gun, not a stolen one from the soldiers like I thought.

"Duck!" Finn pulls me to the ground as a massive tree trunk flies over our heads. I look up and see the four figures still standing at their original spot. Their hoods lowered, revealing their stern faces. All of them male.

I want to ask Finn where did that tree trunk come from but the blue soldiers have caught up to us from behind. Finn springs onto his feet and collides with the crowd of blue in a flash.

I hold up my gun with trembling hands, thinking I can help Finn clear out a few enemies. But the chaotic blur makes it difficult for me to aim. I shift my attention to the purple figures and they too have advanced closer.

Trying to steady my aim, I heedlessly stare into the eyes of one of the Neuronics and find myself immobilized by his intense gaze. No matter how hard I try to look away, my eyes will not comply. I begin to feel something invisible reaching into my mind, like tentacles creeping through my brain, scrutinizing my every brain cell.

NO!

Frantically, I drop the gun and clutch my head with both hands. I need to get these tentacles out of my head. But they are growing in number and are now in every orifice of my head.

AHH!. . . gross!

I can see their ends flailing from my nostrils. I grab onto one with my fingers and I pinch as hard as I can. But the damn thing won't die. The feeling is horrible, like a sickening itch in my brain that I can never scratch.

The sensation intensifies. I drop to my knees with a piercing cry. "Get off me!" I scratch, squeeze, rake, and peel at every bit of tentacle that I can get my hands on. They are too slimy and quick. The terrible itch spreads down my neck, threatening to take over my whole body. I yank one tentacle out of my neck just before it creeps down to my chest, but three more take its place with a vengeance.

"AHHHH . . ."

My hands are furiously battling with the creatures when my knee bumps into something solid. Through the flailing limbs, I see the gun on the ground, the gun Finn told me to use when the time is right.

I grab the gun and press the cold barrel to my head. The agony is insufferable. I wrap a finger around the trigger, ready for my sweet relief.

CHAPTER 8

A low humming wakes me from my sleep. I expect to see my bare walls and my lonely desk in the corner. Instead I see a room filled with medical tools. I struggle, but the leather shackles around my neck, wrists and ankles hold me down, forcing me to lie flat on the hard metal table. A face appears in my line of vision, revealing only the eyes under the surgical mask. He's speaking to me, but I can't make out anything more than just mumbles. He inches closer and closer to my face, with something shiny in his hand.

NO! STOP! I yank as hard as I can.

"Gabi, wake up . . ."
No. Don't cut me.
"*Gabi!*"

I slowly come to. I'm not shackled. The man in the surgical mask is gone. It was only a dream.

The loud thumping of my heart suggests that I'm still alive, or am I? The agonizing itch is gone, leaving me with a paralyzing numbness. Liquid is dripping into the dirt, creating an interesting pattern of red swirls on a brown canvas.

Are the creatures dead? That must be their blood. As triumph revitalizes my senses, a wave of sharp stings jolts me fully awake.

"It's okay Gabi. Look at me, you're gonna be okay," Finn kneels beside me, "but we must go, *now*."

He helps me up and that's when I notice my hands are covered in red mush—the nauseating combination of blood and mud. I touch my face to see what kind of damage the tentacled creatures have done and instantly regret my action. The contact sends an electrifying sting that radiates down my neck, erecting every hair on my skin. Those damn things must have done a good number on me. My body feels heavy and my lungs are screaming for oxygen.

I try to stand with Finn's help, but my knees collapse the moment I bear weight on them. Without a word, Finn scoops me up and breaks into a run so swiftly that you can't tell he's carrying a hundred pounds of me.

After a few running steps, we come to a pile of bodies in purple. But the idea doesn't kick in until the bodies are a good distance behind us.

"You killed the Neuronics?" my voice weak and raspy. Finn just nods. I can see the lines between his furrowed brows.

"We have to find a place to hide. They've sent more guys after us. We can't go back to the headquarters. Can't risk revealing our entrance." His breathing becomes more rapid.

I look past his shoulder and see another pile of bodies not far behind the dead Neuronics. Then I remember the chaotic crowd of soldiers surrounding him before my attack. There had to be more than a dozen of them.

Gratitude and guilt seep in. I can't believe I almost ended my own life while Finn fought a dozen soldiers *and* the creepy Neuronics to save me. He barely knows me yet he would risk his own life to protect me. And there I was, ready to kill myself like a coward. I'm too ashamed to even look at him right now. I rest my head against his strong chest and silently weep as he takes us to safety.

After fifteen minutes of solid uphill running, Finn finally finds a safe hiding spot in a dense forest over looking the wreckage that was the train station. Someone far behind us is shouting directions to his soldiers. I assume it is to track us down. Who are these people and why are they so eager to kill us?

Finn puts me down and points to a ledge, "We'll have to climb down."

I walk over to the edge and look down. It's a dangerously steep chasm surrounded by thick foliage and sharp broken branches. I'm glad most of my strength has returned because I will need every strong fibre in my muscles to get down. One careless slip would mean death.

I gather my courage by telling myself over and over that I can do this. Meanwhile Finn fishes out a small device from his blood-matted jacket and begins unwinding a string-like material coming out from the rectangular box. Without asking for permission, he wraps the string around my waist.

"I can climb down myself. I'm feeling better now." I tell him. I don't want him to think that I'm useless.

"I know but this is much faster. They're closing in on us." He's not giving me an option because he's already got me wrapped around him. "Just hold on tight."

I let out a puff of disappointment but I'm actually relieved that I don't have to climb down by myself. Finn shoots a small grappling hook into the trunk of a thick tree and tugs it a few times to ensure it's secured.

I'm amazed at how many gadgets he's discreetly carrying on him. Maybe I should check his crotch for that grenade.

Get your mind out of the gutter. I shake away the inappropriate thought.

"Why are you smiling?" Finn asks.

"Uh. . Nothing. Just amazed by your gutter. . Uh, I mean gadget." *Oh shoot me now.*

"Oh, okay," he chuckles. "Here we go."

The initial drop makes my heart sink and I tighten my grip on him. Then I bury my face in his neck, afraid to look down. The metallic scent of blood and sweat overwhelms me for a second, but I don't care. I don't remember if I have ever gotten this close to a guy before but my rapid heartbeat and flushed cheeks suggest this may be my first time. Despite that we're being hunted and that we're repelling into a deathly gorge, this is the most content moment I have had since the crash. I wish this descent never ends, but like with all wishes, they never come true.

We safely touch down at the bottom. The ground under my feet is soft and wet. The temperature down here is much cooler.

My arms linger around Finn's neck for a little too long. I can tell by the awkward shift of his body. I release him quickly and turn away, not wanting him to see my flushed face.

"Sorry. I . . . I was . ."

"I know. You can't get enough of me."

"What? No! I . . ."

Finn chuckles, "Relax, I was just teasing."

Before I can complain, he takes my hand and takes me deeper into the woods. "We need to be out of sight. They can still see us if they try."

My heart skips a few beats when his hand touches mine. Why am I so nervous? I hope he doesn't feel my tremours.

Finn carefully leads me into a small cave which, from the outside, looks completely obstructed by trees and bushes. No one will notice us if they don't know where to look and Finn seems to know exactly where he's going. I wonder if he's brought other girls here before.

The inside of the cave is almost pitch black. Finn produces another gadget from his many pockets and this time it's an orb. He shakes it a few times and it begins to glow. Finn has to adjust the intensity so our enemies won't see the light from outside.

I can see now that the cave is not nearly as big as I thought. The height is perfect for me but too short for Finn to stand up straight. It's just wide enough for the both of us to sit side by side but deep enough for Finn to lie down. I'm happy that the floor is not as jagged as the walls, which makes it easier for us to sit.

"What now?" I ask.

"Now we wait," he says. "I've sent our coordinates to headquarters. They will send some Cores to take down the remaining infantry. Until then, we wait here and tend to our injuries." His voice sounds different—like he's having trouble breathing. His face doesn't look too good either. He winces as he sits down against the wall and in that brief moment where his shirt gets pushed up, I notice the multiple cuts on his torso. When did he get hurt? He showed no signs of it until now.

"Lie down, let me check your wounds." I quickly tend to him. He slides further down until he's lying flat on his back. I can tell he's in a lot of pain. I gingerly unzip his jacket. The zipper is crusted in semi-dried blood. I pray that it's not his.

My mouth goes dry the moment I open his jacket, revealing a pool of blood on his chest and ribs. His blue T-shirt becomes dark red with a glaring shine. The blood is fresh.

I'm not a fan of gore but the fear of Finn dying beats all other fears. I would bathe in gore if it could save his life. But the new courage doesn't seem to make me anymore useful. I don't remember anything about first aid.

"Why aren't you healing?" I try to mask the tightening in my throat.

"I am . . . just very slowly," he croaks. "I might be fast in combat, but my healing ability has always been lower." His face is turning ghostly white as we speak.

"Tell me what to do. I can't let you die. Not here, not for me." I've never seen my hands shake like this before. Not even during any of my anxiety attacks.

"Just keep pressure on here." He takes my hand and puts it on his left chest just under the collar bone. He has many minor wounds on his arms and legs but nothing is as serious as his chest wound. He lets out a small groan as I apply pressure. My heart melts. I can't help but feel responsible.

"Why didn't you say something before? I can't believe I was grabbing onto you so hard coming down the chasm . . . and . . . oh God . . . you were carrying me up the mountain that entire time. I must have made you worse. Why didn't you tell me? Are you crazy?" My shouting echoes loudly in the gloomy cave.

He puts a shaking finger to my lips. "Shh . . ." His voice low and weak. "It was adrenaline that got me through. It's my responsibility to protect you," he winces again. "I can't let those scumbags harm you. Although, I gotta say, I'm surprised that it took all of them to invade your mind. You are—"

"Wait, what?" I ask in shock. "Who invaded my mind? Why were we under attack to begin with? Did *they* blow up the station? Where did those tentacled creatures come from?"

Finn takes a deep breath as if to prepare for a long speech but he moans in pain instead.

"It's okay. You can tell me later. Now rest."

"I'm okay. You need to know," he says. "Yes, they're the ones who blew up the station. I suspect this is one of their planned attacks. We just happened to be there. The blue soldiers are not Neuronics by nature, they're Ordinaries who got brainwashed into serving as infantry to the mind benders. Because Neuronics can't really fight physically, they have to breed soldiers to do the dirty work for them. I barely escaped the explosion. Then you saw the rest."

I feel his chest rising and falling through his laboured speech, and the bleeding seems to have slowed down under my hands. But I'm still maintaining pressure, worry the wound would burst open any moment.

"Those in purple, they were the actual Neuronics?" I ask.

He nods. "Indigo purple is one of the colours that is said to enhance brain activities. I personally think that's a load of crap." He wiggles his hand into one of his many pockets. He holds out a small mirror the size of my palm. Out of all the things he could produce, a mirror would be the last thing I'd guess.

I lift my eyebrows as he passes it to me. "What? Guys can't carry a mirror? How's your face feeling?"

My face? Oh, my face.

I had forgotten about my own injuries. Come to think of it, the stings had reduced to a mild ache in most places, but it still hurts when I move my face a certain way. The bleeding has also stopped.

"Where did they get those nasty creat—" I gasp, almost choked on my own words as I stare into the tiny mirror. The horrific reflection is like a scene from a horror movie. The grotesque figure is covered in blood-crusted scabs that spread like worms across every inch of her face—some are still oozing blood and pus. There's no single patch of clean skin to be found.

I'm gaping at my reflection, unable to move. I curse at those creatures for inflicting such atrocity on my face. My right cheek is so swollen that part of my right eye is blocked. I was totally oblivious to my somewhat obstructed vision until now. The bandage on my nose where Finn hit me is missing, revealing the swollen and bruised bridge. The only spot that has yet to begin healing is the outer corner of my left eye where a patch of skin the size of a small coin is missing, exposing the white of bone amid crimson muscles. The only area I can touch without hurting is along the hairline where dried blood has plastered chunks of hair together. Considering the condition of my face, I'm lucky that I still have my eyeballs.

Anger boils inside me.

"They were from your mind." Finn sounds cautious, like he's afraid to provoke the hideous monster beside him. "They trapped you in a horrible hallucination. Whatever you saw wasn't real. I heard you scream, and I knew then that they had you. Their attack is something I can't protect you from."

Then I remember he had told me not to look them in the eyes and not to believe what I see, but remembering it now is a little too late.

"We were lucky that it took all four of them to invade your mind," he says, "which made them defenceless. Or else I couldn't have killed them just in time to save you."

"I . . . I was about to shoot myself." I glower into the mirror.

The terrifying memory comes rushing back like a dangerous tsunami. All that time, I thought I was fighting some tentacled creatures. But it was me. *I* was that creature.

I drop the mirror and look at my fingers, the nail beds are still coated with blood and bits of my skin. The fact that I didn't trim my nails in more than three weeks made my fingers all the more deadly.

"They may not be good fighters, but their attack is far more cruel and sneaky." Finn says. "They can kill their target without even lifting a finger."

"That tree trunk, how did they manage to throw that then?"

"Telekinesis. All Neuronics possess this power. That's why they only commit long range attacks and let their brainwashed thralls do melee." Finn looks better now that some colour has returned to his face. He sits himself up slowly with my hand still pressing on his wound. "Most of them can also induce hallucinations, but only a handful are powerful enough to completely take over a person's mind. Those would be the leaders, and they never leave their lairs. The ones we faced were probably just low ranks sent to scout our base."

Hearing Finn's description sends chills down my spine. Just a low-ranked Neuronic was already capable of making me want to kill myself. I don't want to imagine what gruesome tricks the more powerful ones can do.

Still kneeling beside Finn, I imagine the war Celine mentioned. I see the Sarcomeres, one by one, falling to the ground, clawing the flesh off of their own faces, screaming, searching for any weapon that would end their misery.

A hand strokes my cheek, wiping off tears that I didn't know I had shed.

"I'm sorry I let this happen to you," Finn says. "I should have better prepared you for it."

"Why are you still protecting me when I blatantly refused to join your group? I acted like a total wuss." More tears roll down my cheeks, stinging the few cuts that have yet to heal.

"You're not a wuss," he says. "You were traumatized from the training. I admit we have a very harsh curriculum when it comes to training our people. Now you know why. A wuss would not walk into the face of danger to come looking for me." He gives me a thankful smile.

"I . . ." I lower my head, don't know what to say.

Finn gingerly lifts my chin and we lock eyes. "If the commander of the Elite Force says you've got what it take, then you better believe it. Because he's never wrong."

"But the commander never even saw me in . . . " he lifts one eyebrow and I finally clue in.

I stare at him, astonished. The leader of the Elite Force is sitting right next to me all this time.

"And don't worry about your face," he continues. "Based on your rate of healing, the marks will fade before you know it." He strokes my forehead one more time. "My team will take care of those guys, we've had our fun, so let's rest up before we make the trip back to camp."

He assumes I will go back with him. He knows that he has won me over. I can't exactly say no considering he just saved my life. I should take another stab at training, I owe him at least this much. The leader of the Elites doesn't look like a liar.

I watch as Finn dozes off beside me, looking so peaceful and innocent. Outside, the sun has set, I think. It's hard to tell when sunlight doesn't reach this far down to begin with. The wind has definitely picked up though, causing branches and leaves to sway back and forth. I hope the foliage covering our hole doesn't get blown away.

I shiver and goosebumps begin to raise on my skin. The temperature is dropping and I have nothing to keep warm, I left in such a hurry this morning that I didn't bother to take a windbreaker with me. They had one hanging behind the door of the guest suite. I guess the only option now is to stay closer to Finn. Hope he doesn't mind.

With my hand still on his chest, I slowly and quietly lie down beside him. Since I can't sleep, I take the opportunity to study his face. It'd be awkward to do this while he's awake.

I start with his brown tousled hair. It looks black in the dim cave. Then I trace each feature as if my eyes are a paint-brush, going over line by line, crease by crease.

He can't be more than a few years older than me, yet he's already among the top ranks of his people. Commander of the Elites, such a powerful title. How many battles did he have to fight; how many people did he have to kill to get there?

If I look closely, I can see the faint scars along his neck and arms, his battle wounds. Some bigger than others, but I bet every single one has a story, a story of the hardship he had to endure. And now, because of me, there will be a big one added to the collection.

Curious to see his progress, I slowly release my hand, making sure there is no more bleeding. I lightly palpate over the shirt, but the fabric prevents me from distinguishing between skin and scab. I carefully peel his shirt away from the wound, spread open the ripped hole, and reach in with two fingers. The bleeding has indeed stopped and the deep laceration feels smaller.

He's healing. I sigh in relief.

I assume in a normal case, a stab wound this deep would have killed a person, but Finn is anything but normal.

A faint smile touches my lips as I feel the slow rise and fall of his chest. If only we can stay like this forever. Just the two of us, so close, so intimate. I know the minute he wakes, this will all be history, something that will probably never happen again. He's a commander and I'm a nobody. He will never see me the way I see him.

I slide my fingers out from under his shirt and I inch closer to him, until my forehead is brushing against his. My heart is pounding so loud that I'm worried it will wake him. But seeing his deep breathing, I don't think he will know what I'm about to do.

I angle my head so my face can lean closer to his.

Just this once. He won't know. I tell myself.

Then slowly, I put my lips on his.

CHAPTER 9

For a brief moment, I'm floating on cloud nine. His lips feel cool and soft against mine. There's no fighting, no Neuronics or Sarcomeres. Just us. Me and him, an ordinary girl and a handsome boy next door. Falling for each other. Protecting each other.

The pleasure is cut short when Finn's head suddenly jerks back. A pair of stunned dark blue eyes stare at me, like I'm some kind of a monster. I should be ashamed. I took advantage of him while he was unconscious. But I'm not. A surge of courage pushes me forward. I close my eyes and lean in, hoping my lips will catch his once more. But there are no lips, just a gentle force pushing me away.

I open my eyes to see Finn holding me at arms-length, eyes looking at my shoulder rather than my face. I quickly shift backward, almost hitting my shoulder on the rugged wall. Shame finally catches up, bringing embarrassment with it.

"I'm sorry." Finn says, breaking the awkward silence. "I . . . um. It's just, I promised myself not to get distracted from my responsibilities. We're on the brink of another war, and I just can't afford to lose sight of my duties. Sorry."

"Ya, of course. I'm . . . sorry too. I shouldn't have done that. It might be the after shock. I'm still feeling it." I lie.

I want to slap myself for being so stupid and spontaneous. What was I thinking?

Too embarrassed to do anything else, I wrap my arms around my knees and slowly rock back and forth, hoping the motion will erase everything that just happened.

A sudden beep startles the both of us. Finn checks something on his wrist and says that we are safe to return.

Thank God, because I don't think I can take this awkwardness any longer. I need to dig a hole and bury myself in it right away.

Hot water is hands down the best remedy for itchy skin. I've been soaking for more than half an hour with no intention of getting out. The relaxing bath eases the pain from the gruesome memories of today's events. At least temporarily.

All the wounds I inflicted on myself have scabbed over. But I look more grotesque now than before. Chuncks of red scabs crawl randomly over my face and neck, like dried up blood-sucking leeches. My swollen cheek has subsided to a bluish bruise, stretching from my right eye down to the corner of my lips.

Ever since we left the cave, I haven't been able to take my mind off of the humiliating situation I've put myself in. Finn's rejection seems to hit me harder than the horrific hallucination I experienced.

When we returned, Finn didn't even look at me when we split up at the Dome Hall. He was instantly escorted to the medical facility for treatment. Since my wounds were superficial and mostly healed, they just sent me back to my guest room with dinner and some ointment.

Over an hour of soaking and ten wrinkly toes and fingers later, I finally climb out of the bathtub. A look in the mirror reminds me of exactly how hideous I am. I can't blame Finn for pushing me away. Who wouldn't when approached by a face that was dripping blood and pus. Maybe this is the real reason he pushed me away—he was too appalled by my appearance.

Then he's shallow and mean, therefore not worthy of your feelings. I try to comfort myself. But I know that's probably not true. How will I face him from now on?

I resume training in two days. Maybe that will keep me distracted enough to forget about all this. If I really try this time, maybe I can unleash my potential and be a real Sarcomere, which is what I really should focus on.

Yes. That's what I'll do.

I get to the arena a bit early like last time, but the place is already packed with mostly Cores, practicing their aiming and sparring in the eight fish bowls.

Someone taps my shoulder. I turn around and see Alex standing there with his arms folded. A slight smile is carved on his face. Maybe he decided to cut me some slack after hearing what happened to me at the station.

"Those Neuronics had a little fun with you didn't they?" he says.

I raise my eyebrows.

"Your face." He wrinkles his nose like he's disgusted.

I put a hand on my face, suddenly conscious of my ugly scars. Most of the scabs have fallen, leaving smaller pink stripes, like baby worms chasing after one another. It was worse yesterday. A little girl got scared by me in the village while I was getting a coffee. She screamed, pointed, then ran to her mommy.

"Too bad they couldn't catch all those bastards," Alex says, "a lot of innocent people died in that station. Those bad ass mind benders are no joke. You were lucky that Finn was there to protect you. No one else could have taken them on alone. Anyway, I'm glad you're okay."

I did not expect that. Am I suffering another hallucination here? Alex is actually capable of being nice. Who knew?

"Ya, the way he fought was out of this world." I say. "Was . . . there anything else you heard?" I hope he doesn't know about the rejection. But if he does, I doubt he can keep his mouth shut about it.

"What do you mean? There was more?"

"No, that was bad enough," I say quickly. "I just thought they might have told you every little detail. Anyway, I'm ready to try again. Hopefully I won't disappoint you this time."

"Good, cuz you really sucked last time." And his annoying personality is back. "Since scaring the crap out of you didn't do squat, we're gonna try another approach." He begins walking toward the guns. I follow close behind.

"Has that technique ever worked on anyone?" I ask. I suspect it's more of an intimidation than anything.

"More than you think," he says. "The latent potential is just hiding inside waiting for an opportunity to pop out. Usually it finds the route in extreme dangers. You had it easy. Finn used to throw his trainees off a cliff."

WHAT?

A scene pops into my head where Finn lures his new recruits with his charm, then pushes them off the cliff without warning. I shake my head to get the image out of my mind. I can't see Finn doing that. But what do I know? I barely know him. Besides, he did say they use extreme training methods. Maybe that was it.

"Does he still train recruits?" I ask.

"He only trains Elites now." Alex randomly picks up a pistol, "Today we'll let you try different weapons and hopefully you'll show some talent in at least one of them." He doesn't sound too encouraging. He's expecting me to fail again, which means I'll have to try extra hard just to prove him wrong.

As we get ready to start, Celine walks over with a grin. I give her warm smile in return. I like her.

"Hi guys," she says. "This is Samantha Briggs, she's a new recruit. She'll be joining you guys for initial training."

"Sure, the more the merrier. I'm Alex and this is Gabi, your fellow recruit. This will be fun. I've never trained two girls at once." He rubs his hands together as if he can't wait to devour us.

This could be good. His inappropriateness won't just be directed at me from now on.

Samantha dips her head at me without a smile but immediately hovers over Alex like bee to honey. Her neatly pulled back dark-brown hair reveals her defined jawline and a disproportionally long neck. She's taller than me by quite a few inches but too slender for her frame, in my opinion.

Celine gives me a big hug, telling me how glad she is to have me back in one piece. Then she's off to do her other chores.

While Alex briefs Samantha, I take the opportunity to examine the firearms on the racks, hoping to find one that feels right to me. The pistols and revolvers are hung on the same rack, with their corresponding ammunition sitting on a short shelf below them. The submachine guns have their own rack while the rifles and shotguns share one near the wall. Every weapon has its name and features listed. But none of them carry red symbols.

I pick up one of the shotguns and find it quite heavy to handle. I doubt I can manoeuvre it efficiently. I put it back carefully and go for the handguns instead. I hold a revolver in my left hand and a pistol in my right. They both feel comfortable and oddly familiar, like I've handled them before. But I didn't feel this way with Finn's pistol during the attack. Maybe because I'm not surrounded by ruthless Neuronics ready to rip my brain out right now. I push the thought aside and continue my exploration.

I compare the two guns in my hands and decide that I like the pistol better. It's lighter, slimmer and holds more bullets. I will give this one a shot.

With my weapon of choice in hand, I walk over to a display case by the wall. Inside are two muskets and a blunderbuss, according to their name cards. Whatever they are, they look ancient. Just when I'm about to read their write-ups I spot a door right beside the display case. It blends in with the wall so well that I wouldn't have seen it if I wasn't standing right next to it. They must be hiding something good in there. I try my luck at the door and it swings open.

"Whoa!" I whisper as I lay eyes on a glorious collection of machine guns, small canons and bazookas. It's like standing in a military base getting fitted for battle. What if the weapon I'm proficient at turns out to be a bazooka? Imagine carrying that thing around. They'd call me the "Bazooka Girl" and I'll be the "big gun" they'll bring out during combat.

"Why are you giggling in here by yourself?" I jump at Alex's voice.

"Um... nothing, just stupid stuff." I say, slightly embarrassed.

"Why am I not surprised?" Alex rolls his eyes.

I want to smack him. But I'm at his mercy for the time being. I catch Samantha's eyes just as she turns around to leave and they are far from friendly. What's her problem?

After Alex explained briefly about the different firearms, I decide to stick to my semi-automatic pistol while Samantha chooses a submachine gun. I have to bite my lips to not laugh when she cradles the gun like a newborn baby, with arms so skinny that they look like twigs against the hefty gun.

My eyes shift upward to her high cheekbones and strong jawline, which I don't find particularly attractive. The arrogance she exudes also doesn't help her case. But there is certain charisma to her that others might find her exotic-looking, like Alex for example.

She catches me staring, so I give her a quick smile to mask my scrutiny. Instead of reciprocating my politeness, she eyes me up and down, then turns her back on me.

What an obnoxious bitch!

She and Alex should be best friends. In fact, I think she's already half way there with the way she's been sucking up to him. Hopefully I don't have to train with her for too long.

We follow Alex into the shooting range, which is through a set of doors between the second and third training chambers. Movable targets are scattered at various distances in front of ten empty booths—five for handgun practice, five for rifle shooting.

I step into one of the handgun booths, feeling rather calm. Why couldn't my first day be like this? Then I wouldn't have freaked out and ran for the door. My nose wouldn't have been broken. We wouldn't be at the station and I wouldn't have thrown myself at Finn and be rejected. If only we could turn back time.

"Stop daydreaming!" Alex knocks on the glass panel that separates me and Samantha.

I give him a dirty look. It's not like he's ready for me. He's still getting Samantha ready.

I look around my booth, which is not that big. There are no shelves nor a door, just two ballistic glass panels on either side. A row of buttons along the side of the right panel catches my attention. I press the lowest one and a target begins to glide toward me. I press the top one and the target moves further away. I'm about to press the middle one when Alex screams behind me. "Quit that will ya? It's not a toy!"

"Sorry! I was bored." I say in a huff.

"Well I guess patience is not one of your virtues then." Alex says and hands me a set of electronic earmuffs. "Put them on, they protect your ears as well as maintain communication with me. He taps his, which is already fastened on his head.

I try it on but the strap is too loose. I take it off and try to tighten it when Samantha fires her pistol in the next booth like there's no tomorrow.

"Jeez!" I drop my earmuffs trying to cover my ears. But the damage is done. The ringing lasts a good minute after.

She hurries to pull her target in. None of her shots made it on the bulls-eye. Now I understand why they don't allow submachine guns in here. It's because of lunatics like her. Just as well. I have no intention of being killed by her reckless bullets. It doesn't boast well for my reputation, not that my current reputation is commendable, but still.

I give her an angry stare. If she notices, she doesn't seem to care.

What a show-off! Is what I want to say, but again, I choose to be the bigger person here.

Not to my surprise, Alex is all too eager to show her the correct body mechanics for handling the gun. *Perv!*

I ignore them and focus on my own task. The sound of

gunfire has brought forth a sense of familiarity. I close my eyes and reach deep inside my mind, hoping to find some guidance. A wave of nostalgia creeps through. *Somehow, I miss doing this.*

"I think she's scared," I hear Samantha's murmur as I find my concentration. "A tiny little girl like her won't be able to handle a gun. Is there a smaller and less dangerous weapon you can show her?" Then both of them chuckle at her not-so-funny joke.

I inhale and open my eyes. I extend my right arm with the gun pointing toward the closest target at about five yards away, hand steady as a rock. Instinctively, I widen my stance in preparation to counter the recoil force. I wrap my middle finger around the trigger and make sure my grip is strong and tight.

Yes, this feels right.

The room lapses into absolute silence as Alex and Samantha watch from next door. I shift my arm ever so slightly and pull back on the trigger. It releases a loud bang followed by the force of the recoil. I lock my wrist and let my forearm absorb the force. I immediately make two more shots at the same target.

I lower my gun. My spectators are staring at the target eagerly. Alex steps into my booth and pushes the lower button on my panel. The closest target slides toward us.

They break into a hysterical laugh when the target reaches my booth, clean as new with not the slightest scratch.

"Oh . . . you should see your . . ." Alex is laughing so hard that he can't even finish his sentence. "Your face . . . you almost fooled me. Where did you learn to pretend like that? Good thing the target doesn't lie." Both of their faces are flushed from laughing.

"You're right, the target doesn't lie." I push the middle button and the furthest target starts gliding toward us. The laughter is fading as the target gets near. I glance over casually, first to Alex, then to Samantha. Their expressions are priceless when they count the three holes on the tiny, innermost red circle of the board. Then their eyes shift down to the lower right corner that marks the distance. Fifty Yards.

CHAPTER 10

It's apparent that I'm proficient with guns. Not just with pistols, rifles as well. But they are heavy and clumsy, so I still prefer my light weight automatic pistols.

This must be what Dr. Mard mentioned in the hospital, muscle memory. My body still remembers the skill even if I can't recall. Maybe my dad taught me how to shoot. But why am I so good at it? Or maybe I belonged to a gun club? Or even competed? At least I've showed them that I'm not completely useless.

Alex has stopped teasing me since the first firearm practice, but Samantha is more hostile now that she knows I'm more competent than she is. Doesn't matter how many times she tried, she just couldn't hold a gun steady enough to shoot a cow. She has guts but no skills, a bad combination for a gunman. Firearms are not her calling.

Today, we are moving onto melee weaponry. I walk into the arena with renewed confidence, but the sight of Finn immediately kills it. I haven't seen him since that embarrassing day. Training did serve as an excellent distraction.

He's talking to a girl enthusiastically, showing her different swords on the wall. Is it the girl or the swords he's so interested in? I hope it's the latter.

The girl looks tall and slender, with straight dark hair that goes down to her shoulders. They look good together, from the back.

The girl turns around.

Samantha!

How can she be flirting with Finn? Do they even know each other? She laughs somewhat exaggeratingly then puts her hand on his biceps. Then she flicks her hair. Oh, the hair flicking. I want to chop it off and see what else she can flick.

The longer I look at her, the more I feel a storm building inside me, swirling like a tornado threatening to swallow anything in its path.

Suddenly Linda's face appears, telling me to calm down. I look away and steady myself with a few deep breathes. It's working. The urge to rip her hair out or scratch up her face is gone. I'm definitely making progress. I wish Linda were here to see my improvement.

I head over to one of the gun racks and pretend I didn't see them. But someone calls my name, and I recognize the voice.

I take a deep breath and turn around. Finn waves and signals me to join them. I don't want to come off being petty or resentful. I have no choice but to walk over with a smile.

Finn seems glad to see me though, or at least he's pretending to.

"Hey Gabi, are you feeling better?" Finn asks. "Your face is definitely looking much better," he smiles handsomely.

I didn't even think about my face the last few days. Now that Finn mentioned it, I remember the itch had stopped and the scars are disappearing, leaving only faint pink lines that are barely visible.

Before I have a chance to answer him, Samantha interrupts. "Oh, you were injured? I was wondering about your face but I didn't know if it was my place to ask." She sounds like a totally different person. What a fake and manipulative piece of work.

"Oh, I didn't know you'd notice. You know, you and Alex were too busy *'talking'*." I pretend to wink at her, hinting to Finn that she and Alex are an item. I can play dirty too.

She just stares at me, with no retaliation. I can sense the hatred in her eyes though. I'll have to watch my back from now on.

I turn to Finn and say, "I'm feeling much better. I guess I do heal quickly. What about your wound?" I look down at his chest. The sight brings back the bittersweet memory.

"It's closed up now, but with a nasty scar. It'll add to my collection of glorious battle wounds," he says proudly. "Anyway, I should get going. My team is helping with the rebuilding of the station."

"They're sending Elites to do hard labour?" I arch my brows in surprise. Through my peripheral vision, I see Samantha's eyes brighten at the word *Elite*. I guess she didn't know. Great, I just made Finn more irresistible to her now.

"Well, it has been quite peaceful up till now. So it's time to put them to work. Plus we're gonna be doing some recon around the area to find clues about the attack." He turns around, shouts orders to a few people behind him, then turns back to us. "Nice meeting you Samantha."

"Yes, same here." There's such eagerness in her voice.

Finn nods and turns to me, "Good luck with your training. I'll see you around."

I smile.

My gaze follows him and three other men as they make their way toward the back door of the arena. I wonder how many Elites are there in total. Can't be just the four of them, who bear no red stripes on their shirt. Just the old boring dark blue T-shirts and sage green khakis. None of them seem overly muscular, but the curves of their muscles and their balanced gaits suggest that they are seasoned martial artists. One guy has two swords secured on his back in an X while another guy has a submachine gun on his shoulder. The red markings dance brightly on their weapons, which confirms my guess that this feature belongs to the Elites. Maybe Alex will know what they actually do.

Alex taps both of us on the shoulder. "Don't let those boys fool you. They may be easy on the eyes, but they're poison to your heart."

"I think someone's jealous." I tease.

For the first time, I see a hint of agreement from Samantha.

Alex scowls.

"Oh come on, it's just a joke." I say. "So tell me, why do their weapons have red symbols on them?" Samantha is waiting for the same answer.

"It's none of your concern. They'll explain to you *if* you get into the Elite Force." He pauses as he studies our dissatisfied faces. "Fine. All I'm gonna say is that they're used against the Neuronics. Now are we gonna train or just stand here doing stupid Q & A?"

I know this is as much as I can get out of him for now, so I let the topic drop and shuffle to the melee weaponry racks to choose our blades.

Alex starts by teaching us a sword-fighting routine, then we are to practice with different blades using the same routine.

I'm eager to try the katana. Seeing how light and effortless Finn wielded it, this should be a breeze.

Fifteen minutes into training, I realize I have never been more wrong. The mildly curved blade hates me. Doesn't matter how I wield it, it will somehow disobey my direction. I don't know if it's the weight of the blade or its length, but every motion I try seems to be off-balanced. I end up nicking myself several times.

Alex says that it may be the curve of the blade that's throwing me off. So I switch to a longsword. But the result is just as bad if not worse.

Alex then suggests I practice the routine without a sword. I do as he says and have no problem duplicating every move to perfection. But when I include a sword, the coordination goes awry.

It's obvious that I have no aptitude for sword fighting. I look clumsy and silly, very much like Samantha with a gun.

Alex shakes his head as he watches.

By the thirtieth time running through the same routine, my frustration boils over and I lose the last bit of control. Without thinking, I swing the sword from right to left, intending to do a overhead swipe. But my dumb body doesn't follow through and the sword comes straight for my neck. I have exactly half a second to decide whether to move my neck or to stop my arm before I slash myself.

CLANK!

Alex's blade intercepts mine just in time.

Thank God. I sigh.

Seeing his death-threatening stare and the taut muscles in his jaw, I know he's had enough of my child's play.

"You should stop before you kill yourself, or hurt someone else." He yanks the sword from my hand. "It's like watching a drunk playing with a sword. Where's the poise and control you had at the shooting range?"

"I'm sorry, I . . . I don't know." I murmur. "I just can't grasp the techniques. It's like my hand is doing one thing and my brain is controlling something else." I'm flushed and exhausted, and not to mention embarrassed.

"Well, it's safe to say that you won't be fighting with a sword. Go take a break," he orders.

I drag myself to the wall and slump against it, feeling defeated. What Alex doesn't know is that my shooting ability has nothing to do with my potential. It was pure muscle memory. So my supposedly strong prime gene has yet to show itself. This little secret needs to stay with me. I cannot afford to disappoint Finn. I cannot afford looking weaker than I already portray.

In the fish bowl next to mine, Samantha is having a blast with her katana. She weaves it into high and low combinations and executes diagonal slashes in the air. She has found her niche, and it pains me to see her with Finn's weapon of choice. I can already picture the two of them fighting side by side with their gleaming katanas.

By the end of the session, she begins adding her own jumps and twirls to the routine. Alex's eyes are fixated on her like a hawk.

After a long moment of analyzing, his lips curl up into a grin, eyes sparkling with pride, like a father watching his own child achieving something extraordinary.

He grabs his sword and thrusts toward her. Stunned at the intrusion, she almost loses her balance. But she recovers quickly and is able to deflect all of his strikes. After a few rounds of defence, she gradually begins her offensive moves toward Alex.

Dumbfounded, I just sit in my chamber and watch through

the glass partition that separates the two rooms. I wonder where she got those skills. Does she also have latent muscle memory?

Ten minutes into sparring, Alex finally stops. Both of them are sweating but not out of breath. Samantha looks perplexed like she has no idea what just happened. Alex just stares at her with renewed respect.

I catch on before she does. As much as I hate it, I have to admit that she was brilliant in that duel. Although they were not advance moves, every strike was calculated and executed with precision. It's frustrating to see that Samantha has just awakened her potential.

CHAPTER 11

It's ten o'clock in the morning and both Alex and Samantha are yet to be seen. In fact not a single soul has shown up. I begin to suspect something is amiss. Samantha has been competing with me even in punctuality. It's bizarre that she's not here by now.

As I'm about to leave, Celine bursts through the door, looking flustered.

"There you are," she says urgently. "We almost forgot about you."

Of course. I'm always the last to know about everything around here.

"What's going on?" I ask.

"Quick, come with me," she grabs my elbow. "Everybody's gathered at the Dome. Chief Trousing has an urgent announcement to make."

I jog after her, wondering what kind of announcement would render the whole place empty.

By the time we arrive, the hall is already packed with people. No wonder everywhere else was so quiet. I have never seen so many Sarcs in one room. Balconies are full. Kids are on their parent's shoulders. There's over a thousand people present, which means it must be something huge.

Celine holds my hand as we weave through the crowd to find her spot. Her hand feels delicate and soft, making me suddenly conscious of my callus-covered man palms. Everything about her is soft and delicate—her golden hair, her sweet demeanour. Sometimes I wish I'm more like her, girly and lovable.

Since neither of us is particularly tall, we have to walk on tiptoes in order to see over people's shoulders. But I can't see Finn anywhere.

"Where's Alex and Samantha?" I have to almost yell so Celine can hear me.

"They're here somewhere," she replies.

"Well isn't it nice of them to ditch me." I roll my eyes.

"Don't worry, I've got your back." Celine says with a smile. "Everybody's here. Good thing they haven't started yet."

We finally find a spot. It's less crowded but quite far from the stage. Celine seems to know everyone in our immediate surroundings, but none of them looks familiar to me. It's not surprising considering I have only been here for a few weeks. Especially when I spent most of my time in my room or at the training hall. They even have our meals delivered to the arena so we can capitalize on our training time. One thing I'm glad is that food is free during initial training. But there's also no earning during this period. It's only when we are placed in a rank and a job will we get paid accordingly.

"I see they've been training you hard." A familiar voice breaks my chain of thought.

I turn around and see a woman in her fifties with short, permed brown hair.

"Linda!"

"There's my girl." We fall into each other's embrace.

Seeing her makes me feel warm and fuzzy inside. She's as close to a family as I have now. If it wasn't for her, who knows where I'd end up. I regret not treating her nicer back in the hospital, so I'm extra pleased to be given another chance.

When we finally come out from each other's arms, our eyes are pooled with tears.

"Do you like it here my dear?" she asks.

I nod, trying to swallow the lump in my throat. "I'm getting used to it. It was rough at first." I look down at our interlocked hands. "I still haven't discovered my potential yet."

Linda raises a hand to stroke my hair like a loving mother. "Don't worry dear. It takes time. This is something you can't force. The gene decides when it wants to be activated. Are you able to remember anything from your past?"

"A little actually—"

A loud squeak from the speakers interrupts me. I'll have to tell her about my shooting ability later.

They test the microphone once more and ask everybody to settle down. It takes all but two seconds for the entire hall to go from clamorous to complete stillness. Chief Trousing makes her way onto the stage like a queen about to address her subjects. Meanwhile a copy of her is projected on a big screen for those of us in the back. Her sense of presence is undeniable. Especially with that bright red fitted dress hugging her like a second skin. The hem of the dress drapes just below her knees, showing a pair of toned legs. If I were to walk in those stilettos everyday, I too would have toned legs. But I have better things to do than to torment my feet just to look pretty. Her blond hair is pulled back in a bun with perfectly styled bangs sweeping across her forehead. Not a single strand of hair is out of place. But behind her flawless facade is a sense of urgency.

She clears her throat and begins. "Hello, fellow Sarcs. We have been informed by our external agents that there will be an impending attack very soon." Everyone gasps in unison like it's been rehearsed. "Please remain calm. We have trained and prepared ourselves for exactly this. I hereby announce that Protocol Red is in place. Please listen to your rank leaders for further instructions." She puts her hands on her hips. "People, we have to trust each other and ourselves in order to carry out what's assigned to us, by fate, by God. We must preserve our invaluable gene and fight for democracy and free will. We cannot allow those cruel and manipulative Neuronics to pollute the purity and freedom of mankind. We are Sarcomeres, we are the guardians of Earth!"

Everyone breaks into a cheer and for the first time, I feel the pride. Guardians of Earth. I wonder who gave us the name. As unlikable as the chief is to me, she is inspirational. She just made me believe that we are indeed invaluable and we can protect the weaker Ordinaries.

She steps off the stage and her spot is replaced by three guys, all fit for battle. The cheers subside as the first guy walks up to the microphone. He's wearing a black fitted jacket zipped up all the way to his collarbone and a pair of black khakis. Two pistols rest on his holster. His over-sized nose is visible even from my vantage point.

The Touch leader taps the mic lightly then says, "Listen up Touches, we all know what our roles are. I want all R&Ds to gather your equipment and board the west tram at exactly 11:30am. Make sure you destroy all backups. Recruitment, board the east tram at exactly 11:00am." He rejoins the other two leaders without any closing remark.

My mind didn't quite register his words, because I'm too busy deciphering what I just witnessed. Alex didn't show up at the training arena not because he was a jerk, but because he needed to prepare the Touches for their escape. Who would have thought that I've been training with the Touch leader all along.

My eyes are fixed on that screen, on Alex's face. His usual sarcastic and offensive demeanour is replaced by pride and honour on that stage. He's not quite at the bottom of the barrel like I thought.

As I ponder on the new information, the next person takes centre stage. The Core leader is in his late forties. Or he could be way older. Who knows. I have never seen him before but I doubt I would forget his face after today. He is short, sturdy and wide, with eyes so dark and deep that they look like two hollow holes topped by two thick caterpillars that are his brows. The bottom half of his face is covered by a thick beard. The only part of him that's not hairy is his oily bald head, gleaming proudly under the spotlights. His battle attire consists of a black tactical jacket, a navy blue heavy duty vest with bulging pockets, and a pair of matching tactical pants with their legs tugged under his boots. Then there's his weapon of choice—the *entire* gun rack. Seriously, is he the leader or the walking armoury of the Cores? One thing is certain though, none of the guns bear the red markings.

"Cores, listen up," his voice is deep and jagged. "Gear up! It's time to defend our home and our people. Let's show those grisly mind-benders and their useless bootlickers what we're made of." He throws his fist in the air and people bellow in agreement. There are *a lot* of Cores. "Meet me here with your weapons ready in fifteen." He spits angrily and walks back to join the other two.

My heart starts to pound as Finn makes his way to the mic. His calm and controlled manner is a sharp contrast to the Core leader. He has ditched his casual jacket for a fitted black high-collar vest that also has an asymmetrical zip-up design, and it shows off his toned arms nicely. His katana is fastened to his back with the two pistols on his hip as usual. But a third gun is added to his right thigh in a leg holster. His waist belt is also embellished with daggers and ammunition. It still seems surreal to me that this young and high-spirited guy is the deadliest killer in this crowd. And I don't know if it's just me or the pulsing glow emanating from the weapons seems brighter, like they too are anxious for the battle.

My legs begin to move uncontrollably toward him. I hear Celine calling me, but my tunnel vision only sees Finn. I need to get closer to him.

"The next hour is going be crucial. Please remain calm and faithful. We will succeed if we all work together as a team, as a family." His words are comforting, unlike the previous two who seemed brusque. "Sarcomeres, this will be our biggest challenge yet. Remember who we are and what we're fighting for." He unsheathes his katana and holds it in the air. The red glow amplifies under the spotlights. "May our blood vanquish the dark and evil, and bring peace and equality back to where they deserve to be." A big roar erupts and those with weapons are waving them in the air. Finn's simple yet encouraging words are just what the crowd needs—a big boost to morale before the battle. Something a true leader can do.

He lowers his sword and everybody follows. "Everybody, take your positions."

On cue, the crowd breaks in different directions. Some move about frantically while others look more focused.

Not knowing where I belong, I just stand there, lost. I truly feel useless seeing everybody with a purpose and a role to play in this desperate time. Yet here I am, a statue waiting to be knocked over.

Celine shakes my shoulder, "You'll come with us. We're going to the east tram. Come on, we only have thirty minutes to prepare."

"Where's the tram taking us?"

"To Alaska," she says. "We have a contingency base there."

Not giving me time to think, Celine and Linda pull me with them.

CHAPTER 12

This is my second time to the recruitment wing. The first was when I came to look for Celine to help me escape this place. Nothing has changed since my last visit. It still consists of several small rooms and one big empty meeting room along a short hallway east of the Dome. Except this time the many computers and electronic devices are either unplugged from their cables or shattered to pieces.

Celine and Linda guide me into one of the computer rooms where the floor has become a sea of wires and cables. They immediately jump to their tasks and leave me standing by the door. On the desk beside me is a bin full of broken plastic. Hidden among the shards is a complete piece the size of my two palms combined. I pull it out carefully and the screen flashes, asking for a login and password. Then someone yanks it away from me abruptly.

"This is sensitive information." The woman scowls. She then takes a hammer from further down the desk and smashes it a few times until it looks exactly like the loose shards in the bin. She walks away before I can tell her that I didn't mean to pry.

"It contains information on our field agents," Linda says as she dumps another bin of broken devices on the desk. "It has anything from the person's height and weight to where she has worked in the past ten years."

"Is there anything I can help?" I ask. Eager to be useful.

"Don't worry dear, we're almost done." Then she disappears into the next room.

I remember Celine told me that Touches who work in Recruitment are actually scattered around world, taking up jobs like nurses, teachers, even police officers. Wherever they can potentially discover a lost Sarc—like when Linda discovered me by chance at the hospital. That's why there's only a handful of them here at the moment. It's unfortunate that Linda got sucked into this mess when she's only here for training. Even though they're short-staffed, they seem to have the back-up procedure well rehearsed. They work like a flawless assembly line.

I'm not offended that none of them wants my help. I know time is of the essence and all data pertaining to the Sarcomeres must be safeguarded. It would be catastrophic if any of this gets into the hands of the Neuronics.

Then the Research and Development team comes to mind. I wonder how they're handling the evacuation. I imagine they'd have to destroy all weapon blueprints and prototypes if they can't move them out fast enough.

I've been standing at the same spot for twenty minutes now, observing people as they move from computer to computer and room to room. In such a crucial moment, all I can do is stand and watch, waiting to be dragged to the next destination. The word useless cannot even begin to describe how I feel about myself right now.

Alex bursts through the door like a bull in a china shop and begins barking orders around the room. The recruitment staff evidently more anxious with him around, which makes me wonder what kind of a leader he is. My guess is the type that exploits his subordinates to elevate his own importance.

He accidentally bumps into me and scowls like he has laid eyes on something repulsive.

"Do me a favour would ya? Stand aside so you're not blocking the others who actually have a job to do. Jeez, I just can't catch a break with you." Then he storms off.

Anger swells, my hands curl into fists, eyes locked on the back of his head, wishing for a gun so I can aim it precisely at that. Then suddenly a flashback comes to mind—I was standing very still, in an empty room enclosed by four concrete walls. I was consumed by vengeance but felt helpless, very much like how I'm feeling right now. Then the memory vanishes, as quick and abrupt as it appeared. It wasn't a dream this time. It was definitely a flashback. And it frustrates me to no end that every glimpse of my past that ever surfaced was too vague to comprehend. It's like being lured by a mirage of water when you are in the middle of a desert—you see it there, but you can never reach it no matter how fast you run toward it.

Celine tugs at my arm. My anger almost caused her a black eye. She backs off a bit warily.

"Are you alright Gabi? We gotta go now," she says tentatively.

"I'm sorry. Let's go."

I take over a load of hardware from Linda and together with the rest of the group, we jog toward the tram station.

"Where's Samantha?" I ask Celine, who's jogging beside me while carrying a bin full of MUDs.

She hesitates just enough for me to notice. "She's with the Elites." She says through her panting.

I know why she hesitated. She thought it would make me feel bad knowing Samantha, who started later than I did, has made it to Elite before I even got ranked. Well she's wrong. It doesn't just make me feel bad, it makes me furious. I can just imagine her and Finn practicing their katanas together in a provocative sword dance. He tried so hard to convince me to stay, and here I am, staying with the Touches.

We get to the station with only two minutes to spare. The tram we'll be escaping in looks nothing like the detachable egg pod Finn took me on. This one is shaped like an airplane fuselage minus the wings and wheels. Its nose and tail are pointy like a bullet and it also hovers a foot above the track like the pod. The white, glossy tubular body has ten circular windows along each side. I don't see the point of having windows when we are completely surrounded by rocks. I also wonder how it's going to maneuver itself in the winding tunnels. Unlike the pod which was small and agile, this tram is the opposite. I guess I shall find out soon.

The tram starts to move just as I get on. I do a quick scan around the cabin. The words old and meek immediately come to mind. I didn't notice this in the recruitment wing when everyone was frantically busy. But now, with everybody under one roof, their characteristics become obvious. I don't know why but they don't quite fit my definition of Sarcomeres, with Alex being the exception. Is it because I've only been around the athletic type? Or is it the lack of fire in their eyes? The attack hasn't even begun, yet defeat and despondence already etched on every face. I thought Sarcomeres were supposed to be brave. But sitting in front of me is a group eager to leave this soon-to-be battlefield so they can bury their faces in precious data while praying that the world doesn't crumble around them.

I can't see myself living like this. I may have wanted to escape in the beginning, but ever since the horrific attack at the station, I realized that I am a Sarcomere wherever I go. I will be marked as one whether I like it or not. So the best thing is to train like one. If we are just as strong as the mind benders, why should we hide from them? Our number may be low, but running will only prove that we are cowards. I have to stay and fight. This may be the only chance to prove myself.

The train is picking up speed. It's now or never.

I hand my load to Linda and give her a brave nod. She knows what I'm thinking. A bittersweet smile spreads across her face and she nods with encouragement. She's the only person who understands me and I'm about to leave her knowing that I may never see her again.

With no time to dawdle, I grab the door handle, slide it open and jump. I hear Alex and Celine's voices behind me. I hit the ground hard, but I dive into a roll to diverge some of the impact. I get up quickly, ignoring the bruising pain in my knees and shoulders and break into a run without looking back. I'm technically rank-less. No one can order me what to do. Not even Alex. This is the first, and probably the only time that I don't mind my status.

CHAPTER 13

I need to find a gun, so I go to the one place I know. On my way there I pass by a group of Cores by the tramway entrance. They're busy setting what I assume are traps.

It has been forty-five minutes since Chief Trousing's announcement and there's still no signs of an attack. Could we have been pranked?

Just when I begin to doubt the intel, the ground shakes violently under my feet, throwing me off balance. I stumble forward, landing on my face and palms. Before I can get up, a muffled explosion in the far distance jolts the mountains, followed by another violent shake that pins me to the ground. The attack has begun.

I reach the training arena when a third explosion shudders the entire compound. This one is much louder. To my disappointment, all the racks have been swept clean. Not a single weapon is left behind.

Panic sets in as I imagine a flock of infantry breaking through our barrier right at this moment and finds me here, alone, defenceless. I wouldn't last a second.

I need to find Finn, so I decide to try my luck at Dome Hall.

I get there to find the place covered in debris. Just an hour ago this very place was filled with Sarcs who were eager to defend their home. Now there's only squeaky windows that are barely hanging on their hinges, like autumn leafs dangling from their branches.

Standing in the centre of the Dome, I consider the possible locations where Finn and his team could be. Would the Elites be outside fighting the intruders already? My logic tells me no. If anyone, it would be the Cores who would engage the mindless thralls. Finn and his team are expertly trained to target the Neuronics, who won't be among the soldiers. They must still be somewhere in the compound.

Just as I turn around, a very faint shuffling sound stops me. I freeze and concentrate on the noise.

Ten seconds later the shuffling begins again but from a different direction. A light bulb turns on in my head. *I'm in the middle of an ambush!*

But the realization comes too late. A loud blast from the south entrance sends me flying. Shouts and gunshots erupt at once from all directions even before my back hits the ground. The landing knocks all sense out of me and I lie there, fighting to breathe.

Someone grabs my shoulder and drags me into a wall. I kick and scream, expecting to see a mindless soldier. But Alex's face appears. He pins me down with such rage that I think he's going to kill me.

He props me up against the wall inside a nook where the bullets can't find us. Then he crouches in front of me with his right arm pinned to my collarbone. If he presses any harder, I will suffocate.

"Your stupidity almost got everyone killed. You know that?" He's yelling at the top of his lungs. Partly due to the loud gunfire surrounding us, but mostly because he's livid with me.

Seeing the veins in his forehead and the battle around the

corner, I finally realize the severity of what I have done. I *did* almost blow their cover by blindly walking into the ambush they planned. I've put them in a precarious position.

"You deliberately disobeyed my order. Do you know how dangerous that makes you? You're a liability to everyone!" Alex shakes my bruised shoulders, causing pain to shoot down my arms. I know I deserve it but I will take Alex's chastising no more.

"I am NOT under your order," I retort. "I don't have a rank, so don't pretend you own me."

"You're still my trainee, therefore you ARE my responsibility." He releases me with a hard push, my shoulders hit the wall. "I'm not gonna let you run free while putting everyone in danger. You're reckless and selfish!"

"You've hated me from day one. You've deemed me a failure from the moment you laid eyes on me." I push myself to stand, ignoring the pain. "I never wanted your supervision. Why don't you just go back to your pathetic group of cowards who are now so comfortably hidden while others fight for their lives." I know my two dearest friends are part of that group, but it doesn't change the fact that they're fleeing and we're here fighting.

I push Alex aside as hard as I can and run for the submachine gun lying beside a dead Core. I ignore the blood on the handle and quickly take aim at a soldier who's busy shooting at a balcony. They came prepared with their elaborate armour but no amount of helmets and chest pads can protect them now. My gun fires three shots at once and the first bullet penetrates right through the soldier's helmet. The other two hit his buddy behind him. Just like that, both men are lying on their back, dead.

Exhilaration flows through me like a forceful tsunami that destroys anything in its wake—except this time, I'm the tsunami. I hope someone is watching, taking note of my kills, because I have never felt so proud. I thoroughly enjoyed the perfect kill.

A cry from behind interrupts my triumphant moment. Then a forceful impact knocks me to the ground, pinning me under something heavy. I hear my name. Someone is calling to me from afar. I push the heavy object off me and turn toward the voice.

"We'll cover you, take Alex to safety." Finn yells from thirty feet away, with bullets flying everywhere.

I thought I heard him wrong until I look down at the heavy object slumped by my legs. My stomach twists when I recognize Alex, who's drowning in his own pool of blood.

Seeing him in such agony erases all resentment I have toward him. I bend down to lift him up, but my clumsy hands cause him more damage than good. He lets out a painful groan and tightens his grip on his chest. Blood is fast draining from his face. No time to waste. I have to tend to his wound right here. I kneel down beside him when several bullets fly by, one hitting the ground just inches from Alex's leg.

"Sorry, I really have to move you." I say.

I'm not sure if he heard me but I have no other option. I hook my forearms under his armpits, a deep breath to collect my strength and begin dragging him back to the nook where we hid earlier. A thick trail of blood paints the ground.

I lay Alex flat on his back behind the elevator shaft. This should be a safe spot for now.

"Why did you come back?" I ask with genuine concern.

As he opens his mouth, a thin trail of blood streams down the side of his lips.

"You . . . you're my . . . responsibility. I . . . I can't . . . let you get hurt." He stutters through his pain.

It takes me a few seconds to comprehend what he did. *He was the sudden impact that knocked me down. He . . . took a bullet for me.*

"Why? Why did you do that? You'll be alright. You heal fast right?"

Please say yes. I pray.

He gives me a bitter smile. "Listen . . . to me . . . one last time. Stop being reckless. Consider . . . the consequences before you act," he stops to catch his breath. "You . . . are . . . brave but bravery also . . . requires . . . tactic." He begins to tremble and his lips are turning blue.

I prop him up gently on my lap so I'm cradling his head and shoulders. I press one hand firmly on his chest just like I did for Finn in the cave.

"Then you'll have to teach me tactics when you get better." I say. "You can't die . . . not for me . . ." A drop of tear lands on his cheek.

He looks up with tired eyes and slowly, shakingly, lifts his pistol from his belt.

"This is . . . yours from . . . now on. Take good care . . . of her for me. I'm sorry . . . that I couldn't bring . . . out your potential." I take the pistol with my blood-soaked hand. "One day . . you will . . have your . . red markings on it. Think . . . of . . . me . . . when that day . . . comes . . ."

"NO!!!! Please . . . you can't . . ." I hug Alex as tight as I can, hoping my squeeze will wake him. "No, no. Stay awake. Please."

I put his head back on the floor and start performing CPR on him. *One, two, three . . .*

I don't know where I learned it, but I remember now to push and count. I push hard and fast on his heart, then listen for his breath.

Nothing.

I continue until my arms go numb.

Still nothing.

I know he's gone. Nonetheless, this is the only thing and the last thing I can do for him.

As I count my compressions, I remember our short time together. Though most of it involved us fighting and bickering at each other, it seems sweet and invaluable to me now. My arrogant and harsh teacher is now lying lifelessly on the ground when it should have been me.

I don't know how much time has passed when I finally stop. I straighten his shirt and gently wipe off the blood on his face. He looks young and peaceful. The usual creases between his brows are gone. He has no reason to frown anymore. I stroke his hair slowly and plant a kiss on his forehead.

"Thank you." I whisper in his ear.

I regret that I never got to know the real Alex. The talented, self-sacrificing leader of the Touches.

I stand up, holding Alex's gun in my hand. Those mindless rats killed my teacher. They will pay.

CHAPTER 14

I walk out from our hidden spot and aim for the first enemy I see.

A perfect head shot. Alex's gun feels right in my hand.

In spite of the amount of protective gear these thralls are clad in, our specially designed weapons can penetrate the toughest armour.

Finn and several of his men are engaged in a close combat with a group of soldiers near the north door. Many Cores are scattered around the Dome Hall, some on balconies and some behind window sills. All shooting at the south entrance where soldiers are filing in like ants. When one dies, three more replace the fallen.

A massive pile of bodies has accumulated in the centre of the dome. Most are in blue uniforms. But a lot of our people are also gravely injured if not dead.

Twenty feet to my left, a group of six blue soldiers are sneaking up on two Cores ducked behind cover, busy reloading their weapons. They work fast, but the soldiers are too close.

Without thinking, I leap forward in a rolling dive and collide with the pack of thralls, catching them by surprise. One gets knocked down by me instantly. I shoot him in the head at point-blank range and steal his pistol. I'm now standing among five disoriented soldiers with one dead by my feet. They regain their footing almost immediately, but not fast enough. My pistols are already pointing at two temples on either side of me. A second later two more bodies drop to my feet. The three remaining men—one in front of me and two behind, fire at me simultaneously. My reflexes kick in and I spin to the right as they pull the triggers. Their bullets graze my shirt but hit each other instead. The two who got shot collapse with grunts. Five down, one more to go. The last soldier gets stupefied for a brief moment, long enough for me to kick the gun out of his hand and feed my bullet into his head.

This is for Alex, you filthy mindless rats!

The kills make my blood boil. I'm ready for more. I need to kill every single one of them for Alex.

I glance around for my next target. A group appears on the far right. I start running toward them when a hand grabs my elbow, yanking me back. I swing my other arm around, fist first. My punch connects with Finn's hand with a loud thud, inches from his face. I glower at him, flushed with rage.

"How dare you. Let me go! Alex didn't die for nothing. Now let me go!" I yank myself free.

I turn to run, Finn's strong arm wraps around my waist yet again and lifts me off the ground. I kick and twist violently trying to free myself as he pulls me away. My sharp nails dig into his forearm creating streaks of red.

"Let me go!" I scream.

Alex's dying face is etched on my mind like a fresh burn mark, hot and sizzling. I hate Finn for interfering. I loathe the Neuronics for killing Alex. I despise myself for being such a hopeless wreck.

I thrash and kick. I yell and scream. I think I might have bitten Finn's arm at one point but I don't care. I need to avenge Alex.

But Finn's more stubborn than I am. No matter how many times I have kicked him or how loud I scream, his iron-like arms never let go.

Eventually my energy dips and I'm finally too exhausted to struggle. Finn has his arms around me and he's gently stroking my sweat-soaked hair as I gradually begin to feel like myself again. Then I realize the sounds of gunfire and battle clamour are no longer audible. No more dead bodies around either. Just an empty lab.

"I'm sorry about Alex," he muffles in my hair.

The name brings another wave of pain and sorrow. My mentor died for me . . killed in cold blood . . .

I bawl into Finn's chest, no longer care that I'm crying in front of others. He holds me tighter, slowly rocking back and forth like he's comforting a crying baby. Tears collect on his shirt, marking a wet spot.

I quiet down after a while, feeling sluggish and run down. I stay in Finn's embrace, reluctant to face him—partly because I don't want to leave his comforting arms, but mainly because of the guilt. I got Alex killed. I almost compromised their whole plan. I don't know how to face the Sarcomeres.

Finn eventually pushes me off his chest and forces me to look him in the eye. He looks just as tired.

"You were brave," he says. "What happened to Alex wasn't your fault. If a fellow Sarc were in danger, any one of us would have done the same. I can imagine you would do the same too."

"If I had listened to him . . . if I stayed with the Touches, then he wouldn't need to run after me and he'd still be alive." I sob. "Not to mention I almost blew your cover. All because I wanted to prove myself."

"We can't change the past, but we can work toward a better future. Yes, this is a horrible situation, but it's also fate.

Alex's death has awakened your potential." Finn shakes my shoulders.

I gaze at him, confused. *What potential?*

Then I remember the quick battle I had with the thralls. "How do you know for sure?" I ask him.

"I saw you out there. One against six in mere seconds?" he raises his eyebrows. "Not to put you down, but I don't think you can do that without the help of your gene." Finn has a point.

"I was so enraged that I just let my body take over." I say.

"That's exactly it. Your mind shut down, and you stopped fighting with your inner energy." Finn explains. "It showed you a glimpse of what it's capable of, but it has yet to release its full potency. You'll know when that happens."

His hands are still on my shoulders as I stare at him with empty eyes. He waits quietly for me to absorb it all.

My gene finally makes an appearance, but at the worst time possible. My supposed excitement and sense of accomplishment would only demean Alex's sacrifice. I don't deserve any celebration.

"Alex did not die in vain." Finn continues. "He brought out a new, powerful Sarcomere that we desperately need right now. If you want to avenge his death, then focus your energy on improving your skills, to become a true guardian of Earth." He puts Alex's gun back into my hand. "We can't let the Neuronics dominate human kind. They *will* destroy anyone who's weaker than them. We need to fight for all humanity."

His words have lifted a small stone off my chest. Enough for me to breathe.

Someone bursts through the door just then. "We know where the Neuronics are," he gasps.

Finn pulls me up immediately and says, "This is the real deal. I want you to hide until I come find you."

"No, please let me go with you." I grab his arm desperately. "I promise I will obey every order and stay hidden. Please, just don't leave me by myself."

Finn contemplates for a second and nods. "You stay behind me at all times, you get that? No trying to be a hero." His voice stern.

I nod doubly fast.

"One more thing," he stops in mid-track. "Do not look them in the eyes. If you feel a strange presence in your consciousness, focus on something real, something you hold dear to. Just keep thinking that image, this will make their mind intrusion more difficult. Remember!" I nod, knowing full well the effect of their power. He takes my hand and we run after the Elite messenger.

Something real, something I hold dear to. I repeat Finn's words in my head.

This will be hard considering I don't have enough memories to rely on. I look down at our interlocked hands as we run, the feeling is as real as it gets and I can't help but think what if this is the last time we touch? What if he dies? I tighten my grip— something I hold dear to.

"What's wrong?" Finn feels my sudden tremour.

"Promise me . . . don't get killed." My voice cracks.

He squeezes my hand and says, "I don't make promises. And I don't go down easily." He gives me a wink and together, we run toward the biggest challenge yet.

CHAPTER 15

I'm utterly lost after Finn takes me through a series of maze-like hallways. What Celine showed me when I first arrived was only a fraction of this compound.

After about fifteen minutes of following Finn through unknown sections, we finally arrive at a big warehouse about half the size of Dome Hall but rectangular. I can see rows of stacked crates and barrels through the glass double doors. The ceiling is about three storeys high with exposed steel beams and pipes.

As soon as we step into the warehouse, my stomach growls from the fruity aroma that permeates the place. I have not eaten since breakfast and it's now late afternoon. Apparently adrenaline can block your desire to eat.

Finn and I join the ten Elites huddled in a corner to the left of the entrance, cleverly covered by a stack of crates labelled PRODUCE. The six men and four women all lift their heads to face us as we approach. I see Samantha, all donned in Elite gear with a katana on her back and a row of daggers on her belt. So they gave her daggers instead of guns. Not surprising considering the disaster in the shooting range. Still, she made it to Elite and I'm no where close.

She's shocked to see me, but so are the others. Their

antagonizing stares suggest that they know me even though I've never met most of them before.

A man in his forties is the first to speak. "Why is she here?"

"She's with me." Finn says solidly.

A girl joins in. "But she almost blew our whole ambush. Plus she's not an Elite." She is easily the least attractive female I have ever seen, with disproportional facial features and an over-sized head that's too big for her petite body.

Finn crosses his arms and the look on his face is as serious as ever. His team knows he will not give in easily, so more join the argument, trying to get rid of me.

I see Liam, the twelve year-old prodigy, standing with his arms crossed, looking disinterested.

I lower my head and direct my glance elsewhere. Everyone's steely gaze is too much for me to handle right now. Especially when *I am* guilty of their accusations.

Something moving in the shadows catches my eye. I grab Finn's arm without making a sound and tilt my head toward where I saw the movement. Seeing my warning, everyone finally shuts up.

"Everybody, take your position!" Finn orders in a hush. Then the Elites discreetly disperse among the wooden boxes. My eyes locked on Samantha until she disappears behind a tall shelf of construction tools at the far right. Finn grabs my hand and pulls me behind a stack of crates that's taller than me. "Your gun will not work on them." He points to the pistol that Alex gave me. "It hasn't been enhanced. Take mine. But don't use it unless you really have to. I don't want you out there fighting. Just stay here."

Though his voice is suppressed to a whisper, his tone leaves me no room for objection. I take his gun, the same one he loaned me during the train station attack, and put Alex's in one of the many pockets on my khakis. Now I'm certain that the red markings are specifically designed to kill Neuronics. I resolve to ask Finn about them if we get out of here alive.

Someone fires. It comes from one of our men to the right. I peek around the stack and see a floating crate suspended in mid air.

The Neuronics are here.

Ten seconds later, three more men in purple robes enter through a small opening in the back of the warehouse. How they managed to get in, I have no idea. I don't doubt they can create a tunnel by parting dirt and rocks using their telekinesis.

Finn signals to the others, telling them to flank the purple figures. As the Elites begin to move, the crates covering their approach swiftly shift aside, revealing their positions. Seeing that their element of surprise is lost, the eight Elites begin to fire.

I thought Finn would go help his team, but he has other ideas in mind. Stealthily, he climbs up the nearest stack of crates and leaps to the side, catching a narrow pipe near the ceiling. He swings himself up and onto the pipe with ease and fluidity.

Through a gap between two crates, I see a group of seven Neuronics gathered near the middle with their backs against a wall of barrels. I look up at Finn, who is already making his way toward the centre of the warehouse on the narrow pipe, walking as quietly as a hunting cat on the prowl.

Gunfire erupts on the other side of the warehouse. I clutch Finn's gun against my body, hoping the enemies would be distracted long enough to give Finn the element of surprise. Otherwise he could easily be struck down on that precarious ledge.

My heart beats faster with every step he takes. I don't know what he's about to do but whatever it is, I'm sure it won't be a walk in the park. Yet here I am, safely tucked in the corner so no one can bother me. But this time I won't move a muscle unless Finn tells me to. I'm not about to repeat my previous mistake and put my fellow Sarcs in danger again.

High up on the beam, Finn closes in on the group of crouched Neuronics who are still oblivious. Faster than my eyes can follow, he leaps off in a forward somersault and lands right in the middle of the group. All of them spin out of harms way except one. After one quick sweep of the katana, the unfortunate Neuronic drops to the ground like a stone. But the remaining six now have Finn surrounded.

I cover my mouth so my gasp doesn't give away my location. I watch in horror as two guns point at him and four others standing by. All they need to do is pull those triggers and that will be the end of our Elite leader. How could he be so careless? I thought he had a better plan.

Nobody moves for ten gruellingly slow seconds. Finn slowly sheaths his katana but instead of drawing his pistols like I thought he would, he slowly lifts his two empty hands in the air, surrendering.

This can't be right. My vision must be distorted by the narrow crevice I'm peeping through. I shift to the right to look around the stack of crates, exposing half of my head to our enemies. Luckily no one notices me. The crowd of Neuronics are still in a circle, enclosing Finn whose hands are up in the air. A part of me wonders if I overestimated his willpower. But the other part is glad that he is still standing.

I lean against the crates, about to accept defeat when a sudden burst of movement erupts in the group. Finn grabs the two guns pointing at him with lightning speed and wrenches them upward as the bullets fly out, hitting the ceiling. He yanks on the guns so the two Neuronics stumble into him. He then snaps up his elbows, punching them right in the nose. The two men drop their guns as they cry out in pain. They don't suffer long when Finn pulls out his pistol and lodges a bullet in their skull.

The other four begin to shoot but Finn spins into a tornado kick, dodging their shots. He then leaps upward, avoiding another spray of bullets, and lands in the splits. His arms extended to both sides, guns firing.

Two more bodies drop to the floor.

My eyes lock on him, bewildered, like a teenage girl staring at her favourite rock star. Finn spins, kicks, jumps and twists to avoid the dozens of flying bullets aimed at him, all within the proximity of the circle the enemies created.

The remaining three are taken aback, unnerved by the skills they just witnessed. They begin backing up to gain some distance between themselves and the deadly Sarcomere.

Finn doubles his speed, making him too quick for the Neuronics to keep up. It's apparent that their nerves have gotten the better of them when their aims become clumsy. Not only do they miss Finn by a long shot, but they take aim at each other by accident.

I watch with wide eyes as their own bullets ricochet off their robes like rubber balls bouncing off a wall.

What the . . . how are they doing that?

Finn doesn't seem surprised. While in a full twist back flip, he guns down another Neuronic and finishes with a round kick landing. Now it looks like he's just showing off.

But why are Finn's bullets able to penetrate while theirs just bounce off? I squint and see the red symbols glowing fiercely in his hands.

The enhancement!

After another flurry of motions, the last two mind benders join their dead comrades on the ground.

I stand half exposed, fully mesmerized by the spectacle when a cold hand grabs my throat from behind. I manage a loud squeal just before the hand completely closes off my trachea. My mouth desperately gasping for air but finds none. I frantically claw at my attacker but my brittle nails can't even cause so much as a scratch on his thick, leather-like skin. My vision begins to blur as random stars flash before my eyes. One thought comes to mind—*this is how I will die.*

CHAPTER 16

"Drop your weapons, or she dies!" The man squeezes my throat to emphasize his point.

My face contorts in pain and more stars appear in my line of vision. The world begins to dim. On the brink of collapse, I see Finn dropping all of his weapons. Just when cyanosis kicks in, the man releases my neck just enough for me to gasp a big lung-full of air before he tightens his grip again. The brief relief makes things worse. It's like being woken up from the edge of unconsciousness so that you can feel another stab of pain. The agony is renewed and intensified after that short reprieve, further sending me into excruciating hell.

I stare at Finn with bloodshot eyes, trying to capture every detail of his charming face, because I know this will be the last time I lay eyes on him.

He walks slowly, cautiously, toward us with such fierceness in his eyes. His fists held so tight that even I can see the blanched knuckles. He looks beyond angry—like his suppressed rage is barely contained in a pressurized bottle, and some of the steam is already hissing and leaking from the seam. He is about to burst at any moment.

"So we meet again Mr. Finnegan O'Riley." My captor says with venomous sarcasm.

Hearing Finn's full name for the first time shocks my system, temporarily reviving me.

Finn glowers at the man. "Let. Her. Go."

The man loosens his grip on my neck as if in compliance. I regain airflow to my lungs, but only in short, restrained breaths.

"Why do we always find ourselves in this situation Mr. O'Riley?"

My senses are back and I can hear the man's deep, raspy voice clearly. It belongs to someone older. But there's a strange familiarity to his scent—cheap cigar mixed with poor oral hygiene.

Have I met him before? I certainly hope not because he is clearly a Neuronic. Still holding my neck with his right hand, the man sighs, releasing a warm stinky breath against my hair. The putrid stench is almost as suffocating as his grip. He seems calm though, too calm for someone who's about to kill or to be killed.

"She has nothing to do with this. Release her and we'll settle this once and for all." Finn says warily.

"She has *everything* to do with this," the man snarls.

Then I feel a subtle squeeze on my left arm. Is he trying to signal something to me? Maybe he has no intention of hurting me.

He just tried to squeeze the life out of you. Do you call that unintentional? I want to slap myself for being so naive.

Finn is now joined by the rest of the Elites. They all came out of the crossfire relatively unscathed. The enemies on the other hand are sprawled across the warehouse in blood-soaked purple robes.

The Elites stand a few paces behind Finn, looking firm and unyielding. I can tell by their expressions that they're more annoyed than concerned. To me, it translates to *what has she done now?* I know full well the hatred in their eyes is not directed at my captor. I have become their liability once again.

I close my eyes briefly, hoping to gain some clarity. The man is clearly using me to get back at Finn. They must have a long and harrowing history.

"What do you want?" Finn growls. He's about to explode.

"To make you suffer," the man hisses. "I had so much fun last time."

Finn's face tightens, showing a hint of sorrow but its quickly replaced by fury. The unattractive girl grabs her gun and points it at my captor. The man tightens his grip on my neck and lifts me higher so I'm on my tiptoes.

I thrash violently at the sudden pain and tears pool in my eyes. They are not tears of pain, but rage. I've had enough of this brutality. Either kill me now or release me. Quit playing this cruel, taunting game. I have nothing to do with this sentimental reunion of theirs.

Finn quickly extends his arm to stop the thoughtless girl from doing anything stupid. Despite his effort to de-escalate my torment, there's a look of defeat behind those darkened blue eyes. Whatever this man has done to him in the past has left him paralyzed at this very moment. This is when I realize he doesn't actually have a plan.

My anger and desperation begin to well up, like the stir of an undercurrent in the ocean—swirling, picking up speed as it spins the water into a deadly whirlpool. An unexpected spark of energy shoots through my body, like a mild electrical current zapping every body cell, starting with my cardiac muscles. My heart rate spikes as the increased circulation forces new blood into every vein and artery. My body temperature rises as a result and I feel a rush of heat spreading from the sole of my feet, slowly moving up toward my torso. Then it splits into three branches—one continuing its path upward and two reaching out to my arms. I can distinctly identify three separate heat sources moving toward their destinations.

The travelling warmth touches every fibre as it scans over me, causing my muscles to relax. As the warmth dissipates, the muscles reflexively tense up and quivers like they are excited. The pattern continues at different intervals as the three branches of heat make their way through me.

My attention draws inward, focusing on the subtle changes as the foreign but elating sensation sweeps through me, blocking me from the outside world.

Abruptly, the energy waves end, leaving me rejuvenated and vigilant. For the first time since the crash, I know *exactly* what to do.

CHAPTER 17

With the new surge of energy, I grab the man's hips behind me with both hands. Using them as an anchor, I propel my legs upward into a back flip. Startled, the man desperately tries to maintain his grip on my neck, but as I flip up and back, his hand slips and I'm finally free from his suffocating grasp.

My momentum causes him to bend backward and he falls onto his back as I land my backflip on top of him. Before he can react, I turn on my heels and pin him down with one knee on his neck, and his arms are restrained by my other knee and my hands.

Let see if you like this. I dig my knee deeper into his throat and he gasps just like I did a few seconds ago. In spite of the pain, his lips are still locked in a triumphant smirk. *What a psychopath!*

Then I remember his strongest weapon is not his hand. I knee him harder into the ground to break his focus and shift my gaze from his eyes to his lips. He groans in pain, but the smirk never leaves his face.

My realization comes a second too late though. The intrusion has already begun.

Focus on something real, something dear to my heart. Finn's voice weaves through my thoughts, but my mind has already been reduced to a jumble mess. I close my eyes, trying to focus on Finn's face, but he is no longer there.

Before the man completely takes control of my mind, I feel my body tensing up. Then I hear someone's agonizing groan. The next thing I know, I'm staring at myself—not in the mirror, but another me.

She is sitting hunched over at a desk, wearing a simple white tank top and shorts. The bedroom is poorly lit with only a dim table lamp. The bare walls are made of concrete with no windows, and the space is significantly lacking in colour. The bed is neatly made up with simple black and white linen that looks rough and uncomfortable. The first impression of the room reminds me of a jail cell.

I take a step closer and the soft yellow glow illuminates her profile just enough to show her troubled and distraught expression. Her round eyes are focused on something on the desk and her lips are pressed in a hard line.

Cautiously, I walk over to her, contemplating if I should touch her. She doesn't seem to notice me.

Am I the ghost here or is she? I think to myself, trying to wrap my head around this out-of-body experience. I reach out and lightly tap her shoulder, expecting a mystified expression when she sees me. But my hand passes right through like a ghost. I stare at my hands, then rub them together, feeling the heat the friction creates. Convinced that I am dreaming, I disregard the apprehension and redirect my attention back to the pseudo-me, who is still sitting in the same position.

I look over her shoulder and see that she's stroking a photograph delicately, as if any more pressure will reduce the picture to ash. My gaze trails down her slowly swaying hand and a faint scar on her inner forearm catches my attention. I quickly check my own inner elbow and shocked to find the same scar on my skin. It's amazing how I managed to miss such major detail on my own body. The light pink and round mark resembles either a bullet wound or a cigarette burn. But the raised fleshy rim doesn't indicate a simple burn.

Maybe it was from the plane crash. I think.

But the nurses said I didn't sustain any physical injuries. Besides, I don't recall being in this room after the accident. This is very intriguing yet unsettling at the same time.

I shift my attention to the picture, hoping it will give me some hint as to where I am. The photo looks old and wrinkly, like it has been handled many times. The couple in it looks happy and very much in love. The young Asian woman looks beautiful with her dark round eyes and soft pink lips that curved up in a sweet smile, looking up at her handsome beau. She is petite compared to him. The young Caucasian man looks just as happy, gazing lovingly down at her. His dark brown hair is messily styled and his nose is tall and straight. It's too bad that I can't see his eyes from the angle but his perfect white teeth are visible through his face-splitting grin.

My throat tightens as I study the photo. Familiarity turns to recognition, and my heart begins to throb. I know this couple.

Mom, Dad!

The overwhelming emotion paralyzes me for a moment. I blink away my tears and the scene changes abruptly.

"NO!" I yell, reaching for the photo.

As unwilling as I am to leave the only memory of my parents, this cruel dream dictates the landscape and there's nothing I can do.

I rub my eyes frantically as another scene unfolds. Seconds

later, I'm standing in a field surrounded by breathtaking peonies, my favourite flower.

The beautiful terrain quickly washes away my struggle and I'm no longer saddened by the photograph. I feel like I belong here, under the blue canopy that is the summer sky, where the velvety breeze carries a fresh fragrance of peonies. I take a deep breath and let my nose be filled with the sweet, rose-like aroma.

Just when I'm enjoying the beautiful scenery, a bone-chilling scream pierces through my bubble of serenity, almost causing me to trip. The disturbing sound came from somewhere beyond the small hill over-grown with daffodils. Hesitantly, I make my way over the hill.

Mid-way down another field of greenery sits a beautiful country house that is half blown apart. Fire still burns on its roof. About twenty feet from the wreckage, a little girl kneels beside what looks like a body.

I rush over, but just like the previous scene, the girl is oblivious to my existence. I see the dying woman on the ground, severely burnt from her waist down. Both of her legs are barely recognizable; patches of flesh are missing, revealing the white of bones from under the shredded muscles.

My stomach twists and I can almost taste bile in my throat. I have to look away from her gruesome wounds to prevent myself from fainting—though I don't know if you can faint within a dream.

Her face is still relatively unharmed compared to the rest of her body, but blood is foaming in the corners of her lips as she mouths something to the little girl. I force through my queasiness and kneel down beside the woman. I angle myself so I can see only her face, her dark round eyes, soft pink lips . . .

"Mom!" I scream.

"Kazumi . . . take . . . this . . ." Mother lifts her shaking, bloody hand to the girl, the child-me. In her hand is a silver chain draped by a silver pendent in the shape of a hollowed peony. A sparkling diamond is crusted in the centre. The necklace looks exquisite, but tainted with my mother's blood.

I eagerly extend my hand to grab the necklace but only find air. The child-me slowly reaches out with her adorable little hand and grabs the necklace.

"My love . . . my Kazumi . . . I love you . . so much. Be strong . . . don't . . . tell anyone . . . who you are . . . run my angel . . . don't look back . . . just run—" My mother's hand slips and lands on the grass with a thud. Her eyes glaze over, staring blankly into nothingness.

"Okaasan!" We both scream.

CHAPTER 18

I wake with a start. A sense of profound sorrow and confusion lingers. A few people are leaning over me, concerned.

"Focus on me, Gabi." I vaguely hear Finn's voice.

"Finn, we have to get out of here, now! The north and east entrances are lost." A man says nervously.

I can see Finn better now, but my head still feels heavy, like I just woke up from a long coma. Finn scoops me up in his arms and begins to run. I don't complain. This is exactly what I need right now, his warm and comforting chest. I tighten my arms around his neck and bury my face on his chest, distraught by the thought of my parents. Why? Of all the memories, why bring back this one?

My mom may have died eleven years ago, but reliving the horrific scene has revived my grief. It transcends my whole being into a dark place, surrounded by despair and guilt. The precious necklace my mother left me is probably gone. And my father, the only memory I have of him is from that old photograph. I can't even remember if he's still alive, but a nagging feeling tells me he is gone as well. And their names . . . what were their names? I am the worst daughter in the world!

Finn's shirt is once again soaked with my tears. But he

doesn't seem to mind. He has more pressing business on hand, like escaping the besieged complex. There's just too many of them to fight, especially when he has to tend to me. Maybe they'd stand a chance if it wasn't for me. I'm slowing them down, I know it. I'm nothing but a liability.

We left the main compound and are making our way into a tunnel. A dark winding tunnel that doesn't have enough lights to see where we are going.

"You can put me down now." I say. My voice low and flat.

"It's okay. We're almost there," Finn says.

"I'm slowing you guys down. Just leave me here. I don't want to be a burden anymore."

Finn tightens his jaw. "That's not an option." The finality in his tone tells me that this conversation is over. A small part of me is glad that he's not letting go. If he puts me down at this moment, I would just tuck myself in a corner and let the dark sorrow engulf me. I drop the topic and allow the bobbing motion numb my mind.

The dark tunnel opens up into a big cave where a lonely tram sits in waiting. It looks similar to the one the Touches took but significantly shorter. The tubular body only has five windows. I assume it was built specifically for the eleven Elites.

Finn gently lowers me onto a plush bench that runs lengthwise inside the cabin. A few others take their seat at the opposite bench. It's wider than it looks on the inside, with a good five feet of space between the two rows of benches. I don't recall the one I jumped off was this spacious.

A minute later, we are zooming through the tunnel. Finn presses a finger to his ear, like he's communicating with someone. I just stare blankly into the dark tunnel ahead, which is as bleak as my mood.

I had a goal before today, that I'd find my family, my home. They would remember me even if I don't remember them. They would welcome me back with open arms. But the truth is, I'm homeless—have been since the age of seven.

Finn turns around to face us, one hand on a red button. His eyes look dark and mysterious, with obvious sadness behind them. He narrows his brows and takes in a deep breath.

"I just got confirmation that all surviving Cores have made it to the standby trams." He looks down and closes his eyes briefly, then lifts his chin again with renewed courage. "Final destruction in three . . . two . . . one." He pushes the red button.

The ground shudders mildly when the explosion sets off far behind us. Then the tunnel shakes more violently as the subsequent explosions get louder.

I'm suddenly afraid. Afraid that we'll be crushed by a thousand tons of falling rocks. I look up at Finn, his eyes meet mine. They look impassive, empty even. I think I know why. Their home, the Sarcomere's last headquarters has crumbled into ruin, forever buried under a mountain.

I wonder how many Neuronics and their puppets are killed in the process. Imagining their bodies being blasted into bloody pieces gives me satisfaction. They deserve it.

Finn sits down beside me and I notice no one is operating the tram. He sees my apprehension and says, "It's on auto mode. It'll get us there safely." He sounds tired.

I nod and look down at my fingers as my emotion begins to fold inward into the deepest, darkest part of me. The tram becomes very quiet. I can't even hear the rumbling of the engine. Everyone is lost in their own introspection, thinking and absorbing the events that led us here.

"You did well back there." Finn's voice sounds like a morning alarm, waking me from my stupor.

Is he mocking me? At a time like this?

I stare intensely into his darkened eyes, enraged.

"You didn't see yourself, but we all did." He glances at the other Elites who are now looking at me. I follow his gaze around the cabin and see that the men now look less hostile toward me. They even give me an encouraging nod. On the other hand, the four females still carry the same you-don't-belong-here look. Especially Samantha and the ugly girl. If anything, their stares have gotten more antagonistic.

"Did you feel something different in your body? Just before your counter attack on Jack?" Finn asks.

I think for a moment. Then the alien sensation comes to mind, strange but exhilarating. And the energy buildup, the heat rush.

I nod slightly, not sure of its implication.

Finn lets out a long sigh, then a warm smile spreads his face. "Congratulations. You've unleashed your *full* potential," he says.

His words render me speechless. *Was that it? My moment of truth?* I ask myself.

Should I be excited? I have been anticipating this moment from the time I set foot in the Sarcomere headquarters, which really isn't that long ago. I even thought of how I would react and under what circumstance it would occur. Never in a million years did I think it'd take a precious human life to achieve it. Now that the moment's here, the excitement and pride elude me. What took their place is a tremendous pang of guilt, an overwhelming despair, and a certain hopelessness.

"Thanks for saving my life, again." It's all I can manage to mumble.

Finn wraps both of my hands in his. The sudden warmth resonates through my entire body. I didn't notice how cold my hands were and that I was shivering.

"I didn't save you this time. And I owe you an apology." He tightens his grip. "I . . . I was caught off guard when Jack got a hold of you. I should have . . . could have done something. But . . ." He trails off like he is remembering something aweful. His face locked in a grimace.

"So you would watch me die?" I sound harsher than intended, but I'm angry and confused by his statement. Looks like I thanked the wrong person. He was indeed helpless, just as I thought before my mind was invaded.

"Look who's talking," the ugly girl suddenly breaks her silence and storms toward me. "If it wasn't for you, everybody would have gotten out much earlier. And Alex . . . he would still be alive!" She is about to launch herself at me when a middle-aged Elite pulls her back.

"Easy now Chloe." The man drags her back to her seat diagonally across from me.

"She deserves to die!" She thrashes in the man's grip, completely losing it.

"That's enough!" Finn scolds and Chloe falls silent, but tears continue to roll down her cheeks. Her death stare is a good indication that we will never be friends.

"Look Gabi, it's not Finn's fault." The man who stopped Chloe explains. I've never met him before today. He has a kind face—eyes full of compassion and lips that curve upward. His face doesn't carry too many wrinkles but his hair does contain more gray than black. His relaxed demeanour might suggest that he's quite easy-going as well. He looks to Finn for confirmation and is given a slight nod. Then Finn releases my hands and rests his right arm on the window sill, eyes blank.

What the heck is going on?

"It's hard for him, Gabi. He lost his fiancee four years ago, to the same bastard."

My eyes widen, feeling like someone just splashed me with a bucket of ice water.

"She died in a similar situation," the man finishes.

I turn to Finn, his eyes closed, brows creased. I can't stand seeing him like this—so tormented, so filled with grief. I want to wrap myself around him, to comfort him, but I don't have the courage.

"I'm so sorry," I say. "I didn't know. I . . . I wasn't really blaming you. Sorry, I'm really . . ." Finn clasps my hands again before I can finish my apology.

"Don't feel bad. You did what I couldn't. I should thank you for avenging Jane's death."

"What?" I gape at him, muddled.

"You remember the sensation when your potential was building?"

I nod.

"You remember pinning him down with a backward flip?"

I pause, searching my memory. Then I nod again.

"What do you remember after that?" Finn seems to have put away his grief for now.

"Uh . . ." I think hard. Then the words flows out of my mouth like a river. I recount how I tried to avoid his eye contact, but it was too late; how I had the out-of-body experience, the photograph of my parents, and finally, the gruesome death of my mom when I was seven.

After listening to me, the whole tram falls into an awkward silence. Chloe sits sideways on the bench, looking out into the black tunnel. She's still weeping quietly. Despite her nastiness, I feel for her. I know what losing someone dear to you feels like.

"So what happened to the attacker?" I ask.

The kind-faced man sits down beside me. "You killed him when you were under his spell. I've never seen anyone do that before. Even our leader couldn't have pulled that off," he pats Finn on the back. "Finn's right, you *are* strong." He puts a comforting hand on my shoulder. I begin to like this man.

"But how?" I'm still confused.

Finn says, "I suspect your body's self-protective mechanism kicked in when your mind was being invaded. Your muscles responded and your knee suffocated him. It took three of us to get you off his body. Then you passed out."

"But why didn't he just kill me when he had the chance?" I ask. "Why chose to revive my memories instead?" I can see the same question daunting the others.

"Are you sure they weren't fake memories implanted in your mind?" Finn says dubiously. "He may have created your mom's dying scene to mess with your head."

I jump up, shaking my head defensively. "No! They were real. My mom died in front of me!" I'm hollering over Finn. "I remember the peony pendant. I remember holding it dearly in my hands. I remember I was only seven. I remember how traumatized and helpless I was." My voice cracks and I can no longer contain myself. I'm not going to let anyone discredit the only memory I have of my parents.

Finn wraps his arm around me, holding me close, silently apologizing for his insensitive comment. I want to release all my emotions at once, in the arms of the person I trust. But I can't. The other Elites, they're standing by, ready to judge and scrutinize my every move.

"Be strong, Kazumi." My mother's last words ring loud and clear in my head.

Yes, that was definitely my mother.

I slowly break away and wipe my face with the back of my hand.

"Gabi," Finn breathes.

"It's Kaz, actually. My real name is Kazumi Clarke."

"You remember who you are?" Finn smiles.

I lower my head. "Not exactly. What I told you is all I remember. I can't even recall my parents' names." I sit back down between him and the nice man.

"Murray Flemington," he extends his hand to me. I shake it tentatively. "I'm sorry that we have to meet under such circumstance Miss Kazumi Clarke."

I nod. It's nice to finally hear my own name again. "You can call me Kaz." I say.

"Now that we have your dad's last name and your mom's ethnic background, we can do a search and see if we find anything," Murray suggests.

My eyes brighten at his idea. "You'd do that?" I suddenly sound like an excited twelve-year-old girl.

"I'm sure it can be arranged," he smiles. "But it may take some time since we need to re-establish all our networks and systems at the new base."

"Thank you." I smile.

"My second in command never fails," Finn adds proudly. "Let me introduce you to the rest of my team." He starts with the Elites at the opposite bench.

Samantha, whom I already know, sits directly across from me with her arms crossed. She looks even more arrogant now that she is officially an Elite. Next to her is Chloe. She has stopped crying but still carries that I-want-to-kill-you look. I skirt her eyes so as not to provoke her. Bridget, who has a massive amount of hair that's both curly and frizzy, looks to be in her early forties. She's wearing a tight sleeveless shirt that shows off her athletic build. She stares at me warily then finally nods so I don't focus on her anymore. Sitting next to her is Lilly, who could be around Finn's age or a couple years older. She has an average-looking face dabbed with freckles but a body that's both curvaceous and toned. She looks somewhat familiar though.

"How's your cheek?" she smirks.

It was her, the girl who sliced my cheek with a flying dagger. I instinctively rub my face where the cut was.

The skin is as smooth as new.

"It was healed before I got back to my room. Thank you for asking." I reply.

Finn eyes us curiously then moves on to introduce the guys. I recognize Liam, the youngest member of the team. He's quite tall for his age. He casually salutes me with his index and middle fingers without looking up from his MUD. Sitting at the very end is Nick, who appears to be in his thirties, has a shaved head and a big tattoo snaking up the side of his neck.

"Gotta say, your reputation precedes you," says Nick.

"It wasn't my intent to create a reputation for myself." I try to control my tone but the tension is already mounting.

"Don't listen to him, he doesn't know when to shut up," a young guy at the end of my bench stands up, "I'm Kayden by the way," and he waves.

"Hi." I give him a small smile.

Kayden has darker complexion, like caramel. His wavy black hair is short and tamed, with thick eyebrows that are obviously trimmed to perfection. He is cute, but I also get the feeling that he tries too hard. How he managed to get out of a battle looking like he was fresh out of a salon is beyond me, but he seems like a nice enough guy.

Ryan and Benji are the last two guys I get introduced to.

Ryan is young and somewhat shy. I can tell by his reserved smile. For some reason he reminds me of Chief Trousing. Maybe it's the golden hair. Next to him is Benji, which is short for Benjamin. His hair is gray to almost white and the cut is short and messy. Finn says that he's the oldest and the most experienced Elite on the team. He demands people call him Benji because it makes him sound younger.

"That's right. I refuse to get old. I have a face-lift appointment next week." Benji pushes his cheeks higher.

"He's the oldest *and* the most childish one here. As you can see." Kayden puts his arm on Benji's shoulders.

Thanks to their comic relief, the earlier tension is gone. People seem to be less on edge now, except for Chloe.

After the exhausting round of introduction, Finn tells us that the trip will take about fifteen hours.

Excellent!

How am I going to survive the next fourteen hours with some of these not-so-friendly strangers in such a confined space? I can see Miss Ugly Blond over there is dying to cut me open with her sword.

Finn continues to explain our travel arrangements. Two people must take guard duty at all times and we will rotate shifts. He presses a button and the floor between the two benches slides open, revealing a hidden compartment filled with canned food, water, and blankets.

What about washroom breaks? *I wonder.*

As if reading my mind, Finn presses another button and a toilet rises up from under the floor at the end of the short tram. That's why the opposite bench doesn't extend all the way. What else does this tram *not* have?

"Sorry gang. This is an escape plan, not a luxury cruise." Finn says. "You'll have to make due with what's here." As he finishes, a silver screen cascades down from the overhead compartment above the toilet, becoming a privacy curtain. But the sound will still be completely audible by everyone on board. *Note to self: Don't drink water.*

Samantha volunteers eagerly to take the first watch with Finn. Her disappointment is too obvious when Finn volunteers Chloe to accompany her instead. Then he takes his seat beside me and folds his blanket into a pillow for his nap. Ugly Blond drags her unwilling legs to the control panel, while Samantha gracefully strolls by us. I know her ploy—she wants him. But she won't succeed, just like how I will never have his heart. Now I know why.

The feeling of being rejected resurfaces. I curl up in a ball beside the man I want, but can never have. Eventually sleep claims me.

CHAPTER 19

I am dozing in and out of sleep when Finn taps my shoulder.
A blanket is cozily wrapped around my torso, but I don't recall
fetching it myself.

"It's our turn to take watch." Finn says softly.

I get up, taking care that I don't step on anyone's toes. Finn
dimmed the lights earlier so we could sleep. I join him by the
control panel. Everyone else is fast asleep behind us. We must
be nearing Alaska because the temperature in here has dropped
significantly despite the heating system. I blow hot air into my
palms and rub them up and down my quads. Finn opens an
overhead compartment and produces a fluffy white blanket.

"Here," he takes my elbow and sits me in a small seat beside
the control panel. He then wraps the soft blanket around my
legs. "It'll warm up once we get out of the tunnel where there's
sunlight. Summer there is cooler than in the Rockies."

Why do you have to be so caring?

He then sits down directly opposite from me.

"Thank you." I mumble.

He nods.

"How did it happened?" I ask without realizing that this
may be too personal. "Um . . . sorry. You don't have to tell me
if you don't want to."

His eyes lock on mine, gazing intently like he's contemplating what to say. Finally he takes a deep breath and recounts the tragedy.

"We were on a recon mission four years ago, at what we thought could be a Neuronic base just outside of Seattle. Everything looked fine at first, nothing suspicious. As we were getting ready to leave, an army of soldiers jumped out and had us surrounded," his face twists as he recalls the painful event. "It was an ambush. We were outnumbered, by a lot. Our commander ordered an immediate fall back, which . . . we could very well make it out. But . . ." he stops again, elbows prop up on his knees, face buried in his hands. Is he crying?

He straightens after a moment. He's not crying, but the torment on his face is almost unbearable for me to watch.

"I was hot-headed back then. While my team was fighting their way out, I marched forward instead, thinking that I was strong enough to take them on by myself. I didn't want to leave empty-handed. My team made it out of the building without me. I held my own for a while against their mind intrusion but my mental guarding was rapidly depleting. Soon they would have taken complete control over me, and that was when Jane came back for me." His eyes darken, like all the lights have been sucked out of them.

"We could have gotten out, but I was too proud. Too stupid. Before I knew it, Jane blocked a flying metal crate that was coming for me. She must have broke several ribs from the impact and it was all my fault." He is getting more agitated as his story leads closer to the climax. I hurry to his side and put a comforting hand on his back, half kneeling.

"He got her. Had her throat in his hand . . . just like how he had you." I'm holding my breath as the image of Jane withering under the man's deadly grip—just like me mere hours ago. Except, I made it out alive and she didn't.

"I was pinned down by six guys and was forced to watch as he killed her, slowly, painfully . . ." I can barely make out his last muffles.

I sink to the floor beside him, my knees wrapped tightly in my arms. Jane's dying scene replays again and again in my head, like a video caught in a glitch. But in my version, Jane's face is replaced by mine, struggling violently as my last breath is being slowly squeezed out of me.

We sit like this for a long while—each trapped in our own version of the tragedy. Then Finn's unexpected comment breaks the eerie silence.

"You remind me of her," he murmurs.

What?

My eyes wide, lips parted.

"Your hair, your eyes . . ." his luminous eyes trace my hair, my eyes, and down to my lips." My mouth goes dry, and my heart pounds through the roof. "And your courage." He says as he gets up from his seat and leans against the low row of buttons, hands in his pant pockets.

I stare at the back of his head, not knowing what to make of his sudden comment. Is that why he rejected me? Because I remind him too much of his dead fiancee? A tiny gleam of hope begins to emerge.

I get up to stand beside him. "I'm sorry you had to go through that." I don't know what I can say to make him feel better. I can't begin to imagine the depth of his sorrow and guilt. He closes his eyes briefly, accepting my condolences.

"So what happened after?"

"I was kicked out of the Elite Force for disobedience causing death. Then Gerry, our commander resigned," he sighs. "Too light a punishment if you ask me. For me I mean, Gerry was a fine leader. But he felt it was his fault that we got ambushed."

"Where is he now?" I ask.

"Somewhere out there. He became a field agent and I haven't seen him since."

"I see. But how did you get back into the Elite Force and become a commander?"

Finn chuckles. "Good question. Sometimes I still wonder the same thing. Alex took over the position after Gerry left—"

"Alex?" I cut him off. Please don't be the same Alex who just died for me.

Finn lowers his head. "Alex was an Elite, yes. And a fine commander."

I feel my lungs collapsing. *"He's not quite at the bottom of the barrel."* was what I thought when I found out he was the Touch leader. I have astronomically underestimated him this entire time. An Elite leader, sacrificed to save my sorry life. How will my conscience be okay with this from now on?

"But . . . he was the Touch leader?" Self-denial kicks in.

"He volunteered when the Touch was lacking a suitable leader two years ago," Finn explains. "And he fiercely persuaded the chief to make me the Elite Commander, because according to him, I'm one of the most capable Sarcs he's ever seen. It also helped that I've cleaned up my act while serving as a Core."

"So he demoted himself. What a true selfless leader," I mumble to myself.

"That, he certainly was," Finn says. "He said the Touches were too weak as a group compared to the rest of us. If we were to stand a chance against the Neuronics, they need to step up their game. So he went and strengthened every single one of them, both mentally and physically."

"But the Touches, they just fled. They left you guys to fight the battle. I don't think that qualifies as strong. I saw them in that train, they all looked so defeated."

Finn turns to me. "I don't know about the defeated look, but they did *exactly* what they were trained to do—to preserve our history, our work, and most importantly, our genes. They aren't meant to fight. They are scholars, scientists and doctors. Without them, we would not have the technology and the ability to kill the mind benders."

Why does he have to tell me all this now? Knowing Alex's true nature adds another thousand pounds of guilt on my shoulders. I take the pistol Alex gave me from my pocket, almost overjoyed that I didn't lose it during the attack. It just became my most treasured possession.

"Maybe he didn't show it, but he thought highly of you," says Finn. "That was why he came back for you. Willing to sacrifice himself for you. And gave you his most treasured weapon."

Great! Another blow to my conscience.

"I thought he hated me. He . . . he made my life miserable." A tear drops silently on the silver handgun.

"He might not be the most lovable person, but he had his own unique ways to bring people out, potential wise. That was one of his strong suits."

Did Alex know he had to die in order to bring out my potential? The idea disturbs me greatly. And I will never know the truth.

Finn holds my hands, wrapping the pistol tightly in our palms. "You will train with me from now on. You're one of us now, Kazumi Clarke." Finn's lips curl up in a smile. His eyes bright and hopeful, the earlier sorrow gone. But all I can see is Alex's dying face.

CHAPTER 20

After an exhausting fifteen hours on the tram, we finally see sunlight. The track ends in a wild field not too far from the tunnel exit. Nothing but a tattered shed overgrown with long grass and weeds stand among the wilderness.

The first thing that welcomes me as I get off the tram is the air, so fresh and brisk. For the first time since the attack, my dark mood brightens. I lift my head to bask in the warm Alaskan sun. The temperature feels just right with my training shirt and khakis on. Then all too soon, Alex's face reappears.

He will never see the sun again. I can't help but think.

Will my conscience ever leave me alone? Will Alex haunt my every waking moment from now on?

"Okay people, we have to move," says Finn.

Without a word, everyone starts running westward. They seem to know where they are going, so I follow close behind. It amazes me how I can easily keep up with their pace now that my potential has awakened. The group runs past the abandoned shed and into the thick grass that's the same height as me. I thought this was one of their illusions to keep out enemies but the cuts on my exposed arms from the grass blades are all too real. They might very well have planted this to deter people from treading through. Seriously, this grass is evil, and I'm not the only one complaining. Samantha is rubbing her arms and whining to the boys a few paces ahead. They just chuckle and shake their heads.

We emerge from the scratchy grass and are welcomed by a breathtaking view of the Gulf of Alaska. The water is so vast and calm, like a deep blue wavering blanket. We make a right and jog along the banks. Murray tells me that we're on Kenai Peninsula, the southern tip of Alaska. I can see the picturesque snow-capped mountains in the distance, creating a splendid backdrop for this magnificent coastline. It's beauty is further accentuated by a canopy of blue sky above. I could live here. Maybe just in the summer though. I hate cold weather.

I look around for signs of civilization. Nothing stands out as far as my eyes can see, just a few half-collapsed wooden sheds scattered along the coast. Where did the town go? Finn said this used to be a fishing town called Homer. We make another bend to the right and sitting at about fifty feet in front is an ultra modern jet on a short runway—sleek and new. I'm not too thrilled about travelling again. My legs are still numb from hours of sitting.

As we get closer, I see that the jet is built from the same white, glossy material as our escape tram. It looks half plastic, half metal, probably some high-tech material created by the R&D team. The single turbine engine sits steadily on the rear of the fuselage, just in front of the vertical stabilizer, which incidentally resembles the tail of a whale. The wings are curved fluidly upward into their winglets, giving the visual effect of a big white bird in flight. The entire design is smooth and curvy, without any sharp angles. The most attractive aspect is the faint red glow that illuminates the entire underside of the jet.

I turn to Finn. "What's with the red glow?"

"Oh it's just for show," he smiles playfully. "You should see it at night." Then he rushes me into the cabin.

The interior is just as impressive. The walls and furniture are made of soft white leather. The floor is covered in a plush gray carpet. A curvy sofa runs lengthwise on one side ending with a pair of reclinable leather chairs facing forward. On the other side are two rows of the chairs with a retractable table in between. A soft glow illuminates the ceiling, transforming subtly from yellow, to orange, to red and back to yellow. I notice the soft music crooning in the background, making the waltzing glow ever more intriguing.

A man's voice rings through the speaker, overlapping the music. "Good morning ladies and gentlemen. This is your captain speaking." Giggles break out among the group.

Where's Finn? I look around but can't see him in the small cabin.

Benji shakes his head with a smile. "Every time."

"Our cabin crew will distribute snacks and drinks once we're in the air," the captain says.

But where is the cabin crew? We're the only ones here.

"Ah hem . . . this is you Lilly," says the voice in the speaker.

"Hey not fair! I did it last time already!" Lilly whines, and everybody breaks into a teasing laugh.

So this is the Elites when they're not on a killing spree. I can't help but smile at the lively group in front of me. Half of them are just teenagers growing into adulthood. It's hard to imagine that this is the very group that just killed almost an entire army of Neuronics.

"Miss Clarke, would you please join me in the cockpit please," the voice says, which I now recognize. "Enjoy your flight ladies and gentlemen."

Everyone now directs their attention to me as I make my

way to the cockpit, making my steps all the more awkward. As I enter, Finn signals me to sit beside him in the First Officer's seat. "I figure you don't mind keeping me company. If you do, then I'll have to bribe you with the view." He gives me a quick smile then goes back to pressing buttons and checking gauges.

The view is indeed spectacular through the cockpit windows. In the foreground are white-crested rolling waves crashing again the rocks, jetting up sprays of water like two unstoppable forces colliding. The wind must have picked up because the water was a calm sheet of blue just minutes ago. Nature can be just as unpredictable as life. One minute we are living peacefully inside the Rockies, the next minute we are fighting for our lives and forced out of our home. Who knows what's waiting for us in the new base? I want to be optimistic but it's hard when my life has been nothing but a disastrous joke.

I look up from the crashing waves and see the serene mountains in the background, beastly beauties thousands of years in the making, juxtaposed with the turbulent sea. They're majestic and glorious.

"Well I suppose this is slightly better than being stuck in the cabin with people who want to cut me open." I say to Finn.

"No one is cutting anyone open today."

I grin at his comment. This is exactly what he said to me when we first met back in the old headquarters.

"What?" he asks, seeing my smile.

"Nothing."

Finn shrugs and we begin to move.

"Just so you know, I'm not a fan of flying." I say as knots form in my stomach.

"Oh you'll love it after I show you what I can do," he winks as he takes the jet into the sky.

After the sinking feeling of take-off passes, I steal a glance at Finn as he plays around with the intimidating number of buttons in front of us. His eyes wide, alert and beautiful. My mind dashes back to the cave where my lips touched his for a brief second. The same lips that are talking into his headphone right now. And I remember the goosebumps, the electrical current that sent my mind spinning when I stole that kiss. What I'd give to have that feeling again.

"You can relax," Finn's voice breaks my reverie. "I'm the best self-taught pilot you'll find."

"WHAT?" I almost jump out of my seat.

Finn laughs, "You're so gullible."

"This is why you want me here isn't it? So you can poke fun at me." I pretend to be mad, but the truth is, I'm enjoying our little tease.

"Of course," he replies. "My team is tired of me."

I can see that. But I don't think I'll ever get tired of him.

"Anyway. So, this jet's pretty cool." I say.

"Ya, she's a keeper," Finn pats the throttle. "Our R&D designed it for the government and they only manufactured four in total. All for high government officials."

"So how did you get a hold of this one?"

"We did a mission for them last year. They suspected that there was a mole from the Neuronics in their National Defence. We found him and got rid of him before any big damage was done. So as a thank you to the Elite Force, the government gave us Natalie."

"You named it Natalie?" My voice jumps two octaves. What an absurd name for a powerful jet.

Finn snickers. "What? Natalie's a good name. The whole team voted on it, not just me. It was a toss between Natalie or Cameron. But she's totally a Natalie."

I grin ear-to-ear. I love seeing the carefree side of Finn, despite the fact that we practically *just* got kicked out of our home. Maybe this is his coping mechanism, like how some people would cry, some would mope, he just shoves it to the back of his mind and locks it tight, pretend it's not there.

"It's good to see you smile again. I was worried . . ." I say.

Finn sighs. "It was my team's first time too."

I cock my head, not understanding what he means.

"To see me like that," he adds. "Well, other than Murray. He was there on that mission too. Anyway, I don't like to dwell on the past. We need to be optimistic and hopeful. It's the only way to push forward in hard times. And that includes having a little fun once in a while."

I want to tell him it's easier said than done. I'm the type who would always think of the worst case scenario. So when it does happen, there's no disappointment. And if it doesn't, then it's a bonus. Maybe I can benefit to lighten up a bit. My frown lines are getting deeper and I'm only eighteen.

After Finn switches to auto-pilot, I ask, "Is that what the red glow is for? To identify that *Natalie* belongs to the Elites?"

"Well anyone who's authorized can use her. We're not greedy. But yes, we figure the red glow matches our weapons." He grins like a little boy who's proud of his toy.

"Oh right, your weapons. What exactly are those red symbols?"

Finn pauses for a second then says, "You really want to know?"

I nod enthusiastically. I've been curious about it since the beginning.

"Our blood."

"You're kidding." I frown. "Come on. Just tell me. I'm a part of your team now, you said so."

"I did say that. And I'm not kidding." Finn says with a somewhat straight face.

"Well would you care to elaborate?" I'm still not convinced.

"It has something to do with our DNA being an antagonist to theirs. In battle, Neuronics would create an energy field around them that deflects pretty much all attacks—physical, thermal, electrical, you name it. The only way to penetrate that is with our blood, which carries a specific type of molecule that can break down their cellular barrier. I don't remember the whole biochemistry behind it. I'm not a scientist. As long as it works, that's good enough for me."

"Then how come the Cores don't have these markings on their weapons?" I ask.

"Because their gene is not potent enough. They've tried. Never worked. Only the DNA of the Elites has enough juice to do that."

"How interesting," I tap my nose with my index finger. "So what you're saying is people who qualifies as an Elite would have the right DNA to enhance these weapons?"

"You can say that." Finn replies.

I take out Alex's pistol from my pocket and hold it in front of me. The silver weapon catches a ray of sun and gleams proudly in my hands. There's not a single scratch visible. Alex must have taken great care of her. My fingers gingerly run along the slide, remembering Alex's final words. *"One day you'll have your red markings on it, remember me when that day comes."* He knew all along that I would be an Elite.

I smile at the gun and swallow the lump in my throat. I need to be strong, for Alex.

"Are you alright?" Finn asks.

I nod, eyes still on my pistol. "I will work very hard from now on. I will have my own markings."

"I know you'll make Alex proud." Finn puts his hand on mine.

It's fascinating what having a goal can do to one's mental strength. The black hole that threatened to devour me back in the escape tram is now a guiding light, leading me toward self-redemption.

CHAPTER 21

From our short flight, I learned that most of Alaska has been deserted for many years. Mainly due to the floods caused by melting glaciers. Then huge tsunamis took down the remaining establishments. The town Homer, where we boarded the plane, used to be a great fishing village some eighty years ago, known for their fresh halibut. But most of it is now under water.

Finn lands the jet steadily on the isolated island in southern- most Alaska. As we slow to a complete stop, I see a broken, half-fallen sign that says: WELCOME TO KODIAK ISLAND. A quick glance around the surroundings makes me realize how defensible this location is. Making a base that can only be accessed by planes or boats is a smart strategy.

Finn said the new base is built with a massive foundation that runs deep underwater and it should combat any earthquake or tsunami.

I'm pumped with anticipation as we get off the jet. But my excitement melts just like the glaciers when I lay eyes on the terrain.

Where is the base?

There's nothing on this small island but rolling hills and wild grass. Probably the same thorny grass that assaulted my arms. Did Finn make a mistake? I want to ask him but he's already leading the group down a dirt path heading east. He seems to know where he's going so I keep my mouth shut and follow.

Everyone is keeping to themselves as we make our way up the slight hill. Apparently Samantha and I are the only ones intrigued by what lies ahead. The others just look indifferent, bored even.

The group stops at the top of the hill overlooking a wild field that stretches into the horizon. Beyond that is the cobalt blue sea. The whole area just looks abandoned and unkempt.

Finn pushes a series of buttons on a circular device strapped to his belt. The air in front of us shimmers and just like magic, a huge structure made of steel and glass appears out of nowhere.

"What the . . ." Samantha mutters as the massive structure looms over us. Both of our jaws hit the floor.

I can make out three distinct buildings that are combined into one impressive architecture. The one directly facing us resembles a silver spaceship—sleek, disc-like, and somehow suspended in mid air. I crane my neck to see better and I think it's actually being supported by the second structure behind it, one that resembles a tall rectangular 3-D puzzle. Its exterior is made from the Sarc's favourite material—the one with the glossy white finish. Then they carved in lines and gaps to create the illusion of a jigsaw puzzle. Some pieces even protrude outward to give a more three dimensional effect. Attached to the puzzle building is a smooth spiralling tower, entirely made of glass, reaching high into the sky. Sunbeams glinting brightly on its surface, making it sparkle like a crystal wand anchored to the ground, wielding the magic that made all this possible.

I know the Sarcs have ridiculous technology, but what I'm seeing right now is out of this world. I look over to Finn, who is standing at the front of the group looking at me, amused.

How long has he been staring? I feel embarrassed all of sudden, thinking that he must be laughing in his head at my comical reaction.

I make a face at him and follow the group as we make our way toward our new home.

"So, welcome to our humble abode." Finn says when I've caught up to him.

"Humble indeed." I say as I stare at the structure. I still can't quite compose myself. This is too crazy.

I tilt my head back as we approach the main entrance so I can admire the underside of the spaceship. The glass floor looks bright and fuzzy, which I assume is to protect the privacy of its occupants. I can't wait to find out what's inside of it. The chief's office maybe. I can totally see Annette hogging the coolest part of the complex.

I bump into someone, didn't know that the group has slowed down to funnel through the main entrance. Chloe squeals exaggeratedly.

"Watch it, you reckless drama queen!" she hisses.

"Hey Chloe, cut her some slack would you?" One of the guys comes to my defence.

She narrows her eyes at him, then storms into the building without another word.

"Uh . . . Kayden is it?" I think that's his name.

"Yeah. Don't worry, I've got your back." He winks at me then disappears through the sliding doors.

That was odd.

The Trousing Hall, obviously named after the self-absorbed chief, is grand and opulent. I step onto the white marble floor, completely amazed by what the architect has achieved. The design is modern yet majestic. No more plastic-looking walls like the Dome Hall. This one consists of mostly natural stones in white and gray. Twenty silver plinths line the two sides; on top of each is a hologram of a full size person, slowly spinning. I walk up to the first hologram to read the engraving on the plinth: CHIEF JONATHAN BLAIN (FOUNDER OF SARCOMERES) 1953-2052. I look up, intrigued to see what our ancestor looked like. The image slowly makes it way around, eventually his face becomes apparent. Clean shaven, dark hair, dark eyes. He was handsome, very handsome actually. The three dimensional portrait must be showing him in his prime. The tailored suit could barely hide his bulging muscles. His life must have been one heck of a story.

I quickly count the rest of the holograms from where I stand; nine women and eleven men in total. Our current chief is among one of them. Hers is situated closest to the stage in the far end of the hall. Two pillars that remind me of the spiralling noodles I had at Italo, twist upward from both sides, attaching the semi-circular stage to a dais three storeys above. I bet that's the throne where the chief reigns over her people.

Behind the palatial stage is one of four glass elevators with its transparent shaft extending all the way up to the ceiling, giving access to each of the ten floors. The other three elevators are spaced out evenly around the perimeter, one being right next to the main entrance. Ten rows of balconies, made of transparent blue glass, line the sides, overlooking the great hall. Rays of sunlight cast down through the huge skylight in the ceiling and reflect off the blue glass, creating a cascading shower of blue and white lights around the hall. No more weather hologram needed.

Fidgeting with eagerness, I can't wait to see the rest of the place. But our tour is cut short when a petite, stocky woman greets us by the stage. She sends Finn away after a brief discussion, then leads us into a food court, which is off to the left of Trousing Hall. I didn't even think about food until now and realize I'm famished.

We gather around a table where Gretchen, the stocky woman, hands us our new MUDs, which are preloaded with three hundred dollars. The old cards are no longer valid in this base. It's not an issue for me since I never had an official Sarcomere MUD to begin with, only a temporary "New Recruit" ID.

My face darkens the moment she hands me mine. It's transparent but with a black tint. It even has my picture on it. At the bottom are big block letters that read TOUCH.

"Sorry Gretchen, I think there's been a mistake. I'm not a Touch." I try to sound as polite as possible to hide my frustration.

Gretchen gives me a pointed look. "If you got a problem, talk to your commander." Then she storms off.

"I would if you hadn't snatched him away the minute we walked in." I call after her but she pretends she can't hear me.

Chloe jumps in, of course, never missing an opportunity to degrade me. "Do you have no shame? Don't think that by unleashing your potential is enough to get you a spot on our team. Every Sarc here has unleashed their potential but none of them is comparable to the Elites, including you!" Just when I thought she couldn't get any uglier.

There's no point arguing since there was no witness when Finn invited me to join his team. I will have to sort this out with him. I ignore her and head to one of the food stations. They have all sort of cuisines available for our indulgence. I decide to go for Japanese.

Hmm!
The sushi here is exquisite. So fresh that I can almost

taste the sea. I close my eyes to savour the deliciousness, and something triggers inside of me. I see Okaasan dancing around the kitchen in her lovely lilac apron. Then Daddy came in, swept her into a romantic waltz. I sat in my chair, clapping delightfully to their rhythm.

"Mommy, Daddy." I mouth the words silently as the scene replays in my mind. I remember my mother always made these cold soba noodles along with her divine salmon and tuna hand rolls. She would tell me stories of our ancestors and how her parents survived the deadly tsunami that wiped out all of Japan; and how Greater China then took in all the survivors. Since then, the once strong and advanced nation of Japan was nothing but an underwater ruin. Because of that, my mother was adamant in preserving our culture. She taught me the importance of who I am at every opportunity she had.

"Oh Gabi, I was so worried . . . oh are you alright?" Celine grabs my shoulders, hauling me back to present.

I quickly wipe off the beads of tears on my cheeks with the back of my hand. "Hi Celine, I'm alright." I force a smile.

"Why are you crying?" she sits down beside me.

"I just remembered something about my parents. Nothing major. Don't worry."

She hugs me. "Oh Gabi, that's great news. Is your memory coming back slowly?"

"Um . . . my name is actually Kazumi. You can call me Kaz."

"Wow, that's a beautiful name. That doesn't sound English," she says.

"No. My mother was Japanese and my dad had some British in him I think." I look down at my fingers and my throat begins to tighten up again.

Having sensed my mood, Celine stops interrogating me about my past. "Well I'm definitely very happy that you're safe and sound. Oh, do you know where you're staying yet?"

"No, we just got here and Gretchen just gave us our MUDs." I say. "To be honest, I have no clue where I belong. Finn told me I'll be training with him from now on," Celine takes a sharp breath and covers her mouth in shock. "But . . ." I show her my Touch ID.

It takes her a second to recover. "Oh my gosh. Another Elite! We're in such luck . . ." she pauses, realizing what an oxymoron she just made. I don't think she knows how many casualties we just had. "I mean . . . Elites are hard to come by these days. We were thrilled to find out about Samantha. And now you too. Two back to back, we've never had that before. Our last Elite recruit was Liam and it was almost three years ago."

I look down at my Touch ID. "Well it's not official yet. Finn hasn't made the announcement and I don't know where to find him. It's so huge here," I look around. "I thought we were going to some temporary shelter or something, but wow, this is so . . . unexpected."

Celine smiles proudly. "Our plan was to move here anyway. The attack just pushed us a little ahead of schedule. The Rockies have become more unstable in the past few years. Earthquakes and landslides have threatened our compound multiple times."

She gets up as I finish my last piece of sushi. "If you want, I can show you around, just like old times. I know my way around here pretty well. Then I'll find Finn for you," she grins.

Maybe being a Touch isn't so bad. At least they are less arrogant and chastising . . . Nah! Who am I kidding? Now that I've had a taste of the pie, I want it all. I won't stop until I have the marks of Elites.

CHAPTER 22

I am lying in bed, in a well furnished guest apartment, sorting out the events that happened in the past twenty-four hours.

The spiralling tower turned out to be a residential condo. The Touches occupy the lower third while the Cores take the majority of the floors. Both groups need to share rooms with at least one other person if they're single. Families of course, occupy one unit. The Elites are fewer in number and because they're Elites, they get their own room in the highest section. And of course, Chief Trousing gets the panoramic penthouse.

I stare at the white ceiling, thinking how everything seems so surreal—Alex's death, me being held hostage, unleashing my potential, the underground travel, and now here—in an even bigger, better modern day sanctuary.

After the exhausting tour Celine took me on, I now have no urge to do anything else. She was thorough, too thorough in my opinion, but I endured it seeing how proud and happy she was.

Out of all the different sections, the training centre impresses me the most. It's situated inside the spaceship, the coolest part of the compound. The size is twice as big as the old arena and with state of the art equipment. No more fish tanks as training chambers, but glass partitions that would descend from the ceiling to create customizable training space.

The weapons are placed in stations throughout the arena, based on their size and use. There are two shooting ranges, one indoor and the other outdoor. Celine didn't have the clearance to show me the outdoor range but it pretty much involves an extensible platform from the windows, hologram targets, and special sensing bullets that track your accuracy. I have the jitters just imagining standing out there, high up in the air, shooting into the Gulf of Alaska. I can't wait to start training in that spectacular arena.

Next stop the Promenade, a square lined with shops and restaurants. It was open-air when we visited, but it has an automatic glass roof that opens and closes depending on the weather. It would come in handy in the gruelling Alaskan winter. And I'm definitely glad that we don't need to stare at a fake sky anymore.

The other sections like the huge Research and Development Department, the Medical Centre, and Recruitment all have similar layouts as before but bigger and with newer technologies.

I cover myself with the fluffy blanket and realize what tremendous luck I had to be lying here, comfortable and safe. Alex's face appears again but instead of just overwhelming guilt, there's also hope.

I will make you proud. Your sacrifice will mean something.
Eventually, I fall into a deep, dreamless sleep.

A loud chime wakes me instantly. It's my MUD.

Feeling frustrated that someone woke me up, I pick up the call. It's Celine.

"Morning Kaz," she sounds too happy in such early hours.

"Hm . . . morning." I mumble followed by a yawn.

"You're still in bed?" she sounds surprised. "It's almost noon. The memorial will start in fifteen minutes."

"Shoot, it's noon already?" Celine made it very clear yesterday that attendance is mandatory. Besides, I want to be there, I need to be there.

We hang up and I scrabble out of bed and put on my dirty clothes from yesterday. I brush my teeth hastily, and rush out the door. It's good that my guest suite is on the second floor. I will make it in time.

I reach the Trousing Hall just as the anthem of the United Nation of North America starts. The hall is packed with people, but there's a palpable sense of emptiness in the air. Some are weeping. They must have lost their loved ones in the attack.

My mind is still flustered and my breathing has yet to calm down when someone whispers in my ear.

"Did someone sleep in?" I turn and see Finn's half smile. He traded in his battle wear for his casual zip up jacket and pants. But he still has his weapons with him.

I nod with embarrassment and turn my attention back to the stage.

Chief Trousing, looking elegant as usual, has begun her speech. I wonder where she went during the attack. I highly doubt she stayed and fought, though I would love to see her in full battle gear. I'm sure she has a pair of stilettos just for that.

Her speech is long and tedious—going on and on about how our role as Sarcomeres is to protect and sustain mankind. She says that the Sarcs believe in equality and strive to create a better tomorrow for generations to come on our rapidly dying Earth. Whereas the Neuronics believe they are far more superior and strive for world domination by weeding out the weak.

It sounds like a noble cause we are fighting for, but for some deeper reason, I am not entirely convinced. Could it be because these words are coming from the pretentious Annette Trousing? But if I were to be a true Sarcomere, I need to believe. I need to trust our highest leader, like everyone else here. Somehow it's unsettling, but I can't quite put a finger on it.

She finally finishes with a closing remark and the crowd breaks into a loud round of applause. People's moods seem to have brightened slightly by her encouraging words. She is definitely good at motivating her people. I'd give her that.

As she makes her way down the stage, a big screen slides down silently from under the third floor dais. A solemn music begins to play in the background as words in big block letters appear on the screen. WE WILL ALWAYS REMEMBER. WE WILL BE FOREVER GRATEFUL.

I stiffen as pictures of those who died materialize on the screen. They all look so proud in their formal head shots. Below each picture is a name and rank. There was only one Touch who did not get out in time. The rest were all Cores . . . until . . . Alex's face appears last on the giant screen. ALEXANDER BOWLES—TOUCH COMMANDER & FORMER ELITE FORCE COMMANDER

He looked young in the picture, cute even. What would his family think? Does he have a family? How would I face them?

In the corner of my eye, I see people begin to turn their heads my way. Low murmurs begin to form within the crowd and I begin to feel the hostility pricking on my skin like pins and needles. Words must have gotten out that I am the reason Alex died. They all seem to recognize me and the fire in their eyes are heating up my body. My hands begin to tremble and I can no longer bear their malicious stares.

Please stop! I squeeze my eyes shut, with the tiniest hope that people will disappear if I don't see them. *Why? Why didn't I die instead?* I wrap my arms around my torso as if the self-embrace will protect me from the condemnation. Blame becomes insults. I even hear a few death threats somewhere in the crowd. I want to run, but my feet are planted firmly on the ground. I can't move. I can't scream. I'm spiralling down a deep tunnel filled with evil laughs and hateful curses. Everyone despises me. The hope of making this my home is disappearing as fast as a wrinkle on a shirt under a hot iron.

Then suddenly, the accusatory voices stop. The hall is silent once again. *Did they go away?* I almost don't believe my ears.

I slowly, tentatively open my eyes, realizing that I'm leaning on something warm. No, *someone* warm. I peek under my lashes and see that people are no longer staring at me, but at something slightly above me. I release my breath—the same breath I have been holding all this time. I recognize the strong arms and the familiar meadow fresh body wash. I look up and see that Finn is eyeing the audience slowly, from one end of the hall to the other. His jaw clenched and his eyes stern, almost threatening, as if they're saying *if you hurt this girl, I will kill you.*

The commander of the Elite Force, the most powerful Sarc is siding with an outcast. People must be thinking that Finn is nuts. But they're too intimidated to speak up. My conscience urges me to push him away.

Don't drag him down like you did Alex. I tell myself. But the actual me is too weak and too afraid.

What happened to the Kazumi that never wants to show her weakness?

SHUT UP!

My inner voices are just as relentless.

"Ah hem." Chief Trousing's voice breaks the incredible tension. "Let us remember our heroes and heroines. Let us not to forget their contribution and move forward to accomplish what they set out to do." Her gaze lands on us, more specifically, on me. There's something hidden behind those impassive eyes. Something dark, something that sends a chill to my bones.

CHAPTER 23

I watch as Finn gobbles down his sandwich in the training centre. Mine just sits on the plate, barely touched. I have calmed down from the memorial assembly but my appetite has yet to come back. Finn insists that I need energy for this afternoon's training so I try to get a few bites down.

I don't know if I'm ready, not for the training, but to face people again, especially the Elites. They have such negative opinions of me. I know that they will never accept me as a teammate. But Finn's right, I can't hide in my room forever. Alex would have wanted me to be strong, to train with the best, to become the best. That was why he gave me his precious pistol.

We're sitting side by side on the glass floor, overlooking the Gulf of Alaska. The windows are tinted to the perfect shade so they don't distort the panoramic view, yet protect our eyes from the burning rays of the sun.

I look down at the new ID that Finn got me. It's sitting proudly on my lap with the same hideous picture they took of me at the initial medical scan. Instead of the tinted black, it's now red, the colour of the Elite Force.

I want to be excited. I want to be proud. But all the positive sentiments are overlapped by guilt, fear, and self-doubt.

"So, have you managed to remember anything new?" Finn breaks our comfortable silence.

"No. Why?"

"Oh . . . nothing. I'm just curious," there's uncertainty in his voice.

"Are you okay?" I have never seen him so fidgety.

"Ya, I just want to make sure you're okay," he says as he stares at the floor.

"What you did, um . . . at the hall, it meant a lot to me. You have no idea how glad and grateful I am." My face is turning as red as my ID. All I can hear for the next few seconds is the loud thumping of my heart.

Finn offers no reply. His eyebrows are locked in a crease, lips slightly apart, staring blankly into the vast landscape. He looks desolate and lost.

Is he thinking of his dead fiancee? My heart twitches with jealousy. *Just let go Kaz. He will never be yours.* I have to keep reminding myself.

Then he suddenly mumbles. "Kaz, I can't make you happy."

What? My head turns toward him so fast, I almost strained my neck. "What . . . do you mean?"

"I—" Before he can finish, my beloved teammates crash through the door, all loud and excited, except for Chloe. They look less deadly now that they've changed into their training uniform. Samantha and Lilly are wearing the same outfit Finn gave me just now, a sleeveless black round-neck shirt with two red stripes curving inward along our torso, and a pair of flexible black pants with a red strip along the sides. I assume the others are wearing the same thing under their black hooded vests.

"Great, perfect timing!" I scoff under my breath.

Finn reverts back to his normal self so quickly that I question the existence of his previous words. Did he really say he can't make me happy? If so, why on Earth would he say that? I guess I'll never know, thanks to my new teammates.

I have to bite my lips to suppress my irritation. The team is not too fond to see me either, except maybe Murray and Kayden who acknowledge me with a smile. Liam, as usual, just looks like he could care less. Did he accidentally lose his personality when he found his potential?

"What is *she* doing here?" Chloe snaps the moment she sees me. She looks miserable, with eyes so swollen and red that no doubt she has been crying.

I lift up my red MUD to her face, "I have every bit of right to be here."

Her eyes widen in shock, then the hatred intensifies, like a deadly snake ready to deliver her venomous bite.

"That's enough!" Finn shouts. His voice loud and commanding. "We're a team now, I don't care if you like it or not," he looks to each and everyone. "Do you want to give those mind benders the satisfaction of Sarcs killing each other? We're at our weakest, so you either train hard and work as a team, or get out! We can always use more Cores."

Whoa! Commander Finnegan O'Riley. I almost swooned at his sudden outburst of prowess.

Murray walks over to Chloe, puts his arm around her shoulder and softly mutters in her ear. "Just let it go." And leads her back to the group. I have a feeling this isn't over.

Finn scans the room assertively. "Good." Then he walks over to the blades station. "From our last recon mission, we discovered that the mind benders are now training younger members in martial arts. I happened to encounter one of them." He sucks in a deep breath, looking slightly disappointed. "They're fast. I don't know how or why, but that only means we need to step up," he tosses a sword to each of them. "Spar in groups of two. Try to speed up both your offence and defence without losing precision."

On cue, everyone breaks into sparring mode and I just stand there, not knowing what to do with myself. Maybe I should grab a sword. But I certainly don't want to showcase my awkwardness in front of my Elite teammates.

I watch as they practice. They are ferocious, fast, and deadly—like a pack of wild dogs fighting for domain. Even Samantha is keeping up with the veterans and able to hold her own. How did she improve so quickly?

At the other side of the room, Finn has been studying me intently. I finally get the hint and turn to walk toward him while avoiding eye contact. His commanding stance unnerves me.

"What do you want me to work on?" I ask, suddenly feeling intimidated.

He releases his crossed arms and lets out a small sigh. "I've seen you with a gun. I liked what I saw. But before I make any further conclusion, I want to see you with blades."

Oh no!

"I . . . I'm not good with blades," my throat goes dry. "Alex taught me a routine and I completely bombed it. Can I just stick to guns?" I supplicate.

Finn's eyes darken. Then a resounding "No." rings in my ear. He wants to embarrass me in front of the others, people who already detest me.

"I want to see it for myself," he hands me a katana from the rack.

Hesitantly, I grab the hilt and tense up on purpose to mask my shaking hands, but I'm sure he sees my trepidation. My heart is drumming so fast that you can almost see my pulse dancing on my wrists.

Just when I secure the sword in my hand, Finn launches himself at me with his. My improved reflex saves me from his first attack and I parry off his second stab. But my speed is inferior to his and I can't anticipate where his sword will go next. In a moment of panic, I step on my own toes, both feet entangle, and I fall flat on my back. The impact jars my skull and I have to shut my eyes to deal with the pain. Then I hear faint laughing from the group.

"Get up." Finn orders without empathy.

I don't like Commander Finn, so strict and unyielding.

I scramble to my feet and my face is burning with embarrassment. Before I can get my bearing, he lurches at me again toward my left side. I lift my sword just in time to block his side sweep. The collision of our blades sends a vigorous vibration through my arm and up to my shoulder joint. He just hit me with full force. I'm appalled by his lack of leniency. Is he always this serious in training?

Alex's words come to mind: *"He threw recruits off the cliff."*

"Concentrate!" He yells as he spins to my right and jabs at my right shoulder. I turn a nanosecond too late and the tip of his katana pricks my biceps.

I wince at the sting and a thin drop of blood rolls down my bare arm.

In the blink of an eye, I think I see a flash of concern on his face, but it's so subtle that I immediately doubt what I saw. I ignore the stinging and resume my defensive stance. It will heal before our sparring is over.

Finn comes at me again and this time I am ready. I manage to deflect his first two attacks with unexpected ease, and as I parry his third overhead sweep, I see an offensive opportunity. I kick my right leg high and straight, hoping to connect with his flank, but Finn spins away at the last second so my foot only grazes his belt. I didn't succeed at my first attack but my increased flexibility just gave me a dose of confidence.

A smirk finds his face, then he extends his right arm, katana in hand and slashes right into my neck. I bring the sword up just in time to block his blade with a loud clank.

He went straight for my neck!

I gape at him in disbelief. Swords still locked together. Thank God I happened to be holding my sword just under my collarbone. Or else . . .

To make matters worse, his apathetic expression tells me that he thinks it's okay to hack at an untrained newbie. Out of fury, I grab his wrist with my free hand and quickly bring up my knee to his lower abdomen. This time it connects with a thud. He lets out a low groan and backs off a couple steps. I don't wait for him to recover. This is my chance. I lunge forward to stab at his mid waist, except I change direction at the last second and perform a diagonal upward slash instead. Finn anticipated my fake move though and fluidly parries my katana with his and punches my chest with his free palm. The impact pushes me back several steps and I lose my balance again. As I fall backward onto the ground, Alex's pistol falls out of my holster and slides three feet across the glass floor.

I let out a painful grunt as the back of my head hits the floor. The crushing pain in my chest where Finn hit is no longer a concern. I'm now worried that I might have cracked my skull open.

Vaguely, I hear a sharp yelp then followed by some urgent mumbling. Then a violent shake on my shoulders further aggravates my headache.

"Where the hell did you get this gun?" Chloe keeps repeating the same question while shaking me vigorously. Her face is flushed with rage.

Why is no one coming to my rescue? Why isn't Murray pulling her back?

I grab my head to feel for an open wound and find none. Good, at least my head is still intact. I tilt my head to see past Chloe and there I find my answer. Finn stands in front of his team with an outstretched arm, stopping them from interfering.

My heart sinks to the bottom of my stomach. I can't believe Finn just turned against me as well. No wonder he went all out. Maybe he wanted to avenge Alex's death all along. Or maybe he finally realized that I'm more of a liability than an asset. The sparring was just a test.

The pain in my head finally subsides enough for me to push Chloe away. I stumble onto my feet and the whole room spins. The only thing keeping me upright is the katana that I'm leaning on.

I stare angrily into Chloe's eyes when the spinning stops. "Alex gave me his pistol before he passed." I enunciate each word perfectly so Miss Ugly-Blond gets the point.

That finally shuts her up. She cradles Alex's gun like a treasure then slowly shakes her head in denial.

"No. Alex would NEVER give his treasured pistol away. You have NO IDEA how much this meant to him," she looks down at the pistol. "It belonged to his mother. It's a legacy of her sacrifice. You're the LAST person he'd give this to. You must have stolen it from him after he died. HOW. DARE. YOU!" Tears roll down her cheeks as she hisses the last three words.

She turns the gun slowly in her palm, wraps her right hand around the grip and slides her index finger around the trigger. With a shaking hand, she points the loaded gun at me.

CHAPTER 24

A minute ago I was training as an Elite. Finally given a chance to redeem myself. Now, I am held at gunpoint by a vengeful lunatic along with a group of resentful spectators. Is God playing a trick on me? How many times do I have to escape from death for Him to understand that maybe I want to live?

Or maybe you deserve it. A voice in my head says.

If so, then Crazy-Blond better make it quick. I take a small step back, but Chloe follows with a step forward. Her expression is a combination of sorrow and desperation.

I want to ask why is she so mad, but I know anything out of my mouth will only aggravate her. Her hand is shaky enough as it is. She realizes that too, because she puts her other hand around the grip to gain more stability. It helps, which means her aim will probably be accurate.

I take a quick glance at the audience not far behind her. Finn's arm still extended. People behind him begin to stir with great concern but are unwilling to disobey their commander. Murray is whispering something urgently to Finn, but he looks as determined as ever.

So he's really going to let Chloe kill me. My heart aches at the thought, but not the same pain I felt with his punch. This is deeper, darker, worse. It drains my soul.

I close my eyes, thinking back to the time when I was at the brink of death, under Jack's suffocating grip. Finn had a good excuse for not coming to my aid, due to the debilitating memory of his dead fiancee. So what about now? What excuse does he have now?

My eyes snap open when I hear Murray's voice, "Chloe, Don't! This is not what Alex would want. We're a team. We don't hurt fellow Sarcs," then he turns to Finn. "For God's sake, do something! Didn't you just give a grand speech about us not killing each other?"

But Finn doesn't move nor respond. Murray's outburst does nothing but fuels Chloe's anger.

"She's a murderer, and a thief!" She yells as she steps closer, forcing me to back into the row of windows.

"This is ridiculous." Murray pushes past Finn and storms toward us.

Chloe tightens her grip on the gun when she sees Murray approaching, and just as he comes in contact with her arm, she pulls the trigger.

A loud bang echoes in the arena, then the world stops. In front of me are eleven completely stunned Elites, staring at me with wide eyes and parted lips. Chloe is still pointing the gun at me with Murray's hands gripping her forearms, looking as still as wax statues. Finn is locked in a grimace, but there's something else in his expression, something I can't read.

My eyes blink a couple times and I'm still standing.

I'm not dead. Chloe missed!

I look down. Just inches from my heart is my katana, help up by my right arm. Visible on the edge of the blade is a small chip. I take a deep breath and that's when I feel it—the sharp, excruciating pain in my left shoulder. I trace the source and find a bullet hole in my upper chest, about an inch medial to my left shoulder joint. The bullet went through my muscles and exited through my shoulder blade in the back. Seeing the blood oozing from its opening intensifies my pain, making it unbearable. I drop my sword and a loud clank echoes through the quiet arena as it hits the ground.

Finn dashes toward me and the sight of him brings out my bagful of mixed emotions, but it doesn't take long for rage to climb on top.

He's coming to finish you off. I warn myself.

I grit my teeth and shoot for a door just to my right. My action catches everyone by surprise. A commotion erupts behind me but I don't care. I need to get out of here. Luckily the door is an alternate exit. I run as fast as my body allows, like my life depends on it, which it actually does. I don't know where I'm going, but all I know is to run.

I make a sharp right at the end of the short corridor and bolt down another endlessly long hallway. My limbs are getting weaker by the step, but I push on. I maintain pressure on my front with my right hand but blood is freely flowing out the exit wound in my back. My vision begins to blur and my labouring breath is getting shallower.

"Be . . . strong Kazumi." My mom's dying words echo in my mind.

The hallway begins to sway left and right like a drawbridge, and my legs finally give out, followed by the rest of my body. I brace myself for the hard landing, but it doesn't come. Two strong arms catch me as gravity pulls me down. Then the drawbridge is gone. Everything is gone.

CHAPTER 25

"Don't worry sweet heart, this won't hurt. Think about your parents, this is all for them." A man in a surgical mask says.

"Make sure she doesn't remember any of this." The same man then says to the other doctors in the room.

I want to tell them that I don't want to do this. I'm scared. But it's too late, the drill is on. I can hear it buzzing. Then the shiny scalpel appears, it's coming closer and closer to my forehead.

NO! I don't want this. Please. . . Marko!!!

My senses slowly return. First is my hearing; nothing but the white noise emitted by the air vent. Second comes my vision as my eyes peel open reluctantly, but are forced to shut as the bright light directly above stings. It takes a few blinks to finally adjust. That horrible nightmare is gone. But where am I?

Then my mind comes alive. I look around and find myself in a medical room with white textured walls and a matching ceiling of white lights. A lonely white armchair sits in the corner across from me.

I try to prop myself up but my left arm is wrapped in a sling, non-responsive. I wriggle my fingers and relieved to find them working. Then I remember . . . I was shot.

After a couple of attempts, I finally sit myself up on the blood-stained bed. The red of the blood creates a sharp contrast against the snow white bedding. I almost feel guilty for ruining the pureness of this room with my filthy blood.

You wanted the colour of the Elites, here you have it. I think to myself. *Is it worth it?*

The loss of blood makes me weak and shaky. But thankfully the searing pain is gone. Whatever they gave me was life-saving.

I spot a glass of water on the white cart beside my bed and I down it in seconds.

Ah! I can easily drink another gallon. The water clears my foggy mind, but then the sickening episode springs back into my memory in vivid high-definition.

The Elites want me dead. Well maybe not all of them, but certainly Finn and Chloe. I am not at all surprised at Chloe's action. She hated me from the beginning and it was only a matter of time before she goes haywire on me. I just didn't think she would actually have the guts to kill me.

But Finn . . . the thought of him makes me want to punch the wall, yet I can't say I hate him. My heart has been shattered, almost literally, but . . . why can't I hate him? Why do I still long for him after what he has put me through?

I need to go. I can't stay. But where to? Where is home? I need fresh air to clear my mind before my emotions make me do something stupid.

I clumsily get off the tall bed and find my shoes beside the armchair. Sitting on it is a clean tracksuit, black with red stitching. I carefully and awkwardly get out of the medical robe. I hope whoever changed me was a female.

I push the distracting thought away and put the track pants on with some difficulty. But then I can't possibly put the top on unless I take off the sling. Frustrated and impatient, I fold the robe I just took off in half and wrap it around my upper body like a tube top. I tie a tight knot in the front using my good arm and my barely functional hand. I wiggle a little, to make sure the robe doesn't slide down. Then I slip the top through my good arm and drape the left sleeve over my left shoulder.

I exit the room discreetly. The whole place seems to be empty. It must be after hours. I wish I knew the time but I vaguely remember it was late afternoon when the incident happened. As I quietly make my way down the corridor, things begin to look familiar. Celine gave me a tour of the medical section and I'm grateful for it now.

This place has multiple floors. The corridors of each floor are arranged in a square, overlooking a man-made garden on the ground. I don't need to lean over the glass railing to know that I'm on the top floor. There is a glass elevator on the other side that I can take but I opt for the stairs, to avoid being spotted.

I push the door open and the number 10 is the first thing I see on the wall. *Great!* I know I'm high up, just didn't think it's 10 storeys high. This is exactly what I need right now, going down ten flights of stairs with weak knees and a useless arm.

I begin my descent carefully, grabbing onto the railing for support. My legs are not as bad as I thought but I begin to feel the pain in my wound again. The throbbing intensifies after every flight.

I just made it down to the fourth floor when I hear a door opening high above me.

I hold my breath, hoping the person will exit without detecting me.

Keep moving. I tell myself.

I take another step and my name echoes through the empty staircase. I break into a run as soon as I hear that voice.

"Kazumi! Stop! You'll aggravate your wound." Finn calls pressingly as he tries to catch up to me.

My knees almost buckle as I recall how his katana came straight for my neck, and how he just watched while Chloe put that bullet through me.

I shake off my fears and focus on climbing down the stairs as fast as I can. I finally reach a door at the bottom but it won't open. It's MUD-protected. I quickly fumble through my pockets but my MUD is gone. Of course, they switched my clothes. I curse at my bad luck. "Kazumi, please don't run." I almost jump out of my own skin when I hear his voice right behind me.

I slowly turn to face him, tired and out of breath. I try to look as fearless as I can even though I know this is a fight that I can't win.

"Just so you know, I won't go down easily." I stare right into his eyes, telling him I am not afraid of him, even though I am terrified.

His intense stare is slowly softening into a hurtful gaze. "I'm not here to hurt you," he says softly as he takes a few steps forward.

I stiffen. I have no where to run as my back is already leaning against the locked door.

"You tried to kill me," my voice cracks and I fight hard to keep my tears in check.

So much for acting tough. I hate myself.

He stops. I don't know what halted him, my tears or my accusation? He looks down to the floor, contemplating.

"I'm sorry I let you get hurt," his voice is so soft I can barely hear him.

"So you *did* try to kill me!" I yell.

"No!" he shouts, then sighs and rubs his face with his

hands. "But it was my fault that you got hurt. I should have stopped—"

"Should have?" I interrupt. "It didn't occur to you to maybe stop the crazy woman with the gun?" He wants to object but I don't let him. "You tried to kill me even before Chloe got a hand on that gun. You came for my neck with your sword! You could have slashed my head off." I'm surprised I still have the energy to yell at the top of my lungs.

"That was a test, to see how far your ability can take you. I could stop at the last second if need be, but I have faith in you. And you didn't disappoint." His lips curl up in a bittersweet smile.

"Then what about Chloe? You had plenty of time to stop her . . . but did you?" I let out a hurtful sob.

Finn shakes his head and there's a pinch of sorrow in his eyes. "That was my fault. I'm sorry. I . . . I pushed too far. I was desperate to see how much you could handle, because you've shown me so much potential. And I was right, you *are* strong. You deflected that bullet!" He steps forward with an outstretched hand. "Please . . ."

"Don't!" I yell. "Don't come near me," my back is probably bruised from pushing into the door handle so hard.

I don't know if I trust his words. It's such a bizarre excuse. He would push my life to the brink of death just to prove how strong I am?

But why would he bother lying to you when he can take you down right here, right now? The other voice in my head asks.

I bury my face in my one good hand.

"Kaz, please," he says softly. "Just let me take you back to the medics. You need rest so your body can heal properly."

I shake my head, still feeling hesitant. Which one is the real him? The cruel commander or this sensitive and caring guy?

"Even if I believe your feeble excuse, you made a fool of me in front of everyone. How am I going to face them from now on?" I ask. "I thought I could trust you. All the heart-felt talks we had, were those your plan to find out how strong I am? Everything you've done up to now . . . were they all tests? To see if I'm fit enough to be your tool? I thought you were my friend, someone who I can rely on, someone I can turn to when I'm trapped in the dark. But instead, you pushed me into the abyss." I take a shuddering breath as I clutch my wound. The pain is becoming insufferable.

Finn is upon me in an instant when he sees my painful struggle. He holds my wounded shoulder with one hand and with the other, he strokes my hair soothingly.

No, don't let him manipulate you Kaz. I tell myself.

I push him away with what little strength I have left. "Is this a test too? See how I react when you are nice to me again? Do you know what hurts the most?" Finn just stares at me, speechless. "Not the bullet through my flesh . . . not hitting my head on the solid glass floor . . . but here!" I put a trembling hand on my chest where my heart is.

Finn gazes at my hand for a moment, then lifts his dark eyes to find mine. His expression is a cross between confusion and heartbreak.

"What do you want from me?" I say softly, unable to find my voice anymore. "What—"

Finn's lips fall onto mine, stopping me from talking. I gasp at the unexpected contact, but my lips reciprocate like they have a mind of their own.

Seeing that I don't object, he leans into me so I am pinned between him and the door. His tongue finds mine and they begin their tender, sweet waltz.

The phenomenal sensation is more than I ever imagined.

All my pain has vanished, only to be replaced by currents of electricity, zapping at my every nerve ending, making my skin tingle. He smells like a summer meadow, so revitalizing. And he tastes like fresh mint. If this is a dream, I never want to wake up.

CHAPTER 26

Finn finally releases my lips. The feeling is as surreal as it gets. His hands on my cheeks, stroking tenderly with his thumbs. I reluctantly open my eyes, half expecting it to be a dream. But no, he's still here, still so close to me that I can feel his every breath.

I stare astoundingly into his gorgeous dark blue eyes. They contain a spark that can light up the night. My heart begins to race as reality hits—Finnegan O'Riley, the leader of the Elites just kissed me. A hundred questions run through my head. But the first one that comes out surprises the both of us.

"How old are you? . . . I mean, I don't even know your age." *Oh God, kill me now. Why do I have to speak?*

Finn chuckles softly. "You don't do this much do you?"

I lower my head, face burning.

"Sorry sorry," says Finn. "If that's important to you, I'll be turning twenty-four in a few months."

So he's five years older than me.

"That means you were engaged at only twenty? That seems young." Finn looks down, his smile gone.

Oh Kazumi, can you be anymore of a mood-killer? I want to kick myself in the rear. "Sorry, I didn't mean to—"

"It's okay," he sweeps a strand of loose hair away from my

forehead. "Sarcs tend to marry early. There's not many of us left, so it's important to sustain our population and extend our family tree."

His answer was not what I expected. I can't imagine Finn being a father, or any of the Elites for that matter.

"Um . . . did you and Jane . . . um . . . create a family?" My voice is so low that I am surprised he heard me.

"No. But we were planning to after we got married."

Jealousy invades. So much for not bringing up his dead fiancee. Now we're talking about kids they would never have.

He lifts my chin up so I can look him in the eyes. "It was a long time ago. We need to look forward don't we?"

I release a long and heavy sigh. "I don't understand. I thought you didn't want to . . . um . . . what changed?"

He shifts his gaze from my eyes to my lips, looking pensive. He doesn't speak for a while. I grow wary as every second passes. What's he thinking now? He's so hard to read sometimes. Maybe he regrets kissing me now that the moment is over.

"When that bullet went through you," he finally says. "Everything became clear. Like someone has knocked some sense into me. I haven't felt this way since Jane. I didn't think I could feel this way ever again . . . for anyone . . . until you showed up."

I want to pinch myself. Is this for real?

He brushes my forehead with his fingers. Then they move down to my temple and to my lips. Every touch makes my heart leap.

"I've already lost Jane. There's nothing I can do about that. But you're still here, well and alive. I realized I should seize the moment, before it's too late."

I want to tell him that I won't be well and alive for long if he doesn't change his training methods. But his expression suddenly changes.

"We need to get you back to the medics now," he says urgently.

"Huh?"

He swiftly swoops me up into his arms and says, "Your wound's bleeding again."

I glance down at the robe and it's now soaked in blood. I groan as the previous adrenaline fades and pain returns. He speeds up his strides, taking three steps at a time up the stairs.

My rapid breathing turns into hyperventilation. Cold sweat coats my skin. "Why am I . . . not healing?" I croak.

Without looking at me, Finn says, "You *are* healing, but a bullet wound is no easy job. You can still bleed to death before your tissues can repair themselves in time."

His words make me think of Alex. The bullet went right through his bulletproof vest and into his chest. It was only a matter of minutes before he died. I guess we are more vulnerable than I thought.

By the time Finn gets me back into the medical room, I am barely coherent. Finn's voice, joined by another, reduce to a mumble. Slowly, I fall back into my dark void.

I had that dream again, where I was being cut and poked by masked doctors. This time was so vivid that I swear I almost felt the pain when they sliced my head with the sharp scalpel.

Finn jumps out of the white armchair and leaps to my side. I must have startled him with my blood-chilling scream.

"It's okay. It's just a bad dream," he says while wiping the sweat off my forehead with his sleeve.

"You're still here?" I ask.

He sits down on the edge of my bed, "I'm not going anywhere. You're my responsibility now."

I stare at him, still convinced that this is just a dream.

"When can I get out of here?" I ask after a minute of pause.

"Don't try to run again," his tone half-serious. "You lost a lot of blood. You need to finish your transfusion first. Maybe in a couple days." I try to complain but he raises a finger to say he's not finished, "Then after that you need rest, in your apartment. It'll be at least a week before you're allowed to train again, and that depends on how quickly you heal."

"But—"

"No but," he puts a finger on my lips. "This is an order."

I grab his finger with my right hand and hold it tight.

"Don't worry. I'll visit," he stands up, finger still in my hand. "I have to meet with the chief to talk about Chloe's punishment."

"Oh." I let go of his finger. I almost forgot about my attempted murderer.

"Be good. Don't cause trouble for the poor doctors." He turns and heads for the door, but stops mid-stride, like he is forgetting something. He turns around and plants a kiss on my lips. I cup my free hand on his stubbly face. Then he walks out the room, leaving me with an ear-to-ear grin. All the pain, all the horror, forgotten.

CHAPTER 27

I am finally in my own apartment after three days of being studied like a lab rat. They were so fascinated by my speed of recovery that my primary physician invited more associates to study my case. She said she had never seen such rapid recovery in a Sarc before.

Finn only visited once during that time, and it was all too brief. He mainly wanted to check on my progress with the doctor and didn't even stay to chat, never mind a kiss or a hug. When I was ready to go, he didn't come. Celine was the one who showed up to take me to my new apartment in the Elite section of the spiralling tower.

"How do you like your new place?" Celine asks enthusiastically as we settle in.

"This is great. Thanks for everything." I give her a warm smile. She is probably the only person that I can fully trust, besides Linda, whom I didn't even get a chance to say goodbye before she left. But at least I know she's safe.

"You know, you're making me jealous. I had no idea the Elites get such a nice place," she checks out the room for the third time since we walked in.

"Really? Yours don't look like this?" I ask. Celine shakes her head. "Interesting. I thought the Sarcomeres pride themselves in equality and all that. But, really, I do see a lot of hierarchy and favouritism going on."

Celine looks at me with a bitter smile. "Well, you're not the first to notice. But we all trust Chief Trousing with our lives. Without her bringing together the remaining Sarcs after the war, our legacy would have probably died out. Societies are built on hierarchy, whether we like it or not. Without some form of it, there would be no order."

I give an agreeing nod, "So, about the Sarc's family values. Finn told me you guys have the tendency to marry young. Something about sustaining our population?" For some reason I want to verify his words.

She immediately brightens up. So it's true. "Yes, we do have that tradition," says Celine. "Those of us who grew up in a traditional Sarc family are taught the value and the importance of our legacy."

"Did you grow up in the headquarters?" I ask.

"Yes, both of my parents are Sarcs and I was born in the old headquarters," she says.

"Can Sarcomeres marry an Ordinary?"

"Technically yes. No one's stopping you but it's kinda frowned upon, you know. Because there's a chance the kid might not have our specific genes."

"Ah, got it. It's all about reproducing people like us." I say.

"Yeah. But too bad my potential is so low, unlike my parents. But it all worked out. I love what I do and if I were anything other than a Touch, I wouldn't have met my fiancee."

"Oh I didn't know you're engaged."

She beams brightly, "Just recently. Our wedding's in two months."

"Congratulations!" I give Celine a big hug. She seems too

young to be getting married if you ask me, but I keep the opinion to myself. "Where are you having the wedding?"

"Here. It'll be the first wedding at this new base. I feel special," she grins like a twelve year-old. "It's a fresh start . . . for everyone," she clasps my hand in hers. "Oh, oh. I meant to ask you earlier. Would you like to be my bridesmaid?"

"Wait. Me? But . . . I mean . . . you barely know me." I am baffled by her unexpected request, but also incredibly touched.

"I don't have many friends because my parents moved around a lot, for missions and stuff. I feel like we get along great. I was so worried when they told me you were shot. I came straight to you when I came back from my assignment. Please, it'll mean a lot to me."

I can't say no to those adorable blue eyes. Besides, it's nice to feel needed after all I have been through. "I'd be honoured to." I say, "But you know, I'm not the most popular around here." I can just imagine people throwing garbage at me as I walk down the aisle as her bridesmaid.

"Don't worry about that. People will forget. Plus they wouldn't dare to disrupt the chief's son's wedding." She smiles, and I suspect it's partly at my bewildered face. "You probably know him too. Ryan Trousing. He's on your team."

I have to think for a minute, mentally screening each face I met on Finn's team. Then I remember a guy with golden hair just like Annette's. I had a hunch when I met him. I was right, they are related. He was there too when Chloe shot me.

"Yes I know who. I remember him being quite shy."

"Yeah, he doesn't talk much. It took him a long time to warm up to me, but he's super sweet," she says.

"I can tell he's a very nice guy. You two look great together." I say.

"So that's a yes?" she bats her long, mascaraed lashes.

I smile and nod. "But you have to catch me up on my duties. I don't know a thing about weddings. I don't want to make a fool of myself again and ruin your wedding in the process."

"Yeah!" She launches herself at me, knocking me backward. "And don't worry, my sister will handle all of the details. She's my maid of honour."

This is the most excited I have seen her and I can't help but feel her excitement too. But our girly moment gets interrupted when Finn barges through the door.

"Don't you knock?" I scoff. I have had enough of his hot and cold attitudes.

"I did, a few times," he says. "I heard noises, and the door wasn't locked. We're all family here anyways, right Celine?" He winks at her.

Celine returns a smile and says, "Guess what, Kaz has agreed to be my bridesmaid."

Why is she telling him? I look at her curiously.

"Oh really?" Finn arches a brow. "How did you get Ms. Cranky Pants to oblige?"

I know he's joking but I'm still mad. More so now that he seems totally oblivious to my seething.

"Finn is the Best Man." says Celine.

Of course he is.

"I can't wait. This is going to be so much fun. After everything that happened, we all deserve to have a little fun, don't we?" she nudges my good shoulder. "Anyway, I gotta go meet the caterer. See you guys later."

As soon as Celine closes the door behind her, the awkwardness begins.

"How are you feeling?" Finn asks, still standing near the door.

"Fine, thank you for asking." I stare at the floor.

"What's wrong? You were so happy just now."

"Ya, until *you* showed up."

"Wait, *I'm* the unwelcome guest here?" he points to himself. "Well that's a first. Girls usually flock to me when they see me."

"Please!" I roll my eyes and turn my back to him.

He hugs me from behind, arms wrapped tightly around my waist. And just like that, all my resentment is washed away.

"So what do you think of this place?" he asks softly.

"It's very spacious. So why were you acting so distant the past few days?"

Finn turns me around and there they are, the pair of irresistible eyes gazing down on me. "I *knew* you were mad about this. You're just like an open book," he chuckles. "I wasn't ignoring you, if that's what you're thinking. I was dealing with Chloe's case."

"So what did you guys do with her?" I ask as we make our way to the couch.

"She's no longer an Elite," he sighs. "We demoted her to a Touch. When she's done her therapy, she'll be working in Recruitment." He doesn't look too happy about the result.

"Was that your decision?"

Finn leans forward with his elbows on his knees. "The chief and the other commanders wanted to just give her a warning, but that's too light a consequence for her action. Besides, she's too emotionally unstable to be on my team. So I convinced them to demote her indefinitely."

"What do you mean emotionally unstable?"

"Well, she was Alex's favourite student. She idolized him like no one else. When Alex died, she was devastated. So when she saw you with Alex's gun, it was like a slap in her face, and she lost it."

"Oh." Now I feel guilty for pushing her to near insanity. "Did you guys call the police?"

Finn shakes his head, "We don't usually involve the police with our internal affairs. We have a very extensive agreement with the government in that we govern our own people and only involve them when there's political issues or the involvement of an Ordinary."

"And the government trusts you to do that? Don't they feel threatened by our abilities?" I ask.

"They didn't trust us before the war. In fact, the Ordinaries didn't know much about us, nor the Neuronics until the war broke out. But the mind benders suddenly decided to make themselves known and scared the hell out of high government officials. They were the ones who instigated the war behind the scene. But in the public eye, it looked like the United European government had declared war against UNNA and Greater China, but they were merely controlled by the Neuronics. Then the Sarcomeres unveiled themselves and offered the governments protection and military backup. Without us, they wouldn't stand a chance. So they realized we were the good guys. It was really a war between the Sarcs and the Neuronics. After all, we have been blood nemeses for generations. The poor Ordinaries were just their pawns."

"Then what happened?" I ask.

"Thank God no one was dumb enough to bring out the nuclear weapons. Despite the world-wide ban, I still believe someone, somewhere still has access to those massively destructive weapons. I just hope it's not the Neuronics. Anyway, so the war dragged on for years and many were killed and numerous cities destroyed. We lost most of our headquarters around the world and countless numbers of Sarcs, including some very powerful Elites. So finally we retreated to the Rockies and they retreated to somewhere in the United Europe. For some reason the Neuronics eventually stopped attacking. The Sarcs suspected that they ran out of resources. Our own resources were badly drained as well, so we didn't pursue further. And here we are, thirty years later."

"You tell it like you were personally there." I admire how much he knows.

"The history was drilled into my head pretty well," says Finn.

"So where are your parents?"

"Dead." His answer straight and simple.

"In the war?"

He tilts his head up, staring at the ceiling.

Then I realize how stupid my question was. If his parents died in the war, he wouldn't have been born in the first place.

"They were both killed on a mission when I was three, by Neuronics."

The image of three-year-old Finn, all alone, hungry and crying makes my heart throb. No wonder he showed no mercy on killing the Neuronics. "I'm so sorry. I didn't mean to pry." I put my hand on his lap. Poor Finn. At least I had my parents till I was seven.

He takes my hand and says, "I barely remember them. It saves me from a lot of heartache I guess."

"So who brought you up then?"

"Chief Trousing."

Oh. Now *that* I did not expect. I picture a younger Annette with baby Finn, but instead of coddling him, she trained him into an elite killing machine.

"What are you thinking?" asks Finn.

"Nothing. So Ryan is your brother, in a way?"

He nods.

No wonder he's the Best Man. I wonder what his relationship is like with Annette. He definitely doesn't talk about her like a mother figure.

"Anyway, I should go." Finn says.

"Already? You just got here."

"I know but I still got things to take care of. To get our new base up and running you know?" he pokes my nose with his finger.

"Fine. I'll see you later then." I see him out and watch as he steps into the elevator.

I lean against the door frame of my apartment, staring at the empty hallway, unable to get Finn's story out of my head. Is it a blessing or a curse to have experienced so much so young? People say ignorance is bliss. Is that what it's like being an Ordinary? Living life as they see it, oblivious to what's really going on. Unaware of the sacrifice people made to protect their home. If I get to choose again, would I want a blissful normal life or one that fights for those who can't defend themselves? It is a hard decision.

CHAPTER 28

I go back into my new apartment and realize the sun has already set. With Celine then Finn occupying the past hour, I have yet to explore my new home, which is contemporary and fully stocked with necessities. The white, glossy curves of the interior remind me of Natalie, the jet we arrived in.

I start my exploration in the kitchen, which is off to the right from the front door. It has state-of-the-art built-in appliances most of which I don't even recognize. I press the "Instruction" button on the fridge's touchpad and a slideshow appears on the screen, detailing the workings of the high-tech fridge. For simplicity, or laziness, you can also key in the item you want and a window opens to deliver your request without having to open the door. This will be my go-to function.

Then there's the flat-top stove, which is a big white circle that runs two feet in diameter. I can customize which section to turn on and it easily fits several pots and pans at once, but I don't ever see the need to cook that much food.

On the wall next to the stove are the cabinets, curvy and smooth. The counter top closest to me has buttons that say: MICROWAVE, TOASTER, DISHWASHER. I try each button and a panel slides open to reveal its respective appliance. I wonder if the Ordinaries have such high-tech features in their homes. I somehow doubt it. These have our R&D team written all over them.

Opposite to the kitchen is a glass dining table that sits four. Even the chairs are made of glass. I sit down in one and it's surprisingly comfortable. Then something activates when I lean forward. A hologram appears just above the table in front of me. I think it's showing some TV program. Curious, I try the other three chairs and they all activate a hologram of their own. I can just imagine a family of four, sitting around the dinner table, each watching their own show on their personal hologram. It's a nice touch, but shouldn't a family interact with each other instead? But what do I know, I don't even have a family.

Next I move to the cozy living room with a huge bay window that runs from floor to ceiling. I sit down on the white leather sofa, or at least I think it's leather, and put my legs on the glass coffee table. I expect a hologram to show up but it doesn't. It's just a regular coffee table, how boring.

About ten feet from me is a wall, blank and glassy. I can see myself in the reflection, looking tiny on this big, five-person couch.

The open concept layout definitely gives the apartment an airy and spacious feel. The white palette adds even more brightness to it. But seriously, there's not one dab of colour anywhere.

I spot a remote control fastened on the wall beside me and decide to try it.

"Jeez!" I jump, startled by the sudden noise as the glassy wall comes to life with vivid colours and surround sounds that fill the room.

I zip through some channels but find nothing interesting. Just news on the instabilities around the world and some stupid comedy.

I head to the only bedroom in this apartment and the plush white carpet cuddles my feet the second I walk in. A nice contrast to the cool white tiles I was stepping on. I immediately see a circular bed rests in a corner, paired with two round nightstands extending from either side. It looks very comfortable with big pillows and a soft comforter. To the right of the bed is a work station complete with a desk, a chair and a plastic screen fastened to the wall. A long chaise lines the wall to the left of the bed. Facing the chaise on the far side of the room is a row of closets equipped with automated sliding doors. I don't even have enough clothes to fill one drawer never mind a whole row of them plus rails. Finally, the last stunning feature is another floor-to-ceiling window that overlooks the vast Gulf of Alaska. The chief sure does know how to take care of her people. I'll give her that.

Feeling thirsty, I go back into the living room and realize I forgot to turn off the TV wall. Then I notice the words APARTMENT CUSTOMIZATION on the top left screen. I point with the remote and a manual opens up.

This is a blank canvas! I finally clue in. No wonder it's so bland.

Apparently I can change every item in this apartment to any colour or pattern available in this manual. Or I can download more if I pay. It uses reflective illusion technology, a much simpler version of how they hid the entire building from the naked eye.

My first design is to change my kitchen cabinets to a glossy black with a red under glow. I keep the white glossy floor, but turn the wall behind the couch to a collage of pastel-coloured glass tiles. I keep the sofa as it is and add a soft white glow to the ceiling as my primary lighting. Then I go onto customizing my bedroom, washroom, and closet.

By the time I finish, it's already ten at night. I quickly fix myself a simple dinner from my high-tech fridge and head straight to bed. I know I'm going to sleep very well tonight.

It has been five days since I got released from the doctor. At first I complied with Finn's order to stay in my apartment but I became restless after two days. By the third day, my wound was fully healed. So I decided to go explore.

My Elite MUD gave me access to most sections except of course, the chief's office and her personal compound as well as some other restricted areas for authorized personnel. I refrained from going into the training centre knowing that Finn would not be happy to see me milling about.

At R&D, I bumped into Murray. He was going over some blueprints with a group of engineers. He got flustered as soon as he saw me, like they were afraid I'd eavesdrop. I wasn't interested in their prototype anyway.

Yesterday I called up Celine to see if there were any wedding related chores I could help with. Not that I was at all interested in wedding stuff, but it was something to help pass the time. Plus it would be nice to see my friend and fulfil my duty as a bridesmaid. Turned out I called just in time. The fashion designer designated by the chief, surprise, was there to discuss Celine's gown. So I got dragged into the meeting along with Celine's sister Bethany, who had just came back from a five month recruitment mission. What a beautiful creature she was—same bright blue eyes and silky blond hair as Celine, but with long legs, an ample bosom and a flat stomach. It hurt my self-esteem to just stand next to her.

Evidently the designer designs everything for Chief

Trousing. No wonder she looked immaculate every time she made an appearance. After five hours of designing, measuring, and picking fabric, I was utterly exhausted. I can't imagine having a personal fashion designer at my disposal. It gave me a headache just thinking about how much time and effort it involved.

I've been dying to get back to training. So today, I decide to pay my team a visit. I spot Finn right away as I step into the circular training centre. He's talking animatedly with a girl in the far end by the windows. I haven't seen him in days. But as I stroll closer, I recognize the stunning girl. Bethany. She's chatting intimately with *my* Finn. They're too wrapped up in their conversation to even notice my presence.

Should I interrupt them? Or should I just eavesdrop?

Finn spots me before I can decide. A subtle change in his demeanour notches up my suspicion, like he's been spotted doing something he's not supposed to. The last thing I want is for him to tiptoe around me. Or is he actually flirting with Pretty Blond behind my back?

"Oh hi Kaz." Finn gives me a *friendly* greeting.

"Hey Kaz. So nice to see you again." Bethany doesn't seem surprised to see me though. It would be easier if I resented her like I do Samantha or Chloe, but the fact is, she is a genuinely nice girl. Patient, polite, and sweet. Our five hours of dress-picking together was a good indication.

"Hi Beth. Likewise. Am I interrupting you guys?" I purposely avert Finn's gaze. He didn't bother to look for me the past four days. Things would be much simpler if I can just view him as my commander and nothing else.

"No, I'm just about to head out," says Bethany, "We were just catching up. I've been away for so long, can't believe so much has happened."

I wonder if Finn told her about us. I highly doubt it.

With her hand, she strokes Finn's arm tenderly. "Anyway, I'm so glad to be back. I've missed you," she leans in for a hug.

A red alert sign flashes in my head.

At least she didn't lean in for a kiss. I try to calm myself.

Beth hugs me next then walks out of the arena.

"You two make a very cute couple." I say.

Finn suppresses his frustration and takes my hands. "She's a very good friend. She's been gone for months. We were just catching up." There's obvious exasperation in his tone.

I sigh and Beth is gone from my mind. I really don't know what to do with him sometimes.

"Though I recall someone is not supposed to be here." Finn says wickedly.

"I was only gonna be a visitor. But . . ." I look around. "I guess I won't see much action today."

Finn releases my hands and saunters to the middle of the arena. He turns to look at me with a mischievous smile and I arch my brows in wonderment. He pushes a few buttons on his wrist device, and the floor around him opens up. Six full size robots dressed in red bulls-eyes emerge from the floor, each with a pistol in their mechanical hand.

"So you want some action huh?" asks Finn, who is now standing in the middle of the circle created by the robots.

I don't know what to expect but this is looking very intriguing.

"You're in for a treat. I usually do this in private," he says.

"You clearly like these robots *a lot.*" I arch my brows again.

"Oh Cranky Pants, you have no idea. Now step back."

I comply and he initiates another sequence on his device. Eight sheets of glass glide down from the ceiling, enclosing him and the robots in an octagon.

Two robots fire at him as soon as the glass partitions connect. Finn quickly draws his two pistols and swiftly arches his back into a back flip, effectively avoiding the bullets. Immediately upon landing on his feet, he widens his legs into a full split, lowering himself to the ground, dodging the third robot's shot. The fourth one joins in as he leans back and lifts his legs into a helicopter kick that propels him into a handstand, all the while dodging more incoming bullets.

Then the craziness begins when all the robots fire at once. Finn's movement speeds up to a blur. All I see are legs flying here and there, forward flips, backward somersaults—all performed within the confines of the glass octagon. One second he's flat on the ground, the next he's in the air.

A minute later, the gunfire stops. Finn is standing in his original spot, looking captivating in his post-battle glow. The target dummies on the other hand, are all covered in patches of red dye.

I walk toward the battle zone, eyes never leaving the robots. Finn deactivates the protective glass so I can enter the space. He looks irresistible in his tight sleeveless training top that accentuates his taut muscles.

"Looks like someone wants more." Finn teases.

"How . . . what did you do?" I'm too mesmerized to speak properly.

He chuckles, "I showed off a little gun kata for you."

"Gun what now?"

"Gun kata, it originated from Greater China. More specifically, in the city of Hong Kong," he says. "Some call it gun-fu or bullet ballet. It utilizes firearms in a melee combat, combining martial arts and close-quarter gun play."

Just when I thought I've seen it all, Finn manages to awe me yet again.

"And what's with the paint?" I ask.

"We don't load real bullets in the targets. Just in case anything goes wrong. But mine are real. Just to be cool, you know." He brushes his finger past a hole on one of the robots. I look closely and see that all the robots are covered in bullet holes. Now I understand what the protective glass was for.

"Pretty cool isn't it?" asks Finn. "What if I told you *you* have what it takes?"

I freeze, wondering if this is one of his jokes.

"I'm the only Elite who can do this, and it's been years since I witnessed someone else with the same potential," he grabs both of my shoulders. "I saw you. Back in the Rockies. How you fought those soldiers with your gun, right after Alex had fallen, remember?"

Of course I remember. I promise myself never to forget what happened. But I was too mad that my mind just shut down and my body took over. I doubt I can ever duplicate that again.

"I've never seen anyone do it without learning the techniques. Even those who learned cannot perform in real battles. But you . . ." he shakes my shoulders, "You opened my eyes. You are a natural!" His eyes beaming with pride, like he has found a crown jewel. He's not joking.

Gun kata . . . gun kata. I repeat the words in my head, imagining myself in that circular arena. Excitement begins to build. "So you would teach me?" I ask.

A satisfying smile crosses his face. "Every bit of it."

I leap into his arms, knocking him back a step. Finally, a chance for me to shine.

CHAPTER 29

I thought I would get to train with guns and robots and be able to kick butts in a matter of days. But life is never that easy. I was stuck in a computer room, for eight weeks, learning trigonometry, finite, physics, and all sorts of fun maths. Finn said I need to know how the body moves in relation to bullet trajectories as well as their probabilities. I need to predict where the bullets will go based on the angle the guns are held, then quickly calculate in my head how to direct my body at the right time and the right position to avoid the bullets. To add to the difficulty, I also need to consider the angles of *my* bullets so they can bring down my enemies in the shortest time possible.

It didn't take long for me to realize that this is impossible to achieve. The math alone was daunting enough, not to mention how I need to execute the sequences to perfection, with blinding speed. The more I learned, the more I respect and admire Finn's ability.

Two weeks into training, I was ready to quit. I convinced myself that I can still be an Elite without gun kata. All my other teammates can't do it either.

But Finn didn't allow it. After hours of persuasion, he finally showed me a short cut to remember all the numbers and equations. I smacked him on the head, hard, for not showing this to me sooner. It would have saved me a lot of time and headache. He just loved torturing me.

The method worked like magic. It was all about how you process the information in your mind using visualization techniques, and how to weed out all the unnecessary information that's taking up your memory. By the end of the third week, I began to get the hang of it.

Finally, after two months of drilling numbers and equations into my head, I'm ready to handle the physical part of the training. Finn has booked off the training centre for a few hours each day and we'll begin with him throwing marbles at me.

A dark cloud hovers over me when Finn says it took him two years to get over this stage and onto real bullet training. His teacher, who died in a mission several years back, took five years. This is not going to fly well with someone who has zero patience like me.

"So are you ready?" Finn tosses a bag of marbles up and down in his palm seven feet from me.

I swallow and get into position.

No need to be nervous, they're just marbles. I tell myself.

With no warning, Finn whips a marble at me, and it hits squarely on my right quads.

"Ouch!" I squeak. "Do you have to throw that hard?" I scowl, hands rubbing my thigh.

"Or else you won't have the motivation to dodge." He throws another one at me and this time it lands on my stomach. "You're not focused!" he yells. "Remember what I taught you. Learn my stance, my hands, predict where my arms will go next."

I take a deep breath and focus on what I learned in the past weeks.

He's about to throw another one as I study his stance, and this time I predict exactly where he will make the throw. He aims for my neck, so I side-bend to the left by about ten degrees while rotating my body to the right slightly. The marble whizzes by and lands on the glass floor behind me with a few bounces.

I did it! I want to jump for joy, but I stop myself just in time. Don't want to look like a little girl in front of Finn. I'm a confident young woman.

The key to all this is to keep the movement tight and not to over rotate in order to cut down on recovery time, so I can move into the next position efficiently.

Finn flicks another marble at me and my right cheek is bruised from it. Another follows and I manage to spin away just in time.

"Your movement is too big. Keep it tight," says Finn.

I do just that and manage to dodge three out of ten marbles.

"Now let's speed things up shall we?" he says with a devious smile and flicks two at my torso, one after another in double speed. Both hit me right in the chest.

"Hey not fair. I wasn't ready." I scold.

"Life isn't fair. Stop whining." He whips another one at my groin. Thank God I jump up just in time or else my lady parts would be bruised.

After four hours of training, I'm thoroughly marked with red and purple dots. Finn didn't even hold back. Who treats his girlfriend like that? But come to think of it, he never acknowledged me as his girlfriend. I doubt anyone has any idea of our secret relationship.

"Um . . . does anybody know about us?" I decide to ask after our training.

My question catches him by surprise. "That's random," he says.

"I was just thinking," I mumble while massaging my sore spots. "What are we?"

He goes silent for a long while, just staring blankly at the floor. My heart aches at the realization that he indeed doesn't want anyone to know.

I slowly stand up, feeling like an old lady. "You clearly still can't let go of your baggage. I get it. We'll just be friends." The word 'friends' stabs my heart like a sharp knife.

I turn to leave but he grabs my forearm. I flinch at the pain of my bruised arm. "Sorry," he lets go quickly. "That's not what I meant."

"I'm naive, but I'm not stupid," I say. "I can tell by your look."

He stands up to face me, "I do like you Kazumi," he places his hands on my shoulders. "I'm just . . . I just need to make sure I'm ready before I commit any further. I do want to be with you, but it's a big step for me."

"So . . ." I don't understand why it has to be so complicated.

"So we'll take it slow. Is that okay?" he gives me a light shake on the shoulders, prompting me to look at him.

He doesn't give me much of a choice. I either accept his request or leave altogether. The latter is certainly too hard for me to do.

I nod, but feeling dreadful and conflicted. I'll have to wait for this scarred, mysterious, but irresistible man to come to terms with his own feelings.

We continue with the same training routine for the next three weeks. My personal feelings are locked up for now so that I can concentrate. The training will only be more brutal and intense as we go. In the meantime, the Elites train at a different time to avoid any unnecessary tension that might interfere with my training. I couldn't be happier with this decision.

By now, I'm used to the cycle of getting bruised, go home, healed by the next morning, and get bruised some more. I haven't seen a clean patch of skin on myself for weeks. Though slowly the number of bruises decreased and by the end of the third week, my speed has finally improved. But still not enough to precisely predict where the marbles will hit during a sequence of shots.

Impatience and exhaustion loom over my confidence. I'm tired of Finn telling me that the hardest part is perseverance. We haven't made any big progress and today is already the last day of training before we take a break for Celine's wedding. I know we both will benefit from a little time off. My crankiness has reached a new height and Finn won't be able to endure me much longer.

"Alright. Let's make today count." Finn's ready to whip more marbles at me.

I drag myself into position, dreading the next few hours to come. We begin our usual sequence of marble throwing and dodging. To my surprise, I dodge the first twenty marbles with ease. Five shy of my record.

Finn speeds up his throws and my body and mind match his rhythm. I jump from a full split to a single handstand, then a forward somersault into a side cartwheel, all within the parameter of the glass octagon. My eyes are focused and my mind is in overdrive, trying to anticipate his next throw. On top of that, my muscles are elastic and responsive.

Oh this is elating!

Finn throws a double for the first time and I see them coming, as if they are in slow motion. I spring three feet into the air in a wide split, avoiding both marbles just under my legs.

I shift my balance in mid air, ready to dive forward to dodge the next throw when a loud voice breaks my concentration. Instead of landing on my hands, I falter at the last moment and hit the ground, head first.

CHAPTER 30

"Oh God, you're awake. I'm so sorry Kaz." A girl kneels beside me, sobbing. I feel a hand lightly stroking my head, but it doesn't belong to the girl. I flinch and the hand is lifted.

"How are you feeling?" A man directly above me asks. He was the one stroking my head.

I instinctively push him away but he doesn't move, because I'm still lying on his lap. This time I push myself up, but immediately regret it. The overwhelming urge to vomit tells me that I just had a major concussion.

I wrap my hands around my head, hoping the symptoms will clear soon. Meanwhile the hand is back but I'm too disoriented to do anything about it.

After a long five minutes, my nausea finally fades away. I look up slowly, avoiding any sudden movement. Two sets of eyes stare at me anxiously.

"We should get you to the medics," says the guy with the dark blue eyes.

"What's going on?" I demand, feeling sick and confused.

His face turns ashen. "Shit. Kaz, no . . ." he grabs my hands in desperation. I want to move away but his touch feels familiar, and he knows my name.

"What is this place?" I ask.

The girl shakes her head violently. Tears falling from her bright blue eyes. The guy squeezes my hands tighter and dips his head down in defeat.

"Answer me!" I yell.

"Training centre, our new headquarters," he mumbles.

"Who's headquarters?" I ask.

His jaw tightens and a combination of shock and anger spread across his face. "Sarcomere," he says.

I let out a small gasp.

I've made it.

I stare into the pair of harrowed dark blue eyes. *He must be one of them.* I look over to the girl, who is still sobbing. She looks weaker compared to him. I can take her down with no problem, but the guy may be an obstacle.

"So what am I doing here?" I act as if I am lost, so I can assess the situation first. There will be plenty of time for a bloodbath.

The girl leaps onto me, wrapping me tightly in her arms. "I'm so sorry Kaz. It's all my fault. I . . . I shouldn't have interfered with your training. I was . . . I was just too excited for you to try on your dress." She's full on crying on my shoulder, soaking my collar with her tears.

I grab her head with both hands and am about to push it off my shoulder. No amount of Sarcomere tears can wash away my hatred. But something unnatural happens. My arms automatically move down to wrap around her in a hug.

What am I doing? Feeling disgusted by my own action.

Then a sudden stream of images flash in my head. All of them involving the girl I am hugging—us in a cafeteria, us eating pizza, us running fiercely to a tram.

"Celine?" I breathe.

She lifts her head so fast it almost gives me another

headache. "You remember me? Do you really remember me?" she wipes her tears with her fingers.

I know her name and we did all of that together but . . . something's missing. Did I manage the infiltration? How long was I out for?

"I . . . you're getting married right?" I ask.

She embraces me again, this time with heartfelt laughter. "Yes! Yes! And you're my bridesmaid."

WHAT?

I can't believe what I'm hearing. As I struggle to make sense of this, more memories come rushing back—the horribly long meeting with the dress designer and her beautiful sister Bethany. But the pleasant memories are tainted by my purpose.

How can I feel this way toward my enemy? There has to be an explanation. There is no way I befriended my enemies for real.

I look over to the guy, who is sullenly staring at us, with Celine still wrapped around me. Then who is he?

I study him intently. He looks familiar. Could he be . . .

"Then do you remember Finn?" Celine asks.

Of course. Finnegan O'Riley. The leader of the Elites. Annette Trousing's second in command. I knew it even though he looked totally different in the picture they gave me. But being charming will not save his life. This is perfect. He will lead me to Annette.

"It's vague, but I know his face." I pretend to look confused. I will go along with their little game for now.

Finnegan slowly leans toward me, his piercing eyes locked on mine. I begin to feel something, something visceral, something I've never felt before. Then my heart starts pumping like an off-beat drum.

He stops just inches from my face, too close for my comfort, but I endure it. No, I actually enjoy it. What is happening to me? Why am I not slapping him away? It's like my brain and my heart are working against each other. For some horrible reason my heart is longing for his touch.

Finnegan places his hand on my cheek, caressing it tenderly. My guts twist and I tense up, unsure what I want to do. My rational-self wants to chop his hand off. But I can't bring myself to doing it.

Without permission, his lips intrude mine, arms wrapped around my waist. I hear Celine's loud gasp behind me.

Get him off! I scream in my head. But my limbs are already wrapped around his muscular back. Every brain cell is telling me to kick him, push him, get his filthy lips off. But every muscle cell is doing the opposite.

Celine coughs, and my mind finally wins the battle and I push him away, feeling utterly appalled and violated.

"Can someone tell me what's going on here?" she demands amusingly.

This is bad. I really need to get this under control. It's like a whole chapter of my life has been erased.

"You still don't remember me do you?" The perv asks, ignoring Celine's question. His brows crease together, like he's heartbroken.

I lower my head, touching my lips with my index finger. I should NEVER feel this way toward a Sarc. I need to get to the bottom of this, but not here, not with them watching. "I just need some time, alone."

"I think it's best that we take you to the medics," Annette's puppet says.

"I'm alright. I just need to be alone right now." I give him a firm stare, which seems to surprise him.

"But—" he begins to speak.

"I'll take her home." Celine offers.

Seeing my unyielding gaze, Finnegan reluctantly agrees.

Celine helps me up and as we walk out, I see her stealing a sympathetic glance at the Elites commander. I ignore my urge to look back, but I can feel his gaze following me out of the training centre.

CHAPTER 31

On our way to my apartment, Celine recounts the details of the past few months, but she cleverly avoids asking about the kiss she just witnessed.

None of this makes any sense to me, but from the sound of it, I managed the infiltration successfully. I just need to retrieve my full memory so I can plan my next move.

As we enter my apartment, the familiarity returns. The first thing that catches my eye is the black kitchen cabinet with the red under glow.

"Are you gonna be okay on your own? I can stay for a while if you want," says Celine.

"I'm good."

She takes my hands, "I'm sorry again. Please get better soon. I won't forgive myself if your memory is damaged because of me. You've suffered enough. And . . . apparently you mean quite a lot to Finn as well." She turns and heads for the door but stops, "Oh, and don't worry about my wedding. Focus on getting better." She gives me a bittersweet smile then leaves.

She seems like a sweet girl. Too bad she's a Sarc. Being nice does not give her immunity.

I take a quick look around the apartment and it's enough to confirm my belief—the Sarcs are materialistic, superficial, and selfish. Marko was right. I need to somehow send him a message. He'd be thrilled. But first thing's first, I need a mirror.

I walk into the unnecessarily big bathroom and find what I'm looking for on the wall. The full length mirror is decorated with a lavish frame. How vain and useless.

I lock the bathroom door, one can never be too safe, and sit cross-legged in front of the fancy mirror. The cool tiles under me begin to warm up. I roll my eyes but I can't say it's not comfortable. I take a deep breath and focus on my reflection. Through it I can see little circular bruises creeping along my skin. But what surprises me the most is how well I look despite the contusions. The frown lines between my brows are barely noticeable, and my face looks brighter with a pink tint to my cheeks. I think I've gained a few pounds as well. Now I'm really curious about what happened.

I close my eyes, steady my breathing, and brush all the distracting thoughts aside. I open my eyes again and stare into the mirror. My peripheral vision blurs as I hone in on the pupils. Then the surroundings darken, leaving nothing but the same pair of grayish green eyes staring back at me.

I successfully bypass my unguarded barrier and begin to enter the preliminary level of my own subconsciousness. This should be a piece of cake since I know my way around my own mind, unlike intruding a stranger's mind where I have to navigate through new territory.

After a brief moment in the dark threshold, I surface into a tunnel of moving images where my memory centre lies. I immediately know why I have no recollection of recent events. Several neurons that transmit memory signals are broken, leaving clusters of wandering images like lost children waiting to be claimed. This should be an easy fix. I'm just glad that the fall on my head did not create any permanent damage.

I extend my mind into each random image in the attempt to rearrange them back into chronological order. But the task soon proves to be more challenging than expected. The second I enter the first memory, a surge of emotion catches me off guard. I begin to sense how I felt at the time: the rapid thumping of my heart, the dryness of my mouth, the unfamiliar urge, and the exhilaration when my lips touched those of an unconscious figure slumped beside me.

I kissed the perv!

I freeze, not knowing what to make of my own action. I wish what I saw was just a dream. I did not just eagerly give away my first kiss to the very person I vowed to kill. And for God's sake he wasn't even awake. What the hell was I thinking?

And there's more, like what I witness isn't traumatic enough, I have to re-watch how my enemy rejected me and pushed me aside, like I'm worthless.

I have to back out of that memory before my rage and whatever else I'm feeling corrupt my mind. I never had so many emotions run through me at once, some of which are new to me. I suddenly don't know what to do.

"Emotions are only there to cloud your judgement." Marko's voice rings loud and clear in my head. A phrase that he used so often that I'd tune it out most of the time. But now, it finally serves its purpose.

I clear my head once more, then bravely dive back into the mess—from the plane crash all the way to the fall on my head just an hour ago. The sorting process is unbelievably distressing not to mention exhausting.

After thirty minutes of probing my own brain, I retreat from my mind carefully, don't want to disturb other brain activities. I see my reflection again and I'm finally back. No more rosy cheeks and line-free brows. Whoever that happy and

228

healthy girl was, she wasn't me. I'm used to seeing my pale and troubled face. But seeing my own self is not enough to calm me down.

I FELL IN LOVE WITH A SARC!

It is the one thing I promised myself not to do; and that is falling in love. This is exactly why my parents were killed and why I became an orphan at the age of seven. But clearly that did not damage me enough. Fate has to play another dangerous game with me. Not only did it throw me into the eye of the storm that is forbidden love, it also brought forth Alex, the enemy who saved my life.

Every belief instilled in me for the past ten years seems to contradict what I have experienced for the past few months. What should I do? My mission is precariously balanced on the tip of a scale; with one wrong move, I will lose everything I have ever worked for. What would Marko think? I can just imagine his disappointed face. I can't let that happen.

I hug myself tightly on the warm floor, reliving my original plan.

I left Nice in the Republic of Europe on a bright sunny morning. It was early May. The scorching sun was creating ripples of hot air on the tarmac. I didn't mind the heat, it made me feel more alive.

I was ready, too ready, as I have trained all my life for exactly this moment. My first and most important mission; to infiltrate the Sarcomere headquarters, assassinate Annette Trousing and her lackeys, and avenge my parents' deaths.

I looked out from the waiting lounge and there it was, the biggest aircraft ever made, sat in waiting. Our small seaside airport could barely fit the beast. I studied it thoroughly from how it was made to how it'd fly but never had the luxury to see one up close. Though its design was similar to the old commercial airplanes that would soon be obsolete, this flying monster was three times the size, had four levels, and a maximum passenger capacity of eight hundred. The upper set of wings blended into the top of the massive fuselage in a wrap-around design to give it a more aerodynamic style. Two gigantic turbine engines sat underneath each wing. The other set of wings were smaller and sat further forward, just above the lowest row of windows. On its roof were the words EUROPEAN AIRLINES painted in bright red, a nice contrast to the silver and white body.

A woman's voice came on the speakers, announcing our boarding. I stood aside, letting everyone board before me so I could see all five hundred and forty-two passengers on this flight. I mentally noted their faces as they walked past me. They didn't know what was going to hit them, but small sacrifices were necessary in order to achieve the greater good for all mankind.

The plane took off without incident. I watched as the picture-perfect pebble beach that hugged the Mediterranean coastline slowly disappeared. I was glad, glad that we were forced to relocate to Nice—the only city in the former country of France that was relatively unharmed by natural disasters. But we were close at one point. A destructive earthquake hit fifty miles north of Nice three years ago and took down about a third of the city's infrastructure. Rebuilding was underway, but with limited resources and cash flow, the journey would be long and laborious.

The Great War had left Europe poor and crippled, so I have heard. But the subsequent geohazards deflated the restoration process. To make matters worse, the wasteful and materialistic Sarcomeres continued to deplete the world's resources in building high-tech gadgets and unnecessary weaponry that would only instigate more wars.

I closed my eyes, reassuring myself that my mission was of absolute importance. It was necessary for the longevity of our planet and the sustainability of a strong humanity. We have to rid the world of its weaklings who give minimal contribution to society, and to eliminate the prodigal Sarcs who are draining the last of our resources into their personal gains.

Seven long hours later, we finally began our descent into Toronto. It was show time.

I purposely chose a window seat on the fourth level where I could see the powerful engines. I needed a visual to control the engines telekinetically.

My eyes honed in on the fast-spinning turbines. Slowly, I extended my mind to visualize their mechanical aspects: air being sucked in at the front, compressed inside the engine, shot out as burning gases through the back to thrust the aircraft forward.

I grabbed hold of both massive engines mentally and with absolute concentration, I imagined the blades inside the compressor breaking, and the intricate electrical connections shredding to pieces.

Instantly, the engines stopped. The plane immediately moved into gliding mode and began to descend rapidly at a thousand feet per minute. I could just imagine the panicked faces in the cockpit, trying desperately to revive the broken engines. But their efforts would be futile.

The depressurization began as the rapid descent continued. Oxygen masks were dropped and passengers were sent into a frantic scramble. The captain's voice came on, announcing the unexpected engine failure and that he would be performing a forced landing near Toronto.

This was exactly what I expected the captain would do and everything was going according to plan. I just had to make sure the plane did not land safely. In order to guarantee my safe entrance to the Sarc's headquarters, the plane must crash with me being the only survivor. My miraculous survival would then catch the attention of the Sarc recruiters stationed in various Toronto hospitals.

I had suggested methods that were less destructive but Marko was right. Every option would require sacrifice. He said we needed this. A grand entrance, something with a bang. Besides, the crash would take down several Sarcomeres who would be on board. That alone counted for something.

Ten minutes into gliding mode, I realized damaging both engines was not enough to bring down the plane. The pilots were more skilled than I thought. From the rate we were going, a safe emergency land was possible. I had to think of something more drastic that even the experienced pilots could not handle. But time was running out, so I decided to go right to the source.

I unbuckled my seat belt and walked toward the cockpit. I made eye contact with as many passengers as I could along the way. Those who looked into my eyes instantly fell into a deep sleep. That was the least I could do in return for their sacrifices.

I put to sleep the four flight attendants who were fastened in their seats just in front of the cockpit. I knocked and the young flight engineer opened the door promptly. He was shocked to see a passenger, but before he could make a sound, he fell into a coma and hit the floor with a thump.

"Is everything alright Josh?" The first officer shouted from his chair, too busy to even look back to see what happened.

Through the windows, I could already see the airport approaching in the distance. Time was of the essence.

"Hey!" I call out.

The muscular first officer finally turned his head. We locked eyes and he was gone before his butt ever left the seat. The captain saw his buddy slumped onto the throttle levers. The plane tilted forward as a result, and began to nose dive toward the ground. I fell forward, hitting the back of the captain's chair.

"Don't do this! You'll die too," the distressed captain said while desperately trying to correct the plane's trajectory.

I knew there was nothing I could do to make him look me in the eyes at this point. I yanked loose my belt from my jeans and vigorously wrapped it around the captain's neck. To my surprise, his hands were still on the controls.

"I know who you are," the captain said with clenched teeth. "Don't think by killing us you'd win, you vile mind-bending mutant. The Sarcomeres will kill you all!"

My muscles began to quiver but the stubborn captain would not pass out. "You've been brainwashed by the Sarcs." I say. "I'm sorry it had to come to this. You're not my enemy and your sacrifice will be remembered."

I mustered the last of my strength to pull on the belt. My Sarcomere gene finally became useful. Even though I couldn't release my potential without the guidance of a Sarc, the gene made me naturally stronger. The poor captain made his last hopeless attempt before sinking lifelessly in his chair.

I looked up, completely exhausted, and saw a sea of greenery fast approaching. No amount of training could ever prepare me for the level of terror I felt at that moment; the looming of death, the knowledge that in mere minutes I would hit the ground at two hundred and fifty miles per hour. My extremities began to tremble and a layer of sweat soaked my undershirt.

If I were to survive, I must perform two more crucial steps.

But my confidence was wavering. Tremors became vigorous shakes that brought my knees to the cockpit floor. I took a deep shuddering breath and began to create my protective energy field. This was the only defence that would prevent me from being blown into pieces.

They couldn't mimic such powerful impact during training, but my DNA confirmed that I'm the only person capable of creating an energy field strong enough to withstand the crash. Being the only hybrid to have ever existed, my abilities are inherently superior to the average Neuronics.

Pushing through the fear, I extended my energy around me. The hardest part was evening out the invisible aura to avoid any weak points. I had trained long and hard for exactly this—being able to create the field instantly under pressure. But it still took me a draining minute to complete.

I never prayed, but this seemed like a good time to start. I prayed that the shield would deflect the thermal and physical impact as it did in training.

ONE MINUTE TO IMPACT was flashing on the flight panel.

No time to think. I quickly dove into my last step, which was to seal off all my memories. Any traces of my past would be detected by the Sarc's advanced equipment. They cannot know my identity.

I took out a small pocket mirror and entered my own mind through it.

I hastily severed all the neuronal communications that held my memories intact. Then I tried to separate the blueprints that created those memories in the first place. But before I could finish, a violent jolt sent everything flying. I distinctively remembered the extreme heat before everything went dark.

I stare at myself in the mirror, rocking back and forth on the warm bathroom floor. The word confusion doesn't even begin to describe how I'm feeling right now. The old Kazumi, who lived solely on the notion that Sarcomeres were evil and needed to be destroyed, is battling with the new me, who saw the Sarcs through a different set of eyes. I saw the ability for self-sacrifice. I saw empathy and love; something I've tucked away and has long forgotten. I was so consumed by vengeance and hatred that nothing else mattered. My lifelong goal was to concoct the perfect deception that would ultimately bring down the Sarcomeres, the murderers of my parents. No amount of selfless acts can make up for what they've done to my family. But this, waking up with a fresh new soul, was never in my plan.

Another accident that was not part of my plan was killing my own mentor in that warehouse. It wasn't supposed to happen that way. Jack was there to help me retrieve my memories in case I failed to do so on my own. We agreed that if I had not sent out the signal after a month, they would attack the compound and send Jack to discreetly revive my memories.

This is another stab to my conscience, something I can never forgive myself for. What would Marko think? He raised me and taught me everything. In return, I killed one of his most trusted advisors.

Then there's Alex. I can convince myself all day long that he was a Sarc and that he deserved to die, but it still doesn't change the fact that he died protecting me. Would that still make him my enemy?

I pull myself up, completely drained. I barely make it into bed when I fall into a dreamless sleep.

CHAPTER 32

A warm hand runs along my hair, slowly and softly as I drift in and out of consciousness.

Hmm . . . this feels nice.

Then suddenly I remember I'm still in Sarcomere territory.

I prop myself up, almost knocking the guy to the floor.

"What the hell are you doing here? How did you get in?" I yell.

"You remember me?" Finn says with a look of relief.

I glower at him with groggy eyes. "I remember."

"How are you feeling?" he asks.

"How did you get in?"

Finn seems stunned by such a simple question.

"Sorry," he says, "I have access to everyone's apartment on my team. For emergency purposes."

"What part of sleeping in *my* apartment counts as an emergency?" I shake my head, "Why am I surprised? You are a Sarc after all."

Finn opens his mouth as if to say something but decides not to. He just sits on the side of the bed, staring at me like he can't quite understand what just happened.

I return his gaze with unwavering confidence—something that returned to me along with my memories. Thinking back to the way I acted among the Sarcs sickens me. That weak and helpless coward was not me. I didn't go through ten years of excruciating training so I could be humiliated by my enemies.

But as angry as I am, I can't risk blowing my cover. I soften my stare, "Sorry, I'm just tired."

My apology works. Finn sighs and allows himself to sink deeper into the mattress.

"I'm sorry I startled you. I know I shouldn't have sneaked in without permission, but I was really worried," he looks down, "I was scared that you . . . will forget me just like that."

Don't get fooled.

But it's too late, my anger has already melted by the thought that Finn is afraid to lose me. I never had someone who cared so much about me. Maybe Marko does but he has always kept his distance like he's afraid to get too attached. I thought I didn't need anyone to care, but now I know what it feels like, I don't want to lose it.

"I remember you, I always will." I mumble. "Oh, did Murray get a chance to check my parents' records?" I suddenly remember this could be a potential threat to my identity if they find out who my parents were.

"No. He did a brief scan in our system and no one from your description popped up."

"Oh." I act as if I'm disappointed, but breathe a sigh of relief.

"Don't worry. We'll get there." He takes my hand. I flinch. He sees my apprehension. "What's wrong?"

"Celine, she saw us kissing in the training centre."

"Right," he says. "I couldn't control myself."

My heart flutters and for the first time, I wish I hadn't retrieved my memories.

"What if she tells others about us?" I ask.

He looks into my eyes. "I don't care anymore. If people find out, so be it. I'm not letting you go because of my stupid insecurity."

You ignorant fool.

He leans in to kiss me. I want to slap his face away but my right hand is already wrapped around his neck, and the other is making its way through his soft hair.

Maybe just this one last time.

Without taking his lips off, Finn leans forward, forcing me to lie on my back. He is on top of me, propped up by his strong elbows so not to crush me under him. It doesn't matter how loud my conscience is yelling, every cell in my body is screaming for his attention. I have never felt such raw emotions before. My body is sucking in every ounce of it.

He lifts his lips and begins trailing kisses down my neck. No one has ever been this physically close to me. No one.

His action just ignited a whole new level of desire that I didn't know I possess. His hand begins its slow descent from my shoulder when a loud beep snaps me out of my dream-like state.

I push him off, a little too hard. He gives me a look and goes to answer the call.

I straighten up and brush my hair with my hands, feeling angry and ashamed. My years of training and discipline just crumbled the moment he touched me. If I can't even resist the slightest temptation, how am I going to accomplish my mission? I wish Marko was here to slap some sense into me.

Finn hangs up after a brief conversation and directs his attention back to me. "Guess what? Our tuxedos are here," he says with a fake cheer. "The Neuronics just destroyed our home, so let's go try on tuxedos, and pick table linens. If they show up again we'll just suffocate them with table cloths and chair covers." He rolls his eyes.

"You should go." My voice flat and harsh.

"What, you didn't find that funny?" he leans over for a kiss but this time I move away. "What's the matter? You alright?" he asks, looking serious.

"Just tired. I'll see you later." I lie down and cover myself with a blanket.

"Oh, alright. Get some rest then." He brushes my hair once more before showing himself out.

I relax after Finn closes the door behind him. It's frightening how my self-control can just fly out the window when it comes to Finnegan O'Riley. I must convince myself that he's just a minor setback, a test to my willpower. Yes. He's only a distraction. I know my priorities. The wedding is just around the corner and it would be the perfect stage to execute my plan. With UNNA government officials being there, what better way to demonstrate our power and make them capitulate to us than to kill the head of the Sarcs in front of their eyes. Without the head and her second in command, the Sarcs will surely disintegrate. Then our army will take them down like killing birds with no wings. Until then, I will play along as the bridesmaid.

I want as little interaction with these pretentious beings as possible. To avoid them, I'd have to be a ghost; retreat to my room during the day and only come out at night when everyone's asleep. I just need to endure five more days and all will be over.

The training centre at three in the morning is such a paradise; quiet, free of wedding craze, and has the provisions I need. I steal a pistol from its station—a newer model than the one Alex gave me but uses the same bullets—and head to the ammunition vault right beside the gun station. With all the wedding chaos going on, no one would notice a missing handgun and a dozen bullets. I slide my MUD through the reader and half expect the system to reject my access, but it doesn't. The device beeps, a loud click from the lock, then the silver door swings ajar. Finn never showed me the inside but I doubt it'd be difficult to navigate. The light flickers on the second I step into the vault, showing rows upon rows of handle-less drawers the size of my palm. The T-shaped room is primarily made of stainless steel, clean and bare. As I search the room for a way to access the ammo, I stumble upon a group of drawers that bear the names of the Elites. This must be where they keep their enhanced bullets—the Neuronic's greatest threat. If only I could destroy them all; it'd render the Elites useless against us.

After circling the room, I finally spot the touchpad on the wall beside the door. I can't believe I missed that. Looks like becoming a Sarcomere has dulled my mind.

I hold up my Elite card and my data is promptly displayed on the small screen. It shows everything from my height, weight, date started, to my weapon of choice and the corresponding ammunition. On the very bottom of the list is the record for how many enhanced bullets I own. It says: ENHANCEMENT PROCEDURE PENDING.

Though it was not in our plan, I now realize I need Finn to show me the procedure of creating these enhanced weapons. This mystery has been baffling the Neuronics for centuries, and no one has ever come close to discovering its secret, until now. If I find out exactly how the blood bullets work, maybe Marko can finally find a way to counter their effects. Then there'd be no more wars, no more Sarcomeres.

I quickly punch in the amount of ammo I need and one of

the drawers down the left wall glides outward. Inside are two packs of ammo, fifty bullets each, and a loaded magazine for the pistol I just stole. Perfect.

"What are you doing here?" I jump at the voice, almost dropping the two boxes of bullets.

I close the drawer and straighten up slowly. I recognize that voice by the door.

"I knew you're up to no good. Sneaking in here, in the middle of the night. Don't think that I'm gonna let this slide," the voice says.

I turn around casually, "Hi Chloe, we meet again."

"Don't play dumb with me. I know who you really are," she says.

"Oh do you?" I raise my eyebrows.

"You're a cunning, deceitful succubus." Chloe spits the words like they taste of bile. "You can fool all the guys with your damsel in distress act but we girls, we see through you. That's why none of the girls on the team trusts you, you evil bitch."

I chuckle, finding it truly funny. "Oh Chloe, you have a very active imagination. I'll give you that. But I have no time for your little whiny game so get out of my way."

"Or what?" She straightens up her back to look more imposing, which I find more amusing than anything. She thinks she can take me on.

"You know, I have yet to make you pay for shooting me the other day." I say.

Threatened by my words, she immediately draws her gun on me.

"This is getting old." I say while mentally grab a hold of her gun and yank it out of her hand. Chloe yelps as the gun hits the metal drawers then slides halfway down the silver floor.

"Wha. . ." Utterly stunned with hands still outstretched, Chloe dashes her eyes back and forth between me and the gun. "Who are you?" she's terrified now.

"I thought you knew who I am." I tease, fully enjoying our little game.

"But . . . wait . . . oh my God," she finally clues in. "You're a Neuronic!" Her finger pointing at me.

"Shh.... don't tell anybody. It's our little secret." I say in a hush.

Chloe freaks out and turns to run but I shut the vault door telekinetically, almost hitting her in the face.

"You think I'm just gonna let you leave?" I take one step at a time toward her. She backs into the door, stranded. "I could kill you right here, right now and no one will know."

"I was right. I was right. You are evil." Chloe mumbles with her eyes shut. "Kill me if you wish. An Elite will NEVER beg for her life."

I have to admit, her words surprise me. I didn't think she has dignity in her. Although not an Elite by rank anymore, I can tell she will always be one at heart.

"Is this what Alex taught you?" I say.

The mention of her beloved mentor spikes up her anger, making her forget the most important lesson against a Neuronic. I enter her mind before she realizes her mistake. She tries to resist but her mental instability has gotten the better of her. I bypass the threshold with minimal effort and extend my mind into her cerebral cortex. I locate the visual and auditory areas, then mentally inject a hallucination into their sensors to trick her into believing what she'll be seeing and hearing are real.

I can feel her brain activities accelerate as the hallucination kicks in. Her cortisol and adrenaline levels shoot up the roof. I thought about using Alex as the catalyst; it'd surely break

Chloe. But he did sacrifice himself for me after all. It'd be a low move to taint his memory. So I gave her an imaginary torture by her own teammates instead.

After about ten minutes of fun, I exit out of Chloe's mind, leaving her breathless and paralyzed with fear. She's curled up in a ball on the cold floor, whimpering like a dying puppy. A tang of sympathy hits me. I shake my head in disappointment. I can't believe I'm feeling sorry for a Sarc. I've gotten weak. This is bad.

I sigh and kneel down beside her, "I hope you learned your lesson of never to screw with me again."

Chloe is too shaken up to understand my words. I take both of her shoulders and sit her up against the smooth wall of drawers. Her eyes dart right and left, right and left, like something's going to come out at any second.

"Look at me Chloe."

No response.

"Look at me!" I shake her a little.

She inhales sharply, eyes fall on me. They carry such profound horror that I get a layer of goosebumps by just looking at her.

"Damn it!" I say under my breath. Then I carefully enter her mind again. This time I encounter zero resistance.

I lay Chloe down by the firearm station just outside of the vault. It's almost five in the morning, the sun will rise soon. Before I exit the training centre, I look back at the figure I just laid down, who looks so peaceful. She won't remember what happened when she wakes. Our little secret will be safe.

CHAPTER 33

The big day is finally here—the happiest day of a girl's life. But the look on Celine's face for the past week suggested otherwise. I don't blame her for feeling overwhelmed, or even terrified for how controlling the self-absorbed chief has been. Celine had no say in most of the details, other than her dress. Even that was heavily swayed toward what Annette suggested. Poor Celine, she's too weak. I can tell she wants to be married to Ryan, just not any of the glitz and glamour her future mother-in-law is forcing upon her. I guess not every Sarc is equally materialistic. Well, her pain-in-the-butt mother-in-law won't be a concern for much longer. I'll be doing Celine a big favour.

One failure though, is that I wasn't able to lure Finn into showing me the bullet enhancement procedure. He was busy playing host to several government officials who arrived for the event. To push him would raise suspicion. Then I tried accessing the weapons lab but found nothing more than simple blueprints and prototypes that wouldn't do me any good. They've securely locked away everything that was pertinent. To make matters worse, I wasn't able to create a secure line in their communication system to contact Marko. They've completely upgraded their network in this new base to make hacking almost impossible. I'm on my own.

The wedding rehearsal last night revealed that the ceremony will only be immediate families and the bridal party, and it will take place on a hill overlooking the water. Then a huge dinner reception will take place at the Trousing Hall where every Sarc in the compound are invited, plus some well-connected government officials.

This whole fiesta further proves that they're a bunch of resource-wasting scums. I can't begin to imagine how much money went into this wedding when it could have been spent rebuilding fallen cities. Despite their willingness to sacrifice their lives for each other, innately they are still a group of greedy, self-righteous pricks.

With that conclusion in mind, I unzip the garment bag that contains my dress, my expensive and beautiful dress. The soft silky fabric drapes in my arm like water running downstream.

I lift it out of the bag and make my way to the bathroom. Despite trying not to think about Finn, I still wonder what he's doing at this moment. But it's for the best that I haven't seen him much since I recovered my memories. The more distance I put between us, the easier for me to finish my job. Celine is already a pain to my plan—being the sweetest human being I've ever met. I can't say I'll enjoy killing the closest thing to a friend I'll ever have. Or maybe I can spare her. She's not a direct threat anyway.

I swiftly put on my bridesmaid dress and check myself in the mirror.

Wow!

I stare at the beautiful stranger standing in front of me. So glamoured up and accentuated in every right place. The expensive eggplant purple dress hugs my figure perfectly. The one-shouldered neckline accentuates my breasts with a hint of cleavage, just enough to be classy yet alluring. The slight ruching of the waistline also looks flattering. The skirt portion is a soft pleated A-line with a hidden slit that exposes my right leg when I walk. I love purple, although not the Indigo purple I'm used to, this I find is even more suited for my relatively fair skin—thanks to my Caucasian father.

I turn around and see that my back is elegantly exposed. All the bruising from training is now gone. My skin actually glows from the body polish I so reluctantly received under Annette's strict order. I've never been pampered but I can't say I didn't like it. It was uncomfortable at first, but my body soon surrendered to the heavenly treatment. The chief even wanted my makeup and hair done professionally this morning, but the body polish was my absolute limit. After a somewhat heated discussion and a testimony to my self-control, I got away with doing my own makeup with what they provided. I swear, I would have ended her life then and there had she pushed any further.

Staring at the big bag of products, I suddenly miss home. We never had such bells and whistles to worry about back in the Neuronic headquarters. We value practicality and frugality. Our goal is clear; to rid the world of its rotten apples that drain the life source of our mother tree, so the strong and capable ones can flourish and produce better seeds.

What would my parents think if they could see me now? Would they be proud of their little girl? I don't know about my parents but I know for sure that Marko won't like this one bit. I can almost sense his disgust and disappointment. Seeing his adopted daughter dressed like this would only fuel his hatred toward the Sarcs.

I blink away my daydream and hastily apply some lipstick, mascara and a dab of blush on my face. I pick up a long, cylindrical rod they called a curling iron and run it through my hair. I can intrude minds, I can deflect bullets but apparently I can't use a little hair tool. I burn my finger a couple of times trying to wrap my stubborn hair around it. By the third time I clumsily touch the burning rod, I've had enough. I don't care if my hair is not in "bouncy curls". I throw the darn thing on the floor, almost cracking the tiles.

There! Still looks like me . . . somewhat.

I walk back into the living room where the flower bouquet they sent this morning sits beautifully on the dining table. It's made of fresh white and pink peonies, my favourite flower. I pick it up, feeling its weight in my hands. Then I strategically conceal Alex's loaded pistol within it. The bouquet is so big that no one will notice my gun.

I examine the peonies more closely, feeling each delicate petal, smelling its aromatic fragrance. We never had flowers this beautiful in our headquarters, because the Neuronics see them as a pretentious commodity that carry no real purpose. The only plants we ever had were purely medicinal. I myself have always loved flowers, especially peonies. Maybe because I spent my first seven years in a flower field. I didn't know if it was planted by my parents or it had always been there, but it was right outside our country home—a meadow blanketed in thousands of peonies and wild roses. My mom and I would hand pick the biggest ones every week and put them in vases around the house. I still remember her face when dad gave her that intricate peony pendant he made. It is now sitting in my room back in the Neuronic compound, stained with my mother's blood, a reminder of my ultimate goal.

"Mom, dad, today is the day," I whisper to the flowers.

I set the heavy bouquet down and try to strap the pistol I stole the other night to my left thigh. To my dismay, the stupid dress is too fitted to hide the gun. I might as well be standing behind a security scan panel for the concealment it provides.

Infuriated, I yank the leg holster off with the gun still in it and toss it to the couch. Since I can't conceal anything on my legs, I manage to hide ten extra rounds of bullets in the bouquet. I'll need to be careful not to waste any shots.

A sudden knock on the door gets me flustered. I quickly hide the useless gun along with the leg holster under the couch and compose myself before opening the door. When I do, I find Finn standing in the hallway, looking absolutely breathtaking in his custom-fit tuxedo. His brown hair is stylishly tousled in a controlled mess, and his closely shaven face is glowing. I wonder if he was also forced to indulge in the body polish as well.

He lets out a faint gasp when he lays eyes on me. His gaze is sparkling with desire.

"Wow. Kazumi, you are angelic!" he breathes in awe.

"Hm." Is all I can mutter, because it's taking every ounce of self-control to keep myself from leaping into his arms.

He takes a step forward in an attempt to kiss me, but I back away, leaving him curious.

"What's the matter?" asks Finn.

"I don't think the chief would be very happy if you ruin this dress."

"No one can stop me from kissing you." He closes the gap between us and wraps me in his arms.

So the internal struggle begins. His touch is like pouring hot water onto ice—melting away every drop of my reasoning.

But our affection is cut short by a cough in the hallway. I forgot to close the door.

Beth clears her throat again, "Sorry, I didn't mean to interrupt."

Her dress is the same style as mine, except hers is lavender.

Her neckline seems a bit small for her ample bosoms though, like they would spill out if she jumps. But the rest of her looks impeccable. She's already in her stilettos, which makes her intimidatingly tall.

"Do you need us?" Finn says while wrapping his hand around my waist. My heart skips a beat, but I can't decide whether I'm happy or angry. The Sarc inside me is grinning but the Neuronic-me is seething.

Beth doesn't answer for a moment, just glaring at us with her beautiful blue eyes. I expect her to be somewhat surprised, like when Celine saw us kissing, but her face is not giving any hint as to what she's feeling. The uncomfortable silence and her awkward stare are getting on my nerves. If only I could read her mind.

She shakes her head finally. "No. Nothing. I'll see you at the wedding." She turns and leaves.

What was that about? Was she here for me or Finn? Then I realize she never laid eyes on me that entire time. She was looking for him.

"The wedding's not for another couple of hours, walk with me? I want to show you something," says Finn, seemingly not affected by Beth's unusual interruption.

"I want to stay here, alone," I say.

Finn arches his brows. "Why? What are you gonna do for two hours?"

"I still need to get ready, and you should go help out."

"You look perfect!" he nuzzles my hair. "And you can't get out of this one." He pulls me toward the door. My legs follow like they don't belong to me.

I quickly take my bouquet with the gun still concealed in it and totter after him in my unnecessarily high silver stilettos.

The elevator descends rapidly to the lobby. As soon as the

door opens, Finn grabs my hand and leads me out. My heart flutters again as our hands lock. He's never held my hand in public before but if I let go, it will make him suspicious. Deep down though, I know this is only an excuse I made for myself so I don't feel guilty for enjoying every second of it.

The residential complex is surprisingly quiet. Maybe everyone's busy getting ready for tonight's big celebration. Celine is probably being tortured by an entourage of stylists as we speak. That poor girl.

More people are milling about as we get closer to the Trousing Hall. Caterers and decorators are busy setting up. Finn tells me they're all hand-picked by the chief from partnering companies— to eliminate any chance of spy infiltration. How ironic.

No one is paying any attention to us. Most likely because they don't know us. Then my speculation is confirmed when we finally bump into some Sarcs. They do a double take as we stroll by, hand-in-hand.

I take a quick glance at Finn and find him looking amused. He's enjoying this. This is his way of announcing to the world that we're officially together. I try to let go but his firm grip keeps my hand in place. But to be honest, I didn't try that hard to let go.

As much as I try to suppress my emotions, I'm still allowing him to drag me deeper and deeper into a bottomless black hole, one that will swallow me if I don't pull myself together soon.

As we make our way across the massive hall, people's stares become more hostile, mainly toward me. But several people are shaking their heads disapprovingly at Finn as well.

I remain impassive, not wanting to stir up any trouble that could jeopardize my plan. But out of spite, I return a few warning glances to those who humiliated me in the memorial. I don't know them by name but I remember their faces.

Finn on the other hand, is soaking in all the attention—negative and positive.

I remember dreaming this day before my full memories returned. But the truth is, I will never know what pure happiness feels like. If my mission succeeds, my life will be tainted with the blood of the first man I ever loved. And if I fail . . . maybe it's better if I fail, so my misery can finally end.

Finn and I exit the huge structure and step into the bright September day. The light ocean breeze feels perfect against my skin, and the fresh air is revitalizing.

Finn takes me over a small hill not far from the main building. My heart stops as the scenery unfolds. A blanket of flowers stretch along the bank in an array of colours; the daffodils and daisies yellow as the sun, the lilies white as clouds above, and orchids the colour of my dress. The luscious man-made garden mimics that of a natural flower field with narrow paths enough for one person to walk on. The plants are arranged by types, which adds structure and depth, and is probably for easier maintenance as well. Those with longer stems are wavering side to side as the breeze catches, like a group of waving arms beckoning to us. I love that there's no pretentious statues or fountains that would only take the focus away from the flowers. The heavy fragrance assaults my nose as a gust of wind blows past. It is so uniquely integrated that each subsequent breath carries a different aroma. My nose can't get enough of it.

"So you like it?" asks Finn.

I turn to face him, speechless.

"Give me your shoes," he says.

"What?"

"Your heels will sink into the dirt. Give them to me," he holds his hand out.

I give him my stilettos more than willingly. Once I hand them over, he pulls me into a run and I almost let out a laugh as we speed down the hill into the alluring sea of flowers.

I make my way through each group slowly, not minding the moist dirt under my bare feet. I delicately touch each leaf and feel each petal, worry that if I go any harder the flowers will disintegrate between my fingers. Finn says that the chief is very protective of this garden. Those who wish to visit will need to sign in with the exception of a few. Finn being one of them. I guess Annette and I have a common interest after all.

I walk deeper into the field and finally see a patch of peonies blooming elegantly at me. It makes me think of the times when me and my mom played hide and seek among the flowers. I would hide behind the tall peonies and my okaasan would pretend she couldn't find me.

I clutch hard on my bouquet as I reminisce about the past. There's no Neuronics here, I can enjoy the flowers without fear of reprehension.

I put my bouquet on the ground and kneel down in the cluster of blooms. I wish I can hide among them just like when I was little—happy and worry-free. But I'm too tall now and any innocence in me was ripped away the day I witnessed my mother's gruesome death.

"So you like peonies?" Finn's words pull me out of my trance. I nod.

He kneels down beside me. "I love seeing your eyes light up like that."

Please, not now. I don't want to deal with my inner torment right now.

"Are you ready for some more?" he asks.

"Some more what?" I can't imagine something more exquisite than this.

Finn stands up, extending his hand to me. I take it somewhat reluctantly and he leads me to another section of the garden.

This area resembles wilderness, with long bear grass and big leafy greens as tall as Finn. He leads the way as we tread through the thick foliage, just like the time when he led us through the forest of defensive thorns to get to the new base. Except this forest of grass is more gentle on my skin. There's no serrated edges or thorny leaves that would leave my arms in bloody cuts. The most I have to endure is the mild tickling as they sway back and forth in the breeze.

Finn stops when we reach a patch of lawn. A bottle of wine and an assortment of hors d'oeuvres are elegantly laid out on a big red picnic blanket. The walls of leafage conceal this little haven perfectly, making it a secluded world for just the two of us.

Finn sits down on the blanket and holds out his hand. "Would you care to join me?"

I stare at him, lost for words once again. My limbs begin to move toward the handsome man like they have a mind of their own.

"You don't have to look so shocked. I can be romantic too you know." He pulls me down beside him and plants a kiss on my cheek.

"We have a wedding to attend." I say quietly, trying to contain the swirls of emotions building inside.

"Not for another hour. So I don't see why we can't enjoy ourselves for a little bit." He hands me a glass of white wine. I take it, somewhat robotically.

"Here's to a new beginning. To us," he raises his glass.

"To us." I copy.

I take a sip of the wine and wince. It tastes bitter and potent. Neuronics don't consume alcohol. It's an expensive indulgence that clouds our minds.

Finn laughs at my contorted face and brings a stuffed mushroom to my lips. "At least pretend you enjoy it. It's an expensive wine. Here, have this. It'll make the wine taste better."

The appetizing smell is too enticing. I open my mouth and Finn feeds me. The savoury flavours of shrimp and chives explode in my mouth, making my empty stomach growl.

Finnegan O'Riley, why are you doing this to me?

Finn studies my face for a brief moment and says, "You don't like this."

"No. This is . . . more than I could ever imagine." I take a shuddering breath and quickly swallow the lump building up in my throat. "Thank you."

Finn pulls me in. I lose balance and fall on top of him. While holding me, he rolls over so I'm pinned under him. He kisses me passionately, hands pulling my hair.

My limbs completely surrender to his affection and I push aside all the warnings my conscience is firing at me.

Maybe I deserve a moment of genuine happiness, a moment of heavenly bliss.

Our kissing intensifies and there it is again, that deep pulsing desire I felt a few days ago with him in my bedroom. I know the consequence. But at this moment I don't care. I owe it to myself to feel what is love . . . before I die.

His hand finds the slit of my dress and slowly makes its way to my exposed leg. Next to my ear, Finn whispers, "Kazumi, I love you."

CHAPTER 34

In an alternate universe where Finn and I are not enemies, would I still fall madly in love with him? Would I consider betraying my people to be with him? Or is it the concept of forbidden love that makes this apple ever more irresistible? Am I really attached to Finn himself? Or is it the thrilling elation my betrayal brings?

I glare at him, not sure what to make of his sudden declaration. I would have reciprocated the same phrase four days ago, but now . . . does it matter how I feel when the inevitable is deemed to happen?

Seeing my lack of reaction, Finn says, "I know it's a bit sudden. I just wanted to let you know that's all."

I respond with a forced smile. He buries his face in my hair and holds me tight, like I will vanish if he lets go. I close my eyes and savour the moment, knowing full well hell will soon descend upon me. If I get killed, at least now I can say I've been loved. My parents gave their lives for it, maybe it's worth dying for.

"Thank you . . . for everything." I say.

Finn smiles, but there's a flash of uncertainty in his eyes, then it's gone. He pulls me up. "Come on. We should get going or else the chief is going to cut both of our heads off."

My bouquet! I suddenly remember.

I discreetly scan our immediately area but find nothing. I search the garden carefully as we make our way back. Finally, I spot the bouquet lying beside the bed of peonies. I quickly pick it up, feel for the gun, it's still here.

By the time we reach the ceremony site, most of the guests have already arrived. White wooden chairs are placed in perfect lines overlooking the water. A rose petal strewn aisle runs along the middle, dividing the chairs into two sections. At the front, where the bride and groom will be standing, is an extravagantly decorated arbour covered in white, pink, and lavender roses. I hate the fact that I actually love every bit of it—how the simple chairs and aisle are the perfect accompaniment to the star of the show that is the rose-covered arch.

No I can't. I can't sink down to their level. This is against my belief as a Neuronic. This is the very definition of profligate.

"You okay?" Finn asks, still holding my hand.

"Ah-uh." I murmur.

He chuckles, "Don't be nervous. Just focus on me, who cares about the others."

I sigh as we approach the crowd, hand-in-hand. Then there's Annette looking flashy as ever; perfect updo dazzled with a silver hairpiece, huge pearl necklace that I just want to rip off and choke her with it, and dark silver lace dress with patches of crystals that blind my eyes every time she moves.

She's too busy socializing with guests to notice us until we're standing right next to her. She swivels around and acts as though she's happy to see me.

"Good good, you guys are here," she pretends to straighten

Finn's bow tie, "look at you, so handsome," then she turns to me, "and you Kazumi, you're lovely as ever."

"Well I sure hope so, you've spent a fortune on this dress." I fan out the skirt while imagining putting a bullet right in her skull. *Patience.*

She lifts her chin as if to swallow what I just said. My words offended her, which was exactly my intention but she won't show her anger, not today. "You're welcome. I will do anything for my son and my wonderful daughter-in-law. Now get into position, we're about to start." Then she walks past us to greet another group of guests who just arrived.

She's out of my sight but her impression lingers in my mind. Why wasn't she surprised to see Finn holding my hand like everybody else? I highly doubt it's because she approves of us.

A soft melody flows through the air, distracting my thoughts. Two musicians—a violinist and a harpist—begin their duet beside the arbour. Guests who are still standing find their seats and we make our way to the alter. Beth and I are to stand to the left of the fancy arbour and the groomsmen are to the right. I walk past Reverend Lee, a tall and slim older man whom I already met at the wedding rehearsal, and take my spot beside Beth who's wearing an ear-to-ear grin, looking into the audience.

There are just under a hundred guests present, all dressed to impress. I recognize a lot of them. I just didn't know so many of them are actually related to Annette and Celine's family.

Ryan sits nervously beside his mother in the first row. He must be terrified right now. I can't imagine a shy guy like him would be comfortable being the centre of attention in front of hundreds of people. But he does look sharp in his fitted black tuxedo. And his freshly cut hair accentuates his features for the better. I wouldn't go as far as calling him handsome, but he's certainly not ugly. Now that I have time to study him, I realize he's quite short for a guy. But unlike his mother, he has a kind and innocent face. I can see how he and Celine make a great couple.

The music reaches the main chorus, a cue for Ryan to go join the Reverend at the front. Kayden gives Ryan an exaggerated smile. He too is looking smart. His warm, caramel skin looks silky smooth. Must be the work of the body polish.

Finn shakes Ryan's hand, then pulls him in for a hug. I can only imagine the immense competition growing up as adopted brothers. I can totally see Annette favouring her biological son over Finn. But if there's any resentment, it's not evident today.

I study the crowd as we wait for the bride. Annette and a few women whom I don't recognize are seated near the groomsmen. From what I can see, Annette doesn't seem to have a husband. Sitting near me are Celine's family. I've never met her mother before today but I know exactly who she is; she's the one who looks like an older version of Celine. I probably can't tell them apart from the back. The similarity is uncanny.

Finn's eyes catch mine and a warm smile spreads across his face. I avert his gaze and in my peripheral vision, I see his smile quickly turns into a frown.

For the first time in my life, I understand why my parents did what they did. They were bounded by love, passion and hope—enough for them to betray their own people. I swore never to walk in their footsteps because I thought they were weak and foolish to give in to temptation. But now, after what I've been through, I think they were the bravest. I'm not so sure I can do any better.

In the distance, Celine emerges from behind a cluster of trees, with her father leading her by her arm. All the guests stand at once to welcome her. She looks absolutely stunning in a white chiffon dress paired with a long cathedral veil. The wind picks up just enough so the train of her dress and the veil cascade behind her like a Greek goddess floating in heaven. Sparks of crystals glint in the sunlight, giving her an angelic glow that further accentuates her beauty.

I envy her, because I will never have a chance to walk down the aisle as someone's bride. Even if I survive, life as a Neuronic will never allow a marriage never mind a lavish wedding. We don't believe in marriage, at least not since the war. Our number was drastically reduced and we couldn't achieve our ultimate plan without man power. So boosting our population became top priority. As soon as a girl is deemed suitable to "breed", she'll be tested for the strength of her genes. If she falls within the top quadrants, she'll be matched with a mate who is just as strong. Their goal is to breed the strongest Neuronics, which renders marriage pointless. That's why our population has been increasing at a staggering rate and our younger Neuronics possess much stronger powers than any of their ancestors.

I was the exception only because they couldn't afford to have their secret weapon busy making babies. But if I manage to go home in one piece, breeding might be my next destiny.

Today, seeing everyone's joyous faces—a scene that would never occur with the Neuronic—makes me wonder how much I've been missing out. What if I was brought up here? Would I be a different person then?

But the truth will never change. My parents were blasted to pieces by these monsters. So it doesn't matter which side I agree with, the Sarcs will have to pay for their crime.

I squeeze the stem of my bouquet, feeling the tip of the gun hidden within it. Maybe I can just kill Annette and spare Finn. But the consequence will be the same. I will lose him regardless. He will never side with me. And the commander in him will not spare my life when he finds out who I really am.

". . . you may now kiss your bride," Reverend Lee says.

Cheers and applause break out in the audience as they stand to greet the newlyweds. I follow after Beth as the bridal party prepares to exit. I grab Kayden's arm as instructed in the rehearsal and recess down the aisle.

"You look gorgeous by the way," Kayden gives me a wink.

"Sure." I mumble absently, not wanting any small talk.

Kayden just shrugs.

My focus shifts to Finn and Beth's interlocked arms and a twinge of jealousy shoots out like a jet of flames. They make a great couple—both tall and attractive. My heart aches at the thought and I look away.

I break contact with Kayden as soon as we reach the end of the aisle. The ceremony is officially over.

Most of the guests make their way to a table of refreshments off to the side—something the catering team discreetly set up during the ceremony—while the immediate families return to the rose arbour for pictures.

I had planned out my escape route during the rehearsal but I survey the area once again for reassurance. The closest entrance to the building is about a ten-minute run, more than enough time for them to catch up or shoot me down from behind. So that won't work.

I look to the other side and there's nothing but a steep cliff that falls into the ocean. That won't work either unless I want to commit suicide. The only way off this island is by air or sea. I can fly a plane, a skill the Neuronics made sure I learned, but Natalie is parked all the way at the opposite side of the island.

So my only option is a narrow path I found that wraps around the building and ends up at the dock, which is now anchored with boats from wedding vendors.

As best as I tried to plan my escape, I knew this would be a suicide mission from the start. Whether I kill Annette here or in her sleep, it won't make a difference. The Elites will make sure I can't escape. I was not afraid of dying. I had nothing to lose. But now . . . I can't say the thought of betraying the Neuronics didn't cross my mind.

And the funny thing is I know what Marko would say at a moment like this, *"You could have lived a happy and normal life with your parents. But the Sarcomeres took that privilege from you."*

Then my mom's dying words appear in my head. *"Be strong Kazumi."*

The thought of my mother's dismantled body revives my determination.

Deep breath. I wrap my hand around the handle of the pistol and begin inching toward Annette, who's mingling with a few guests by the arbour.

"Hello Kazumi." Someone taps my shoulder just when I'm close enough to shoot.

I whip around and see a middle-aged man with graying hair smiling at me. He reminds me of the man who escorted me to the Rockies. I think his name was Bill. But this guys seems taller and stronger.

I don't even bother to cover my scowl. I just want to punch him in the face and toss him aside.

"You probably don't remember me. I'm Kyle Bobly," he leans in and whispers, "I knew your parents."

I take a step back, trying to suppress my reaction.

He knows who I am!

"What do you know about my parents?" I keep my voice low but firm.

"I knew them, personally." His tone low and soft. He's also afraid that someone might overhear.

I can't tell if he's a friend or a foe, but being here means he's a Sarc, which makes him my enemy. If he's telling the truth, that means he might know my identity. I have to do this now before he ruins my mission.

I ignore him and turn to face Annette again. Kyle grabs my arm. I twist around, grab his shirt and pull him close to me without making a scene. My gun is pointing at him under my bouquet.

"Don't make me hurt you." I say.

"Easy," he lifts his hands in surrender. "I mean no harm. I know you lost your memories. What I need to tell you is utmost important though. You need to know, trust me. You'd want to know." I ease up as he continues, "But we can't talk now, not here." He looks around and pretends to smile at people. "Besides, I don't want to miss my niece's wedding." He looks over to the beautiful bride. "Meet me in the storage room behind the main elevator shaft in Trousing Hall after the fifth song tonight. We'll talk then. And don't tell anyone about our conversation. It's for your safety." He nods, then backs up slowly as I release his blue shirt, now with a wrinkled spot.

I watch him as he makes his way to join the others. My feet solidly stuck to the ground. Every reason tells me not to trust him, but the mention of my parents is an excellent bait to lure me in and he knows it. Annette can live for a few more hours. I have to find out what's cooking in that sneaky mind of his.

CHAPTER 35

"Are you enjoying this evening?" Finn whispers in my ear.

"Uh huh." I reply, hugging him tightly as we dance to a soothing tune under a canopy of stars.

The Trousing Hall has been transformed into an enchanted forest. Tall trees line the walls, and real grass replaced the hard stone floor. We were sitting on the stage during dinner, the most painful two hours of my life. I'd rather get hit by bullets while being chased by a wolf than to go through that again. Not only did I have to be on guard in case Kyle blew my cover, but I also had to act normal so not to bring suspicion while enduring speech after speech of the same crap.

I was all too relieved when dinner was finally over but as soon as the dancing started, my anxiety was back. This time was for meeting with Kyle.

The lights are dimmed and the roof is opened, revealing the dark summer sky filled with twinkling stars. Or are they just holograms? I don't know and I don't care. I just don't want this song to end. This is our last night together.

I frown as the fifth song draws to a soft decrescendo, meaning the end is near. I pull away and excuse myself, claiming that I need to use the ladies' room.

The ground gives in as I walk. Who's clever idea was it to use real grass when half of the guests are in heels?

I walk past the stage and cut left to get to the elevator. A washroom sign illuminates above me, pointing to an extra wide door to my right. How convenient. I push through the door and enter a long, well-lit corridor. The ladies' room is ten steps to the left. I walk past it and head straight to the back where another door awaits. After making sure no one's watching, I push through it.

"I'm back here," Kyle says as I walk in.

The room looks deceivingly large on the inside with some sections hidden in shadows due to the dim lighting. The smell of plastic invades my nose. The layout reminds me of the warehouse where Jack held me hostage, where I killed him mercilessly. But instead of crates and barrels, this contains obsolete electronic devices in plastic boxes.

Kyle beckons me over to a tight corner where he's cleverly concealed by packed shelves. He eyes my bouquet as I approach but asks nothing of it. My skin tingles with caution as I stand less than two feet from him.

"So, what do have to tell me?" I go right to the point. But I don't think he hears me. He's too busy studying my face like I'm some kind of specimen.

I have no time for games. Just when I'm about to intrude his mind, he says, "You look just like your mother. She can finally rest in peace knowing you're safe and all grown up."

"No she can't." I say. "Her murderer is still out there."

He comes closer. I tense up as he puts his hands on my shoulders. His deep-set eyes glare at me with mixed emotions.

"I'm sorry that things turned out the way they did." His condolence seems genuine enough. "They entrusted you to me if anything were to happen to them. But I was too late."

WHAT? I freeze.

He sighs, "I know you don't remember me. Even if you still have your memories, you probably won't recognize me anyway." He's right. I don't recognize him at all. "You must have a lot of questions about your past and who you really are." He sits down at a chair by the wall, revealing his entire face in the dim light. His brown eyes look sad. A visible scar carved on the bridge of his nose. "I knew your dad. We were Elites back in the days."

My dad, an Elite?

"Long story short, he met your mother and fell deeply in love. Unfortunately, she was a Neuronic. They would be severely punished or killed if people found out. The two factions had been enemies for nearly two centuries. Anyway . . ." he shakes his head. "They decided to leave and create a family of their own, away from the hatred and the violence. They just wanted to be happy. I was the only person your father trusted, so I helped them with the necessary arrangements and I was the witness at their secret nuptial."

I stare at him in shock, unable to breathe. Part of me is very suspicious of his words but the bigger part is captivated. What if he's really telling the truth?

"Then they had you," Kyle looks at me with a sense of pride a father has for his child. "They risked everything to have each other, then risked their lives to protect you."

Kyle's face becomes a blurry picture as tears fill my eyes.

"Your parents knew either group would eventually find them. They didn't care about themselves. They were worried about you," he stands up. "They would die a thousand deaths to prevent you from falling into the hands of either side—to be studied like an animal or worse, to be used as a weapon."

"Who killed them?" my voice thick with menace. Will he admit that it was his people?

"They found them, at your country home in West Virginia. They sent in a SK1 bomber jet and blasted the place down to rubble, killing both of your parents." He pinches his nose between his eyes, right where his scar is. He seems deeply affected by the harrowed memory.

"That jet belonged to the Sarcs." I say through gritted teeth as a salty bead of tear touches my tongue.

"Yes," he says. I clench my jaw, fist ready. "But the Sarcs didn't bomb your parents."

"You're lying!" I shout, ready to deliver the punch.

"Two jets were stolen from our manufacturing plant in New Hampshire two days before the bombing. The Sarcs never launched the attack. It was the Neuronics."

"No! Don't you try to blame this on the Neuronics." I tremble with anger. He's trying to manipulate me. I won't let him. He's lying. He's lying.

"Seems like you know more than I thought. Then you probably know that you can access my mind anytime to verify my words," he says calmly.

That's exactly what I should do. But I'm too shaken up to concentrate. Why did Marko tell me the opposite? But why would Kyle lie if he knows I can read his mind?

Kyle grabs my shoulders, "I know this is a lot for you to take in. When I got there, you were already gone. I thought you were dead as well, but thank God I didn't find your body in the wreckage," his voice cracks, like he's about to cry. "Then I spent the next ten years looking for you. I promised your father I would keep you safe. That was why I left the Elite Force and became a field agent so I could search for you. I've pretended to break all ties with your father so no one would suspect. And most importantly, no one knows about you—at least not to my knowledge. It was the only way to keep you safe. I was completely shocked when I saw your name on the wedding invitation. Kazu,mi." He enunciates it as if he's teaching a child to speak. "Your mother gave you this name. It means beautiful harmony in Japanese."

"Beautiful harmony. . ." I repeat the words again and again. A forgotten scene begins to surface in my memory.

Okaasan was brushing my hair in the mirror. I couldn't have been older than four at the time. She was singing a beautiful Japanese folk song to me:

Botan ga saku, fuurin wa utau.
(Peonies are blooming, the wind chimes sing.)

Hito wa te o tunagi, koe wo awasete.
(People are holding hands, swaying in unison.)

Sizen no kodou ni awasete.
(Singing to the beat of nature's heart.)

Botan ga saku, fuurin wa utau.
(Peonies are blooming, the wind chimes sing.)

Korekarano sedai no tameni.
(Let us create a beautiful harmony, for generations to come.)

Kyle suddenly buries me in his arms. "You still remember the song!" I didn't know I was humming the tune as I relived the memory. "Do you remember the title?"

I remember. The title was Kazumi.

But all of this is wrong. I push him away and shake my head in denial. This can't be it. The world I know, the world I grew up in was nothing but a lie? The Neuronics and the Sarcs both accused each other of killing my parents, but who is telling the truth?

I lift my eyes to meet Kyle's. As soon as I catch his attention, I extend my mind into his, bypassing the dark void without resistance.

He's expecting my intrusion!

The moment I land in his subconsciousness, I'm welcomed by an overwhelming mixture of pain and guilt, almost drowning my focus. He has been honest with me. But I still have to see it for myself.

I will my mind further into his memory centre, sorting through a mesh of irrelevant memories. After numerous tries, I finally found what I'm looking for. I dive in and the scene unfolds in Kyle's perspective.

He's driving at a dangerous speed through the countryside. The uneven ground creates a continuous turbulence, causing him to bounce up and down in his seat. I feel his anxiety and fear as he zips through the winding path. There's smoke rising into the sky in the distance, visible between trees. He floors his gas pedal and his head jerks back into the headrest. But he's too late. He knows it. Fear begins to overpower his composure.

The car finally pulls onto the scene. Half of the white and gray country house has collapsed into dark, ashy rubble, and the standing half is burnt through the walls.

Do I want to relive this again? I question myself.

Be brave, Kazumi. My mother's words echo in the back of my mind.

He approaches the crime scene, desperately searching the ground for any signs of survivors. He attempts to call out to us, but the site is eerily quiet, except for the crackling of the dying flame.

His gaze lands on a broken body . . . my father's broken body. I don't have the luxury of shutting my eyes as I watch in horror. My father's grotesque body, or what's left of him, sprawls on a pile of crumbled bricks. His head is almost completely charred. Both of his legs are missing, and his arms are shredded to an unrecognizable state. It's impossible to identify him at this point but Kyle knows . . . and I know that the body belongs to Hendric Clarke.

I can't . . . do this . . .

My concentration begins to falter. My consciousness is flickering like a light bulb about to burn out. If I slip even slightly during a telepathic exchange, both of our brains will likely be fried.

Kazumi, hang in there. You need to know the truth!

Kyle? How do you . . .

Just focus, the worst parts are almost over.

But you're not a Neuronic. How can you communicate during . . .

I'll explain later. Focus!

With Kyle's encouragement, I sharpen my concentration. Then slowly, the oppressive feelings begin to subside. I resume the playback where Kyle continues his search for me and my mother. He finds my mom at where I left her, in the same condition I remember. There it is again, the combination of pain and rage, terrorizes my sanity. But this time I power through it . . .

After leaving the scene, Kyle confronted the old chief, whom I've never met. Then his own investigation ensued and it was confirmed that the Sarcs never launched any aerial attack since the war. Two SK1 jets were indeed stolen two days before . . .

I carefully exit his mind and sink to the floor, feeling drained and empty. Marko lied to me. The closest person I have to a family has been lying to me for ten years. Why?

"I'm sorry you had to see that again." Kyle sits down beside me on the floor.

"How did you do that?" my voice harsh.

"Your mother," he clears his throat. "She unlocked a part of my mind so if the day comes when I have to raise you, you'd be able to practice your telepathy on me."

I let out a cry and bury my face in my arms. Kyle wraps me in his and gently pats my hair. Years of penned up emotions, unleashed at once. I miss my mother, and my father. They went through great lengths to avoid the very fate that had fallen upon me. It was my fault. I trusted the devil and it burned away everything my parents ever did for me. How could I be so stupid?

"It's okay." Kyle gently lifts my chin as I sit up straight. "You're strong Kazumi. One day you may very well be the strongest of the two factions. Whatever you've been told in the past, it doesn't matter now. It's up to *you* to find your path. It's your decision from now on. Remember, you're no body's pawn, you are Kazumi Clarke. Stay true to who you are, in here." He pokes me lightly at where my heart is. "It consists of the essence from both sides." His brows furrow, like he remembers something bad. "But you shouldn't stay here. You're not safe if they find out you're the hybrid . . ."

"Oh no! Murray might find my dad in the system." I realize what a big mistake I've made by telling them my real name.

Kyle shakes his head. "He won't. I've personally deleted any data that related to your father."

Just when I want to thank Kyle, Finn bursts through the doors.

"Kaz. Are you alright?" Finn looks at me, then at Kyle and scowls. "What did you do to her Kyle?"

Kyle lifts his hand saying he means no harm. I get up and throw myself at Finn. He's no longer my enemy.

"What the hell did you do to her Kyle?" He sounds like he's ready to murder someone.

"No Finn," I interrupt. "No, he . . . he helped me." I glance back at Kyle, who's looking at me in a fatherly manner. "I recovered more of my memories and I couldn't handle it," I lie. "I broke down and Kyle was just comforting me."

Finn relaxes but his stare is still suspicious. "I thought . . . I was just worried because you were gone for a long time." He tilts my face upward so he can see me. He frowns as he gently wipes the tears off my face.

"Well Kazumi, looks like you're in good hands." Kyle comes closer and pats Finn on the arm. "Take good care of her. She's a wonderful girl." Then he wraps his arms around me in a hug and whispers, "Don't trust anyone. I will find a way to get you out of here." He nods to Finn as he steps out the storage room.

He didn't say it, but my nagging feeling tells me Kyle knows where I've been the past ten years. But it doesn't matter now, because my mission has changed.

I look up at Finn with new found hope. "Let's go dance some more."

Maybe I won't lose him after all.

CHAPTER 36

Someone's phone beeps. I twitch, almost hitting Finn with my elbow. He answers his phone drowsily, propping himself up on the bed beside me. I look out my bedroom bay window and it's already morning. It's another beautiful day with not even a single cloud in the sky.

". . . got it. I will brief them as soon as possible." Finn hangs up and turns to face me, "Morning. How are you feeling?"

"Uhh . . . what did I do to myself?" I rub my throbbing temples.

Finn chuckles, "You only had three glasses of wine."

"Um, did I cause any trouble while I was drunk?" I hope I didn't reveal my identity to him.

"No. You just passed out," Finn says, "And I brought you back here and I hope you don't mind I stayed the night."

"Oh . . . um . . . did we?" my face turns bright red.

"Oh God no!" Finn jumps up, face contorts in disgust. "You were unconscious for God's sake. What kind of a monster would I be if . . . no, I just fell asleep beside you."

"Sorry." I grab his hands, "I wasn't accusing you of anything." I tug on his arm, telling him to come back to bed.

"Ya okay, sorry. I overreacted." He slips under the blanket

beside me and wraps me in his arms. Both of us are still in our formal outfits.

"Finn," I say.

"Hm?"

"I love you."

His eyes widen in surprise, "I was waiting to see how long before you admit it."

"So you're not mad that I didn't react when you said it yesterday?" I ask.

"Oh I'm mad. And this is your punishment." He tackles me and rolls over to pin me under him, throwing the blanket on the floor. He tickles me on my ribs. I squirm and scream, laughing wholeheartedly for the first time in ten years.

"S-stop!... Help!... Ahh!" I kick and thrash at the unbearable sensation, but I also don't want it to end.

"Alright . . . I think that's enough punishment for today." Finn finally stops and I'm left panting in bed. I guess the prime gene is not impervious to tickling.

"Now we have to go. Get dressed." He flips me swiftly so I'm on my stomach.

"For what?" I lazily climb out of bed, hating the interference to our lovely morning.

"The chief's got a mission for us. I need to brief the team," he follows me into the bathroom. "Your first mission."

I pause for a second, trying to figure out how I feel about this.

"Why are you frowning?" he asks, "I thought you were eager to go on a mission."

"Ya, I am. I'm excited."

"Well you certainly don't look it. You don't have to go if you're not ready."

"No, I will go," I say. "It's my first mission as a Sarc. It means something to me."

"Alright. Then get dressed."

The Elite Force gathers in the training centre, waiting for Finn's instructions. It's only been a week since I was here last, but it feels like a month has gone by.

Murray is the first to engage me in a conversation about random stuff. He apologizes for not being able to find anything on my parents. I act as if I'm disappointed.

The rest of the team doesn't bother talking to me. Though Kayden did give me his signature greeting. What a flirt.

I wonder what went through their minds when they saw Finn and I at the wedding. Astonishment? Hatred? Jealousy?

Finn returns, looking grim. "Alright, listen up," he begins. "This is a rescue mission. One of our field agents and two government officials from UNNA are kidnapped by the Neuronics and are being held in Nice."

My body twitches, but I quickly recover. Finn hands out three pictures to each of us, depicting the captives—two Caucasian men and an Asian woman.

"We believe they're being imprisoned in their headquarters. Our mission is to rescue them in *low profile*—"

"What if it's a trap?" the words rush out of my mouth, cutting Finn off.

He scowls, not too happy about my interruption. "That's why not all of us are going. So we're not putting all eggs in one basket. But it is a risk we have to take. We don't leave our men to be tortured for information. And these officials hold important offices in UNNA, not rescuing them means jeopardizing our relationship with the government. We believe the Neuronics will corrupt their minds to gain diplomatic significance in North America."

"What if they're already corrupted?" Murray asks.

"Then we bring them back, restrained. Chief will deal with them if they've already been compromised," says Finn.

I wonder what can the chief possibly do when only the Neuronics are able to reverse the damage in their minds. Will she lock them up? Or just kill them? Even though I now know she's not the one responsible for my parents' deaths, I still can't find a place in my heart to like her.

After the briefing, we gear up and head to our jet. Nick, Benji, and Liam are staying behind to man the base. I'm glad Finn knows better than to ditch me.

A big thunderous cloud hovers over me as we board Natalie. Going into the Neuronic headquarters means there's a chance they'll uncover my identity. I'm not ready for Finn to know yet. Not until I sort out everything. But risky as it is, it's a great opportunity for me to investigate the truth behind the bombing of my home. I will confront Marko if it's necessary.

The Promenade des Anglais—a celebrated promenade in Nice—lights up vibrantly in a crescent that curves along the dark Mediterranean Sea like a sparkling half moon. But not even the beautiful scenery can calm my rapid heartbeat as we get closer to the sea-side city.

I'm sitting in the cockpit behind Finn and Murray, who are preparing for landing. It amazes me how multi-talented Finn is. He has mastered everything from flying a plane, to sword fighting, to gun kata. He even excels in dancing, which I had the honour to witness at Celine's wedding. Is there anything this man can't do?

Twenty minutes later, we land without incident. Our jet is cleverly disguised as one of the planes from the UNNA fleet.

As much as the Republic of Europe is under Neuronic control, on the surface it's just like any other nation where people can travel to and from rather freely.

Finn and Murray are in pilot uniforms and the rest of us are disguised as flight attendants. No one has recognized me yet. But I'm not expecting anyone to since most of my time growing up was spent in the Neuronic headquarters.

"It's for your safety," they'd say, to prevent me from roaming outside by myself.

My interaction with Kyle has begun to cast light on how I was being treated the past ten years. I was blind to the nature of the people around me. But now that I can see, I would not give anyone the opportunity to manipulate me ever again. The idea of having been tricked into working for them—the exact situation my mother feared—is making me want to burn their headquarters down.

Don't be hasty. Maybe it's not like what you think. Maybe Marko had a good reason. My Neuronic side is still not giving up.

We meet up with our contact just outside the airport. Sebastian is his name, a field agent stationed in Nice. It's his partner who got kidnapped along with the officials. Sebastian is in his late twenties, dark skin and with a smile that can light up the whole city.

We pile into his beat-up twelve-person van and drive off in the direction of Old Town. I remember being there a few times—an historical yet vibrant little area filled with narrow cobblestone paths, boutique galleries, shops and churches. But the name Old Town is not so fitting anymore since all the buildings have been refurbished to modern standards. Though they still resemble the old French architecture—a style that the European government insisted on keeping.

The old van shudders to a halt. I step out onto the

cobblestone street where the air is heavy, like I'm breathing in clusters of water vapour. The smell brings on a sudden wave of nostalgia—manipulated or not, this was my home for ten gruellingly long years. A decade of my life that I can never get back. Resentment and longing wash over me like two opposing forces fighting for dominance.

Keep it together. I take a deep moist breath and follow the crowd into a secret basement under an unremarkable food mart five blocks from the Neuronic headquarters.

So the Sarcs *do* have a base in Nice, contrary to what the Neuronics believe. This would be valuable information *if* I decide to continue my alliance with them. But the chance of this happening is close to zero.

The small and musty basement is crammed with high-tech equipment and surveillance monitors. Suddenly it's clear. This is why the Sarcs knew about the Rockies attack and had enough time to evacuate.

Sebastian had most of the provisions ready and after he explained the sleep arrangements, everyone retreats to their corner and calls it a night.

"Too bad we don't get to spend more time here. Nice is so pretty," says Lilly.

The four girls are crammed into a small room with two single beds about two feet apart. I'm sharing one with Bridget. Lilly and Samantha take the other one.

"You know this is Neuronic-central right?" says Bridget. "There are plenty of other beautiful cities we can visit that don't have filthy mind benders crawling about."

I know Bridget's comment was not directed at me, but it still stings.

"If it were up to me, I would kill them all while we're here," Samantha says while picking at her fingernails.

"I'm sure not all Neuronics are evil," I retort.

All three of them stare at me like they've seen a ghost. Then Samantha opens her mouth, "So all of a sudden you're the expert now that you're dating our commander?"

I glare at her, ready to intrude her mind to give her a little taste of me. But Bridget's hand on my shoulder stops me just in time before I make the grave mistake.

"Okay now, there's no need to be mean. We're all teammates here," says Bridget, hand still on my shoulder. "Kazumi has a point. We're not cold-blooded. We don't just kill whenever we like."

That shuts Samantha up for good. Then Bridget turns to me and says, "But be careful Kazumi. You may be soft, but our enemies are sneaky and manipulative. Don't let your compassion get in the way of what needs to be done."

I just nod but know full well what it takes to get a job done. No need for her to tell me.

"Well I'm going to bed," Lilly yawns. "Big day tomorrow."

Before long, the three girls are fast asleep. Someone even begins to snore. It's coming from either Lilly or Samantha.

The hot stifling air along with the musty stench of mildew are a bad combination when trying to fall asleep. Or is it the constant working of my brain keeping me up? I can't stop envisioning the many possibilities of tomorrow.

The more I try, the more sleep eludes me. I quietly leave the room for some fresh air, relatively speaking, and find Finn in the main room, hunched over a big desk. I walk over, making sure to shuffle my feet so he can hear me coming. I've learned my lesson.

"Shouldn't you be in bed?" he says without looking at me.

I slip my arms around his waist, "I can't sleep. What about you?"

"I don't need sleep. I run on pure adrenaline when I'm on missions," he's still looking at the map on the table.

"I hope you're joking." I give him a squeeze, then peek over his shoulder and find a map of the Neuronic headquarters.

Where did they get such a detailed map?

He turns around and holds my hands, "Tomorrow's mission is very dangerous. I need you to be careful. Don't be reckless. Don't be a hero. You understand me?" Concern fills his eyes.

I'm touched by his words, but I want to tell him that I'm actually very capable; that the reckless girl was not the real me. But will he understand? Will he see me as a threat?

I wrap my arms around his neck and pull him lower, so our noses touch. "I love you." I whisper in his ears.

He shakes his head and chuckles, "I take that as a yes, you *will* be careful," he says and wraps his hands around my waist. "I love you too. I wish things can stay like this, forever."

Me too.

We spend the next day going over the final plan and getting a few last minute items. By sunset, we are ready to go.

The original plan was to have me, Samantha and Lilly as backups, hidden in a dilapidated factory building a block east of the headquarters. But after my ferocious persuasion, Finn finally gave in and allowed me to accompany him inside the dragon's den. Lilly didn't seem to mind but seeing Samantha's about-to-explode face meant that I just delivered the perfect comeback for her obnoxious comment last night.

The sun sinks into the horizon, leaving the sky in a veil of darkness. We wait till the wee hours of the night before making our way to the big square building made solely of concrete. The Neuronic headquarters is located at the most northern outskirts of Nice where the surroundings are nothing but ruins.

Sebastian parks the van by an old factory building, out of sight. He and the two girls prepare the surveillance and communication systems that will aid us in the infiltration. The rest of us begin to make our way toward the Neuronics.

I can already make out the building a block ahead, a dark mass under the faint moonlight—the only light source available in this abandoned area. The ominous giant box is the size of three football fields. It's three storeys tall with only four tiny windows, one on each corner. It was a huge storage warehouse for construction supplies before the Neuronics took over.

We're getting close. I can see the metal pipes affixed to the side of the building, running all the way up to the roof. My hands are clammy and my heart is about to pop out of my chest. I don't even have a word to describe how I feel right now. All I know is that the same structure I used to call home now looks absolutely hideous to me. It looks like a dark concrete prison. No. It *was* a concrete prison designed to confine me, feed me lies and false hope.

I suddenly regret my decision to tag along. What was I thinking? People *will* recognize me as soon as I step into that compound. What then? Will they play along for my sake? Marko doesn't know that I know the truth though. He still thinks that I'm on his side, so he won't readily expose my identity. I just need to be smart and play it safe.

"So according to Sebastian, the captives are locked up in these cells." Finn brings up a hologram map of the interior. "Everyone ready?"

We all nod and set our GPSs preloaded with the same map. Finn and I will go in through the roof on the west edge; Murray and Bridget will enter through the east window, Kayden and Ryan will take the north window.

I'm surprised that Ryan and Celine agreed to postpone their honeymoon so he can participate in this mission. Or was he coerced into it by his older adopted brother? I'm not surprised if it's the latter. Finn can be quite intimidating at times.

We reach the west side of the building without being spotted, thanks to Sebastian for monitoring our locations and temporarily disabling the surveillance cameras as we go.

The west wall doesn't have pipes, so we'll have to do it the fun way. We shoot a couple of grappling hooks onto the roof and scale the wall rapidly.

Finn looks to me when we're about half way up. "Not too bad for your first time," he smiles, showing his perfect white teeth.

"It's not hard." I say as I continue to climb just as fast as him. What Finn doesn't know is that I *have* scaled these walls many times, for training.

We both reach the top at the same time. I wonder if he held back to make me look better. I certainly went easy on him. This *supposedly* was my first time using a grappling hook. How suspicious would it look if I get to the top before he does.

"Don't get too cocky," Finn says in a somewhat serious voice.

I just shrug and follow him to the fire escape entrance a few paces from the ledge. I remember this circular plate that covers the entrance. I've touch that handle all too many times. I used to climb up here alone at night so I could get some fresh air and gaze at the stars. This was the only place I felt comfortable and peaceful—away from pressure, away from pain. Back then, nothing else mattered other than training, the mission and seeking revenge. I never thought further than that. Never thought I'd live beyond my mission to come back and see the stars again, let alone be here with a boy who loves me.

I stop, look up into the starry sky, and a teardrop rolls off my cheek.

"Okay, get in." Finn says in a hush.

I don't want to move. I just want to be here, with him, under the sparkling lights that make up the universe.

"Kaz! What are you doing? Move!" Finn yanks on my pant leg.

I gaze down at him, who already has the cover removed and is crouched beside it. "Thank you. I'll never forget tonight." I whisper.

Finn looks perplexed at first, then annoyance creeps in. "Okay seriously, stop it. We're on a mission." He scolds.

I get in quickly, mumbling a "sorry" on my way down. Finn follows close behind. I climb down the iron staircase, taking care not to make a single sound. But as soon as Finn hits the first step, it creaks like someone's scratching a fingernail against steel.

"SHHH...." I shush as I step onto the concrete floor. "I thought stealth is one of your strengths." I say as quietly as possible.

"Strike two. Pull one more and you'll never come on a mission with me again," he says.

Is he actually serious? I can't tell by only his voice. It's too dark in here to see his expression. But I don't need to see to know that we're inside a small mechanical room the size of my walk-in-closet back in the Alaskan compound.

I feel for the door and find it without much trouble. The metal door opens into the middle of a dim hallway, long and bare. I go left without thinking only to be halted by Finn.

"Where are you going?" he whispers harshly.

"I—"

"I told you to stay behind me. How do you know which way to go?" He's getting more frustrated with me by the second.

"I saw the map too. See?" I hold out my device, showing him the GPS. I lied. I turned left by force of habit.

Finn sighs, "Just follow my order okay? Please? I can't afford you running around recklessly." He looks exhausted all of a sudden.

I nod and let him take the lead, all the while hating how impulsive I acted. I can't afford any more mistakes.

Even with the map, it's still difficult for Finn to navigate through the intricate labyrinth created to throw off intruders. But I can't say anything or else he'll know I've been here before. I can't tell him that the heart of the Neuronics is actually several storeys deeper into the ground than Sebastian thought. In fact only a handful of leaders and high profile personnel are granted access. I was there once with Marko, but he had to erase that memory from me after the visit. At least he thought he did.

"Seriously, can't this place be anymore dull?" Finn says under his breath.

"I know, right." I reply casually.

He's right, compared to the Sarcomere compound, this is the ultimate showcase of simplicity and boredom. Not a dash of colour or design to be found anywhere in the entire complex. I can't imagine how it looks to a Sarc who's used to lavish designs and fancy gadgets.

As we approach a corner, I catch a flicker of movement behind me. Three soldiers happen to walk into the corridor about fifty feet behind us. They see me and one is about to sound the alarm. But they also look directly into my eyes.

Obeying my new command, they turn around and march back the way they came from without making a sound.

Finn looks back at me just as they march out of sight. I assure him everything is fine and we continue forward.

That was close!

I was lucky that they were the infantry. My trick wouldn't have worked on Neuronics. Our minds are sealed from each other, unless permission for access is granted. If I try to tap the mind of a Neuronic, our infiltration would be detected immediately.

As we make our way around the convoluted hallways, I try to look for Sebastian's cameras but find only the ones that belong to the compound. How he managed to put hidden cameras in here is a total mystery to me.

After fifteen minutes of navigating through the concrete maze, we finally see the holding cells two floors beneath ground level. We believe this is where they are keeping Sebastian's partner Myra.

Finn quickly takes down a guard with his silenced pistol and retrieves a set of keys from his body. I stare at the corpse, silently apologizing for his misfortune. I didn't know him. But I know he didn't have to die. I could have easily redirected him but that would risk blowing my identity. I chose my secret over his life.

"I have a bad feeling about this." Finn whispers as we approach the cell door. I agree. How can there be only one person guarding such an important prisoner. But we're in too deep now. The only option is to move forward.

Finn quickly unlocks the door and slowly pushes it open.

The cell is bigger than I thought, big enough to house the eight figures waiting inside. Sitting in the middle of the room is a man in a black suit. "Well it's about time you two show up.

Nice to finally meet you, Commander O'Riley. Marko Gregory, at your service." Marko stands from his chair and bows.

Finn doesn't say a word, but his steely gaze indicates he knows who Marko Gregory is—the leader of the Neuronics.

CHAPTER 37

"Your eyes tell me you're not surprised to see me," says Marko in his scratchy voice. "But I know fear when I see it." He ambles up to Finn, who's as still as a corpse, eyes fixated somewhere on a wall beyond Marko. "I contemplated sending more men out there to welcome you. But then I thought, the renowned leader of the Elite Force can easily take down as many as I send," he scratches his chin with his index finger. "See commander. I value my men very much, the *useful* ones that is." His eyes fall on me.

My heart falls into my stomach. I have a feeling Marko knows more than I give him credit for. Just then, the other three figures donned in purple lower their hood. I recognize them— two boys and a girl—all younger than me by two years. I even trained a couple of them before I left. But they're not here for a reunion. Their eyes bear hatred, even when they're looking at me. Standing beside them are four infantry men pointing their machine guns at Finn. This is a well-prepared trap, and we walked willingly into it like two blind mice.

"You see," Marko walks up to me. I want to duck behind Finn, but it's no use. There's no where to hide. "This one here . . ." he lifts my chin. "Is of utmost importance to me."

I hold my breath, suddenly afraid to look at him. His

face never looked more hideous to me. Those eyes, those dark menacing eyes are the last things I want to see right now.

I turn my head toward Finn, catching his last untainted gaze before the truth comes out.

"Get your filthy hand off her," Finn finally speaks through clenched jaw.

"Oh no Commander O'Riley. I think you're mistaken. This one's mine." He strokes my hair like I'm a little girl.

I freeze. Not wanting to believe my predicament. Maybe Finn won't believe him. Maybe there's still a way out of this mess. But Finn's lack of reaction suggests that I'm too naive to even think that. I have envisioned a hundred different things he might do or say at the moment he learns of my identity. None fits his current state. He's neither mad nor surprised.

"Thank you sweetheart, for bringing him to me. You'll get your reward soon enough." He kisses my cheek.

I bat Marko's face away. "No, Finn. Let me explain!" I desperately grab onto his arm.

He looks at me with hollow eyes and asks, "Is this true?" His voice deprived of any emotion.

"I . . ."

"Oh how touching," Marko interrupts. "Bind him!"

On cue, the four men confiscate all of Finn's weapons and cuff his hands behind his back. He complies without even a hint of struggle, like he's lost the will to fight.

"NO!" I dash for the soldiers, but Marko grabs my arm and twists it to just before the breaking point.

I scream in pain. My agony finally wakes Finn from his desolation, but there's nothing he can do now.

I watch from behind as Finn is being pushed and shoved along the concrete corridor, blind-folded.

"What are you going to do to him?" I walk with Marko's hand on my achy arm.

"You'll see." He replies without looking at me. His tone neither angry nor happy.

"Why did you lie to me?" I ask.

"I don't know what you're talking about."

"You can stop with the act. I know it was the Neuronics who bombed my parents. WHY?" I can easily yank his hand away if it wasn't for the gun he just pulled out.

"I have no time for your child's play right now. Shut up and maybe I'll let you watch the show." He yanks me harder and that's when I see the red markings on the gun—Finn's gun. There's only one reason Marko needed the enhanced gun. Dread hovers over me as we're being escorted to our imminent death.

We get shoved into a big room that looks exactly like the holding cell except it's ten times the size and installed with bright white lights. In the middle are four slumped figures on their knees. Their hands are restrained behind their backs by a heavy manacle, and their feet are locked in metal shackles that are fastened on the concrete floor. I would have thought they're unconscious if not for the subtle rise and fall of their shoulders. More than twenty men are scattered around, all pointing guns at the captives.

My shoulders fall and I feel heavy, like an invisible force is pushing me down and it won't stop until I'm completely crushed. All hope is lost. The Elite team has been captured.

Finn is pushed to join the hostages while Marko is holding me back. I haven't seen him for a few months but he looks like he has aged a few years. His black deep-set eyes seem deeper and with wrinkles wrapped around them. His usual luscious black hair is finally showing hints of gray. Looks like stress has gotten to him. Was it because of me? A smidgen of guilt dabs my heart but it's quickly wiped away when my eyes fall on Finn again.

After a flurry of hands working, Finn gets fastened in with the same heavy-duty restraint as his teammates.

"Now we finally have a full house," Marko says. "We rarely have such high-profile guests. Let's have some fun." Marko pulls me to stand in front of the five Elites, who are on their knees. Four of them are staring at me with inquisitive eyes. They soon will hate me like Finn does. He can't even look at me anymore. A mixture of guilt, shame, and anger boil inside me like a nasty concoction ready to spill over.

"Now my dear Kazumi," Marko releases my arm and begins circling around me slowly. I know this tone. This I-know-what-you're-up-to tone. I heard it often enough growing up. "You were entrusted with the most important mission," he looks down at Finn. "Yet you failed me. You failed your own people."

The four Elites finally catch on, giving me the reaction I anticipated. But Murray possesses something else in his eyes, like something has been confirmed.

He knew!

Marko squats down in front of the Elites, so they can see eye-to-eye. "You see, my talented Kazumi was supposed to kill all of you back in your lavish home. She failed. Because she was stupid enough to fall in love," he sneers.

How does he know?

"So I had to bring you here instead. A bit of inconvenience on my part, but I guess it's more exciting to see your execution live. Isn't it Kazumi?" he stands to join me.

I don't bother to answer him. My eyes never left Finn, who is just staring at the floor.

The four Elites try to rise but quickly get pushed back down with gun barrels on their heads. Finn still frozen. I wish he would yell or fight back. I want to go into his mind to tell him everything, but he won't even look at me.

"Let's show them what you're capable of Kazumi," says Marko.

I know what he wants. I know those dark eyes all too well. But I won't get manipulated anymore. "All these years . . . I trusted you. I saw you as my family." I say. "Did I even mean anything to you?"

A flash of emotion appears in his eyes, but he blinks and reverts back to his emotionless-self.

"Of course my dear. You're everything to us, *if* you succeed." He steps closer, so uncomfortably close that I can smell his stale breath. "We groomed you. We trained you. But you've destroyed all our efforts without even a second thought. Your pathetic little game is getting old, and my patience with you is at its limit." He grabs my arm and squeezes it so tight that it begins to go numb. "Perhaps this will motivate you."

He turns to the Elites on the floor and I immediately know what he's about to do. Before I can warn them, Ryan lifts his head and stares right into Marko's eyes.

"NO! Look away!" I launch myself at Marko, but two sets of hands catch me from behind and pull me down. Neuronics are most vulnerable during telepathy, but the infantry men are there to make sure no one gets too close. Knowing their strength will not match mine, the two guys quickly cuff my right hand to a metal chain attached to the floor, preventing me from lifting my arm higher than my waist. I unlock it telekinetically but my effort is immediately reverted by the other Neuronics in the room.

Here I am, forced to watch while Ryan suffers from what I can only imagine is the most horrific hallucination. Marko is known for a lot of things, being merciful is definitely not one of them.

Although the Elites are trained to guard their minds to make mental intrusions more difficult, Ryan is up against the most powerful mind bender yet. It doesn't take long for him to be completely engulfed by the Marko's power. His blood-chilling scream and contorted face are telltale signs.

Finn finally snaps out of his reverie when he hears the scream. He springs forward, trying to knock Marko down. Five men immediately jump on him, barely holding him back.

One of the men unlocks the shackles on Ryan's ankles and is instantly trampled by him. With his hands still cuffed behind him, Ryan frantically runs toward the wall and smashes himself into it at full speed. A loud thud echoes through the entire room. Blood is trailing down his nose, but he doesn't seem to feel it. He repeats the process again and again, until his nose is completely shattered.

The sight of him brings me back to the tentacle attack where I experienced the cruelty first hand. If I have to choose, I'd rather be slayed by a Sarc's weapon than be killed under the Neuronic's gruesome hallucination. No one deserves such execution, not even the worst of criminals.

While Ryan continues his blind rampage, one of the Neuronics I don't recognize, pulls a lever beside the door. Sharp spikes jut out from the wall, stopping at about an inch long.

"RYAN!" The five of us call out to him, hoping our faint effort will wake him. But I know our scream is futile at this point. His mind only knows horror. His survival instinct will become his worst enemy.

I close my eyes as he sprints into the metal spikes. The agonizing scream that follows pierces through my heart like a thousand daggers. I open my eyes and see him stumbling back from the wall, barely holding himself up. Blood rapidly seeps through his shirt, but it's not enough to demobilize him.

The man pulls the lever further and the spikes extend by another inch.

"Marko, please stop! I will do whatever you want. Just stop . . . please!" I beg. I can't let him do this to Ryan. I can't let him do this to Celine.

I know he heard me when he extends his thought into mine. *"Sweetheart, you're too late."*

Ryan makes another attempt. This one visibly weaker, but he still manages to break into a sprint from the other side of the room. His eyes are dark and focused but empty, like they're deprived of a soul.

I close my eyes at the point of impact. His tormented cry is twice as loud as before. Tears begin to blur my vision and I think of Celine, the happy bride who's waiting anxiously for her new husband to return so they can start a life together. It's me who brought this upon them. I should have carried out my mission, because a bullet to the head would have been a mercy.

Sluggishly, Ryan pulls himself out of the spikes, staggers backward, and falls onto his side. But he's not quite done yet. He rolls onto his front and with great difficulty, he manages to stand back up. His face is as pale as a ghost and his walk resembles a broken zombie. His hair no longer blond.

The spikes are now extended all the way like swords. This will be his final run. A part of me is glad that his misery will soon be over.

I look over to the Elites. Murray is throwing a litany of curses at Marko, Bridget can do nothing but wail and Kayden is utterly traumatized. Finn on the other hand makes not a sound but his knuckles are held so tight that they're pale white.

Ryan heads for his third and final run with a loud,

primal growl. His face is so smudged in blood that he's barely recognizable. This time, I force myself to watch. I will have this imprinted in my memory as a reminder of Marko's cruelty. If this is what being a Neuronic is about, then I am definitely not one of them.

Ryan picks up speed as he stumbles and at the last second, launches his body forward, fully penetrating himself onto the spikes. Just when I thought Marko can't be anymore cruel, he exits out of Ryan's mind just before he dies. Ryan lets out an excruciating moan as he regains his sensory functions. Slowly, he turns to face us, mouth moving but inaudible. Then I realize he's not actually talking to us, he's calling out to Celine, for one last time.

I'm staring at his limp, gory body, held up by the spikes. My own body feels heavy, yet my heart feels hollow, like someone has punched a hole in my chest.

Marko hands me a gun and says, "I know you don't have the stomach to do what I did Kazumi, because the Sarcomere in you makes you weak. They're not your family or your friends. *I am* your family. Do not throw away the ten years we've had together for a heartthrob. He will only cause you pain. Kill him, then everything will be like the old days."

I step closer to him, so he can taste the rage in my breath. "I despise the old days. And you're *not* my family, because they are dead."

Marko shakes his head, "Such a shame. I knew the minute you fell for that boy, I'd lost you. I know *exactly* what you're thinking even if you don't say a word," he snarls.

He's bluffing. I have sealed my mind from intrusion just like everyone else.

"So you think I'm bluffing huh?"

What? How does he . . .?

"You see, I could never just send my most treasured weapon out in the world unsupervised. So I planted a little something in your head." Marko taps my forehead with his finger. I bat it away in disgust. "I heard all your thoughts. I knew you weren't able to recover your memories on your own, so I sent Jack to help. But you *killed* him."

"Then you should know I didn't mean to." I shout. But the guilt has already resurfaced, nipping away chunks of my soul. Maybe I do belong here, with these merciless killers.

"And then . . . you allowed his filthy hands to touch you. You have no shame!" Marko's suppressed anger is brewing behind his eyes but he will never show it publicly. He believes that showing any kind of emotion is a sign of weakness.

"No he didn't!"

"Oh quit the innocent act. We both know you wanted to."

Heat rushes to my face, spreading down my neck and reaching for my fingertips.

I look to Finn, his eyes finally fall on mine and they're flooded with rage. I don't have to intrude his mind to know what he's thinking. He must regret everything he has ever done with me. He must be appalled that a Neuronic has crept into his heart.

Marko jams Finn's pistol in my hand and unlocks my cuff. "I don't have all day. Kill them. You owe me this."

The gun feels cold in my sweaty palm. The same gun Finn gave me at the train station, but it feels a thousand times heavier today.

"Who killed my parents?" I ask again. "Answer me!"

Marko narrows his eyes at me. "You fool. You think intruding some random Sarc's mind would give you the truth?" Of course, he knows about my conversation with Kyle as well.

"Then tell me the truth!" I scowl.

He tilts his head toward the Elites. Then he sighs and signals to the men around Finn. "Be careful Kazumi, you're hanging on by the skin of your own teeth. One wrong move and you're done. I don't care if you're the hybrid."

He waves his hand and the mindless soldiers pounce on Finn like a pack of wild cats, beating him with their long guns and kicking at his vital organs. Finn is taking it like a true commander, but as strong as he is, he is still human. He still bleeds. He can still die.

"STOP!" I run toward him but get pulled back again.

I look over to Murray and Kayden for help, but they're just as helpless. They themselves are being pinned down by ten massive guys.

The merciless beating continues and Finn is beginning to lose endurance. Blood is running freely from his nose and mouth. They will surely beat him to death if I don't do something.

Seeing my noncooperation, Marko walks over and directs a soldier to unlock one of Finn's arms. The assault temporary stops but Finn's still not safe yet. Five gun barrels train on his head while five others pin him down so that the one can unlock his arm. I'm sure Finn can still take them down if he wants to, but he knows better—for his teammates' sake.

Marko grabs Finn by his free arm and twists violently in an awkward angle. The loud popping sound of the shoulder joint coming apart sends a punch to my stomach, and the scream coming from Finn makes everything that much worse.

I can't take this. I can't stand here and watch him suffer. If I can't save him, maybe it's best that I put him out of his misery.

I lift my gun with both shaking hands. Murray and Kayden watch in horror as my trembling legs move toward Finn. Bridget is yelling at me at the top of her lungs but I tune her out. I can't hear anything except for Finn's agonizing groans as they resume their assault.

I'm sorry Finn. I wrap my middle finger around the trigger and take in a deep shuddering breath. Then I contract every muscle in my body and spin to the right as quicky as I can, grabbing Marko by the throat. My pistol is now pointing at his temple. Fortunately, he's a short man.

"STOP! Or I'll shoot him," I demand.

The assailants stop at once. I'm glad their minds can still process basic reasoning. Then Marko's shoulders begin to shake, and soon the other Neuronics join in the humourless laugh.

"Oh my dear Kazumi. You are clever. But seriously, do you really think I would trust you with a Sarcomere weapon? Go ahead, shoot."

I tighten my grip on his throat and shoot at his foot. There's a click but no bullet.

"I know you Kazumi. I know you too well." Marko shakes his head.

I drop the gun, but before it hits the ground, I pull out a hidden blade from the back of my right boot.

"And do you see this coming?" I dig the tip of the enhanced blade into his neck, puncturing the skin so everyone can see the thin trail of blood running down Marko's neck. The guards didn't do a very thorough search.

All the guns are now pointing my way. The Neuronics are ready as well, but we all know there's nothing a Neuronic can do to me mentally other than hovering over my thoughts.

"You know full well what I'm capable of. I'm the hybrid and you have yet to see my Sarcomere side in action." I whisper in his ears. "Do you want a race to see who's faster? Their bullets or this knife in your carotid artery."

His jaw tightens as his calculated mind spins. "Is this how you repay me, huh? After all these years—"

I inch my blade deeper, causing him to wince. I need him to shut up. His words can be as dangerous as his mind.

I take this brief second to unlock Murray's handcuff telekinetically. He then quickly cuts out the others' shackles with his pocket laser pointer designed to burn through metals. The soldiers must have forgotten to confiscate that as well, thinking it was only a key chain.

The three Elites pull Finn up, who is now unconscious, and support him on their shoulders. The soldiers try to stop them, but I dig a little deeper with my blade to show them who's in charge here.

"Drop all your weapons and do not follow us. Or else *this* will happen." I jab the dagger into Marko's thigh, avoiding his femoral artery. Now it's his turn to scream. "This one is for Finn." I whisper in his ear.

I half drag Marko out the door while Bridget leads the way and the other three follow close behind. Finn's moan is like a shot of adrenaline into my veins, giving me strength and hope. He's still alive.

We make good time winding through the labyrinth with no pursuit. Soon after, we are out into the dark summer night where the air is so fresh that I want to just stop and breathe. But we don't have the luxury.

A black SUV pulls up just as we exit the building. Samantha and Lilly jump out before the car even stops completely. After loading Finn into the car, Sebastian begins shouting something to me in the driver's seat, but Murray stops him abruptly.

Are they planning to leave me behind?

Marko chuckles, having read my thought. "I would if I

were them. You just played them like a game of chess," his voice weak from the blood loss.

"No, *you* played me like a game of chess." Without warning, I stab his other thigh, causing him to curse on my mother's grave. "This one is for Ryan." Then I pin him down onto the ground. "Tell me, who killed my parents?" I yell in his face.

He doesn't say a word. Instead he begins to laugh. Both of his thighs are lacerated yet he's laughing. He's really laughing, like I'm the world's funniest joke. *Well let's see if you find this funny.* I hold up my blade, ready for a final blow. But a voice in my head stops my hand just inches from his heart.

He did raise you the past ten years. He did teach you everything you know.

Images of him training me and tending to my wounds flash before my eyes. Although he was never affectionate, he was the closest thing I had to a family, at the time.

"See, you're weak!" Marko has stopped laughing.

"No I'm not. I'm just not a monster like you." I plunge the knife into his right shoulder. "Consider this my repayment. We're even."

I stand up with the wet knife still in my hand and that's when Murray pulls me into the black car. I lock eyes with Marko as we drive off and that's when I hear his voice in my head one last time.

"It was a Sarcomere jet that bombed your parents, but I was the pilot."

CHAPTER 38

Something cold chafes my forehead. My face is burning yet I still shiver. Then there it is again: broken images of me being strapped to a surgical table, a blurry man holding a sharp tool. A distant voice, sounding unpleasantly familiar saying, *"I don't want her to remember any of this, you get that?"*

I jolt awake, all too glad that it was only a dream. But I recall a glimpse of Murray's fist before he knocked me out. Why did he tackle me? Did we escape? Ryan . . .

I push the horrible memory aside and try to get up, only to find a head brace holding me in place. Bright fluorescent lights illuminate every corner of the room including the stranger in a big mirror. Strapped to a semi-reclined surgical chair, her grayish green eyes look alert yet her dark eye bags say exhaustion. The most striking feature is her bald head where every strand of hair has been cleanly shaved off. Written on it are lines and numbers like coordinates on a globe. Dangling above that globe is a spine-chilling device equipped with needles of various lengths. A cart full of medical tools is parked just next to the surgical chair, showing three shiny scalpels standing by.

I almost choke on air as I study my gleaming head. A combination of shock, terror and disbelief wraps me in a tight cocoon, squeezing the life out of me. The only image that occupies my mind is alien dissection where I'm the alien about to be cut open.

I have to get out of here before they come back. I try to ignore the fear and concentrate on releasing my straps and neck brace with my mind.

No response.

I try again, this time really honing in on the metal and leather. Still nothing.

Then I realize something in this room is blocking my brainwaves, rendering my telekinesis powerless. I don't even think such thing is possible, but this is the only reason I can think of.

Gripped by fear, I yank on the restraints with all my strength but the damn chair refuses to budge. My heart is pounding so loud that I'm afraid it will wake the monster who put me here. I can only guess by the layout of the room that I am back in the Sarcomere headquarters. A click from the door and my guess is confirmed when Annette Trousing walks through it.

She's wearing a form-fitted black pantsuit with hair pulled back in her usual French twist. She looks tired and aged, like her skin has withered overnight. Her eyes are swollen with a rim of red. The extra makeup doesn't hide the fact that she's been crying profusely. She must have found out about Ryan.

She locks the door behind her and ambles toward me. The way she's sneering at me sends a chill up my spine.

"I'm glad you're awake," her voice is coarse and strained.

"What is this?" I struggle to make my point.

"Don't waste your energy, it's no use," she crosses her arms. "I will make sure the process is long and painful."

I inhale to cover my tremour. "What are you going to do?" I ask in as calm a voice as possible.

"If it wasn't for your invaluable genes, I would've torn you to pieces and it still wouldn't be enough for what you did to my Ryan." She hisses and circles around me slowly like a venomous snake teasing its prey.

"I'm sorry about Ryan. I tried to save—"

"Shut your filthy mouth!" Annette snaps. "I will make you pay. I will make you regret ever stepping foot in the Sarcomere headquarters."

"I know there's nothing I can say, but can you at least tell me if Finn is okay?"

"He's not your concern anymore."

"I need to see him. I need to explain—"

"There's no need. His mission is accomplished," Annette says.

"What are you talking about?"

She laughs and shakes her head. "Aside from your grand deception, you're pretty dumb for a hybrid."

How did she know? My eyes widen, betraying my surprise.

"Don't look so shocked. I knew what you are from the moment you accidentally revealed your real name. Just didn't think you belong to the Neuronics that's all. Didn't calculate *that* in the equation did you?" She strokes my bald head gently and her voice suddenly softens. "I thought you were dead, along with your parents ten years ago. But here you are, the only hybrid who ever lived. You have immense power, but you already know that. That's why you're tremendously valuable to us."

"What does this have to do with Finn?"

"Isn't it obvious? I need you to be on *our* side. What better way to buy someone's loyalty than with the power of love."

No she's lying. She's lying to get under my skin. I know it. She will say whatever it takes to break me at this point.

"I see that you don't believe me," she say. "You're the mind bender, you are welcome to examine my memories. I have nothing to—."

I enter her mind and zip through the dark void in record time. Then I clumsily sort through the irrelevant and finally find what I'm looking for. But before I can enter that memory, a voice interrupts.

Don't get any other ideas while you're in here. You're in the "read-only" mode, you don't get to play with my brain.

How . . .? You're a Neuronic!

I feel a sense of revulsion coming from Annette. Then the voice says, "*Don't insult me! I'm one hundred percent Sarcomere, as pure as one comes in. Do you want to know the truth or not? Last chance.*"

I shove my curiosity aside and dive into her memory.

"You're saying Gabi, I mean Kazumi is a Neuronic?" Finn asks in disbelief.

"I have evidence to believe that her father was the traitor who left us for a Neuronic woman," Annette says.

"But that doesn't mean she's a Neuronic."

"No, it's not conclusive at this point. Her brain scan from recruitment shows that her frontal lobe is indeed damaged. But we found her brain activities similar to that of a Neuronic," says Annette

"How's that even possible? She is definitely a Sarc." Finn is still not convinced.

"Hybrid. She's probably Henry and that bitch's kid." I can sense fire burning up inside her. "Just imagine what she can do with both powers. She'll be unstoppable!"

"So what do you suggest we do? Kill her?" Finn asks.

"No. She is not to be harmed physically. She's too valuable." Annette nibbles on her fingernail. The fire in her eyes is replaced by guile. Then her mood is lifted by an overwhelming sense of excitement. "Here's where you come in."

Finn looks confused.

"She's a lovely girl don't you think? And you've grown into such a fine young man. Make her see the irresistible side of you." She brushes Finn's collar.

Finn's gaze drops to the floor like he's lost in thoughts.

"Love is the most potent poison if administered correctly," she smiles deviously. "She will be loyal to you and to the Sarcomeres. So even if she *is* a Neuronic, your 'love' will ground her to us. Then she becomes *our* secret weapon."

I exit out of her mind, having seen enough. Ryan's death was not the worst cruelty after all.

Kazumi, this is what you get for being hopeful. You really think there's still people out there who care about you? You're nothing but a mistake. An abomination. An orphan. A pawn to be used.

"I was going to groom you into the finest Elite we've ever had. And you and Finn could have had a happily ever after. But since your master decided to kill my only child, I too, decided to change my agenda with you." Annette turns to leave but stops at the door. "By the way, your Neuronic power is useless in this room." She leaves and two female doctors enter.

I try to unlock my cuffs again but fail. I try to move smaller objects on the table, but they're as still as if they're in a photograph.

I catch the blond doctor's eyes and extend my mind into hers. I see the assortment of her memories and I can go as far as reading them, but that's the limit to what I can do. Learning their memories would not get me out of here. Whatever she did to this room was designed to block my neural transmissions.

I finally give up and sink into the chair. Their activities become background noise to me. The pounding of my heart slows down as the last ounce of hope just fizzled away. Why struggle when I have no where to escape to. My home turned out to be a prison designed to mold me into a weapon. I have no parents and no friends. There's no sanctuary anywhere for me.

The blond woman injects me with something, but I don't even feel it anymore, it's like all my nerves have given up as well. The chair begins to tilt back until I'm almost flat. The view changes from the morbidly depressing figure in the mirror to the cluster of needles suspended above. If I squint my eyes, the silver needles become a group of abstract lines that glimmer at random intervals as they sway ever so slightly. Looking at them no longer gives me trepidation. I welcome the sight of the torture machine, because it signifies the end is near—my misery will soon be put out.

"What are you doing?" Annette's voice rings loud and clear through the speakers.

"I'm just injecting anaesthetics," the blond replies.

"No anaesthetics or sedatives. We need her one hundred percent alert," Annette orders.

"No anaesthetics? That's torture!"

"If you're not going to do as you're told then I shall find a replacement."

"But—" the brunette doctor puts a hand on the blond's shoulder to shut her up.

"She's a Neuronic," Annette emphasizes. "Do you think her people thought twice before killing your friends and family back in the Rockies?"

No one speaks for a few seconds, then the doctors resume their preparation like the conversation never happened.

That's right. Have your revenge on me. I deserve it. I took hundreds of innocent lives on that plane. I killed Jack and I'm definitely responsible for Alex and Ryan's deaths.

I close my eyes and let the throbbing of my heart surge like a wave, crashing into my soul. The thought of Finn's betrayal further pushes me under the crushing rapids. I imagine myself curling up and sinking deep into the chilling ocean where no one can find me, where no one can hurt me.

Two streams of tears roll down the sides of my face as the cluster of needles begins to move, separating into two groups like two alien claws ready to rip me apart.

I blink away the moisture in my eyes and go back to my happy place—the deep, dark ocean . . . when suddenly a sharp sting brings me back.

"Phase one initiated," someone calls out.

The first sting disappears. But two more needles find their home. I squeeze my eyes to fight the pain.

"Try to relax, or it will hurt more." A voice whispers in my ear.

Then I see them again—the images that were creeping in and out of my dreams. But this time I'm not dreaming. They come back as pieces of memories; the scalpels, the man's voice, the bright lights. . .

Marko!

He was the voice I kept hearing. Those weren't dreams at all. They were sealed memories trying to claw their way back into my mind. Why do I have to be the hybrid? I never asked for any of this. I don't care about my genes or potentials. I just want to be with my family and live like a normal person.

Before my temples stop throbbing, another set of needles

find their coordinates on the globe. I grit my teeth and the pain intensifies. Before I can take another breath, another set sinks in. I shriek and more tears run down my face.

"We found something."

"What is it?" It's Annette's voice again.

"A micro chip, just underneath her frontalis muscle."

"Extract it. It's probably the telepathic device they planted on her," says Annette. "And remember, I don't want a drop of anaesthetic."

The blond begins to object but the brunette stops her once again. She then picks up a scalpel and a wave of panic trickles down my spine. I struggle, forgetting that the needles are still in my head.

"You better hold still if you don't want me to cut deeper than necessary," the brunette says.

Two hands grab my shoulders, holding me still. "Try to focus on a happy moment and stay there," the blond whispers.

As soon as she said "happy moment", my mind races back to the time of my sixth birthday when my mom had baked me a chocolate birthday cake topped with a fresh pink peony from our field. I still remember the scrumptious smell of the cake and—

"AHHGG. . ."

Focus. Think. . .cake . . .sweet smell . . .peony . . .Okaasan beautiful smile . . .

"AHHGG! Stop!" My spine arches from the blinding pain as the scalpel slices deeper. "Stop!"

"Hold still!" someone yells, "It's lodged deeper than I thought."

My mother's face is flickering as my consciousness wavers. The next thing I know, she's replaced by Finn and Annette's evil smiles, inching closer and closer. Annette leans forward with two hollow sockets where her eyes used to be. I scream and she slaps me across my face.

My eyes blink open, still feeling the hot sting on my cheek. Annette's skeletal face is gone but the brunette doctor is not looking pleased. I see her lips moving but I only hear a loud ringing in my ear. She slaps me again, this time on the other cheek.

"Wake up!" The invading pain wakes me completely. "We're done for today." She presses a button and all the cuffs pop open. "Get up."

Shakingly, I push myself up, but the massive headache is debilitating.

Seeing that I can barely move, the blond doctor gives me a lift on my back and I'm finally sitting upright. The mirror is once again in my field of vision. I look like someone who just had all the blood drained, and the black coordinates on my bald head are now dots of red. A white bandage the size of my palm is taped to my upper forehead where they took out Marko's tracking device. At least my thoughts are free from his eavesdropping, but he's hardly my concern now.

"Come on, move!" The brunette impatiently shoves me off the chair. My legs can't catch up and I fall to the floor, right shoulder first. A crushing pain ignites and it radiates through my body, waking up old wounds. Soon after my whole body is consumed by pain.

The nice doctor quickly helps me up but a cough from the brunette stops her. I grab the side of the chair, ignoring the scream in my right shoulder and pull myself up. I have no freedom but I will have my dignity. I pull harder until I'm finally standing. The mean one shoves me toward the back of the room where a small den awaits. It looks approximately ten feet wide by five feet deep and it's furnished with a single mattress and a toilet. I drag my stiffened legs forward, one painful step at a time. As soon as I get into the cell, a glass door slams shut, confining me.

"Rest up. We'll pick your brain again tomorrow," the brunette smirks.

The nice one gives me a sympathetic stare and before she disappears from the room, I catch a silent "I'm sorry" from her lips. The door locks automatically behind them and the bright light shuts off, leaving me alone in the dark.

I curl up in a ball on the hard mattress, but the thin robe hardly tames my chills. Despite my pathetic attempt to not think, my mind decides to replay the "happy" moments Finn and I shared: our first kiss in the staircase, the romantic picnic, the dancing under the stars . . .

Everything was staged to wheel me in like a meaty sea bass on a fish hook. And now I'm dangling by that hook, suffocating and helpless.

I hug myself tighter as tears become sobs and eventually I let the emotions spill. I no longer need to suppress my feelings because nothing matters anymore.

CHAPTER 39

"STOP!" I cry out in pain.

"Bloody hell! Stop screaming! I'm trying to work here," the man who replaced the blond doctor shouts. He's even more ruthless than the brunette. That's why he's been running the procedures for the past days.

I wonder what they did to the nice doctor. Did Annette just demoted her or simply kill her for disobedience? She reminds me of a boy who once came to my rescue and got banished from the Neuronics.

Ethan was three years older than me and he would always bring me treats after a particularly hard day of training. He was sweet and smart and my one and only friend. But none of that mattered to the Neuronics. To Marko, Ethan was a failure. He wasn't born in the top quadrant of the gene pool. When they started me on energy field training at the age of nine— significantly younger than most Neuronics would start, Ethan was worried. He had every reason to. They were too eager to move things along before I was ready. They shot at me, just to test if my energy field would stop the bullets. Except it didn't, and I have the scar on my elbow to remind me of that. As a feeble protest, he stole all the ammo from the weapon room so the next day they would have no bullets to use. Marko was infuriated, because it delayed my training by a few days. That was the last time I saw Ethan.

The thought of Ethan distracted me briefly from the pain but the machine clicks again and another searing pain ignites in my neck. No flashback of any kind can distract me anymore. I bite down on my already lacerated lips and grip harder on the chafed armrests. I have lost count of how many needles are in my neck and scalp.

Just to make things more fun for Annette, they have been very precise in inflicting just enough pain to reach my threshold but not over, so I can't pass out.

"Phase two initiating," the man says.

"Go ahead." Annette has been behind that mirror since day one. I'm clearly putting on a good show for her.

"Hold on tight," the brunette says.

I hear the flick of a button. A different machine charging up just like the sound of a plane before take off. Then a wave of electricity shoots through my veins and arteries, leaving burning imprints in its wake. I screech as my spine bends from the electrocution.

"STOP THAT!" Someone yells from a distance, or was that me? "What the hell are you guys doing to her?"

"You're not authorized to be here. Get out!"

I want to lift my heavy eyelids but the electrocution left me paralyzed.

"Keep going!" I think that's Annette's voice again but the sounds become so distant . . .

They stab me with another shot of electricity and my screech becomes a raspy croak. I feel myself slipping. At the brink of losing consciousness, a sharp bang sends everyone into chaos.

". . . not supposed to be . . ."

"Your mission is done . . . no longer . . ."

"Why? Why did you lie to me? . . . you were . . her... our ally. Is this the way to treat your allies?"

". . . valuable to us as an experiment. Imagine adding telekinesis . . .strength . . . the possibilities."

"I don't care . . ."

"What about your brother huh? . . . he died? She's a Neuronic. They killed my Ryan!"

"She saved . . . makes you no different . . . I'm not going to—" The muffled conversation suddenly stops.

After a while, Annette's voice comes on again. "Take him . . . That's it for today!"

I slowly climb back to lucidity but still unable to open my eyes. I know what comes next. It has become a ritual: injection of liquid nutrients; spend the night in the cell; resume torture. The cycle continues day after day.

The man carries me from the chair and drops me callously on the hard mattress, which normally would hurt but the electrocution has temporarily numbed my body.

I lie where he tossed me, basking in this euphoric freedom from pain. My body has been so accustomed to agony that it rises to the verge of ecstasy the moment pain vanishes. I've lost count of the days and hours I've spent in this retched lab and frankly, I lack the will to care. I'm deteriorating by the day and I find myself looking forward to the sweet relief of death. I did try to speed up the process by banging into a wall in the attempt to break my neck—or to give myself a major concussion at the least. It was the only option I could think of with the lack of weapons and the ability to manipulate my own mind. Unfortunately they caught on and have since padded my walls and toilet with foam. All I got was a broken nose and a heavily bruised forehead.

As I begin to doze off, I think back to the beautiful chiffon dress I wore at Celine's wedding. I've never looked more stunning with my luscious wavy hair and smooth glowing skin. *"You are angelic"* was what Finn said to me that day. I did possess the beauty of an angel at that moment. Unlike the hideous witch I am now—bald and shrivelled. It hasn't been that long but I feel like I've aged considerably. The angel, once in Heaven, was dragged down to Hell in a matter of days. What a shame, I will never see that beautiful Kazumi again. With that thought in mind, I eventually fall asleep.

"Kaz . . . Kazumi . . . wake up."

My eyelids flutter. *Daddy?*

Someone taps the glass. "Kaz!"

I turn toward the voice and see Finn crouching on the other side of my glass partition, fully equipped with his katana and pistols. The lab behind him still dark.

"You should come back tomorrow. The show's done for today," I say then turn away.

"I'm here to get you out," he says while disengaging the lock.

"Really? Where are we going? Did you prepare me another lavish picnic?"

There's no answer, just a beep and a click and my glass prison is opened. Finn rushes in and as soon as he touches me, I punch him right in the face. The assault stuns him but doesn't hurt him. I grab his collar and push him against the cushioned wall. I don't know where my strength comes from, I just know that I want to hurt him. I want him to feel my pain.

He lifts his arm and I bite into it, as hard as I can. I feel his muscle tensing up in my mouth but he makes no attempt to stop me. The smell of him brings back too many painful memories. I squeeze my eyes and sink my teeth deeper. But my adrenaline is depleting and I feel the ground slipping away under me. Next thing I know, I'm slumped on his lap.

He picks me up and the jolt sends another shooting pain through my body. I can't do much other than groan.

"Hang in there," he says.

As Finn carries me out of the lab, I see two guards slumped on the ground just outside the door. A third one is passed out in the viewing room next door where Annette must have been spying.

"I'm gonna get you out of here, but I need your cooperation," says Finn. "I need you to fight on."

I hazily look up at him, with the last bit of my strength I say, "Why do you even bother? Just let me die."

"That's the thing, they will *never* let you die. At least not until they figure out how to extract your Neuronic power," Finn says as he takes me through a series of hallways.

"Don't pretend you don't want my power," I spit the words in his face.

"I do. Just not by torturing another human being for it." Finn rounds another corner and runs straight toward a door lit by an exit sign at the other end of the long hallway. I realize I've ever been to this part of the compound before.

"Where are you taking me?" I ask, suddenly nervous that Finn might not be taking me to safety like he said he was. It wouldn't be the first time he lied to me.

"We're taking one of the back exits to Natalie," he says, "she's not far from—"

Something bursts through the wall right next to us, knocking Finn to the ground, taking me with him. Finn loses his grip and I roll out of his arms, stopping several feet from the damaged wall where a big hole has be blasted out.

Dust and fine pieces of debris fill the air, making it almost impossible to breathe. I can hear Finn's muffled coughs but the dust is too thick for me to see further than my own hands. A sudden flicker of movement by the opened wall catches my attention. We're not alone. Annette's minions finally caught up.

I look behind me and see a blurry red light hovering above. The exit sign. Somehow I've been thrown closer to the exit. I still have time to run before the dust completely settles to reveal my location. I push myself up slowly and quietly, hoping the pursuer can't see me just yet.

A horrible cry erupts just when I begin to inch toward the exit.

Finn!

I press my lips together so I don't give away my position. But it proves to be useless. I can already see the outlines of two figures, five feet from me, which means they can see me too.

Another terrible groan comes out of Finn and this time I see the source of his pain. I almost don't believe my eyes. A half human, half machine thing is electrocuting him with its mechanical arm. If it's not for his exposed face, I'd think it's purely a robot with silver and black metal components protruding from its body. I've never seen anything like it.

Without thinking, I leap forward but only to be met by its other robotic arm. Its punch sends me flying until my back hits the exit door with a painful thud. Whatever that things is, it's inhumanly strong, and huge. Finn, who's being held up by his neck like a limp doll, only goes up to its chest. Before I can get my bearing, the thing tosses Finn over its shoulder and storms down the hallway, away from me.

CHAPTER 40

I stay frozen in place, alone, in a long hallway with a blasted wall. I can't comprehend what just happened. If it isn't for the debris on the ground, I'd thought I just had another hallucination. But why? Why would the cyborg abduct Finn instead of me? Maybe it wasn't sent by Annette. Did Marko send it? I highly doubt it. From what I understand, the Neuronics don't have the resources or the technology to create such a nasty beast.

I sit there, still at the spot where I was tossed, dumbfounded. I lean back and suddenly remember I'm right beside the exit. And Natalie is right outside, waiting for me.

I get up, hands on the door handle but something is preventing me from opening that door. Something from within is tugging me toward where the cyborg took Finn.

Why should I care? I ask that invisible force inside me. He lied to me. He used me. He toyed with my emotions. If anything, I want him to suffer.

But can you live with yourself knowing that Finn might get killed. Do I hate him so much that I want him dead?

Yes.

But as much as I hate him, I also love him, despite how much I loathe myself for it. I know I can't bear to see him dead.

It could be a trap. Annette apparently is a master at it.

But what if it's not? What if this is something new? Something that even Annette doesn't know about?

I squeeze my head with my hands, completely overpowered by the dilemma. But time is ticking and I need to make a decision now. Leave or go after Finn?

I take a deep breath, tighten the straps of my medical robe around the waist and run back to where we came from. I know I'm going to regret this later but I'm not a coward. This is not my first time running into traps anyway. Bring it on.

I follow the path that Finn and I just took and find myself in Recruitment. There's no sign of Finn or the cyborg anywhere. Where could they have gone? I wonder if anyone heard the loud blast? If so, there should be Cores investigating as we speak but the place is totally empty. Just when I'm about to leave, a hand taps my shoulder. I swing my fist around. Kyle catches it just before I hit his nose.

"Shh.... it's just me." He whispers even though there's no one around.

"Don't ever do that!" I scowl.

"Sorry. But you need to come with me," he says, eyes studying my dotted scalp. "Those bloody bastards." He mumbles under his breath, not really talking to me.

I ignore his concern, even though I do appreciate it deep down. "Finn's been kidnapped." I speak without as much emotion as possible.

Shock flashes across Kyle's eyes. "What? By who?"

"A cyborg, half human, half machine of some sort. Have you seen anything like that?"

Kyle shakes his head while searching his mind. "That's impossible. Where did it come from? Why would it take Finn?"

From Kyle's perplexed look, the possibility that Annette is

behind this is becoming less likely, which makes it imperative that we find Finn.

"We have to find him. That thing was strong. Too strong even for Finn."

Kyle contemplates for a moment, then determination appears on his face. "Then come with me. I have to prepare you."

I don't know what he means by 'prepare me' but I trust him. He's the only person who has yet to lie to me.

Kyle leads me into an adjacent room where the Recruitment team works. He then tints all the windows so no one can see through. He sits me down on the floor, doesn't even bother with the chairs.

"Listen, I know you're injured," Kyle's eyes fall on my head again, a flash of anger ignites behind those eyes, "that's why you need this if you want to help Finn and get out of here alive." He produces a syringe containing a murky yellow serum. Not waiting for me to ask, he continues, "It's a gene booster. I stole it from R&D. It will temporarily boost your potential, increasing your power exponentially."

I take the syringe from Kyle's hand and look him in the eye.

He knows what I'm thinking, "I know we are the last people you'd want to trust after what they've done to you." He lowers his head in shame, unable to match my stare anymore. "I should have gotten you out the minute I met you. I failed your parents. I failed you."

"Hey," I put a hand on his slumped shoulder. "The whole world has been lying to me, but I can tell you're different. I don't know how to explain this, but . . . I can sort of see my dad in you. And I think *that* is a pretty good instinct to trust."

He grabs my empty hand and squeezes it in his. "I promise I *will* get you out. No matter what. Now the serum might make you disoriented for a bit, and I don't know exactly how long the effect lasts. It's different on everyone. So we need to hurry."

Without hesitation, I plunge the syringe into my vein. The drug kicks in almost immediately, blurring my vision. Then the world teeters like the night when I had three glasses of wine. I bury my face in my palms and it feels a little better. But not for long. A rush of heat ignites inside me, like the time I released my Sarcomere potential, but ten times the intensity. I fall onto my side, shaking and panting with beads of sweat running down my face. I hear Kyle's voice but he's far far away. I open my eyes and see strings of images laced together. Numerous neurons and axons intertwine, like I'm floating inside someone's brain. This goes on for minutes, or maybe hours. Then as suddenly as it began, the awful sensation disappears, taking all my aches and pain with it. My muscles suddenly feel like they're ready for a thousand push-ups. My mind has never been more clear and alert. Like someone has dusted off the hardware and upgraded the system.

"How are you feeling?" Kyle strokes my back gently. It reminds me of how my dad used to stroke my back to get me to sleep. I miss this. I miss him.

"I'm ready." I wipe the sweat off my face.

"Not quite." Kyle walks across the room, opens a drawer and takes out a set of clothes. A black t-shirt and a pair of green khakis, the Sarcomere's signature outfit. He then opens another drawer and produces a pistol and a small dagger. "Every room has contingency weapons"

I change out of my flimsy robe and strap on the weapons while Kyle waits outside the room. I open the door and he welcomes me with a proud smile. "*Now* you're ready."

We decide that I'll check Trousing Hall while Kyle will check the other wings for signs of Finn and the cyborg. He tries to urge me to just take Natalie and leave and he'll look for Finn himself. But I know there's no way he can take on the cyborg alone. I'm not even confident if I can fight that thing *with* the gene booster. But this is something I have to do. At least to the point where I know Finn is safe. My conscience is firing at me for being stupid; for trying to save someone who broke my heart into pieces. And my conscience is right. I can't justify what I'm doing here but I just need to know if Finn is safe.

I step into Trousing Hall from the north corridor where the elevator shaft and the stage are located. A sense of unease rises within me when I see all the lights are off. Trousing Hall never sleeps. But tonight, even the holograms of past chiefs are turned off, leaving the place in absolute darkness. The moon is hiding behind layers of clouds, rendering the skylight useless as well.

I stand still where the corridor opens up into the hall and listen. Not a single sound can be heard. For all I know, Finn and his captor could be standing right in the middle of the great hall and I wouldn't be able to tell.

As I plan my next course of action, something silvery flashes in the hall, near one of the plinths that support the hologram. I stare straight ahead, eyes focused on the general area of where I think I saw the flash of silver. Just when I doubt what I saw, there it is again, a quick movement of silver metal. Just like the robotic body of the cyborg.

I dash forward with my gun ready. As soon as I get to the middle of the hall, all the lights suddenly come on at once. I shield my eyes with my arm and that's when someone crashes into my back. I fall forward onto my knees, bruising both my knee caps on the hard stone floor. My gun flies out of my hand and slides across the smooth floor.

I scramble to my feet as quickly as I can but a circle of Sarcs already has me surrounded. Another trap indeed. Now the notion of Annette sending the cyborg to fake Finn's abduction becomes undeniable. Maybe the electrocution and the choking were staged as well, to make me really believe that Finn was in danger.

I stare at the floor, shaking my head. I can't believe I get tricked into their little game again and again. I begin to suspect that invisible force tugging deep inside me, pulling me toward Finn, is planted by Annette. Why else can you explain the willingness to go into enemy territory to save another enemy?

"I knew you'd come running." Annette's voice rings loud and clear in the great hall as if she's speaking through a microphone, so everyone can hear their queen.

I look up at the little balcony above the palatial stage where Annette stands with her hands on the railing. Her fitted red dress is the colour of blood.

"Admit it, you'll always have a soft spot in your heart for our Elite commander. Doesn't matter how much he broke your heart, doesn't matter how disgusted he is with you, he has seeped into your heart like poison, hasn't he?" she smiles wickedly.

I wish there's something I can say, some nasty words that I can toss back to her face. But I have nothing. She's right and she knows it. No matter now bad he has hurt me. I still can't get him out of my mind. I can't imagine how disgusted he must have felt to be forced to kiss someone he didn't love. I try not to think about it because the heartache is too much to bear; like someone is reaching inside me and squeezing my heart until it bursts.

"So why do you still struggle Kazumi?" Annette's voice softens like she feels sorry for me or something. "You know there's nothing out there for you. So why not do something useful with your life before it ends? You are half Sarc, after all. You have the obligation to protect the world. With a little sacrifice, *you* can build the strongest Sarcomeres we've ever seen. We just need your genes, your invaluable and rare genes." Annette's almost begging now.

Maybe she has a point. There's nothing out there for me. No one needs me. No one cares. So what if they experiment on me a little? If my genes can help the future Sarcomere population, maybe it's worth it.

I slowly, solemnly scan the hall, passing my eyes along faces that I recognize and those I don't. I see the Elites. They are scattered among the crowd, minus Finn. Most of the Sarcs skirt my eyes when I look at them, like they're afraid of me, or maybe even disgusted by me. I don't know anymore.

In the far right corner, a familiar face appears. My heart sinks when my eyes land on her shadow-covered face. Drenched in sorrow and pain, Celine looks broken. The happy and hopeful soul in her is gone; torn apart by the Neuronics . . . by me.

I want to tell her how sorry I am; how I'd go back in time to make things right if I could. But her seething gaze tells me that our short-lived friendship is over. She hates me now. Just like everyone else in this hall.

I close my eyes as tears threaten to fall. I was once a trained assassin—focused, strong-minded. But ever since I embraced my Sarcomere side, I have fallen weak, cowardly even. All because of emotions I've never had to deal with before: love, sympathy, guilt, shame. Altogether they have consumed me. They've shrivelled me into a ball of hopelessness.

As I'm about to tell Annette that she can use me anyway

she wants, I suddenly remember what Kyle said to me in the storage room the night of Celine's wedding. *"Your parents tried to protect you, to prevent you from being made into a weapon. . ."*

The word *weapon* echoes in my head long after the memory has faded. It keeps ringing in my ear like an alarm.

Just like being slapped across the face, I realize how stupid I've been. Annette would be unstoppable if she gets my Neuronic genes. My power should *never* be in the hands of people like her. She's corrupted. She talks big but her ulterior motive is dark and evil. My parents knew, that was why they had to hide me from the world. If my guess is right, the cyborg was probably created by her. Finn's abduction may be fake but the cyborg was as real as it can be. I can't imagine the destruction she'd cause if she finds the key to my hybrid power. No. I can never let that happen.

The thought that I had almost given up sickens me. How could I be so stupid? Even if I was in a complete trance, clouded by emotions, it was still disturbing to know how easily I could have given up.

I straighten up with my head held high, looking right at her. "You're nothing but a manipulative devil. You already have your little creation. It's far more destructive than what I can offer. In fact, even your Elite commander had a good beating from the abomination *you* created. So why do you still need me?"

Whispers begin to form in the crowd. Apparently they have no clue about the cyborg. Even the Elites look somewhat confused.

"Why don't you tell your people what kind of a monster you've created." The faint mumbling erupts into full on questioning among the Sarcs. "Better yet, show them." I taunt, hoping she'd actually reveal the cyborg. A small part of me still wishes the abduction was real. If so, forcing Annette to address the situation might give me hints of Finn's whereabouts.

"People!" Annette appears a bit flustered now, but she's too clever for her blind subjects. They will trust her no matter what. "Do you actually believe a word coming out of this Neuronic spy? She was sent here to kill us! I gave her a chance because of the Sarcomere in her, but looks like I was wrong to do so. Elites, seize her! I need her alive!"

Together, the eight Elites step out from the shadows. Samantha, being the first one in the pack, throws a dagger at me. I dodge with ease. My muscles pulsate under my skin, like they're excited for a fight. We'll see if this serum is as good as Kyle claimed it to be.

Seeing that she missed, Samantha is more determined to take me down. After all this time, she still hates me for no reason. She rushes in with her long sword aiming at my shoulder. I rotate my body at the last second and knee her in the waist. She grunts but regains her footing immediately. She slashes at me again and this time I kick her with full force, right in her stomach. She flies back a dozen feet then sprawls on the floor, still conscious but barely. The boost serum does work wonders.

I turn to face the other Elites just in time to see Nick firing his gun at me. My body moves instinctively from the gun kata training, dodging the incoming bullet by less than an inch. Someone yelps behind me then the sound of a body collapsing sends everyone into a frenzy. Nick watches in horror as his bullet hits a fellow Sarc in the torso. I feel a pang of guilt as I watch the injured Sarc being carried away. But I have no time to be sentimental as the entire group of Elites pounces on me at once—daggers and swords sweeping left and right. To my surprise, the serum not only makes me stronger but faster also. None of them can match my speed. Not even veterans like

Murray, Bridget and Benji. Despite my increased ability, there are still seven of them against one of me. My arms and legs have been nicked a few times during the close-quarter melee but nothing major that can slow me down.

Frustrated with them ganging up on me, I steal Kayden's sword in a flurry of punches and use it to parry off their subsequent attacks. I send Kayden flying with my helicopter kick so he's out of the way for now. Since he was one of the few Sarcs who was actually nice to me, I decided to go easy on him.

Next Bridget and Lilly come at me with their blades. I catch Bridget's eyes before her sword can reach me and both her and Lilly fall to the ground like puppets who got their strings cut off. Shocked at what I just did, I can only think of one reason. The serum. It must have amplified my neuronal transmission to nearby bodies. Hence I was able to take down Lilly when Bridget was the one I actually extend my mind into.

Elation and triumph wash over me as I realize this is the first time in a long time that I feel comfortable in my own skin. If only the effect can last forever.

Not only the remaining Elites are taken aback by what they just witnessed, disbelief is etched on every single face in the audience. Even Annette seems a bit unnerved.

"I don't want to fight you guys." I speak loud and clear to the Elites. "My business is with her." I point to the regal queen on her pedestal, who has retreated to the back of the balcony. She tries not to show it but I know she's scared at this point. She knows the Elites won't be able to stop me.

"You won't get near her as long as we're still breathing." Murray says with a clenched jaw. But he's smart enough to glower at my lips instead of my eyes.

What a bunch of stubborn meatheads. How can they not see that their chief is manipulating them. I'm getting impatient at this taunting back and forth. If I have to take them down then so be it. I ready the sword I took from Kayden, who is now among his teammates. As I'm about to charge, a loud clank stops me mid-stride, like metal hitting stone. Then a mechanical arm magically slides out from behind one of the hologram stands and into the middle of the hall, just steps from us. Everyone swivels their head to the direction of where the arm appeared. I can only hear faint muffles in the general direction at first. Then the group of bystanders begin to part, opening a small gap for someone to pass through. I gasp as soon as the person's face comes out from behind the crowd. The blood-soaked man half walks and half limps toward us, leaving a crimson trail in his wake. My hand shakes and I drop the sword, half wanting to run to Finn but the other half wants to run to Annette and rip her head off. I was wrong. The abduction wasn't an act to trick me. By the look of Finn's condition, he barely survived that thing.

I can't believe she sent a cyborg to kill her adopted son. What kind of a cold-blooded monster would do that? I turn my head to the witch, whose eyes are glued to Finn, filled with concern and anger. But I know she's not concerned about his well-being but her own little secret being revealed in front of everybody.

Even the Elites are in utter shock to see their leader so beaten up. Murray drops his weapon and runs to support Finn by the shoulder. "Who did this to you?" he asks, anger is evident in his voice.

Finn answers by looking up at Annette, eyes seething and fists clenched. Murray and the Elites follow Finn's gaze, confused.

Finn reaches me with Murray by his side but the glance we exchange is quick and awkward. Mostly for me. I suddenly feel embarrassed, or nervous. I don't know but I look away before any emotion was shown. He's still the guy who manipulated me. He's still the guy who I want to hate but can't.

Someone finally breaks the silence, "Finn, speak! What happened?" Bridget asks.

Finn backs away from Murray so he's no longer being supported and leans forward, hands on his knees. He coughs and a couple drops of blood splash onto the white marble floor, which incidentally reminds me of what Annette looks like right now in her blood-red dress standing against the white stone balcony.

Before his teammates can say anything, Finn puts one hand up to stop them. Seeing him like this breaks my heart. But I need to remind myself that he's not the Finn I thought I knew.

Finn inches forward and picks up the mechanical arm that surely was broken off from the cyborg I saw earlier. Finn has defeated it. He holds the arm toward Annette and says, "What do you have to say about this?"

Annette lifts her chin, folds her arms and thinks for a moment. I can't quite make out her facial expression from where I stand but I can only guess that sneaky mind of hers must be churning to come up with a good answer.

After a long moment, she finally says, "Finnegan, you disappoint me," her voice flat but loud enough for everyone to hear. "Of all people, the leader of the Elites should know better than to dawdle on a single tree, an important tree I agree, but still a minute prospect when compared to the wellness of the whole forest."

"Don't change the subject," Finn replies, "tell me, is this your doing?" He shakes the metal arm to emphasize his point.

The Elites look more perplexed now than ever; they don't know that Finn tried to rescue me from the despicable experiment, they have no idea who injured their commander, and now a mechanical arm appears out of nowhere.

"What the bloody hell is going on here?" Benji asks. The Elites are finally getting impatient.

Hushed conversations break out in the crowd, most of whom are Cores. The chief is losing control of the situation and she knows it. She walks forward so she's almost leaning on the railing again, showing her full face. Her guileful eyes survey everyone slowly, then they fall on Finn.

"I was hoping to teach you a lesson, a small punishment if you will, for betraying me," says Annette.

The Elites all turn to Finn, brows creased in wonderment.

"I can't just stand there and watch you torture her like that." Finn throws the arm back onto the floor. "She technically has done nothing to us." Annette's about to interject but Finn doesn't give her the chance. "Yes, she's a Neuronic. Yes, she was sent here to kill but did she actually harm any of us? She's also half Sarcomere, which means she can be a part of us. In fact—" he walks forward so he's closer to Annette. "She would've sided with us if you didn't experiment on her like a worthless rat."

A concoction of mixed feelings trickle down my throat. First is warmth spreading to my heart, but it doesn't take long for bitterness and anger to take over. I question Finn's sincerity. Why is he trying so hard to defend me? Even to a point where he's deemed a traitor? What's his motive?

"You have no idea what wins war, all of you," Annette's voice loud and harsh. "Man power, Finnegan. How are we to sustain our kind when half of us can't even fight? She can change that," pointing at me, "if we can unlock her genes. Imagine when we don't need to be afraid of the Neuronics anymore. No more hiding in mountains and places thousands of miles from civilization."

I hate to admit it but she does have a point. From what I can gather, the Neuronics are getting stronger, especially with their younger generations. But the Sarcomeres don't really have much going on for them. Other than the handful of Elites who can post an actual threat to their enemy, the Cores are just like the Neuronic infantry—easily destroyable. Then there's the Touches who can't even fight. And the scariest part, I might actually be willing to help them if Annette hadn't revealed their manipulative scheme. I'm now glad that I know the truth, so I don't blindly sacrifice myself for a lie.

Finn shakes his head, looking better now that his healing kicked in. "You can say what you want but I'm getting Kazumi out of here one way or another."

Listening to them talk about me like I'm a damsel in distress is really getting on my nerves. Whether I choose to live or die, it's *my* decision to make, not theirs.

"Stop!" I scream at Finn. Having heard enough. "If I want to get out of here, I can easily achieve that without *your* help. And if I want to stay and be her lab rat, that's *my* choice. So don't pretend you're a hero. You're just a liar. A heartless liar!"

A prick of hurt touches Finn's eyes. "You don't have to like me or trust me, but I'm getting you out and that's final," he says firmly.

"No you're not." I retort, suddenly feeling defensive. "You stay here and do what she asks, since you're so good at being a mama's boy."

Without waiting for a response, I turn and head for the main entrance.

"Stop her!" Annette screams from her pedestal.

"Whoever tries will have to go through me." Finn says behind me.

I don't look back, I just keep walking. If anyone gets in my way, they will get a taste of the boosting serum, which is still running strong in my bloodstream.

I don't hear anything for a few more steps, then hell breaks loose when a thundering thump resonates in the hall, shaking the ground under me.

Curiosity peaks. I turn around and see two massive figures standing side by side in front of the stage. Crumbled marble under their feet. I don't recognize them but the two men seem inhumanly large. Dressed in black leathery bodysuits with knee-high boots and gauntlet gloves, there's not a hint of mechanical attachments present. I'm not even sure if they're the same creatures as the cyborg Finn fought. I have a bad feeling about this. Seems like Annette has built an entire army behind everyone's back—using Ordinaries. The giants' soulless eyes and unfocused gaze look just like the Neuronic infantry, which tells me their minds are being controlled. But how?

I can't see the Elites' expressions with their backs toward me but their rigid stance and balled fists indicate tension. They're just as anxious as everyone else.

"What have you done?" Murray says incredulously. His voice so quiet that I think it is said more in exasperation than as an actual question.

"They're our future," Annette says proudly. "Genetically enhanced and technologically reinforced to my liking. Most importantly, they will *never* betray me."

"So you kidnapped some Ordinaries and turned them into cyborgs?" Benji yells in disgust.

"Of course not," she raises a finger. "They're volunteers. They were fascinated by our strength and were willing to sacrifice just a bit of freedom in exchange for power. Power they could never gain otherwise."

"Then you are no different than the Neuronics!" says Finn through gritted teeth.

"Do you know why I designed them?" Annette asks, but she doesn't wait for a response. "It's because I knew . . . I knew you'd betray me one day. And look, it's happening right now."

I can't believe Annette just said that in front of everyone. If I were Finn, I'd go up there right now and show her what real betrayal looks like. But I know Finn loves his people more than himself, and his loyalty will never let him harm the chief no matter how evil she is.

"Then what about us?" says Murray. "Do you also think that we'll betray you one day?"

Annette thinks for a second, her face relaxing a bit. "I never wanted to believe that. But at the end of the day, we're only human. We're prone to corruption. I'm the chief. I'm responsible for all of you. It's my obligation to do *whatever* I can to protect you, to protect our future."

Once again, I can't believe my ears. If the Elites weren't betraying her before, the statement she just made might have given them the desire to.

Finn ignores her, or at least he pretends to, and turns to the crowd, "Fellow Sarcs," he begins, voice boomingly loud, "please know that me saving Kazumi is not an act of defiance. I'm simply honouring the true meaning of being a Sarcomere. And it certainly does *not* involve torturing and creating abominations for one's own agenda. If any of you are ever in trouble, I'd be there in a heartbeat. But today, I must do what's right."

The reaction from the crowd is mixed; some seem to agree with Finn, having seen Annette's true facade, but others are more scared than anything. Their expressions are of unease and confusion—like they're torn between two sides.

"Then you leave me with no choice but to convict you of

treason. Anyone who sides with him will be convicted of the same crime." She pauses, letting the message sink in. The Elites offer nothing but silence. "That's what I thought. Ultimates, take them down!"

At once, the two giants launch toward us in blinding speed. Finn pushes me aside and meets them head on with his katana. I look over to the Elites who are just gawking at the battle, with no intention to help.

Meanwhile, Finn is fighting two to one, which in most cases is a walk in the park for him. But seeing how the Ultimates fight, I'm not so sure if he can win this one easily. Their speed and skills are just as good if not better. On top of that, their leather-like bodysuits seem impenetrable. Finn's katana has nipped, sliced, and stabbed, but none of the strikes could penetrate that stubborn material.

Standing midway between the action and the main entrance, I can't decide if I should help Finn or take this opportunity to escape. If I just leave, it'd make my grand speech about how I can escape without his help a pile of rubbish. But more importantly, the Ultimates or whatever she calls them, might actually kill him. Annette seems angry and crazy enough to let that happen.

Frustrated, Finn quickly changes his tactic to target their exposed faces, but his sword can't even get close enough before it's blocked by their leathery arms. One of the giants gets a hold of Finn's hand and twists it violently. The katana drops to the floor with a loud clank. But Finn's other hand is already on the holster from which he pulls out his pistol and aims at the man's head. The first shot hits the man right in the chest, but the bullet ricochets off of the bodysuit like it was a marble.

Finn fires again, just inches from the Ultimate's face this time. The giant bends his neck almost simultaneously, dodging the shot like it was nothing.

A collective gasp sounds through out the hall. That was impossible. The man just dodged the bullet with perfection, like he's practiced this maneuver a million times. Even Finn's gun kata can't guarantee success when the shot is fired at point blank. I can't begin to imagine the amount of modification Annette did to these poor Ordinaries. They don't even look human anymore. Are they still in there? Or are they merely skeletons donned in fancy battle gear?

Finn gets distracted for a second by what his opponent just pulled, but that gives the second Ultimate more than enough time to deliver a disastrous blow to his torso, knocking him backward. Finn tumbles and slides to a stop, twenty feet from where he was hit.

I dash toward the Ultimate. The earlier idea of escaping a fleeting thought. The man notices me and turns to look at me.

Perfect.

I extend my mind into his soulless eyes and beyond. Instead of being greeted by his subconsciousness, I plunge into a massive abyss—like I've opened a door expecting a room on the other side, but instead I fall into a bottomless dark pit.

How can this be? Where are his thoughts and memories?

Terrified, I try to pull back but the neuronal path I entered from is no longer there. I have no footing nor steadiness; it's like free falling indefinitely while being blindfolded.

I desperately search for a way out but the devastating sense of doom drags me deeper into the dark void, rapidly overpowering my mind. As my consciousness slowly fades, a glimpse of diminishing light appears in the distance.

That's the path that will lead you out. Focus on it! I will myself to think. But the light is fast fleeting. With the last ounce of will power, I desperately chase after it; what seems to be my only chance to salvation.

CHAPTER 41

After spending what seemed like eternity in the oppressive black hole, I finally manage to retreat from the mindless Ultimate and step back into reality where doom also awaits. As soon as I regain consciousness, the burning in my lungs and the crushing pain around my neck make me almost wish I hadn't come back. The Ultimate has been throttling me, clearly not affected by my psychic invasion.

During my struggle, I manage to glance at his unusual armour. The bodysuit actually protrudes from under his skin, showing a faint scale-like pattern that reminds me of a reptile's hide.

I grab the man's arm above his gauntlet with both hands and the rough yet flexible material exfoliates my palms. I tense up all my muscles, elated that the effect of the serum has yet to fade, and lift my dangling legs to kick him in the gut. The force knocks the man off balance and I free myself from his iron grip. Then I notice something disturbing—the man felt no pain. A kick like that would have at least caused him some serious bruising if not fractured ribs. But he shows no sign of any discomfort. He's back on my heels before I can pull enough air into my starved lungs.

Out of nowhere Murray appears between me and the scaly

man, with a machine gun in his hands. He fires instantly, bullet shells spraying around me. For the next ten gruelling seconds, I can hear nothing other than Murray's gunfire. When he finally stops, the entire hall lapses into a silence that feels odd in my ears, like I can still hear the blasting of the gun even though the magazine has been emptied.

Ten feet ahead, the black figure crouches on the ground, still as a rock. My heart seems to have stopped beating. I can't move or breathe. All I can do is stare at the supposedly dead Ultimate and hope he doesn't get up.

Five seconds pass. Then ten.

Just when I'm releasing a breath of relief, the black leather-clad man slowly lifts his head, face still blank.

In front of me, Murray lets out a litany of swear words, then charges right into the still crouched Ultimate.

Far to my left are Finn and the other one engaging in the most intriguing fight yet. Their speed and fluidity are displayed to perfection, a fully captivating scene. I could stand here and study their moves all day if this wasn't a life-or-death situation.

Now that Murray has come to Finn's aid, this is no longer my fight. The main entrance is not far behind me, and with the serum still pumping strong, I'm sure no one can stop me if I make a run for it. But that's not my plan.

I turn to the source of the chaos, who's perched high up on her throne, fiercely staring at the battle below. Without delay, I climb onto the nearest hologram pedestal and leap onto the third floor balcony that connects to the dais where Annette currently stands. The climb is surprisingly easy, like my body weight has been halved while my strength has doubled. I've never been so exhilarated. I can almost feel my muscles pulsing, telling me they crave more action.

I run along the balcony toward Annette, who's eyes are tracking my every move now. But she doesn't look concerned that I'm coming for her. Maybe she doesn't know that I'm under the boosting serum. Either way, I will seize the opportunity. I lock my eyes on hers and reach out with my mind.

"Do you really think I'm this careless?" A voice welcomes me as I enter her mind. I ignore the taunt and focus on the intrusion. But it doesn't matter how much I will my thoughts, I can't go further than the first threshold, as if her mind is secured by an iron gate.

The voice laughs. *"Oh Kazumi, you have no idea who you're dealing with."*

The next thing I know, I'm being shunted back into my own head; like an invisible hand has grabbed a hold of my consciousness, yanked it out of Annette's head, and shoved it back into mine.

I stand there disoriented, halfway between Annette Trousing and the spot I climbed onto. This is impossible. The most a Sarc can do is slow down our intrusion with some mental training but this . . .

Who *is* she?

I glower at her, boiling with rage and curiosity. She's not a normal Sarc, she can't be. For a split second, I suspect she's an hybrid just like me, but she denied that possibility with a strong distaste back in the lab. She could be lying though. Whatever she is, she's more menacing and dangerous than I ever thought.

With a loud bang, the door crashes open at the other end of the hallway and a sea of blue rushes in. I reinforce the energy shield around me just in time to deflect the first waves of bullets.

Cores, they should know by now the limits of their weapons. Telekinetically, I grab hold of their guns and send them flying over the balcony. A clamour of metal hitting stone echoes down below, followed by a few surprised shouts.

The weaponless Cores gape at me, frozen in their position. I take the opportunity to induce a coma into a man closest to me and this time four others around him fall to the floor. I feel like this is almost too good to be true. A serum like this can make an army ten times stronger. Why didn't they use it during the attack back in the Rockies?

Several guys in the back turn and flee, thinking their comrades just got killed by a look from me. Technically, I *can* kill them with my mind if I choose to but it'll take too long and consume much more energy—something I can't afford to do when faced with a whole army. The remaining Cores just stand there, looking like lost puppies. They're too proud to just run away but too scared to confront me again. I suddenly feel a little sorry for them.

I ignore them and turn back to where Annette is. But these stubborn Cores are just too dumb to take a hint. I feel the disturbance in my energy field as they shoot at me from behind. With a grunt, I whip around, pissed that I didn't confiscate all their guns earlier. Step by step, I press on toward them. One guy looks at me. I shake my head in disappointment. These Cores are not very smart, are they?

Five more collapse in a coma.

I pick up a gun dropped by one of the Cores and that's when the rest of them scramble out of the door from which they busted through.

I look over to the dais and it's now empty. Annette is no longer there. I curse under my breath at the damn Cores who ruined my chance to capture Annette.

I search every corridor and every room on the third floor to no avail. She could be anywhere by now. That sneaky coward.

Feeling defeated, I climb back down to where the battle is, not bothering with the stairs or elevator. Finn has already sustained several deep cuts. Blood is streaming down his bare arms and a few wet patches soak his shirt. The fact that he was injured earlier put him at a disadvantage to begin with. Fatigue has already crept into his muscles, slowing him down considerably. But he seems to be holding his own, for now. Murray on the other hand, is not looking so good. His face is so bloody that I'm surprised he can see. Yet their teammates are nowhere to be seen. These so-called Elites are nothing but Annette's spineless puppets. So are the rest of the crowd actually, standing on the sideline, too afraid to stray from their chief's orders.

Just then, Murray gets slashed on his leg, dark crimson liquid spews onto the white marble. I'm about to help when a sword slides to my feet. I pick it up and quickly look in the direction it came from. Kayden discreetly dips his head in the crowd. I am grateful for the weapon, but this is no doubt a cowardly move. If he's concerned about his leader, he should have joined the fight himself and not hide in the shadow.

I get to the Ultimate just in time to parry off a deadly strike that would have killed Murray. He mumbles something to me but I'm too preoccupied to listen. I punch and kick at the Ultimate but my attack can only push him back several steps to give Murray a chance to heal.

Feeling irritated that I gain no ground on this thing, I decide to try something. I continue to press onward with my sword, forcing the Ultimate to move back inch by inch, toward a pedestal. When his back is close enough to the silver stand, I leap past him onto it. Once my legs get a firm hold on the heavy steel, I push off and jump right on top of him. Thanks to the serum, my speed surpasses his.

I'm now sitting on his shoulders with his neck between my thighs. Not expecting to be so up close and personal, the Ultimate thrashes left and right while beating my legs with his iron-like fists. His damn scaly skin is too slippery, making it impossible to hold him steady enough to shoot.

Like riding a bull on steroids, the violent shaking jerks my spine in every direction possible. The crowd and the hall blur together like a swirl of objects moving in light speed.

Just before I get completely thrown off, my fingers come across two holes and I hook right into them. The Ultimate yelps as I pull on his nostrils with all my might. Using this brief moment of control, I pull out a dagger hidden in my heel and jab it right between his eyes.

Both of us collapse onto the floor, with one still breathing, barely.

Kyle suddenly appears by my side. *When did he get here? I had almost forgotten about him.*

I try to inflate my crushed lungs with air but every breath hurts, though not as much as my legs.

"Hold still," says Kyle.

"What?" I prop myself up and see that he's wrapping my left thigh with a rag.

"Don't look," he says. Then he tugs on the rag.

I scream in pain. It's so bad that I can't even tell where the pain is coming from. Every body part hurts.

"There, this should stop the bleeding for now," Kyle says, wiping his hands on his pants, leaving smears of red. "You're lucky he didn't stab you in the femoral artery."

I brush away a layer of sweat on my forehead and sit up. The world seems to tilt left and right, but I regain my equilibrium soon after. The sharp pain is replaced by a deep, dull ache. Still painful but manageable.

The dead Ultimate lies beside me. His expression not so different than when he was alive. He would have been a handsome man. What made him so desperate to agree to such a horrible transformation? Or maybe he was forced into it. The Sarcs will believe whatever Annette tells them.

"FINN!" Kyle suddenly yells, making me almost jump out of my own skin.

My eyes follow him as he runs toward two slumped figures on the other side of the hall. My heart races as fast as Kyle's running steps. He pushes what hopefully is a dead Ultimate aside to reveal a body underneath it. I don't need to see his face to know the unresponsive body curled up in a fetal position belongs to the Elite commander. Murray, who can barely walk, drags himself to Finn. Together with Kyle, they turn him over.

I prepare myself for the worst when Kyle and Murray frantically try to revive him. Time stops as I stare at his lifeless body and everything ceases to exist. A hundred images flash before my eyes—good ones, bad ones, but all contain Finn's beautiful face, alive and brilliant.

No, he can't die like this. I still haven't make him pay for what he did to me. He can't die until I let him.

A rush of adrenaline pushes my body forward. One arm after another, I drag myself toward him. My body feels heavy, too heavy for a petite girl like me, but I'm determined. I have to wake him with whatever it takes. He can't die . . . he just can't.

Just ten more feet to go. I crawl and drag, biting on my lips to distract myself from the pain. But before I can close the gap between us, a crowd of legs hurries in, blocking my path and my view. All I can see are black columns with dashes of red here and there.

The other Elites.

I can't tell whether they're here to gloat or to help, but either way, I loathe them. Finn wouldn't be like this if they helped.

No. I won't allow him to die. He better be breathing because if he's not, these cowards will pay. I will make sure of that.

Before I can push my way through, a gap opens up among the legs and I see Finn, sitting up with Murray's help.

Skepticism hits.

Is he really alive or am I seeing things? I've learned not to believe the first thing I see, for it is usually a deception. Seeing Finn sitting there may very well be a trick my mind is playing with me, knowing deep down how much I want him alive.

I remain skeptical until his eyes meet mine, then I know it is really him. Our gaze lingers, then I'm the one to look away first, feeling embarrassed . . . or angry? I don't know. I don't know how I should react. I want to smile because he's alive. I want to yell at him because he scared the crap out of me. But then I also want to punch him in the face. Can't bring myself to do any of that, I just stare at the floor.

"Valiant effort, I must say." It's Annette's voice again, coming from behind.

Everyone looks to the front entrance and there she is, in her blood-red outfit. Surrounding her are nine new Ultimates covered in the same black, leathery scales, protecting the one tiny ruby that is their creator. But that's not it. As the nine black figures begin to spread out, a tenth one appears from behind his comrades. This one looks exactly like the one that abducted Finn, except he has both of his mechanical arms, which means Annette has made more than one of these hideous cyborg beasts.

I exhale and feel the life source being sucked out of me, like a deflating balloon shrivelling into nothing but rubbery skin. It took all three of us to bring down two regular Ultimates, and it almost took Finn's life defeating a mechanical one. How are we to face ten more when we're barely alive?

"Elites, be smart and do the right thing," Annette says. "You don't want to end up like them." Tilting her head at Finn and I.

"You're the one who's not being smart," Murray says, "what you're doing right now is only pushing us further and further away."

"Speak for yourself. I'm sure your teammates still have a sense of loyalty in them."

"This is ridiculous." I recognize Bridget's voice. "We're fighting each other now? Is that who we are now, huh? For a girl who happens to be a hybrid? Your so-called Ultimates have done more harm to us than she *ever* did. So for God's sake just let her go!"

I search for the voice and see Bridget standing next to Finn, supporting him on her shoulders.

"Just because we're helping our commander doesn't mean we're not loyal." It's Kayden's turn to speak up. His teammate's courage has rubbed off on him.

Annette looks into each of their eyes then says, "Is this what all of you think?"

There's a brief silence. Then a young boy says, "I've got nothing to do with this. I'll be in my apartment if you need me."

Liam. Always indifferent. Always uncaring.

"Sorry . . . but she's the chief." Samantha half whispers to the group, then walks away with Liam. Her decision on the other hand, doesn't surprise me.

A wicked smile spreads cross Annette's face. "I'm glad loyalty and respect are not completely lost in our Elite Force."

She gives Liam and Samantha an approving nod then turns back to us. "I'm very proud of myself right now, you know why? Because this here . . ." she makes a circle with her index finger, "is *exactly* why I created the Ultimates in the first place. And it proves to be the *best* decision I've ever made."

Looks like Annette just took the last bit of the Elite's loyalty to her, shredded it into a thousand pieces, and scattered them into the Gulf of Alaska.

"Finn, are you able to run?" Bridget whispers.

"I'm good. What do you have in mind?" Finn replies.

"We'll keep these things back and you take Kazumi and get out of here."

"I can fight for myself." I say without looking back at them. I get Kyle to pull me up while expecting another stab of pain when I weight-bear. But nothing happens. I bounce slightly on the injured leg, still no pain. I gingerly feel my stab wound with my hand and it has already scabbed over. The serum.

"I've got an idea," Kyle says under his breath, "all of you try to keep the Ultimates busy for a while and wait for my signal."

Before we can discuss any further, the Ultimates charge toward us. I grab the sword Kayden gave me earlier and fend off the first few strikes.

Finn, Nick and Benji are back to back in a tight triangle. On my other side, Murray, Bridget and Lilly are in the same formation. Kyle is nowhere to be seen.

I don't think they intend to single me out but their move just made me an easy target. Two leathery Ultimates come at me while the robot leading two others collide with Finn's group. I can't see the rest when two blades thrust my way. I rotate my body to dodge the left one and hack away the second blade coming for my right side with my sword. Then I realize the foot-long blade is actually protruding from their gauntlet. They thrust and stab, and I twist and block. Neither side is gaining an edge. I have to try something else.

They're too tall for me to jump onto without someone or something to hoist me up, so I decide to stay low. I crouch down when a blade slices toward my head and roll through the Ultimate's legs. They're fast, but I'm faster. I get up quickly and kick one of them in the back of the knee. The leg gives in and the man falls forward onto his knees. I started climbing up his back even as he falls. Then I'm once again sitting on the shoulders of a giant Ultimate. But this one is smarter, maybe having seen his dead friend. He immediately falls to his side, bringing me with him. I hit the floor hard, jarring my left shoulder and hip. During the brief moment when I recover from the crushing pain, the Ultimate is able to get out from under my legs while the other one stabs at me with his gauntlet blade. The first jab penetrates my forearm, sending a shooting pain all the way up to my shoulder. As he prepares for a second round, I bite down on my lips and roll out of harm's way. His blade connects with the marble floor with a hair-raising squeak.

With zero facial expression whatsoever, they come at me again. I spend the next five minutes evading their attacks. I can't imagine fighting this fight without the serum in me. I don't think I would last till now.

Speaking of serum, out of nowhere, my spine begins to tingle—like a worm is slowly making its way up, one vertebrae at a time. Then a sharp pain explodes in my torso. My slight hesitation from the unknown agony costs me a few bruised ribs and a fat lip. I thought the new pain would drown the weird sensation in my back but it doesn't. The tingling intensifies into burning and I find myself locked into a forward bending position. Then the most intense itch spreads through my body. I try scratching, pinching, rolling on the floor. But nothing can subdue the terrible prickling.

Meanwhile the two Ultimates are hitting me like a punching bag, which feels like a friendly pat on the back compared to the horrible sensations going through me.

As I roll back and forth on the cold marble floor, expecting a knife in my back at any second, a gun fires. The sound is muted and dull like it happened from a mile away. The punching stops and my groaning becomes the only audible sound in Trousing Hall.

Seconds later, a warm hand touches my face, "Hang in there, it'll be over soon."

I don't know who that voice belongs to but he has no idea what he's talking about. If he knows anything about what I'm going through right now, he won't so casually claim that it'll be over soon like he's watching the end of a movie. Every second feels like eternity in this medley of intense itch and excruciating jabbing.

I don't know how much time has passed. A minute? An hour? I have no idea but like that voice said, the sensation does eventually disappear, leaving only severe lethargy.

My eyelids flutter open and see that everything is on its side. My face in a puddle of sweat and drool. Searching for the source of the gunfire, I think I see Kyle somewhere ahead, standing beside some lady. I rub my eyes, sweat stinging my eyeballs. The clarity that comes after sends another shock to my system.

This is his plan? It's suicide!

I push myself up and fall right back onto the hard stone floor. My muscles, they're almost non-existence. *What's happening?*

I try to curl my fingers into tight fists—I can do the action but I can't elicit any force. I try other body parts and the same thing happens. My muscles have officially given up.

Someone finally helps me up. I don't know who but all I care is the scene in front of me.

Kyle is indeed beside a woman. The *only* woman who can turn this mess around. And she will do just that or Kyle's gun might blow a hole in that twisted mind of hers—if he can bring himself to do it. How he could sneak up to her without being detected by her bodyguards is beyond me. But Annette is ten times more cunning than any of them. I hate to admit it but somehow I think Kyle has just sentenced himself to a death penalty. They must escape now—every single one of them who defied her orders. I don't even want to imagine what kind of treatment they will get if they are captured.

Everyone lapses into silence. Some look on in horror while others are in complete disbelief that a Sarc would actually do that to their own chief.

Annette on the other hand looks as calm and collected as her usual self. But there must be a wrath of storm building inside of her. She's just that good at hiding it.

All the Ultimates stand down at once like their batteries are dead. Then one by one, they move aside to reveal a path straight toward the main entrance.

Unease sweeps by me. This is too easy.

I signal my legs to move. They comply, but as soon as I bear weight on them, I collapse yet again. Before I hit the floor, outstretched arms catch me. I try to focus but my mind somehow has become sluggish. It takes me triple the time to process everything around me.

Soon I'm moving . . . no, not me, but the person carrying me—whoever that might be. But I have a slight hint of who he is.

We amble toward the double glass doors that lead to open air. My eyes fall on Annette as we pass her and Kyle, just before going through the doors. I expect a furious gaze to come from her but she just stares past me, not focusing on anything particular. I know she'd hate to lose face in front of her people. That's why she's trying to look as dignified as possible under the circumstance. She must have something planned in her mind. She won't let us go that easily. But her blank face is not giving anything away. I look to Kyle just before he's blocked by my carrier's shoulder. I try to convey how bad his idea is, how dangerous his situation is, but based on my level of energy, I might have come off looking half asleep more than anything. He gives me a very subtle nod but his eyes, they are laced with longing and sadness. He knows . . . he knows that he might not come out of this alive. But he still did it . . . for me.

"We'll be out of here soon, hang in there," the guy carrying me suddenly whispers.

The fog in my mind has yet to settle down and all I can think about is how I *sort of* recognize that voice.

The double glass doors open, someone is holding them so the guy and I can go through. A whiff of the guy's scent flows past my nose. Fresh meadow mixed with sweat and blood, so familiar, so comforting. It reminds me the last time he carried me like this. We were also escaping, but from the Neuronics. As much as I hate to be a damsel in distress, I somehow always find myself in Finn's arms.

Instead of struggling, I just surrender to the warmth, too tired and drained to think if this is a good idea or not. All I want to do is sleep; fall into a dreamless slumber that would take away my pain.

We walk into the night Alaskan sky, dotted with thousands of little lights. So pretty. So calm . . .

A breeze blows by, the cool, brisk air invigorates me briefly from the fast-drowning sleep. My eyelids have become heavy but I tell myself that I can't fall asleep just yet. We're still not safe until we're out of Annette's reach. I take in a big gulp of autumn air, the chilly breeze slides down my throat like an icicle, fully waking me. Winter's coming.

Finn takes me to the front of the pack and I can see Natalie, glowing brightly in the distance.

Kyle mouths a few words to Annette and then tightens his grip on her neck, causing the Ultimates to stay put just outside the doors. But the Cores are slowly creeping along behind us— far enough to not jeopardize their leader's life but not so far as letting us out of sight.

We're getting close to the jet now. I can almost smell its leather seats and hear the soft music crooning in the background. Then Annette's chuckle cuts through the soft music in my ear, followed by an agonizing scream.

I look past Finn just in time to see Annette with a stun gun on Kyle's ribs. He goes down with a convulsion, his gun locked in his hand.

"NO!" I scream but Finn won't let me down. I thrash as hard as I can and manage to get my legs on the ground. But Finn pulls me back, running.

I watch as the Cores drag Kyle away. He's still breathing but I almost wish he isn't. Being alive under Annette's custody is worse than death.

"You guys go, we'll hold them back," Murray yells.

"No—" Finn objects.

"No time, just go!" Nick shouts and pushes us along.

I don't know why the Elites suddenly side with me, but I'm not going to let anymore people die for me.

"Let me go," I scream. "She wants me. You guys don't have to do this. She will kill you all!"

"Too late, we're in this together now Kazumi." Kayden winks at me, then a pack of Ultimates jumps on him, burying him in a mountain of black leathery scales.

"Kayden!" A raspy scream escapes my throat.

Nick, Benji, Bridget and Lilly all go after the Ultimates, temporarily holding them back. Murray rushes Finn and I onto Natalie. We get into the cockpit somewhat unwillingly and Murray fires up the engine immediately.

"Where are you going?" Finn asks when Murray heads for the door again.

"They need me down there," he says. "You know where to find help if needed."

Finn clenches his jaw and nods, eyes looking down.

"Kazumi," Murray looks at me, then at my bald head, "I'm sorry." Then he steps off the plane.

Something tugs at my heartstrings. "We can't go. We can't leave them. They'll die."

"You'll die if we don't leave," says Finn in a low voice, his fingers already punching buttons. "They'll be alright. They'll get punished but Annette won't kill them."

"You mean torture?" I say, but Finn doesn't answer. "Why are they doing this? No one needs to be punished if I just go back—"

"Because we're a team!" Finn snaps, eyes wet with moisture. "They're doing this for *me*."

I stop arguing and just let my body sink into the chair beside him. His team, well minus Liam and Samantha, is truly loyal to him. Now I see it. Whatever Finn does, they follow suit even if it means saving a Neuronic. That I get. But what I don't get is Finn's motive. He doesn't have to save me. He doesn't have to put his team in danger. And now he's probably forever banned from his people. He will forever be marked as a traitor.

For what? A tiny part of me thinks he actually is doing this for me; that he really cares whether I live or die. But I quickly delete that notion, erase it completely from my mind before it takes shape and plants false hopes in my head. I will not allow myself to get tricked again, *ever*.

The jet starts to glide forward. I hesitate for a moment before looking out the cockpit window for I worry what I will see. But I do it anyway. I have to know.

The fighting has stopped. The Elites are still alive, but are pinned to the ground and handcuffed. My heart feels heavy at the sight of their fall, like someone injected lead into my veins. I can't help but feel responsible. If I escaped the first chance I had instead of gone running for Finn, none of this would've happened. I hope and pray that Annette will have mercy on them, like Finn said. Knowing how vindictive she is though, I'm not so sure if they'll be safe. There's nothing I can do now, nothing . . . except to surrender to the circumstance . . . surrender to the pull of sleep . . .

EPILOGUE

"You look gorgeous." Finn strokes my hair softly.

Hm . . . I close my eyes and bask in the Alaskan sun. The summer breeze feels like silk caressing along my skin and the sweet smell of peonies fills the air.

Oh how I love this moment.

Finn plants light kisses on my nose, my lips, and down my neck. But his lips are icy cold against my warm skin, giving me goosebumps along the way. He slowly lifts his head so I can see his sparkling deep blue eyes. There's something in those eyes that I hadn't noticed before though, something dark and swirling from within.

"Kaz, I love you." His lips curl up, but not in a smile. His expression turns from loving to something that makes the back of my neck prickle. A low growl forms in the back of his throat. I press my hands on his chest, preventing him from coming closer, but my strength is no match to his. He produces a knife from thin air and holds it above my head. The blade catches the beam of the sun and reflects into my eyes, temporarily blinding me. "Kaz, I love you." He repeats in a ferocious growl, more animal than human.

I open my eyes just in time to see the knife plunging into my heart. I scream but the sound comes out empty. I stare into those dark, menacing eyes that are inching closer and closer. I scream again, this time the sound registers.

"Kaz, it's okay, just a bad dream."

I'm staring into Finn's dark blue eyes again but the menace I saw earlier is replaced by sorrow and concern. I keep my wary gaze on him, ready to fend off any knife or bullet that might come my way. I wait . . . and wait . . . but his tormented expression remains.

"Hey, welcome back," he finally whispers.

Welcome back?

I tentatively shift my focus from his eyes to our surroundings. What I see is a dingy room that smells of mildew and bleach. A dusty mirror is hung on the opposite wall. Under it sits an old black dresser. There's no summer breeze or Alaskan sun, only the faint humming of a fan.

"Where are we? What happened?" I ask, the horrible nightmare now a fleeting thought.

"You passed out soon after we took off. You were going through a withdrawal from the boosting serum. That thing was too potent. It was banned years ago. I'm surprised Kyle got a hold of one. But you should be good now. One dose shouldn't make you into an addict. You're safe here." Finn shifts slightly, hinting for me to release his sleeves, which I've been clutching.

I let go and see two sweat marks printed on his shirt. I prop myself up so I'm leaning against the headboard. My body screams in disagreement. Every joint hurts like I'm an arthritic old woman. Every muscle burns like I just ran two triathlons back to back.

"Where are we?" I ask again. Even my voice sounds like a dying woman.

"A motel in Greater China," he replies.

"What?" I didn't expect to have already flown to the other side of the globe.

"This is neither the Sarcs or the Neuronic's territory, so you should be safe here."

"I see." I look down at my torn pants where the Ultimate stabbed my thigh.

"You know, I lost you for a moment back there," Finn says.

"What are you talking about?"

"Your heart stopped after we landed," he continues without looking up. "I performed CPR on you . . . and thanks to the defibrillator on the plane, I managed to revive you. You have been unconscious since. It's been four days." He wraps his hands around mine but I retract them immediately.

Four days. I've been out for four whole days. No wonder my body's screaming in pain.

"Thanks for saving my life." I swing myself off the bed and head for the door. Overestimated my strength, I almost fall flat on my face. Finn catches me just in time.

"Where are you going?" he asks while pulling me back onto the bed.

"Why do you care?" I stand there, refuse to sit down. His hand still on my elbow. "You rescued me so I could be free right? Or is there another secret motive I don't know about?"

"I know you're mad at me, and you have every right to be. I'm sorry that I've hurt you but please let me help you," says Finn.

"Fine, then answer me this." I look him right in the eyes. "Did you mean *any* of the things you said when we were 'together'?"

"I . . ." he looks away, "I . . ." his voice low and quiet.

"Got it." I quickly say, regret that I asked such an obvious question.

What did you expect Kazumi? That he'd say yes he does love you? That he wants to spend the rest of his life with you?

I shake my head, shake away any remnant of hope. Neither of us speak for a very long while.

I stare out the dusty window and see an array of colours, bright and flickering on massive billboards. Then something clicked in my head—I'm free.

For the first time in ten years, I can go anywhere and do whatever I want. No one can dictate my actions anymore. I can create a future for myself, whatever it may be. I'm no longer anyone's secret weapon. I can live for myself now, something I have no idea how to do but I'm not afraid to learn.

"Are you okay?" Finn asks. "What are you thinking about?"

"Liberation."

Finn opens his mouth as if to say something, but closes it again when he doesn't know what to say.

"You should go back. To make sure your team and Kyle are okay." I say.

"What about you?" he asks.

"I still have unfinished business with an old friend, but I'll be fine. I'm no longer the lost girl who couldn't remember her name." I cross my arms, feeling the return of strength and energy.

"Then you'll need this," Finn produces a gun from his pocket.

Alex's pistol. My pistol.

In his hand is also a MUD, preloaded with money I assume. Just like the time he chaperoned me to the train station. Except this time, we are saying goodbye for good.

"Call me if you run into trouble. Or if you want to continue our gun kata training. I don't want the art to die with me." He smiles and hands me the gun and the plastic card.

I nod and accept both items from him. "Be careful. Annette might have other plans for you."

"Don't worry about me. I know how to handle her," says Finn.

"Let me know Kyle's condition. Get him out of there. I doubt Annette's gonna forgive what he pulled anytime soon."

"I will. You be careful." Longing fills his eyes.

I nod and lower my head to pretend I'm examining my pistol. I don't want him to see the emotions behind my eyes. I can put all this behind me. I know I can, but I need time. Standing in front of him, not knowing if I'll ever see him again makes my heart ache. There will be no more shoulders for me to lean on, no more strong arms to carry me through dangers. And that's okay. Because I'm free. I can finally be who I am. To lead a life my parents wanted for me all along. And it is this thought that lifted me from the dark into the sunlight, into a world full of hopes and dreams.

I lift my head, this time it feels ten times lighter. "Even though we were enemies once, I'm still glad that we met."

Finn blinks. Then slowly, he begins to show his handsome smile. "So where do you plan to go next?" he asks.

"Maybe it's time to see the world," I reply.

END OF BOOK I

CPSIA information can be obtained at www.ICGtesting.com
Printed in the USA
LVOW10s0000260515

439827LV00001B/2/P